Orphan
FLOWERS

CONQUERING SERIES BOOK 1

J.C. ROCHFORD

Cover Design by Chelsea Barnes, CJPB Designs
Editing by Candice Barnes
Stock Image by Adobe Stock

All Rights Reserved. No part of this publication may
be reproduced, stored in a retrieval system, or
transmitted, in any form or in any means—by
electronic, mechanical, photocopying, recording or
otherwise—without prior written permission.

DEDICATION

To those who were failed before they even began
their journey.

ACKNOWLEDGEMENTS

To my mum and proofreader, Angela—Firstly, thank you for giving me life! Since I was little you always encouraged me to follow my heart and never pressured me to pursue any particular career. As you have mentioned, I am the one having to get up every morning to do the job, not you, so I should choose something that I would enjoy doing for the rest of my life. With every ambition and dream I have had, you have encouraged them to be accomplished. Thank you for the suggestions towards making a stronger novel, bringing out the best in my abilities and ideas. Your love and support will be cherished as more novels are created through the years.

To my dad, Gary—For all the daily talks about becoming an author and encouraging all the milestones along the way since day one, thank you. You took each and every milestone to heart no matter how small or big they were, and only wanted the best from all my efforts. You always say, *to strive is to do*, and that is exactly what I have done. The encouragement and love towards my journey of writing will be deeply cherished and never forgotten. Thank you for all the forehead kisses, and enjoying my big bear hugs.

To my sister and editor, Candice—Without your support from the very first day of writing two years ago, this book would never have been considered for publication. Your enthusiasm and love for the characters encouraged me to bring out the best in each of them. The love and proud support I have received during this journey will be embedded into each novel that is planned to be written and released in the future. Thank you for strengthening this novel with your editing skills!

To my grandad, Mike—For all the nights you stayed awake to listen to my numerous ideas during my long nights of writing, and for the daily encouragements that no matter how many words I wrote, they were words to a story from my heart. The excitement you showed and that we shared will always be cherished. Thank you for your love and support though this journey.

To Stephanie Gresham-Wiggins—Thank you! Those words do not sum up the thankfulness I have for our friendship. Thank you for all the times I doubted my abilities—you were right there to remind me of my worth. You have been my rock since the day you found out I was writing my first novel, and the one who heard all the rubbish talk. You stuck by me until I accomplished what I set myself out to do—write a novel. Love you to the moon and back!

To **ALL** my friends, near and far, and to every single person who congratulated each of my milestones, and accomplishments through my writing journey, thank you! Your support means the world too me, and the friendships along this journey will forever be cherished.

To my Rockin' Readers—thank you for your ongoing support and love. You have all been amazing and encouraging. Thank you for giving a debut author a chance!

To Colleen Hoover— your response to a question during a live Q&A meant the world to me as an aspiring author. Thank you for keeping it real and speaking from your heart. You have inspired me to continue the journey, and continue to write from my heart and imagination.

"[I] didn't really care about the outside world and what was selling, and it worked out. I think that as long as you write something that you're proud of, then you won't care if it sells or not."

Collen Hoover
New York Times Best Selling Author

To the teacher who told me I couldn't, who failed me before my journey even began, this is my fight book. This novel was written to prove the world wrong in how those deemed 'disabled' can actually succeed. I dreamed a dream, and I saw that dream through. I fought the stigma around learning disabilities. You were so very wrong about me, and my capabilities. My disabilities don't define me. My abilities define me.

ONE

Darren
Past, April 1998

Wanting to know where she was headed and her plans, I followed her. I should have been dragging her ass back home as I had before—after only just a few miles—but this time I desperately wanted to know her intentions. Was it another man she was after? Why was she doing this? Answers were what I needed.

Pulling the car over under some dark, low hanging trees, I studied her as she led herself up the driveway to a white upper-class home, almost Victorian in style, with red trim, and a red front door. It reminded me of a house you would see in the movies, all prim and proper.

I had no idea why she would have come to this side of the city to begin with. Who would she know here? It was too far out of the way for her, and aside from when

1

she used to work, she didn't have friends, nor did she go out anywhere. We had nothing more than the average lifestyle—we lived in North Vancouver, I provided what was needed selling the animal meats I hunted weekly, and I paid the bills. It didn't require us to be social with anyone. We lived a perfectly simple life, all we needed was each other.

She fumbled in the driveway seeming to stall herself from reaching the front door of the house. What was she scared of? Barely able to keep my eyes on her, I felt my blood start to boil and my brow beginning to sweat. Clenching the steering wheel in front of me with a nearly white-knuckle grip to contain the anger that was boiling under my skin, I knew I needed to calm my nerves. I took a swig from my flask on the passenger seat, feeling the burn travel down the back of my throat—stinging momentarily. It was a sensation I had grown accustomed to—the aroma, the burn, the feeling.

Maintaining my gaze, I watched her intently. The struggle she was having was evident as she made her way further up the driveway towards the door. She hesitated as she approached the doorbell. At first, she dropped her hand, but a moment later I saw her make contact. Anxiety welled up inside me. I feared I would see another man open the door. She appeared to be staring down at a piece of paper and checking it against the number display next to the door. At this point I had too many emotions running through my head, I wasn't even sure which one I needed to express at that moment.

No one can take care of her but me.

With her condition, she needed ample supervision. I was enough for her, I was capable of providing everything she needed. We were happy together, weren't we?

With my mind fogging over, and the outside world nearly slipping away at the thought of another man in her life, I put my foot on the gas pedal and sped off, not giving her actions a second thought.

Looking back in my rear view mirror, everything was a blur. I saw flashes of our wedding day, us happy in our home, watching her paint each room that needed to be precisely as it appeared in her old, ragged childhood book. Needing to erase the visions, the memories, I took another swig from the flask, which was becoming much like a desert. It was one of the only substances that made the feelings go away—at least that's what I hoped was happening. For the time being, it was numbing me enough to gather my thoughts together.

Why would she want to leave me? I provided her with everything she could possibly need, and this was the thanks I received in return? She could play her little games, but she would realize the importance of my existence in her life in a matter of time—she couldn't forget what I had given her, or the fact that she couldn't survive without me. Nobody would love her like I did—nobody. My mind took over, bringing me back to the good old days with her…

She was beautiful, breathtakingly beautiful, to be exact. Her brown wavy hair caught in the wind as it danced around her face. A smile as wide as the ocean, and eyes the shade of green grass pierced through her long lashes. She was not a woman who wore a lot of makeup. Her natural beauty took over, releasing the natural glow of her skin. She was an incredible woman from the day I met her, I knew she was the only one for me. I never could take my eyes off of her, though what man could—she was perfect.

Slowing at the red light, I could see her out of the corner of my eye. There she was, looking light and airy, delicate of sorts, resembling the days of high school. Why would she be out here alone? Was my mind playing tricks on me? There was no way she could have made it from the house to here in the matter of a few minutes. Not even a moment later I noticed the guy standing next to her, fondling her hair. She laughed as he smiled back at her with delight and desire. Flashbacks of her and I together in love flashed before me, movie style.

I swerved, nearly scraping the bottom of the car across the curb as I abruptly made the turn into the small parking lot of a retail strip plaza, not caring. Jolting the car into park and swinging open the door forcefully to the point of nearly pushing it off its hinges, I jumped out of the car. I was angered at this point. This wasn't happening—my woman with another man was not in the books for today, or any day for that matter. As I approached them, my mind continued to reel memories of her and I—her smell, her presence, it was all so fresh, just like the day I met her. I was ready to take him out for messing with my woman. My eyes were locked on his. He knew trouble was coming and knew what he was doing was wrong. Nobody messed with me or my woman and got away with it.

"Hey man. What's going on?" the male spoke in a snared voice.

I didn't pay attention to his words, I had only one mission at this point—getting my wife back. I was mere inches from him when my hands began to clench into fists at my side. I would do anything to get her back—anything.

"Dude, are you delusional? What's your problem, man?"

His voice was annoying, and whatever he was saying was not registering in my mind. I needed to shut him up. Before I knew it, the knuckles of my right hand made contact with something hard. My eyes took some time to adjust, all I could see was a blob falling to the ground.

Serves him right, that's exactly what he deserved.

He tried to stand, but I wouldn't let him get off his knees before jamming my foot into his back, causing him to fall flat on his stomach. I kept kicking at the blob before me, over and over, until no resistance came from the worthless human being on the ground.

Now that the cheating bastard was out of the way, I turned my attention to my love. As I turned, I found her crying hysterically as she stumbled backwards away from me, her eyes never leaving my face as she moved away from me. I didn't want a scene, I only wanted her back where she belonged—with me. Our eyes locked, but all I saw was pain through her eyes as she continued to stumble backwards.

Why was she afraid of me? Did she really think I wouldn't find out about her sneaking around behind my back?

I was livid and wasn't going to indulge in her little game any longer. Reaching out, I grabbed her arm, but she fought me, slapping me on my forearm. My blood was boiling—she knew better than to fight me.

"Why are you afraid of me?" I called out, but she wasn't having any of it. She continued to use her worthless strength on me.

In one swoop I took hold of her, throwing her over my shoulder like a fireman carry. She threw her fists into my back, over and over, kicking and screaming. I needed to shut her up before we caused a scene. Focusing on my car and our escape, nothing else dawned on me.

When we reached the car, the voices grew stronger within me.

Why are you doing this? You killed a guy, to prove...what?

I shook my head of the thoughts. What was this nonsense all about? Pulling her off my shoulder, I turned her to face me. When our eyes connected, a young woman with mascara running down her face stared back at me. Peering around, I spotted a dead body lying on the ground.

Did I do this? What have I done?

Taking a few glances between the body and the woman—which I still had a grip on—confusion began to set in on what had just happened. It felt like I blacked out, I didn't even know where I was. I could hear sirens in the distance as panic washed over me.

What have I done? It was my wife I had been saving? Wasn't it?

Everything blurred together. I couldn't have done what I thought I had done. My mind was so confused. I opened the trunk and instructed the young woman to get into it. I needed to get out of there unnoticed and a screaming woman wasn't going to help. Of course, she was uncooperative as I forced her inside while she was simultaneously fighting her way out. With her finally inside the trunk I latched it closed.

Had anyone seen? Were there witnesses?

I had no idea what was happening, but the sirens were getting closer. Someone must have seen if there were sirens, right? Could the woman have had a cell phone? I never saw one in her hand, but having frequent lapses of time in my memory caused me to not see or remember a hell of a lot.

Reaching the driver's side door, I turned back and unlocked the trunk. There she was, shaking, with a phone in her hand.

"Give me your phone!" I demanded.

She hesitated. I could see her hand clench harder around the slender case. Reaching into the trunk, I began to struggle with her to free the phone from her grasp. She flailed around, trying to free herself. I had no choice but to knock her unconscious, and with one swoop her phone dropped to the ground. As I picked it up, I saw the display was engaged in a call. Placing it to my ear, there was a woman on the other end stating, "The police are on their way."

Sirens must have only been a block away at this point. I closed the trunk and ran, sliding into the driver's seat. I ripped the battery from the cell phone and threw both parts into the back seat—I didn't need anybody tracking me down.

As I looked back in my rear view mirror, I could see flashing lights rounding the bend. I threw my car into drive and pressed my gas pedal to the floor. The car jolted, and before I knew it, I was coasting seventy down a winding road. I needed to get far away. As I left the city limits, the sky began to darken. With no street lights, I was only going by the headlights of my car to lead the way. I wasn't sure where I was headed, as I seemed to be heading away from where I needed to be—at home with my wife. My mind started to drift back to the incident with the guy at the plaza. I knew this was my wife, I saw her there, with that guy. It wasn't a dream. Or was it? What was I going to do with this woman? She was the only witness—at least I thought she was. If I got caught, I could see life in prison, and I would probably never see my wife again. I couldn't let that happen. This girl needed to be shut up—permanently.

I let things settle down for a day before returning home. I needed to get my wife back. She needed to realize she was still married to me, and she couldn't cheat on me like this. Grabbing my coat off the rack, I closed and locked my front door, breathing in a deep breath of fresh air. As I reached my car door, our neighbour Mrs. Adams, approached.

"Good day, Darren".

Oh great.

I thought I could have escaped without being seen. I didn't like people. I kept to myself and took care of my wife. That's all I needed.

"Hi, Mrs. Adams," I indulged her with a reply, but tried to keep my eyes from making any contact with hers. Maybe she would think I was in a hurry and go on her way.

"How are you this fine day?"

Small talk—something that irritated me the most about people.

I was not a sociable person in the least. That's why I was a hunter—I could be on my own and not have to deal with anyone.

"I'm fine."

I opened the driver's door, throwing my bag over the driver's seat, but missed the back seat completely, causing it to land on the floor with a loud thud. I jolted my head in the direction of Mrs. Adams, hoping she hadn't heard it. I didn't need her to be any more nosey than she already was.

"How's your wife? I don't see her much these days, is she sick?"

My heart stopped, causing me to lose my breath for a moment.

Why is she so nosey? Does she know something I don't?

"She's been busy with work," I lied.

That should have distracted her enough, she knew Justine had worked as a medical receptionist at a walk-in clinic years ago—she didn't need to know that she no longer worked. I continued to climb inside the car to indicate my need to leave as she continued to talk.

"Let her know when she has time that I would love for you both to come for some tea and cookies one afternoon."

In your dreams, lady.

With a nod and small wave I gestured goodbye, while thinking to myself that when I got Justine back she wouldn't be seeing the outside world for a long, long time. I couldn't trust her anymore. New measures would be implemented to keep her in her place—for good.

Once out on the road, I returned my attention to the task at hand—how was I going to go about retrieving my wife? I didn't know what this new man was like. Could I beat him down to a pulp? Frankly, that's what I really wanted to do to anybody who messed around with my woman.

As I drove along the winding roads, my mind started to wander—stress often caused my mind to wander. This time, it wandered back to another night when I found Justine with another man. She had adamantly told me I was hallucinating, but I knew better than to believe her lies.

I was angry. She had betrayed me. She was all I had. She needed to learn that she couldn't go around cheating on her husband like that. We took a vow. We made a promise.

These thoughts repeatedly rolled through my mind as I continued the drive. I wanted to stake out the house, to learn how it functioned, which would give me a leg up on how best to handle the situation. I wanted to be prepared for any situation once I had my hands on her again. She had always been a fighter, but now she was becoming weak, complying with my requests. This would be the ultimate request. I would get my woman back one way or another. She was my woman, and if she didn't want to be with me, she wouldn't be with anyone.

TWO

Murray
Past, April 1998

Lost in my work, I ruffled through investigation reports attempting to piece together a murder that had been discovered a couple of days before. It had been one hell of a stressful day— the girl we found was barely eighteen years old. It sent chills down my spine just thinking of a poor, innocent child murdered for no apparent reason. Part of my heart broke over these types of cases. I often wondered what the families were feeling, knowing their son or daughter wouldn't grow up, have a career, or get married.

I shook the thoughts from my head. My partner swung around from the side of his cubical.

"Have you found anything in missing persons yet, Murray?" Pryce inquired.

"Not yet, nobody with her description."

From the autopsy report, we knew she had been dead for less than twenty-four hours when she had been discovered yesterday morning. The phone at my desk began to ring. I ignored it, trying to concentrate on the task at hand. I didn't usually ignore calls, but in this case I was heavily focused because the family of this young woman had yet to be notified of her death. We didn't know who she was, which made the case even more important.

Out of the blue, my personal cell phone rang with the display indicating it was an old partner of mine from back in the days of 'walking the beat'. It seemed out of the ordinary for her to call my cell phone, especially at this late hour—it was ten o'clock at night. Nevertheless, I answered it on the last ring before it went to voice mail.

"Hey, Gresham! How are you? You must need something important to be calling at this late hour. Need me to run some background checks for you?" I said, balancing the phone on my shoulder as I continued ruffling through paperwork and clicking away at my computer keyboard.

Gresham usually only called when she needed a deeper background check on a suspect.

"No, I'm calling because there's been a kidnapping," she went on to say.

"I'm sorry, but I'm swamped with a murder investigation. Could I ask another detective to assist you?"

There was a long, awkward pause before she answered again.

"I don't know how to tell you this..." The pause in her voice caused me to drop everything in my hands and pay full attention to the tone of her voice. I had never heard her hesitate in all the years that I had known her.

"I'm sorry Murray, the one missing is your wife, Lily."

Jumping out of my seat, I barked down the phone—not intentionally, of course.

"Where the hell is she? Where is Callie? Is she okay?"

"Callie is with me. She's shaken up from seeing the kidnapping, but she wasn't physically harmed," she replied slowly.

The detective in me started thinking up a hundred questions. Pryce jumped from around the cubical, but I ignored him as I grabbed my jacket and ran through the hallways and down the four flights of stairs. I had no time to wait for the elevator.

Storming the stairwell, and nearly jumping from landing to landing as I made the trek down, I kept my phone pressed to my ear trying to concentrate on Gresham attempting to explain the situation. By the time I made it to the bottom I was completely out of breath. As breathless as I was, I managed to yell into the phone,

"Where are you? Where did this happen?"

I paused at the bottom of the stairs for a moment, catching my breath while I waited for Gresham to respond.

"We're at your home, it happened here," she said softly.

"I'm on my way, stay with Callie until I get there."

Hanging up abruptly and making my way into the lobby where it was a quiet Monday evening, the duty officer at the front desk called out to see if everything was okay. I gave a wave of my hand to signal it was—I had no time to stop. I jumped into my car, letting the lights and siren blare, and was off like a bat out of hell.

My mind was completely foggy, and did not comprehend what had just happened. I received missing persons and kidnapping reports daily, but hearing it was my own family caused a strain on my heart. It all seemed surreal. I felt like I was moving at a snail's pace through the streets of Vancouver. It was like a dream where you keep running forward, but you don't get any closer to your destination.

As I rounded the bend of Hart Avenue where we lived, neighbours were standing around chatting amongst themselves while caution tape lined the entirety of our front lawn and driveway. I pulled up along the curb behind a police cruiser, and jumped out of my car, still leaving it running.

I tuned out the voices being directed at me as I stumbled my way under the police tape and towards my front door. I had no intent of having anyone get in my way while I tried to discover what had happened. My attention was first on finding Callie. Barging through the open front door, I saw my little girl in the living room with Officer Gresham. Callie looked terrified, rocking back and forth on the couch with her knees pulled into her chest. Gresham stood to greet me, but I brushed passed her—I was now in father mode, and I just wanted to console and protect my little girl.

Not knowing the extent of the situation or what Callie had or had not seen, I had to be there to comfort her. Rushing over, I threw my arms around her. Although her voice was shaky, in between sobs she attempted to tell me what had happened, but I could barely understand her. At that moment nothing else mattered but to have my little girl in my arms.

14

It was approaching midnight, and Callie was weak and completely exhausted. Although it felt like hours, in reality it had only been an hour and half since I had arrived home. I carried her upstairs to her bed, placing her down gently. Gresham offered to stand guard outside Callie's room until she fell asleep in case Callie needed anything.

Looking peaceful, I kissed her goodnight. It was time to hear what had truly happened. I made my way downstairs, peering around to see if anything was missing or disturbed. Finding no evidence of anything odd within the house, I inspected the front door. I noticed a dent in the wall behind the door where it looked as though the door handle had smashed backwards into it. If that was the only damage, Callie had been very lucky.

How exactly had this kidnapping happened? I knew for a fact Lily would have fought her attacker. She had taken self-defense classes the year after we met, because no woman of mine was going to not know how to defend herself when she needed to.

Gresham appeared in the doorway of the living room as I paced around the main floor questioning how this all began.

"Murray, shall we sit and discuss the events of tonight?" she asked.

I didn't want to sit, I wanted answers. Shifting awkwardly in the doorway, I could sense she wasn't sure how to begin. I spoke first, as calmly as I could.

"Tell me everything you know, Gresham."

Taking a moment, she began the explanation of the night's events as she knew them.

"From the little information Callie provided, we actually don't know too much. All we know is a man in dark clothing knocked on the door, Callie heard him and your wife arguing and then heard the door swing open against the wall. She ran to see what was happening, but the man was already pulling Lily outside..." she trailed off.

Motionless, the words hit me like a ton of bricks. I needed more answers, now.

Who would want to hurt my wife, let alone kidnap her in front of a child?

Anger began to escape me. Gresham took a few steps back as I took a few steps towards her. I couldn't control my feelings. I was hurt. Remembering the crowd outside, I stormed past her and out the front door, running towards the crowd gathered on the street in front of my home. I screamed out to the crowd that was being held back by the police caution tape without realizing the tone I was using.

"Did anyone see what happened? Which direction did they go?"

The crowd began shouting out answers, but the world was spinning all of a sudden. Before I knew it, someone was pulling me back towards the house. My audible sense died, everything was blurry, and I felt as if I was dying inside.

The only thing I remembered next was being helped to the couch back in the living room. I could barely comprehend what was happening—the room was spinning, or was I falling? Someone handed me a glass of water and told me to drink it, but I knocked it away. Anger was building inside me, again. I couldn't just sit there and do nothing while Lily was out in the world all alone with some stranger. I needed to do something, but what?

THREE

Murray
Present, February 2004

In the dark of Callie's bedroom, shadows danced on the walls as the wind hallowed through the cracks of her tiny window. The glass rattled loudly as if someone was trying to break in. Callie wasn't one for being alone at night, especially on stormy evenings. When I opened the door I saw her sitting curled up on the floor in the corner of her room, rocking back and forth. I rushed over to comfort her, gathering her up, holding her in my arms.

"There, there Callie. Everything will be okay…"

I could feel streams of tears rolling down her face and my shirt soaking up the wetness as she cried into my chest. We sat on the floor rocking back and forth, while I comforted my little girl as I had done a thousand times before. Each time never became any easier; in fact, as she got older it seemed to have become harder. Being a single parent hadn't been easy.

I had done my best to raise Callie, but it was clear she missed her mother's love, which put her in a state of feeling lost that no child should ever have to endure.

Callie finally began to calm, enough to stand up and walk to her bed. Groggy eyed, she slipped into bed, as I pulled the covers up and tucked her in, kissing her forehead goodnight.

As I quietly made my way to the door, I noticed a picture frame laying on the floor that appeared to have been smashed against the wall. It was a picture of Lily-May, Callie's mother, and my wife of nearly sixteen years. I knelt down to pick up the shattered pieces of glass and the torn picture, taking them down to the kitchen and placing them gently on the table. Pulling up a chair, I sat at the table finding myself tearing up.

Missing my wife for the past six years had been hard. In front of Callie I needed to be strong and show her that I was there for her. I studied the image; it was a picture I took of Lily on our honeymoon in Italy. Lily's long brown, slightly curled hair and beautiful green eyes shimmered around her smile that reached from ear to ear. She was the most beautiful woman that had ever stepped foot into my life. She had changed me in ways I never knew I could change. When I first met Lily, my heart was not as soft as it was now—she helped me value the important things in life, like family. I was too hard-nosed, always busy with work, and would carry that stress home with me. It was as if I couldn't leave work at work, and come home to spend quality time with my wife and daughter. As much as this mystery disappearance had affected Callie, its effects were slowly catching up to me as well.

Morning rose. I didn't even hear Callie until she whispered in my ear.

"Dad, it's morning. Are you okay?"

I jolted awake, sitting up straight. It seemed I had fallen asleep at the kitchen table.

"Yes dear, I'm okay." I replied groggily, while yawning and stretching my arms above my head. As I peaked at the time on the wall, I saw it was eleven in the morning.

"Damnit!" I shouted, "I'm going to be late for my shift."

Pushing the chair back, I rushed past Callie giving her a quick kiss on her forehead as I made my way to my bedroom to change, calling back to the kitchen,

"Do you need me to drop you anywhere before work?"

Callie must have not heard me, because when I returned to the kitchen she was sitting in the chair that I had vacated moments earlier, staring at the broken picture frame I had found in her room the night before. Callie's eyes began to tear, as she rushed to stand to apologize once she noticed me.

"Dad, I am so sorry. I didn't mean to break it..." She trailed off, beginning to sob.

Walking over I took her face into my hands, kissed her forehead and whispered.

"It's okay, we are both missing her."

It was the first time in six years I had admitted to myself, or to Callie, that I was missing Lily. Being a detective for the Vancouver Police Department for the past twenty years hadn't been easy. I worked crazy hours and all-nighters, which was just what you had to endure to crack a case.

I pulled away from Callie to gather my belongings by the table to head out the door, I knew I was going to get in trouble for being late. As I made my way down the hallway towards the front door, Callie followed behind me.

"Dad, don't forget we have the parent-teacher conference with Mrs. Caesar tonight," she reminded me.

It had slipped my mind, but I didn't need her to know that.

"I remember dear. I'll be home by five o'clock, don't worry," I responded with a smile.

I walked outside to my car as she stood leaning against the doorway, waving at me as I pulled out of the driveway. I began the journey to work as my mind drifted into deeper thoughts. By the time I was able to leave the house it was already eleven-thirty-five, and my shift had started five minutes ago.

These past few years the job had taken a toll on me. I was a detective, and part of my job included finding missing persons. Yet, despite my experience, I hadn't been able to find my own wife. I had to admit, working alone, I didn't have access to the same resources as when I was working with my team.

I had been pulled from the case due to conflict of interest—go figure—and had only been given occasional updates when new evidence appeared; but those updates stopped approximately three years ago, when the case was deemed 'officially cold'. I couldn't sit idle and let it go by the way side—this was my wife! I launched my own investigation, which was tedious and seemed to lead nowhere.

We had no solid evidence that led to any one person, no finger prints, hairs—nothing. The person who had committed this crime had carefully covered their tracks, which led me to believe they knew what they were doing.

I pulled into my parking space in front of Headquarters and cut the engine. I didn't want to move from the driver's seat as I was fully aware of the earful I was about to receive from the Captain the moment I stepped foot into the department.

The Captain had seemed understanding the first year or so, but after that I was expected to be back to regular service with no excuses. I had become quiet around work. At first, many would ask if I was feeling okay, merely for the fact I was not as talkative as I had been before my wife's kidnapping. Eventually, they stopped asking and it seemed as though the whole building walked on eggshells around me. What point was there in asking me how I felt, anyway? They wouldn't have understood, unless they had lost someone they loved as tragically as I had. Hope was fading—it had been six years, after all.

Pulling myself out of the car and shutting the door behind me, I walked into the extremely crowded lobby of Headquarters.

"A normal day at the office," I grumbled under my breath.

My focus was on getting to my desk unnoticed, but that was impossible. Captain Sullivan was standing by the duty desk when I walked in. As he saw me, he motioned for me to come over to him. A tall, slender middle-aged woman was standing with her arms crossed at the duty desk as I approached.

"Detective Murray," the Captain called out, as I approached the desk.

"Captain, how can I help you?" I asked, attempting to sound as pleasant as possible, not knowing the nature of the Captain's presence in the lobby—it was not a normal occurrence. Usually, you would find him tucked away in his office, out of sight, only surfacing when he was needed in extreme measures. The slender woman did not budge when I approached. In fact, she was almost stiff as a board, you could say.

"Murray, this is Mrs. Johnson," Captain introduced us.

Reaching my hand out in a friendly gesture to shake hands, she simply gave me the cold shoulder instead. Confused, I slipped my hand back to my side, peering over to the Captain for guidance. Oblivious to the awkward encounter that had just taken place in front of him, he continued on.

"She says she has information regarding some cases we have been working on." He kept his eyes to the ground as he explained this. It seemed unusual for Captain to be acting in this manner. Why wasn't he cutting to the chase? I sensed he was holding something back. I was all for new witnesses bringing forth fresh information, but something about her bothered me. She made me think of Lily. I couldn't pin point it at first, because of the bulky over coat and sunglasses she wore. Her hair was identical to Lily's, brunette, and worn in lose curls.

If this woman had been a witness to a crime, the station lobby was not where we should have been having this discussion.

"Why don't we take this into a private room, please follow me Mrs. Johnson," I suggested.

I led her down the hallway to an interview room. I wasn't sure what case this was regarding, but any news on any case, was always good news. When we reached the interview room, I opened the door and stood back to let Mrs. Johnson pass. Captain was in tow, not missing a beat; although, he elected to stay in the hallway.

"Please take a seat, I will return momentarily," I instructed Mrs. Johnson

She remained quiet and sat in the chair in front of the window. I closed the door behind me, turning to see Captain Sullivan standing against the wall.

"Do you need me to take part in questioning Mrs. Johnson, Murray?" he asked.

"I don't think I'll need assistance. We don't even know what case she has information for, yet."

I sensed the Captain knew what this was all about, but was not willing to provide me with any information. I had no time for mind games. I had a ton of work to do, and now had to question a new witness after barely being there for only fifteen minutes.

"I will let you do all the questioning, but at least let me be present in the room."

What else could I say? He was the captain after all, and I couldn't exactly tell the man no.

"Fine. Let me run up to my desk and grab some items and I will meet you inside," I agreed.

With a nod, Captain proceeded into the interview room while I ran upstairs.

Making my way back downstairs to the interview room, after pulling a tape recorder, notebook, and pens from my desk. I returned to find the Captain sitting in a chair opposite Mrs. Johnson. He stood, offering me his seat. I sat down, placing the items on the table in an organized fashion.

I seemed to take extra care in their placement, fidgeting with the pens, as my nerves took over

Get a grip, this is standard protocol.

Peering up, and staring at the woman sitting in front of me, she still wore her oversized coat and large, round sunglasses. As she slowly removed her sunglasses she looked at me, and I froze.

"Lily?" I whispered.

The woman shook her head and focused on the table in front of her. I stood and began to pace back and forth. How could anyone be calm in this situation? All of a sudden this woman shows up at the police station with similarities to Lily's features, and no one could tell me what this was about? Captain spoke up suddenly. I had forgotten he was still in the room. What did he know?

"Murray, take a breath and sit down," he instructed me.

I didn't know where to begin. Calmly, I took my seat again in front of the woman and pulled my notebook closer to me. I pushed all confusion to the back of my mind—I wouldn't make any assumptions until I knew exactly who this woman was and why she was here.

"What is your name?" I asked as calmly as I could.

The woman hesitated for a moment, raising her face up level to mine.

"My name is Justine Sinclair Johnson, sir."

Scribbling her name in my notebook, I took a double take at the last name.

"Sinclair?" I mumbled to myself, but obviously she overheard me.

"Yes, sir, that is my pre-adopted surname."

I continued questioning her, while still pondering over her name and its connection to Lily's same maiden name of Sinclair.

"Where are you from, Mrs. Johnson?"

"Please, call me Justine, Detective," she replied.

"I'm originally from Burnaby, but currently reside in and around the North Vancouver area."

I continued to scribble down her information. I looked up from my notebook, but couldn't look at her because she reminded me too much of my wife. Noticing the discomfort between us, I stood, facing the window that was behind Mrs. Johnson with my back to her as she still sat at the table. I had too many thoughts running through my mind again, and I wanted answers to them all.

"What information do you have to provide us with?"

The question had been burning inside me from the moment we had sat down to conduct the interview. It was rare we had someone walk in off the street to provide information to a case. Usually, members of the public would use the country's anonymous crime tip line to submit information about cases.

"Your wife's disappearance." Her words stunned me.

Hearing those words from her pulled at my heart, and confirmed what I had been suspecting all along. It would have been a complete coincidence considering the similarities they shared, but I needed to keep asking my questions.

"Where is my wife?" I asked in a barely audible whisper, but the woman clearly hadn't heard me. I turned to face her and slowly gathered my words again.

"Where is my wife?"

The woman dropped her head and began to fidget once again. It took a moment for Mrs. Johnson to answer,

"I don't know for certain, Detective."

At that moment anger began to overtake me, causing me to turn abruptly from where I was and slam my fist onto the table, next to the woman.

"How dare you walk in here, claim you know about my wife's kidnapping, but don't know where she is?"

My breathing was heavy and I was almost face to face with Mrs. Johnson, when I noticed tears forming in her eyes. I took a step back from the table, and began pacing the interview room again. This couldn't be happening, there were too many whys and not enough answers to them all.

I could see Mrs. Johnson was visibly upset, which made me feel like an ass for treating her with such disrespect. As calmly as I could, I sat back down in front of her, picking up my pen to ask more questions. The only way we were going to get through this bombshell of events was if we kept going.

"Can you tell me why you're here?" I asked.

Mrs. Johnson didn't lift her head, and it took her some time to answer.

"I wanted...I suppose...it's complicated..." she stumbled.

Trying to contain my anger, I pressed forward.

"What is confusing? Let's start at the beginning."

"It's not exactly that easy, Detective," she eked out, staring at her fidgeting fingers once again.

I felt as though I was getting nowhere with her. If she didn't want to talk, why was she even here? Shaking my head, I thought maybe we needed a break.

Looking down at my watch, I saw it was already gone two o'clock. Had we really just sat here for two hours without any answers? Peering across to Mrs. Johnson who continued to fidget, I suggested, "If you're not ready to explain anything right now, maybe we should take a break and resume this tomorrow?"

Without a sound, Mrs. Johnson nodded her head in response. She apparently wanted the easy way out. While this was not normal protocol at all—when anyone entered through those doors claiming to witness or know someone's whereabouts, we questioned until answers were provided—I knew we wouldn't be getting any useful information from Mrs. Johnson today—not in her current state of mind.

With that, I stood; but before I excused myself from the interview room, I turned to the Captain.

"Could you please ensure we obtain Mrs. Johnson's contact information and see her out?"

I needed to get away and process what had just happened.

Shutting the door behind me, I paused and took a deep breath to relax the tension that had built up within me. I felt I would have received answers right away if any new leads to the case ever surfaced, but whatever had happened to Lily obviously had this witness severely upset, and unresponsive to my questions. I needed time to think about what had just happened, thus, I began the journey to the fourth floor to ponder about the afternoon events.

FOUR

Callie
Present, February 2004

I was home alone after dad left for work. Sitting back down at the kitchen table, I stared at the broken picture frame I had thrown against the wall the night before during the storm.

I had never become violent before, and that scared me. Storms brought back memories of the devastating night mom was kidnapped. The details I remembered constantly haunted me on a daily basis. I always feared there was something else I could have done to stop the intruder, and save mom from his grip. My mind escaped back to that late April night.

We were under a severe thunderstorm warning and mom and I were in the kitchen preparing popcorn for our movie. Dad was still at work, working a double shift to crack a murder case of a young woman who had been found by the lake the night before.

A heavy knock sounded at the front door, startling us. Mom, of course, went to investigate. We weren't expecting anyone at this hour. It was nine o'clock. I heard the door creak open, the sound of a man's voice drifted down the hallway. It was not a voice I recognized. Immediately the voice began to rise. I could hear mom telling the man to leave and that she didn't know who he was.

"Sir, I don't know you. Please leave"

She kept repeating this, but the man's voice grew louder.

"Get a grip; you know exactly who I am. Stop playing these mindless games. It's time to come home," the man grumbled loudly. I could hear his heavy breathing from the kitchen.

Walking to the doorway of the kitchen, I peered around the corner to see my mother pushing the door closed on the tall, dark clothed man who was wedging himself inside the door and frame. I took a step back; I wasn't sure what to do next. I stood as still as I could, trying not to make a sound, not wanting the intruder to know there was anyone else home. Then it happened, hearing my mother begin to scream, froze me.

"Get off me!"

Panicked screams filled the hollow hallway. I realized something wasn't right. Her voice sounded scared, I had never heard mom like that before.

Peeking my head back around the corner, I looked just in time to see the man push open the door with a loud thud against the wall, smashing the handle through the wall behind it. He was grabbing my mother by the arm, while pulling her outside. I couldn't let

29

someone take my mom! I ran down the hallway, yelling at the intruder.

"Leave her alone, let her go!"

He wasn't listening, I tried to get his attention any way I could, but he continued to ignore me. It was like he was a horse with blinders on, focused only on mom. I managed to make it to the front door and grab my mom's hand, but she just looked at me with tears in her eyes and whispered, "I love you, Callie."

Her eyes pleaded with mine as I stared at her, but I didn't want to let her go. Who was this man? As her hand slipped out of mine, her wedding band fell to the ground.

Shaking myself back to reality, I jumped out of the chair and began to pace back and forth in the kitchen. I hated remembering that night, it was too emotional and painful. I said nothing to mom after she said she loved me. I couldn't even tell her I loved her. I stopped pacing and glanced down at the picture on the table and touched my mother's face with my fingers, tracing the outline of her features.

Mom was beautiful and dad told me how much I looked like her. Carrying the same eyes, and long, semi-curly brunette hair, Dad often said that I was the spitting image of my mother.

With my mind tangled in memories, I didn't realize my cell phone was vibrating in my back pocket. I answered on the last buzz, not bothering to check the call display, but heard a familiar voice on the other end as I answered.

"Hello?"

"Hi Callie, Stan here."

I was relieved to hear his voice. It took me away from the thoughts that were intruding my mind before his call. You see, Stanley had been my best friend since shortly after that tragic night with mom. We had grown up together since elementary school, but it wasn't until I drifted away from everyone at school that he took notice of me. He had been my rock ever since.

"Hi Stan, how are you?"

"Oh, I'm just fine. I was wondering if you were busy tonight? If not, would you be interested in catching a movie with dinner? My treat."

Stan had been hinting for months now that he wanted more from our friendship, but I had always played it down. I was too emotional to engage in a relationship at this time in my life. Never having that mother figure around to ask relationship questions, it was awkward when boys asked me out. Dad always said I could come to him about anything, but some things were better left between a mother and daughter.

"I'm busy tonight Stan, dad and I need some time together, and we have a parent-teacher conference."

"Oh... Okay, I'll see you Monday then?" he asked hesitantly.

I could hear the disappointment in his voice. I knew brushing him off wasn't the best thing to do, but it was true—Dad and I *did* need some time together. Our emotions had been running high lately, and it was time we finally brought everything we were feeling to the table.

"Yes, see you Monday. 'Bye."

Flipping the phone closed abruptly, I refocused back on the photograph. On my mother's face. Something about her was familiar, as if I had seen her recently. It was impossible though, because mom had been gone for six years. Shaking my head, I forgot the thoughts and focused on some chores to take my mind off of the memory.

It was a P.A., day, and I had reminded dad this morning about the parent-teacher meeting that was scheduled for six-thirty with my teacher Mrs. Caesar. I was a good student, with good grades in the nineties, and I would finish all my homework during school hours and spares; allowing me time to take care of the house in the evening and on weekends. With dad at work most of the time, I had to learn to take responsibility around the house—which included cooking dinner pretty much every single night, with the odd takeout. Taking home-economics at school had helped me with the basics of cooking, and other life essentials.

It was the least I could do for dad. He had been such a trooper all these years. Until today, I had never seen sadness or pain in his eyes. It was as if all the years of struggling had poured out of him this morning. All I could do was accept that he was hurting. It was confirmation that dad really did miss mom.

For the rest of the afternoon, I tried my best to keep busy until dad was due home. Eying my watch, I wondered when he would arrive home, as it was already past five o'clock, and he had promised me he would be home in time for the meeting.

I also wanted to sit down and talk about mom with him. Now that I knew dad was hurting, we needed to have a discussion that was long overdue. It had often worried me when he seemed to always have a brave face on. Whenever I brought up mom, he would speak about her for me, but you could tell he was trying to make me happy. I had always felt like he didn't care, but in reality I could now see it was his way of coping, when he distanced himself from the situation.

Feeling anxious, I picked up my phone to dial dad, but it went straight to his answering machine. I was puzzled because that wasn't a normal thing for him. I flipped the phone closed and sat down at the kitchen table, still eying the picture that had been sitting on the table all day. Why did it seem like I had seen her recently?

FIVE

Lily
Past, April 1998

Everything was as dark as a moonless midnight sky. I was walking, wasn't I? No, I was being dragged. Callie was there, wasn't she? I held her hand, the man, who I didn't know, was at the door. I just couldn't piece it together, my mind was foggy.

Attempting to move, I felt chains—my hands were attached to what felt like a pole in front of me. It was cold and damp. Where was I? I heard nothing around me. I began to blink rapidly, peering through the pure black air. What was this place? I faintly saw the outline of a door ahead of me through the darkness, a slight glow showing through the cracks, but nothing else. I felt dizzy, and all I wanted to do was lay down, but I knew I needed to stay awake to figure out where I was. My mind had its own agenda, and all I could think about was wanting a blanket as I was shivering from the cold and dampness this place brought upon me. I called it a place because I was too incoherent to figure out where I currently was. Drifting in and out of consciousness, my head kept hitting the pole like object I was chained to, *thud, thud, thud*.

Stay awake Lily, I reminded myself. I needed to figure out where I was, and being unconscious would not help me find out.

Thud, thud, thud.

I heard it again, but it wasn't my head hitting the pole this time.

Where was the sound coming from? I tried to peer around in the midst of darkness, then all of a sudden I heard the jingling of keys in a lock.

I was briefly blinded by a stream of light ahead of me, while a silhouette stood in the doorway—tall, maybe six-foot, with broad shoulders. From the shape of the stature, I assumed whoever it happened to be, was a male. My eyes were too blurry to make anything else out about him and at that point I was making assumptions. It was confirmed when he flipped on a single-bulb light that hung above me. I looked around briefly as I took in my surroundings of what seemed to be a basement. His facial features came into view as he moved towards me, carrying a hard stare. He had a beard, a little scruffy, which matched his hair. His eyes were small as he stared down at me.

Trying to pull myself back behind the pole and out of his reach hadn't stopped him from coming closer to me. I began to shout at him, not really thinking if it would even help my escape.

"Leave me alone! Let me go! Who are you?"

All the questions ran together, but he refused to answer. Instead, he breathed heavily while he stood over me. Saying nothing, his hand reached for my head. I pulled away from his touch, but there wasn't anywhere for me to go.

"Justine, why are you acting like this?" he asked with a confused look upon his face.

"Justine?" I whispered.

"I am not Justine, my name is Lily!" I shouted back angrily.

Who was Justine?

The man began to laugh hysterically. I looked at him puzzled, and he noticed my confusion. He continued without missing a beat,

"You're telling me that you've forgotten your own name? You really think you are someone else?"

His laughter threw me off course, putting me in a more confused state than when I first awoke.

I wasn't sure what to say, because I had no idea why, or how, he had found me in the first place. I shut my eyes tightly, hoping all of this had simply been a dream; but when I opened them again, the man still stood above me, smiling wickedly, which sent shivers down my spine. In barely a whisper, I spoke again.

"What do you want from me?"

Again, he began to laugh as he replied to my apparent disbelief of the situation unfolding before me.

"You are a funny woman sometimes, Justine."

His repetition of the name rattled me. This man truly believed I was someone else. I spoke up again and confronted him, with fear lacing my voice.

"I am not Justine, I am Lily, Lily-May Murray. Who do you think you are? You have the wrong person, now let me go."

He didn't seem to care, but his demeanour changed suddenly—before I knew it, his hand slapped against my right cheek, causing my head to whip around.

"How dare you try and play stupid with me, you're my god damn wife—whether you like it or not. Your little game is over, I have you back. You'll never be let out of my sight again."

He stormed off, slamming the heavy door behind him. Hearing keys in the lock, locking my only escape out it appeared, I was in disbelief. Nobody had ever hit me before. A tear escaped from my now swollen eyes and rolled down my tender cheek where he had laid his rough, calloused hand. What was happening, and who was Justine

Hours passed before I heard keys back in the lock. This time he returned with food. Placing it beside me, he spoke in a soft tone—nothing like the tone he had used hours before.

"If I unchain you and let you eat, will you run?" he asked.

I had to process what he was asking. Assuming he believed, once he unchained my hands, I would plan to run. Of course this was my plan, I wanted to be free from this man, but I feared for my life because I wanted to return to my family. I couldn't imagine what they were going through.

I shook my head *no* without saying a word. I had to follow his orders, as it seemed to be the only way I had to survive right now. He acknowledged my answer and began to unlock my hands from the now visible pole. I let my hands drop to my lap, allowing blood to flow back into my fingers. I hadn't realized the lack of circulation, and they had become numb from the lack of movement.

The man sat across from me while I ate. It was disturbing to have someone stare at you while you consumed your food. I kept eying the open door, and tried to peer back beyond the flood of light. All I could see was two steps to the left, which I assumed was the staircase the man used when he came down to me. This led me to believe there was another level above us. Of course, as I was not exactly sure of my whereabouts, it was hard to say whether or not I was in a house.

Other than that, there seemed to be no other doors, hallways, or windows around—inside or outside of this room. He noticed my eyes drifting to the door and reminded me what he had already warned me about before he had unchained me from the poll.

"Don't even think about running. If you do, you'll be a dead woman." His harsh tone had returned, accompanied by a look of anger.

His words shook me, I didn't want to die, not by the hands of this man, because he obviously believed I was someone else—someone named Justine.

I finished the last bite of the meal, which was some combination of oatmeal and fruit. The oatmeal was too wet and mushy for my liking, but I couldn't complain—it was food, something my stomach was in desperate need of. I set the plate in front of me, realizing that at this point I needed to use the washroom. Looking around, I didn't see anywhere that could be a washroom. The fear of speaking up over took me, but I didn't like the idea of soiling myself and being left to sit in it. When I had the courage and finally could find my voice, I asked.

"May I use the washroom?"

The man before me smiled, and went on to say, "Oh, going to use that trick to get free are we, because you obviously know the washroom is upstairs?"

It's no trick! I'm in dire need of a washroom! I thought to myself.

I was not who he thought I was, which meant I had no idea where the washroom was. Politely, I dismissed his assumption.

"No sir, I just need to use the washroom."

I realized that I had no idea what his name was, it crossed my mind that using other references may tip him off even more. Finding out his name, and quickly, would give me a leg up on the entire situation. If I knew who I was up against, then I would have better odds at staying alive. This was the plan, forming in my head.

He rose slowly from the floor and motioned for me to stand. Gripping my arm, he pulled me towards him. Leaning down to my height, he whispered in my ear, "Remember, if you run I will hunt you down. Again." Nodding, I complied.

He led me through the open door and to the staircase to the left. It was a long way up, about twenty-five steps. As we made our way up, he continued to grip my arm tighter. I tried to wriggle my arm to indicate his grip was too tight, but, of course, he completely ignored it.

When we reached the top, we walked into what seemed like a kitchen—a cozy room with yellow walls, and sunflowers plastered all over them—reminding me of a cottage. Scoping out my surroundings, I noticed all the windows and door had heavy blinds, which were all closed and causing the room to appear dark. The only light was seeping in from around the outside of the blinds.

Finally, I felt his grip loosen and my arm drop to my side. We stood motionless briefly in the kitchen, when finally he spoke,

"What are you waiting for? You said you needed to use the washroom."

This was true, but I didn't know exactly where it was, because, after all, it wasn't my house. I was too scared to ask, fearing he may become violent. Instead, I simply nodded and turned to my right where a hallway seemed to lead to other rooms. I prayed that one of the doors lead to a washroom.

Opening the first door on my left, I discovered a simple bedroom with white daisies around the crown molding of the room. I quietly closed the door, trying not to draw any attention to the fact I had no idea where I was going. I spotted a door ajar on the right. I could see the washroom through the mirror. *Phew*. Relieved it was easy to find, and only my second attempt.

Once inside, I closed and locked the door. Taking in the beautiful lavender bath accessories, I could tell whoever Justine was, she loved colour and flowers from the few rooms I had seen thus far. There was a small window ahead of me, and without hesitation I quickly dove over and tried to open it—but it wouldn't open. I checked the locks. They were in the unlocked position. As I took a closer look at the window, it appeared to be sealed with a clear, dried substance. Had this man really glued the window shut? While I was pondering this extremely odd discovery, a sudden heavy thud was heard on the washroom door, and his voice muffled from the other side.

"Hurry up, don't be getting any ideas about escaping now."

I chuckled to myself, knowing full well that was impossible. He had the windows glued shut for God's sake. Clearly, the washroom wouldn't be my escape route. Quickly finishing my business and washing my hands, I felt using the facilities made me feel cleaner, considering where I had been kept overnight. I noticed even the soap smelled like lavender. Lavender was actually one of my favourite scents. I was not fond of the look of lavender mind you, although I thought it was a gorgeous shade of purple.

Opening the door slowly, the man stood in front of me with his arms crossed, not looking impressed at all. His mood changed drastically with each minute—was he bi-polar? Grabbing my arm, he led me back down the hallway where I had walked just a few minutes earlier, looking for the washroom. Without hesitation, he pulled me back down the stairs, but I stopped him. Trying to pull myself back up the stairs, I asked, "Why must I be imprisoned to the basement?"

He simply chuckled and replied with a cocky tone and laughter.

"Because you can't be trusted. You left once, and thought you out smarted me, but you won't be leaving again."

Pulling me harder, I almost lost my balance. Complying with him was the only way. He pushed me through the door we had left through, but this time I could see exactly what my surroundings were with the light he had left on. Without another word, he closed the door and locked it again. While I could now see there wasn't much to the room at all, at least I had some light. To my left was a metal shelving unit with boxes on, but other than that it was just a huge open room with support posts—it was not a finished basement in the least.

As I continued to survey the empty space, I spotted the chains that must have held my hands together when I first came to. Standing in the middle of the room, motionless, I felt tears forming in my eyes. Was this going to be my life now? Living in a cold damp basement with no contact to the outside world? What about my family, wouldn't they find me? How I arrived here was still a mystery, because my mind was fuzzy about the night before. Feeling helpless, I collapsed on the floor, more tears beginning to flow down my cheek, stinging as the salted wetness fell onto the grazed bruised cheek I had sustained earlier. My mind wandered back to the night before, and I tried my best to recall what had happened.

Callie and I were in the kitchen, preparing popcorn for a movie. The doorbell rang just before nine o'clock. I went to answer, where a man was standing on the porch dressed all in black and wearing a hood. I didn't recognize him. His voice was low—husky of sorts.

"You can't run forever, it's time to come home."

His words filled the empty space between us as I held my hand firmly on the side of the door to brace myself.

"You must have the wrong house sir, I don't know you."

He didn't seem to acknowledge what I had said, and began pushing the door open with his whole body. He had strength, something I was slowly losing. I knew if Callie heard the struggle, she would come running; and not knowing who he was I wanted to keep her safe. I attempted to push the door closed, but the man was much stronger than I. All the strength I had was gone the moment the door flung open with a loud 'thud' against the wall.

Seizing me by my arm, he began to pull me outside, I continued to fight back and tried to pull myself back inside the house. Before I knew it, Callie was there, pulling at my hand. She began to tell the man to get off of me, but he ignored her. He was focused and on a mission. Nothing was going to stop him.

I mouthed to her, "I love you, Callie," and let go of her hand. I attempted to kick the man who was leading me away from my home and my little girl, but he held me tighter and slipped his hand over my mouth with a cloth-like object that was moist, trying to silence my cries for help. I knew he was trying to render me unconscious, which caused me to fight back even harder, but my strength was weakening by the minute.

I looked around our silent street—nobody noticed the racket that had been occurring. I continued to be dragged to what seemed like a dark coloured car, but my eyes were closing as the man held his hand tightly to my mouth. I heard the door open to the vehicle, then everything was black.

Knowing that was the extent of my memory of that night, I shook myself from it. The next thing I remembered was waking up here in this room, chained to the pole. What was I supposed to do? There were no windows, and the only door seemed to always be locked unless the man was entering. From the information I had gathered about his fluctuating temperament, I knew if I attempted to run he would catch me and God knows what he would do to me.

More hours passed as I sat in the middle of the floor. Then, once again, thudding down the stairs and the faint sound of jingling keys grabbed my attention—the man had returned. The door swung open, revealing him standing there with a pillow and blanket. Without moving from his position in the doorway, he threw them at me.

Was he really expecting me to sleep here in the basement? It was damp and cold, and what about another meal? Did he really think I could survive on only one meal?

I contemplated asking if I could sleep upstairs—after all, to him I was his wife, and wives slept with their husbands, didn't they?

Gathering the words to attempt my question, I proceeded with a strong voice,

"Why can't I sleep upstairs with you?"

The man shook his head vicariously in response.

"You have barely been home a day, and you expect things to just go back to the way they were? How do I know you won't go off running away again?"

Before speaking, I thought about my response.

"I promise, I'll be good. I don't have any intentions of leaving," I replied, knowing full well it was a complete lie.

I wanted out, and I wanted to see what I was up against to plan my escape. The man laughed that irritating laugh of his.

"You have said that a million times, Justine. You're staying here, in this room, until I feel I can trust you again—that you won't run away from me again."

"Well, what about food? I've only eaten once today."

He always had an answer for everything and shot back, "Maybe not giving you what you want, when you want it, will teach you who to respect around here—something you desperately need to learn."

Turning, he pulled the heavy door shut behind him, and locked it.

I gave it my best shot, at least, I thought.

If I could prove to him he could trust me enough to allow me to be upstairs with him, I knew I would have a better chance of escaping. First, I needed to figure out his name. It was hard to play along without knowing any information about him.

I figured it must have been getting late. Taking the pillow and blanket I found a spot in the open room that would have to suffice for the night. Slumping down, I leaned against a cold wall. This was it, day one of my kidnapping down. How many more would I have to endure until this nightmare ended?

SIX

Murray
Present, February 2004

Ring, ring.

Jolting awake to the sound of an incoming call to my station work phone—not realizing I had fallen asleep at my desk—I answered on the last ring.

"Detective Murray, how can I help you?"

I realized I sounded groggy, and cleared my throat, pulling my voice together.

"Dad, it's me, Callie."

I lowered my head. What was the time? If she was calling, it had to have been late.

Glancing over at the clock on the far wall, I saw that it was gone nine o'clock.

"Callie, honey, I'm sorry, I didn't realize the time, I fell—"

Callie interrupted before I could even finish my sentence.

"Dad, it's okay, I was just worried. You weren't answering your cellphone and we were supposed to have my parent-teacher interview this evening with Mrs. Caesar."

Right, I had turned my cellphone off after I came up from the interview with Mrs. Johnson. As Callie talked in my ear, I stared at the computer screen ahead of me where I was completing a search on Justine Johnson. Everything matched the information she had told me about North Vancouver, but nothing about Burnaby— place of work, residence, nothing. It was as if she had never existed. I decided I would need to finish up my work tomorrow.

Bringing my attention back to Callie, who continued to talk in my ear, I was missing what she was saying. I closed my eyes for a moment and breathed deeply. All I could hear next coming from the receiver of the phone was Callie calling out in a panicked tone.

"Dad, hello? Are you there?"

Replying instantly, to assure her I was.

"Yes dear, I'm sorry. I'll be home in twenty minutes. I'm leaving the office now."

"Okay, see you soon"

She hung up the phone, but I continued to hold the phone to my ear. My mind just wasn't into anything; I could feel myself shutting down. The day's events had made me feel different, bringing up feelings which I hadn't experienced before. I was missing my wife more than ever. Placing the phone back on its base, I leaned forward to shut my computer screen off and gather my belongings.

Everyone on my floor had left for the evening, but I could see the Captain's office light on as I passed by, which meant he was still around. I had tried to avoid him after the day's events, feeling embarrassed that he had witnessed my emotions back in the interview room. Contemplating which route to take to the elevators, my thoughts were interrupted by him calling out my name.

"Murray, come in my office please."

Turning in his direction, I saw the Captain standing in the doorway of his office. Feeling beyond tired, I didn't want to stop and talk to him. All I wanted to do was go home and see Callie. After the storm the night before and her reaction that morning, we needed to have a serious talk about Lily.

Reaching the doorway of his office, I stepped inside as he made his way around his large wooden desk. The Captain motioned for me to sit, but instead I shook my head.

"I'll stand, thank you."

Captain Sullivan took a seat in his black leather chair and began talking immediately.

"Murray, I'm worried. You didn't seem like yourself back there in the interview room earlier. I thought you would have held your emotions at bay a little better with the witness."

I was completely shocked at the Captains assumption. How exactly had he expected me to react? A woman came in claiming she knew details about my wife's disappearance. I thought I had been as calm as I could have been.

"Captain, how would you expect a husband to react in this type of situation?"

I was becoming overwhelmed and trying my best to keep calm. The Captain didn't look pleased, but I really didn't understand what he was expecting from me. He spoke again, this time with more authority in his tone.

"If this is how you're going to act, I will have to pull you from interviewing Mrs. Johnson and any fur—"

I was not going to take a back seat in this investigation yet again. I had done it once before, and I didn't plan to do it again—ever. I wanted answers; I could feel the rage building inside me, but knew I couldn't be angry with the Captain. He was following protocol after all, and was already bending the rules with me. Taking in a heavy breath before speaking, I asserted myself and replied more calmly, "I'll do better tomorrow Captain, just give me another shot. What time is the interview scheduled for?"

"Ten o'clock," he replied slowly while gauging my reaction. "Don't be late. Now, get out of here."

We ended the conversation at that. Bidding him goodnight, I stepped back out into the hallway. Making my way to the elevators, I pressed the down button several times, as if the first time wasn't enough.

I was anxious to go home. I needed to see Callie, and to think through the events from earlier that day to prepare myself for tomorrow. The elevator arrived and I stepped in, pressing the lobby button and then the door close button rapidly, as if that would close them any quicker. I didn't need anyone jumping in the elevator with me—I needed this time for myself.

The ride down the four floors felt as though it took hours, in reality it took under a minute. Time seemed to be crawling by. The lobby of the station seemed busy for a weekday night, but I didn't really care as my mission was to get to my car and travel home undetected by any other co-workers.

As I reached the door to leave, Falcon waved me down from across the lobby as I looked back over my shoulder. Grumbling under my breath, I turned in his direction.

"Murray, I'm glad I caught you."

He was too chipper for me, and I thought, *I wish I could say the same*, but of course I didn't say it out loud. I tried to make it look as though I was in a rush in hopes of whatever he wanted to say would be made quick. He continued on, without noticing my shifting from one foot to the other to move the conversation along,

"We all heard a woman came to see you today, about your wife?"

How did everyone know? How long was Mrs. Johnson standing in the lobby before I showed up?

His comment irritated me—I was not one to have my business aired amongst my co-workers. I stared at Falcon, he could tell I wasn't pleased.

"I'm sorry," he mumbled, peering away as if he knew he had struck a nerve with me.

Apologizing wasn't going to cut it. I took a moment to gather the words in my head that I wanted to speak, and once the words were formed I spoke in a calm, even tone. My intention was not to come off as rude, but he needed to know how displeased I was to hear about this.

"I know everyone means well Falcon, but it would be greatly appreciated if my business wasn't passed around the station. I don't know the situation in detail yet. I don't even know what information the woman had, or if it will be relevant to my wife's case."

The look on Falcon's face made me feel like an ass, but it was the first time I had wanted privacy, giving me the time to process whatever events were about to unfold.

I turned to push the door open to leave, but turned back to Falcon one last time to reassure him I wasn't angry at him, but simply at the situation.

"It's nothing against you, I would just like some time to process all of this, on my own. Thank you for your concern."

With that, I exited the building and made my way to my car, blindly jabbing the key into the key hole of the driver's door. Once I was finally seated in my own space, where nobody could bother me, I broke down—weeping uncontrollably, like a newborn baby, slamming the steering wheel a few times in anger. In reality, it seemed to actually help. I had never been one to lose my temper easily, but I had built up tension from the many years of searching for Lily. It was finally time to admit to myself that it was eating away at me.

"Why?" I shouted into thin air. Why was all I could speak—why had it happened in the first place? Why hadn't we had any leads for years, and now someone stepped forward after years of torment to Callie and I?

Tears continued to stream down my face. It was the first time I had let my emotions overtake me, but to be honest it felt good to cry. I had kept all my emotions to myself for this long, and it was inevitable they would need to escape at some point. I sat in my car for fifteen minutes. Time seemed to keep escaping me tonight; Callie had to have been upset with me by now—with me missing her calls, missing her parent-teacher interview, and the fact that we had planned to discuss Lily tonight, something that was long overdue.

Rummaging through the glove compartment, I spotted some tissues to clean up my face a bit before heading home. I had always hidden my emotions from Callie, because I wanted to be strong for her. I was actually relieved I broke down privately, away from her. She didn't need to see her father in a distraught state.

Taking a look at myself in the rear view mirror, it was finally time to drive home. To avoid traffic on the main roads, I chose to take the side roads to help calm my senses and refocus on the task at hand—getting home to see Callie. We had some things to discuss that I believe we had both been putting on the back burner in hopes we wouldn't offend or upset each other.

Reaching the driveway, I noticed the living room light was on, and the blind drawn just a crack. Lights from the television flickered rapidly through the crack of the drawn blind. Had Callie really stayed up? It was nearly eleven o'clock by the time I managed to get home.

Removing my belongings from the back seat, I slammed the car door shut with my hip. Callie was already standing at the front door to greet me when I reached the porch, throwing her arms around my neck in a comforting bear hug. Callie always had the biggest hugs, even as a little girl—strong hugs that you didn't want to end.

After a few moments of embracing on the porch, I led us inside. Callie didn't give me any time to set my things down before she began rambling off her day, ending with asking how my day had been.

I didn't want her knowing about Mrs. Johnson just yet, not until I figured out myself what her story was. I didn't want to give Callie hope when I didn't know the outcome. I thought about what to say, but she was staring at me, noticing my stalling.

"Did you have a busy day?" she finally spoke up.

"Yes dear, it was busy."

As I moved past her into the kitchen, she followed.

"Anything interesting happen, any big cases?"

Normally, I shared my current investigations with her, and I felt lying to her about today would leave an emptiness between us, but it was a sacrifice I was willing to make—at least for the time being. Thinking momentarily, I gave her my response.

"I received some leads for an old cold case today, but we're unsure if they'll lead to much, but it was a start."

She seemed satisfied with that answer, as she pulled a plate out of the oven.

"I've had your plate prepared since five o'clock, I thought you would have been home earlier."

"I'm sorry you went to all this trouble, I got caught up sweetheart." I could sense the disappointment in her voice.

I walked over and sat down at the table with the plate of food she had prepared. As I took my seat, I noticed the image of Lily from this morning was still sitting on the table. Callie noticed my slight smile as I peered down at the image.

"I thought we could have talked about mom..." she trailed off.

I drifted my eyes back to Callie who was standing against the kitchen counter, fidgeting with her hands. It reminded me of when Mrs. Johnson had fidgeted in the interview room earlier that day.

Taking a bite from my plate of roast beef, caramelized carrots, and mashed potatoes, I motioned for Callie to join me at the table. We sat in silence for a moment, before she spoke.

"Do you miss her, dad?" she whispered, barely audible.

The question shocked me a bit—did she really think I hadn't missed Lily? I needed her to know the truth, I couldn't imagine why on earth she would think otherwise.

"Of course, all the time." I said, continuing with bites of beef in between.

"I've been worried about you lately," she went on to say, her voice shaking with each word she spoke.

"I never wanted to bring her up because I didn't want to upset you...you never—"

Callie stopped mid-sentence. I could see her eyes beginning to tear, and it tore me to see my daughter feel this pain. Setting my fork down, I placed my hands on her hands across the table to ensure I had her full attention.

"We have done the best we can since this whole ordeal began, don't lose your faith."

I could feel a tear forming in my own eye, but I blinked it back rapidly. It was enough to see my daughter in pain, I needed to be strong for her.

"It hasn't been easy on either of us and to tell you the truth Callie, it breaks me apart a little more each day your mom isn't here with us—but I am happy to have you here with me. Experiencing all your accomplishments over the last several years has made me proud, and I know she would be proud of you, too."

Callie lifted her head to look at me, and I saw a faint smile form across her face.

"I'm glad I'm not the only one hurting, dad. You're right, we're here for each other, and I know mom would want us to be happy."

Callie had a good head on her shoulders. She had grown up far too quickly after the events that occurred with Lily. I had to agree with her statement—Lily would want to see us happy, regardless of the situation. Our eyes both drifted to the photograph, and I realized the frame was unrepairable, considering the glass was shattered in too many pieces.

"How about we go out this weekend and find a new frame for mom's picture? Does that sound okay with you?" I asked her.

Nodding, she agreed.

"I am sorry about the frame, dad, I was just angry."

"Angry about what?"

I didn't want to push her, but it seemed like the right time to ask. Her eyes drifted back to her continuously fidgeting hands.

"I was angry that mom wasn't here for me to talk to. No offense, but I'm getting older, and I need to talk to her about..." she paused, as if she had lost her train of thought, but suddenly picked it right back up again.

"About boys, relationships, how to act...you know, girly kind of stuff. The stuff mothers and daughters share."

I had to sympathize, those were things that mothers and daughters shared, and it upset me to see Callie feeling angry over not having her mother around to discuss those important moments in her life.

"You know I am always here for you darling. I may not be mom, but I will always have a listening ear and do my best with advice. Don't shoot me down too quickly."

Giving her a wink, I could see her frown turn into a bit of a smile. Pushing the chair back, she stood and took the few to close the gap between us to wrap her arms around my neck.

"Thanks, dad," she whispered in my ear while squeezing me just a little tighter.

In the back of my mind, I wanted to tell Callie everything that had happened earlier that day, but part of me also wanted to ensure the woman was telling the truth. I wanted some solid leads before I broke the news to Callie. I sensed she wanted to tell me something else as well, but was finding it difficult to share.

"Callie, I do have to go into work tomorrow. I know it's not a normal day as I typically have weekends off, but it's important that I do."

I could sense her disappointment, but she never came out and told me directly.

"That's okay, we always have Sunday."

Keeping her tone neutral, she had to have been one of the most understanding young women I knew, and I was proud to call her my daughter.

Callie headed up to bed a short while later, while I continued to sit in the kitchen and take in the events of the day. When I awoke that morning, I had not expected such a roller coaster of a day. Part of me still felt numb—it had been a long time since any new leads on the case had appeared, and to finally have answers to Lily's disappearance felt unreal. Pondering all this, I felt myself nodding off and shook myself awake. It was time to hit the hay and try to sleep.

Creeping up the stairs, I peered into Callie's room to check on her—she was sound asleep, tucked under the covers. Pulling the door shut with a slight creak, I tip toed down the hallway to the master bedroom. I always loved the master bedroom, because Lily had decorated it the week we moved into the house. We were both young and in love, and this was our first home. Both of us had only rented apartments before we had met, but we knew we wanted a family and needed some space for the family to grow up in. Lily insisted the master bedroom had to have lilies and roses somewhere in the room. The walls were painted white, with crown molding attached to the upper walls to create a Victorian-style room. Lily was extremely creative and had hand painted lilies and roses, alternating the pattern, all around the bottom of the crown molding.

When I asked her why she chose the pattern of the two flowers for the bedroom, she told me about a vision she had when she was a little girl, and this vision included her bedroom having lilies and roses. She couldn't remember why, but it was something that was vivid in her mind from her childhood. Each week, she would pick roses from our backyard and place them in vases on the night stands next to the king size bed we shared. Lily absolutely loved flowers. There was only one flower that she loved the fragrance and colour of, but never how it looked—lavender. In her eyes, it wasn't very pretty because it was a tall, thin flower with tons of tiny flowers. She preferred large bloomed flowers. Nevertheless, flowers were beautiful and fragrant in Lily's eyes; and the key to a beautiful home.

It was all I had to hold onto right now, as I sat on the hope chest at the bottom of the bed. It was Lily's, and nobody had ever been permitted to open it. It contained memories of her childhood, special keepsakes she told us. Over the years I had urges to open it, and had hoped it would have held possible clues to her disappearance—but I respected my wife's privacy, and had yet to open the chest. It had made me think, though. Maybe someone from her past came back? Lily hadn't had any enemies to my knowledge, she was well loved by all, but perhaps that hadn't always been the case.

Shaking my head of the thoughts, I undressed down to my boxers and crawled into the empty bed. For the past six years, Lily's side of the bed remained unslept in—refusing to take up any of my wife's space. It was my way of hoping she would return to occupy it one day. As I fell in and out of sleep, I sensed a tear forming in the corner of my eye. It was not easy laying in a bed without your spouse for this long. I struggled every morning to get out of bed, not waking up next to her, but always found the strength to. She wouldn't want us to stop living, even though Callie and I found it hard some days. I believed that eventually, as time moved on, it would get easier; but if anything, it was becoming increasingly difficult.

SEVEN

Callie
Present, February 2004

Sunshine flooded the bedroom floor as I rubbed my eyes of sleep. It was another day, and the weekend, but mostly a weekend spent home alone. Dad had to work, which was abnormal as he usually took Saturdays and Sundays off for us to spend time together. I knew being a detective caused him to work long hours, but he was pretty adamant with the Captain about not working Saturdays in the past.

Last night, when I asked dad about work, it was as if he was stalling, or possibly lying. I let it go because I could sense it was an awkward moment for him.

It was wonderful to finally be able to talk to dad about mom, and to know that we both had been hurting and needing one another. We couldn't be brave all the time, and lately I had realized that sometimes we just needed a good cry to release the pain. Thinking about mom caused a tug at my heart.

Recently, I felt like I was wearing my emotions on my sleeve, because of the sense that I had seen mom while I had been walking to and from school—every time I doubled backed or snuck a peek, whoever I sensed was there disappeared into thin air. I put it down to my overactive imagination.

Shaking my mind from that state I pondered that nothing would get done if I laid in bed any longer. Even if dad wasn't here to spend time with, I was sure I could find something to do. Maybe I would even give Stan a call.

I had given him the cold shoulder recently, so I thought it was finally time to be straight with him and let him know how I felt about our relationship. He deserved that much from me. At this point, I would have liked to continue our friendship, but if something more came of it later, I would let it happen.

Giving one final stretch, I threw the covers off and headed to the bathroom for a quick shower. Dad's door was ajar and I could see him sleeping peacefully. I wondered if he had forgotten he needed to go to the office. I decided to let him sleep until I was finished in the shower, and then wake him.

As the water ran over me, my eyes began to close and the beating water settled into a rhythm against me.

What's happening lately? Where is mom? Is she even alive?

Tears formed in my eyes, but I blinked them back. It had been tough, and dad had been doing an amazing job, but I missed that mother-daughter love. How would I talk to dad about relationships and boys? I had never been a religious person, but I felt as though sending a prayer skyward would help me in this situation, in hopes it would come true one day.

There was a knock on the washroom door, making me realize I had lost track of time with all my thoughts.

"I'll be out in a few minutes," I called out.

The voice responding from the other side of the door was muffled with the sound of water gushing down behind me. I finished up as quickly as I could and hopped out, drying off and changing into my clothes for the day. Leaving the washroom, I headed downstairs, towards the kitchen.

It was always a morning ritual that dad and I started off the day in the kitchen with a 'hearty meal' as he called it. Mom had always believed a hearty breakfast turned into a healthy heart. Regardless how much of a hurry we were in, or if we would be late for work or school, we sat and ate breakfast together. Time was precious, and we had discovered that over the last several years. One couldn't take anything for granted. We lived each day as if it were our last, fulfilling our dreams and ambitions.

Dad was already sitting in his morning chair, newspaper in hand.

"'Morning, doll," he smiled at me, as he peeked over the top of his newspaper.

"Do you really have to go to work today, dad?" I asked him, trying not to sound too disappointed, but it did pain me a little inside.

Dad didn't respond right away, as if he were pondering how to answer. Was he hiding something?

"I'm sorry Callie, I do. I have several cases that need my attention."

I never understood how he balanced work and family before mom disappeared. It seemed he was busier now with work, compared to when mom was

61

around. Maybe mom had been a distraction to dad's work life?

I had stopped asking about mom's case last year, after realizing that every time I asked about it, dad couldn't come up with any more excuses about why the case went cold or not having any new leads. I know he had done everything in his power to find her.

Making my way to the fridge and opening the door to scan its contents, I realized a lack of food had become a problem around here. Grabbing an apple from the crisper drawer, I closed the door and headed to the sink to wash it.

"What time will you be home?" I asked him.

Dad folded the newspaper he had finished reading and placed it on the table in front of him.

"I hope not too late, maybe late afternoon. I suspect I'll only be needed for a few hours."

He didn't sound very hopeful in his voice, but I didn't want to prod him anymore. I walked over to him as he began to stand, kissing him on the cheek and embracing him in a hug.

"Dad, I love you," I reminded him.

"Have a good day, and don't work too hard."

He let out a chuckle as he kissed my forehead and was off down the hallway towards the front door. I followed behind him as he pulled on his shoes and picked up his brief case. Leaning in, he gave me another kiss on my forehead.

"I'll see you later," he said as he handed me a wad of money.

"Maybe you can hit the grocery store for us? I noticed there's hardly anything left around here to eat."

"Sure. Love you dad, see you later."

He walked out, closing the door behind him, leaving me standing in the hallway—the hallway that mom left me in all those years before. You would think all these years later I would have forgotten about the small details, but it was the complete opposite—I remembered more of the details, and always ran scenarios through my head about how I could have prevented it.

EIGHT

Darren
Past, April 1998

Justine had only been home two days and was already causing trouble. It was as if she were playing mind games. Had she hit her head and caused herself amnesia? Who the heck was Lily, whom she claimed to be?

Whatever.

All I cared about was that I had my wife back. Now, the question was what to do with her. I couldn't trust her anymore, not after the stunts she had been pulling. Who did she think she was, running from me, her husband?

Nevertheless, she was home. I had to go out to work, which is why I planned to keep her locked in the basement while I was gone. Knowing her, she would go snooping for the spare keys and take off again, and we didn't need that happening.

Her using the washroom was going to be a problem, considering the only one in the house was on the main floor. Rummaging through the cleaning closet, I pulled out a bucket and set it down by the basement door. It would have to do considering the circumstances.

Taking the keys off the kitchen counter, I eyed the table I prepared for breakfast and smiled. I headed downstairs to collect Justine, still smiling to myself. Once I reached the basement door, I jammed the key into the lock, entering the room quickly and flicking on the single bulb light I had installed during the week Justine had decided to take off. I knew then, if I had her back, there would be consequences for her unlawful actions.

"'Morning, Sunshine," I called over to where she laid against the wall. It took her a moment to become coherent to my presence. Pulling herself upright and into a sitting position against the far wall she replied.

"'Morning"

Her voice was hoarse as she spoke. Crouching down to meet her gaze, I reached my hand out to help her up.

"Where are we going?" she hesitantly inquired. I felt her resistance as I led her to the open door.

"You'll see." I said coyly, giving her a reassuring smile.

Turning off the light, we made our way up the stairs, as I let her go ahead of me. She took her time, as she climbed each step carefully. Reaching the landing, I placed my hands on the back of her shoulders and ran one down each of her arms.

She shivered at the touch of me—why was she suddenly afraid of me?

"Welcome home." I breathed into her ear.

Pushing her towards the kitchen table where I had prepared her favourite breakfast—eggs, bacon, and homemade hash browns—I pulled out her chair and motioned for her to sit, pushing her in after she was seated.

Taking the seat across from her, I peered up towards her face, catching a glimpse of her eyes. She still took my breath away, made my heart flutter, and created a lust deep within me.

"Is breakfast to your liking?" I inquired, sensing her tension the way she eyed the plate in front of her.

Her disgusted look caused me heartache—I had done everything for her, and she never once showed any appreciation since she had been home.

"I'm allerg—"Her sentence was cut off abruptly, but her thought changed.

"It's lovely, thank you," she continued in a soft whisper.

Picking up my fork, and seeing her do the same, we dug into the meal before us.

As we sat quietly in silence, I could see her eyes darting around the room, it was as if she were in a foreign place. She had only been living here for ten years, what was so fascinating that it required such intense concentration?

"Is everything okay Justine? You seem off."

She didn't answer right away, staring down at the half eaten plate of food before her.

"Everything is fine," she replied through gritted teeth.

Her attitude was beginning to irritate me, and I really didn't like my temper being tested—especially right then, because I needed to go to work and needed to be calm for it. Ensuring she knew she couldn't take up my entire day, I informed her of such.

"Hurry and eat up. I don't have all day. I'm due at work shortly and I need you fed before I leave."

She stared blankly back at me before her mouth began to open to say something.

"I'm not hungry."

With that, she pushed her plate towards the center of the table. That was fine with me, she wouldn't be eating again for another eight hours. If this was how she wanted to act, so be it. She could starve for all I cared. Standing, I took our dishes to the sink to rinse.

"You may want to use the washroom now—you won't have access to it while I'm gone."

Peering back over my shoulder, Justine's attention was on the mail I had left on the table.

"Justine, I'm talking to you. Listen when I speak."

Frankly, I was beginning to lose my patience with her, and it was barely mid-day. Walking over and placing a firm grip on her shoulder to pull her attention away from whatever she was attempting to do, I said,

"When I talk, you listen. Do you understand me? I will not repeat myself. Ever."

This would be her only warning. If she didn't care to listen to what I had to say, she would go without, to teach her to respect me as the head of our house.

Her eyes filled with tears, but I could see she was forcing herself not to shed them. Justine never cried. She learned to be tough, because crying was for the weak.

"What have I told you about crying? Stop it."

This pushed her over the edge. Without warning, she forced herself up, pushed me back, causing me to almost lose my balance in the process.

"Get away from me!" she yelled at the top of her lungs, her voice filled with anger.

She began to run down the hall. Lucky for her, she couldn't get very far, but with her slight head start she managed to reach the bathroom and lock the door before I was able to regain my balance. Through the door, I could hear her heavy breathing and attempt to open the window. The sound of her hands slamming against the glass in agony and her muffled yelling through the door, I could tell she was mad.

"You have nowhere to run, why do you think locking yourself in the bathroom will give you freedom?"

No answer came from the other side of the door. Instead, something heavy was thrown, hitting the door with a loud thud. That was it. As she knew, no door or room in this house was ever out of my reach, considering I wired and keyed the place myself.

Pulling my keys from my back pocket, I slid in the correct key, swinging the door open. She was standing against the far wall, breathing heavily and armed with the hair dryer. I had to laugh out loud over her weapon choice—as if a hair dryer was really going to give her a leg up on me.

"What do you think you will do with that now?" I asked, chuckling.

"Preparing myself," she shot back, anger lacing her voice.

"I'm sure this is all a misunderstanding, Justine."

"What's a misunderstanding is you believing I am someone named Justine....I am not Justine!"

Immediately, she came barreling at me, waving the hair dryer in her hand above her head. I caught her just as she took her first swing towards my head.

"You will learn you can't get away with such behavior. This is your final warning."

I was firm with her, while I squashed her wrist, allowing the hairdryer to come crashing down next to us.

"You won't get away with this!" she snarled back at me.

I didn't know where all the attitude was coming from. She usually complied with my requests, and this side of her was irritating me. She was challenging me, and no one *ever* challenged me.

Keeping ahold of her arm, I led us back down the hallway and through the kitchen to the stairs leading to the basement. Before making our way down, I picked up the bucket I had placed by the basement door, earlier. Giving her a shove to go ahead, she began her way down the stairs at a pain-staking slow pace.

Once at the bottom, I pushed her into the room, flicked the switch for the light bulb to illuminate the room, and threw the bucket inside.

"If you need to pee, that bucket is your bathroom."

I began to mumble as I left the room. I was so tired of these games. If she wanted to treat me like this, then I would treat her like a dog until she obeyed me.

NINE

Lily
Past, April 1998

His name was Darren, Darren Johnson. I spotted mail on the kitchen table addressed to him. At least I had a name to go with this mystery man, which was a step in the right direction, as I planned how to take on my kidnapper. I was only able to get a glance at the mail before Darren was in my face about not obeying him. Right now, I was not pleased with him at all—the demanding nature, violent hand, and verbal abuse from him was eating away at me. Did he really think that he could speak to me, or anyone for that matter, the way that he did? What was his problem? I seriously felt as though he had a mental disorder, because at times he seemed completely delusional, while other times he was sweet and sensitive—complete opposites of the spectrum. Whoever Justine was, it was no wonder she ran away, and I was glad she was living a happier life—wherever that was, now.

Peering around the basement room I was confined to these days, I noted there wasn't much to it besides the metal shelving, boxes, and now the cracked bucket I was to use to pee in while Darren was at work. If my surroundings didn't scream prisoner, I didn't know what would have. He truly was correct when he murmured I was an animal, because he was treating me like one.

Taking a seat on the cold floor, I realized that although I now knew his name, I really didn't have much more to go on. How was he expecting me to stay down here while he was off working was not something I was fully understanding. What type of work was still to be determined, because he hadn't elaborated on what he did. I would find out eventually, though—I was on a mission to discover anything and everything I needed to know about Darren Johnson.

I basically had to force myself to eat that morning, let alone I was allergic to spices and I could see some sort of spice on the eggs. Luckily they were not major, life threatening allergies, but it still left me itchy and uncomfortable. I was too worried about offending him to tell him the truth. I was scared of saying or doing the wrong thing whenever I was around him, worried about what the consequences might end up being. It was already clear to me that Darren was hot and cold with his actions—one minute perky, the next angry as hell.

What had me the most, was him really believing I was his wife. Clearly he was delusional to not recognize his own wife, and somehow I managed to become the victim in this terrible mishap. There was only one person who would have looked identical to me, and that was my twin sister who I hadn't seen or spoken to since I was seven years old when she was adopted from the orphanage we were both in back in Burnaby

Those days would never leave me, I couldn't forget I had a twin, but right now reminiscing about the old days was not going to get me anywhere closer to escaping this hellhole.

There was nothing more I could do besides sit here in this damp, musty place and ponder my escape—and I did plan to escape, there was no doubt about that. There was no way I was going to sit by and let this man control me, and think I was someone else.

My nerves were shot, and I simply couldn't sit still any longer, since I had been doing absolutely nothing for the past three hours. I began walking around the room. Up until now I had not taken in the living arrangements that I was facing. Was there a way out of here at all? I began running my hands along the wall starting by the door, which had the shelving unit against it. To me, the boxes all looked old and dilapidated and wouldn't have held much, but nevertheless, I took a peek in a few of them. All I found was old clothes, which was not going to do me any good. I folded the lid flaps back into place and began checking for loose bricks or maybe a secret door. Anything was possible, right? I was not letting any potential idea of escape drift away. I would investigate every inch of the basement to confirm.

Reality hit once I reached the end of the wall. What was I thinking, this was the real world, not some fairytale. There was no such thing as a secret passage. As I made my way along to the far wall opposite of the door, a brick moved when I pushed on it, but not by much. You could tell it was sealed up, or someone had attempted to seal it because whatever was used was cracking around it. It was clear, and out of place when I took a closer look at it.

I tried to get my fingers around the edge to get a grip on the brick. It wasn't budging. Peering around the room, I checked if there was anything that I could pry the seal open with. It was hopeless, as all this room had was the shelving unit with old boxes sitting on it. Turning back I tried one more time, this time I was able to wiggle it forward a few inches. The brick was not light by any means, almost falling to the ground as it finally gave way from the wall.

Setting it down on the floor, I peered into the hole, of course the light was not helping but I could see a box with a book beside it. Pulling them out I walked over and sat under the light that lit the room to take a closer look at my discovery. The book looked tattered with age, in the way that it had been in the wall for years. The book contained a lock on the outside, appearing to be a journal or a diary of sorts. Blowing the dust off the top and setting it down beside me I turned my attention to the wooden box. It was the size of a small shoebox and also donned a latch with a lock. Whoever put them in the wall did not want anyone to find them. If someone were to come across the two items they didn't want anyone to be able to open them. Without any form of tools prying these open was not going to happen.

I shook the box. Nothing could be heard from inside. Being wooden, I couldn't tell if the objects inside were heavy or if it was simply the weight of the wooden box itself. It was something I needed to investigate. How I was going to investigate without the proper tools, was beyond me.

Loud banging was heard coming down the stairs, which meant Darren was on his way. I scrambled to my feet and rushed to put the box and book back into the hole in the wall. Lifting the heavy brick, I struggled to get it back in. Just as the door swung open the brick was set back in place.

"Justine, where are you?" His voice was deep, but not as angered as it was when he had left.

"Right here," I eked out.

I walked back into the light to see him in the doorway, peering in and looking around.

"Work ended early, I thought we could spend some time together before dinner."

This gave me the shivers. I didn't want to be with this man any more than what was necessary. I would have rathered him be at work than have to be in his presence. That way, it was less likely I would make him mad or upset.

"What did you have in mind?" I asked meekly.

He wiggled his eyebrows, the words I heard him say next sickened me.

"Maybe some romance."

I felt a wave of sickness rise from the pit of my stomach. This had crossed my mind briefly before now, but I had tried to push the thoughts to the back of my mind, hoping it would never actually happen. It was bad enough being in his presence, but I couldn't imagine being romantic with him. He wasn't even my husband!

Taking a few steps back, I was contemplating and giving space between us to think. I had a million thoughts run through my head at that moment. I wanted to give an excuse, but what specifically, I didn't know. Needing to sound confident was the most important part when having to lie; so mustering my strength, I finally blurted out,

"I don't feel well."

It was the only thing I felt would keep him at bay. Who would want to be around a sick person? Then again, being a nurse gave me a different view about these things than the average person. I could see his head shaking at my comment, but I had no idea what he was thinking.

"Justine, don't play those games with me. You know when I need something, you'll do it." His tone was still calm but had an edge to it.

He was demanding, it was like he had to be in control of every situation. Nobody had a chance to voice their opinion because in the end it was his voice taking a stance against anyone and everyone else, and right now that was me he was standing up against.

"But if I don't feel well, I don't need you getting sick."

With a weak tone I spoke, giving a little cough to make what I was attempting to do seem more real. At this point I was trying everything I could think of to keep him away.

"You should know by now I don't get sick, Justine. Stop with trying to get out of it. It's been months since we made love, and when I demand love, love is what I will get."

This man really was mind-boggling. What he was calling 'love' was not love. It was fulfilling his wants, simple as that.

He moved closer to me, and as he took a step forward I took a step back, until finally, there was nowhere else to go because my back was pressed up against the cold, concrete wall. Placing his hands on either side of my shoulders, his eyes were filled with passion. Darren leaned in, towards my lips, and in a split second I ducked and dropped to the floor.

As I had moved down, I could smell liquor on his breath, faintly, but it was still present. The thought of him consuming any alcohol could be the result of his unusual request of needing romance from me.

"What do you think you're doing?" he boomed, towering over me.

I looked back up to meet his confused gaze.

"I told you, I'm not well. I don't really want to be doing this right now," I answered confidently.

I crawled out from under him and pulled myself up to stand in the middle of the room. It took Darren no time before he turned around, but I had my own plan— to run. Without another thought, I turned and ran through the open door of the basement and up the stairs as fast as my legs could possibley take me.

The heavy steps of Darren were not far behind me. He didn't miss a beat and was on my tail immediately. As I reached the top of the stairs, it dawned on me that all the windows were sealed shut, so were the doors, too? What was I thinking, running? This gave him more reason to be angry with me. I turned to see Darren reaching the stop of the stairs, the anger present in his eyes told another story—one which I was not ready to see.

"Have you lost your god damned mind? What have I told you about running? Now get over here before you regret your choice."

His tone was laced with anger. This was becoming a natural occurrence, him being angry. Nothing I did pleased him, but rather, angered him. Not being the person who he thought I was, was already taking a toll on me, too.

"No. I don't want to sleep with you. I am not who you think I am. I won't betray my husband," I blurted out, not realizing what I had said.

My mindset was back to being Lily, not Justine; though I didn't really care, because I would protect my body when I needed to.

"Everyone believes I'm the looney one, I think you're the crazy one in this relationship. I am your husband, and you will be with me however, and whenever I want."

Reaching his arm out, he grabbed me by the shoulder, his grip tightened to secure me at his side. With his other hand, Darren gripped the back of my head holding a fist full of my hair as he pulled me in closer to him. I could still smell the light aroma of alcohol, which smelled a lot like whiskey, as his hot breath surrounded me.

Before I knew it he began pulling me down the hallway, I assumed he wanted to do the deed in the bedroom. At this point I didn't have the strength to fight him considering the grip he had on me, I walked with him down the hallway or in my case almost being dragged. Once inside the room he let go, giving a slight push towards the bed. I rubbed the back of my head where he had held my hair tightly.

Darren rummaged through a dresser across the room and pulled out a red see through piece of fabric.

"Put this on, maybe you can tease me with your dancing, you know I love."

Tossing me the item, I began to unfold what he had handed me. It appeared to be a teddy-style lingerie garment. I was not really used to wearing lingerie at all, and had no idea if it would even fit considering I didn't know the size of his actual wife. Darren's eyes never left me as I studied the piece. I assumed he expected me to undress right here, with him watching me. The thought sickened me, and all I could think about was my husband, Keith. I was about to betray him, even if it wasn't my choice—or was it my choice?

"What are you waiting for? I don't have all night to wait for you," he growled at me.

Starring at Darren, you could tell he was growing impatient, the look in his eyes told me he would make me his, regardless of whether I agreed or not.

Why was I not fighting him more on this, why was I complying so easily?

I dropped the piece I was holding onto the bed. Slowly, I pulled off my shirt and dropped my pants. Darren's eyes followed as articles of my clothing began to fall to the ground, while I slipped the organza fabric over my head, and pulled it down over my body. I closed my eyes, realizing how exposed I felt—another man seeing what only Keith should see, disturbed me.

"You've changed... You don't look as firm in the chest as you did a few months ago. You'll need to get back into your exercise program. You know how I like a firm body."

Internally, I was shaking my head, of course I won't look the same to you because I am not who you think I am!

Darren walked over to me, placing a hand on my shoulder and running it down my arm. With a low voice and desire filled eyes, he stated,

"At least you're still soft like I remember."

I tried not to shake or waver but it was a common reaction when someone you didn't know was touching you in a sensual way. Pulling me into him, he kissed my cheek, and continued planting a trail of kisses down my neck. Naturally, my head fell backwards, but I caught myself before allowing his sensation to completely overtake me. I could feel myself shaking. I could hear my heart thudding loud in my ears. Pulling myself away from his grasp, I moved away from him, I noticed my breathing was heavy. I was scared. I closed my eyes to collect my thoughts, opening them to see Darren still soaking me in.

"The things I want to do to you tonight will leave you wanting more. I guarantee you, Justine."

I wanted to throw up. His words were sickening. How could I actually let him do this to me? Why wasn't I running, screaming, or hitting him? Instead, I stood there completely naked underneath a lingerie piece, with another man other than my husband holding me and kissing me.

Reaching out his hand, he walked towards me, taking my hands in his—placing a kiss on top of each of them. His eyes connected with mine, and he flashed me a smile while he led me over to the bed. He motioned for me to take a seat. As I sat, he began pulling off his shirt, letting it drop to the floor without a care. This was the first time I had seen him exposed. I knew that he was a broad, muscular man from the way he had gripped me. He didn't have any definition of abs, but he was toned. One by one, Darren's clothes hit the floor as he stepped out of his jeans, leaving him in only his boxers.

The discomfort I was feeling never subsided, and I had to continuously remind myself that this was really happening, regardless of my inner demons telling me otherwise. Darren pushed me back on the bed and climbed on top of me, staring at me with lustful eyes. I tried to imagine it was Keith, knowing that was the only way I would be able to get through what was about to happen. I had opposite emotions rampaging through my body—my insides were screaming, but I felt paralyzed on the outside.

With his rough calloused hands, he roamed my chest, squeezing and pinching my breasts. Nobody had ever handled me in such a rough manner. Realizing I couldn't hold in my emotions and discomfort any longer, I shouted out at him.

"Ouch!"

"What do you mean, ouch?" Darren pulled back to search my face for an answer.

"Ummm…it was just unexpected…" I trailed off, not sure what his reaction would be. Regardless of me trying to cover up my outburst, this seemed to put Darren in a different mood—but it didn't make him stop what he was doing. He turned his attention back to roaming my body, moving his hands further down my stomach, landing between my thighs. I tensed with his touch, which caused me to clench my thighs together unexpectedly. I had no control over how my body was reacting. All it knew was to reject him.

"Relax woman, you're acting as though I've never touched you before," he grunted.

I needed to pull myself together before I completely fell apart on him. In that moment there was nothing more I could do, except be Justine.

Taking a deep breath, I let my legs relax, although some tension was still present. He slipped his hand between them, finding and fondling my clitoris. I closed my eyes in an attempt to hold back the tears that had begun to flood my eyes. I didn't want to show weakness, and made it appear I was enjoying his touch instead.

He moved off me momentarily, which caused me to open my eyes to see him pulling down his boxers that revealed his shaft. He was aroused from his foreplay.

The moment was here—he was about to commit an act in which I had no choice in the matter. I had hoped he would at least use protection. I was too afraid to ask while he loomed over me. I was not on the pill, as Keith and I used protection whenever we made love.

As these thoughts flew through my mind, Darren had made it back on top of me, with his breath becoming heavy once again. At this point, I just wanted him to get it over with. With the thought of protection at the forefront of my mind, I somehow found the strength to speak up before he went any further.

"What about...protection?" I asked with a squeak to my voice.

I couldn't help but ask, I knew I was taking a chance, but it was causing me too much anxiety.

"What protection? You're on the pill, I give it to you every morning. You know very well I'm uncomfortable with any other kind of protection."

I felt my breath catch at his words—that pill he was giving me every morning had actually been birth control? I hadn't been swallowing it because I didn't know what it was he was giving me. Now, I almost wish I had known what it was he had been giving me, I probably would have complied and taken it. At least that would have given me some protection against what was about to happen.

"Why are you acting weird?" his voice echoed through my confusion.

"Everything's fine, let's get this over with," I said matter-of-factly.

"Let's get this over with? That is no way to treat me. It's a privilege to make love with me. Don't forget that."

Privilege? It sounded as though this had been my idea when it had been all his. All I could do was lay there, motionless with my eyes closed to keep the tears from spilling over. I never expected I would be violated in that manner in my lifetime, ever. I was in a happy marriage with my husband. Well, I *had* been in a happy marriage; with how this journey was going with Darren, I thought I may never be back with my husband even if I survived this. Who would want to be with someone who had been taken advantage of by another man?

TEN

Murray
Present, February 2004

The drive along McNabb Avenue was crawling to a near standstill, with the lack of green lights to move the traffic. I tapped the steering wheel impatiently, as I inched forward towards Gough Road.

Glancing at the illuminated digits on the dashboard, it displayed well past nine o'clock. In the back of my mind, I didn't care, as it was giving me more time to collect my thoughts. I almost felt as if I was trying to avoid going into work, but right now Mrs. Johnson was my only hope to finding answers about Lily's disappearance. It wasn't just important to me, I needed to think of Callie as well—if she had known that someone knew something about that awful night, she would be all ears. Although, it didn't feel right to let her know just yet. I wanted to ensure I was one hundred percent correct and that Mrs. Johnson was actually a lead and not playing games with us. It had been six years, and as much as I needed to take every lead to heart, leads this long after a crime were usually pointless or someone wanting their five minutes of fame, who didn't actually know anything at all.

I pulled into a parking spot by the side entrance, as I decided I didn't feel like going through the lobby today, I didn't want anything or anyone to distract me. I needed to keep my focus on the task at hand—which in this case was the information Mrs. Johnson was about to share today. After all, this could be a meaningless waste of time. However, when it came to my wife, I would follow every lead and do everything and anything in my power to bring her home.

Making my way up a short flight of stairs rarely used off the side entrance, I made my way through the back hallways I headed to the interview room we had used the day before. I came prepared today, as I had already packed my briefcase before leaving the house with a notepad, pen, and a tape recorder. To prove to the Captain I was in total control over this developing situation, I needed to treat this as a regular interview, just like any other investigation. He already had zero faith in me—at least that's how his actions had come across—I needed to convey that I meant business.

As I opened the door, Captain Sullivan was already sitting in a chair awaiting my arrival. He stood and greeted me.

"Good Morning, Murray," he mumbled.

Before I let anything go any further, I wanted him to know today's interview would run more smoothly than it had yesterday.

"'Morning, Captain," I answered cheerfully, setting my brief case down on the interview table.

"Just so you know, I'm prepared for today, Captain. I won't sit by, I need to be active this time. Let me do this, okay?"

With a nod of his head, he agreed.

Opening my briefcase, I pulled out the supplies needed during the interview and placed my briefcase on the floor next to the chair. Peeking at the clock on the wall, I wondered why the front desk officer hadn't brought Mrs. Johnson through yet. I was usually on time, and rarely had to wait for anyone.

The worst thought ran through my mind—she would not show today. Shaking my head of these thoughts, I asked Captain,

"Has Mrs. Johnson checked in?"

Waiting for his answer caused an anxious feeling within me.

"No... she hasn't checked in yet, Murray—"

I cut him off with a hand gesture.

"I don't want to hear it, we need to stay positive. She could be stuck in traffic, or in a public transit delay."

I still had faith as I spoke my thoughts. It was clear by his facial expression that he wasn't very happy at having to wait, but I was willing to wait all day if I had to. Glancing at the clock again, I noticed it was quarter after ten, but just at that moment there was a soft rap on the interview door.

Swinging around, I saw Detective Gresham and Mrs. Johnson—dressed in a black skirt, and red blazer, standing very timidly behind Gresham. Gresham had been promoted to detective in the last few months, but usually worked opposite shifts to me, as she was still used to night shifts.

Taking a deep breath, I nodded towards Mrs. Johnson and motioned her into the room, as I pulled a chair out from behind the metal table for her. I hoped this would silently imply for her to take a seat. As she walked into the room, I noticed the timid demeanour she carried. You could tell it took all her strength to walk the several steps from the door to the table. I reached out to shake her hand. Taking mine in hers, I noticed her grip was weaker than I had anticipated.

As she sat down, I took a seat in front of her, avoiding eye contact with her. Instead, I motioned to Gresham to close the door behind her as she exited. Rustling with my papers and pen to settle my own nerves, I realized the long awaited moment had finally come. Taking a deep breath to relax, Mrs. Johnson spoke first, to my surprise.

"How are you Detective?" she asked in a soft, timid voice.

I looked up to meet her eyes, feeling taken back by her question. I noticed as I stared that her eyes were green, identical to Lily's. Hers looked swollen and tired.

"I am well, thank you." I replied, speaking in a confident voice—we couldn't have two nervous people in the same room.

Feeling the need to proceed, I pressed the record button on the recorder that I had set out before us, then, without any hesitations, I jumped straight into the first consent question.

"Do you agree to an audio recording of this interview, Mrs. Johnson?"

Without a word, she nodded her head in agreement.

"This testimony may be used as evidence if this case goes to trial. A verbal agreement is needed, please acknowledge with an oral yes or no, Mrs. Johnson."

With my formal interview protocol settled in, I proceeded by repeating the question once again.

"Mrs. Johnson, do you agree to an audio recording of your interview, and that you have been made aware this may be used as evidence in a court of law?"

Time briefly stood still. In a soft voice, barely above a whisper, she spoke.

"Yes, I agree detective."

I pushed the recorder closer towards her to ensure her words were being picked up. I didn't exactly have any formal questions prepared, I was more going with the flow of what she wanted to share to be honest; but that was me being human, and not the detective I was supposed to be. There seemed to be an awkward silence filling the room, and thinking quickly, a question came to mind.

"How do you know Lily-May Murray, Mrs. Johnson?"

Her eyes closed and I could see she was taking a deep breath before answering. Her mouth opened to speak, but closed again.

"I know this is a difficult situation, take your time," I assured her, speaking as calmly as I could.

I knew patience was going to be key in this situation, but I could tell the Captain was quickly becoming impatient. Intervening, he stood and placed his hand on the edge of the table.

"Mrs. Johnson, I understand how difficult this must be for you, but please think of the life of Lil—"

I cut him off immediately before I allowed him to continue. I didn't need him scaring the poor woman before we had even begun.

"Captain, can I speak with you privately?" I rushed, pushing my chair back with a loud screech against the floor, giving the Captain a look of horror.

I knew exactly where he was headed, but I felt it was necessary to keep the interview light, without the pressure of the livelihood of Lily looming over the witness. I knew what was at stake, and time was of the essence; but I had seen past cases like this, and scaring the only witness would pull them back. I didn't need to push Mrs. Johnson away, as she was the key to this investigation.

Leading us out into the hallway, I closed the interview room door quickly behind us.

"Captain, what the hell are you doing?" I sneered at him, still moving away from the door to not let our conversation leak back inside.

"My job, one that you seem to be taking very lightly this morning. This is an interview, Murray, not a dinner party!"

I had never heard Captain Sullivan angry, but keeping my cool I attempted to reason with him.

"Captain, I have a feel—"

He cut me off, not allowing me to get a word in edge wise, he continued what he had to say.

"You can't go in there and be all soft to the witness, Murray."

His tone was firm, as if he were speaking down to me in a childlike manner—had he forgotten who I was? I was one of his top detectives. I had conducted thousands of interviews during my career so far.

"She's scared, can't you see that?" I barked back at him.

He was irritating me, but I tried to keep my temper in check and not sink into the temper that was growing in the Captain.

"I can see she is, but you informed me last night you were going to provide an interview. If you can't—"

I butted in before he could even finish.

"I *am* conducting an interview. She is currently our only hope in this mess, Captain. Be patient, nothing about this case makes any sense and there is a possibility Mrs. Johnson has the answers we have been looking for. I don't want to scare her any more than she already is. Please, let me handle this. "

I could still see the disappointment in his facial expression, but he seemed to let it go, crossing his arms in front of himself.

"I understand the procedure, but sometimes we have to bend them if we want answers," I reminded him.

I had seen the Captain be gentle with his witnesses before, which was why I didn't understand why he was giving me hell about my approach with Mrs. Johnson. The demeanor of the Captain softened.

"As long as answers are received, proceed as you see fit, I suppose."

With that, he walked away towards the lobby, without another word. Everyone knew the Captain was irritated when he walked off. It was his way of cooling off, or not winning the argument at hand.

Breathing heavily, I watched him disappear around the corner from me, I needed to level myself again. I knew if I walked back in the room irritated, it would only cause Mrs. Johnson to feel even more anxious than she already was. After completing a few breathing exercises, I headed back into the interview room to find Mrs. Johnson peering out the tiny window, seemingly lost in her thoughts.

"Mrs. Johnson, are you alright? Would you like some water?" I asked her, softly.

A tear fell down her cheek. Taking the tissue box from the table, I passed it to her. Without removing her stare from the view beyond the window, she pulled one out of the box and dabbed her eyes. In a whisper she asked, "Do you meditate, detective?"

I was confused by her question, but answered it regardless.

"Sometimes, why do you ask?"

"Because you always take deep breaths before you speak."

She was observant, and correct. I was taken back, and wasn't exactly sure how to answer her. She only had known me for a short time, but seemed to understand me, and not just on a professional level.

"I do, because it calms my nerves."

Without missing a beat she turned and stared me in the eye.

"Are you nervous, detective?"

Wasn't I supposed to be asking the questions here?

I thought briefly. How exactly was I supposed to answer a witness who asked such a question? Turning away from me, she opened her mouth to speak, but closed it just as quickly, as if what she had to say was not important.

"Mrs. Johnson, can we resume with the interview, please? Can we take our seats at the table once again?"

Continuing to look out the window and ignoring my attempt to resume the interview, words began to pour from her mouth.

"I was an orphan in Burnaby. I grew up with nineteen other children until the age of seven, before I was adopted by the Cousineaus. I can't complain, because we were treated well considering the circumstances we were living in—not being a real family, having the feeling of having more siblings than the average family, and of course, not having anyone you could call mother and father." She paused briefly before continuing in a more confident tone.

"It was just off in the suburbs of Burnaby, in a small community. The home was small, or at least it seemed it with twenty of us running around. The orphanage also provided schooling for us; you could say it was more of a boarding school. The older children helped with the chores around the home—setting the table, sweeping the floors, and making the beds. Flower, a girl at the orphanage, and I were very close. We called her Flower because she was always picking the flowers in the garden. Miss Walker, the head of the orphanage, would allow her to put flowers in a vase as the table center on the kitchen table, as well as in the shared bedroom Flower and I slept in.

She would come running in from the back door with a handful of pulled flowers, daily—roots and all. For the most part, they were wild flowers, and occasionally weeds, but everyone adored her love of flowers—always bringing a smile to our faces. We used to run through the garden and see who could pick the most flowers within a minute. I don't remember ever seeing her upset or angry—she was also the most optimistic of us all.

Flower and I were the same age. Her laughter was contagious, and when I close my eyes I can still hear her laughter now. It didn't seem to bother her that we lived with eighteen other children, her spirit never dampened. As time grew on, we made a pact that we would always be together, and that one day, we would live together and decorate our home with flower paintings.

That dream was short lived, as two years later the Cousineaus walked in and chose *me* to adopt. I tried to convince them to adopt Flower, too, but they shook their heads and told me they were sorry, but they couldn't take us both.

You see, regardless of whether we were related or not, we were always taught we were individual people, because any one of us could be adopted at any time without their siblings. It was a stark reality, and we had seen it happen many times. Most times, families were only looking to adopt one child, and not a set of siblings. The young children didn't understand this concept, but us older ones knew and understood. I only had a day to say my goodbyes and pack the little things I owned—which fit in my small tattered bag. Part of me was happy to finally have a family, but my heart was broken because I had to leave my friends behind, and especially having to leave Flower.

As the years passed, my mind drifted back to the times in the orphanage, and the friends I left behind. I often wondered if they were adopted and living a life with a loving family, just as I was. The Cousineaus were wonderful parents. When I was twelve, they adopted again, but this time from overseas. I remember asking them to check back at the orphanage that they originally adopted me from, but they were set on adopting a baby from France. My adoptive mother was not able to bare children. They tried for many years before me, and many years after they adopted me; but she simply was not able to.

As time went on, I finished high school, which was where I met Darren Johnson, my husband. I fell in love like every young woman does, and felt he was 'my everything.' We moved in together when I was twenty-two, living together for six years before we decided to get married.

The wedding was small. My adoptive parents were there, and Maggie, my adopted sister was my maid of honor. Everything was perfect, and exactly how I had dreamt it to be as a little girl. However, a year later, our marriage turned south.

Darren became more controlling over where I went and whom I was going out with. When I began questioning him about it, he became abusive. It started out verbally, with name calling. I would shake it off and continue forward, figuring it was a phase and due to stress he was facing at work. I remember thinking to myself that all relationships went through this at some point. Months passed and I was confined to our home more and more. He even went as far as not allowing me to work. My only privilege was to go to the grocery store, and even that was limited—I was only given one hour to make it there, shop and purchase our groceries, and be back home. This went on for a couple more years. When the verbal abuse turned into physical abuse, I decided that was enough and ran away. I ran away for a purpose—to find Flower."

At this point, her eyes had welled up, and I could tell she was fighting back tears; but the tears won, with a steady stream of tears leaking from her eyes. I passed her the box of tissues, placing them in front of her on the ledge of the window. I contemplated what my next question should be. She had essentially just poured out her life right in front of me. I was lost as to where to even begin.

I knew this was going to be a rough day from this point forward. As she spoke, I was jotting notes to question her on later, when I looked down at my paper; it was just a scribbled mess. I still wasn't entirely sure what her connection was to Lily, because she had made no reference to her with what she said.

"Thank you for explaining your story, Mrs. Johnson," I consoled her, while searching my paper for a question.

"Please, call me Justine, detective," she replied.

"I must ask, what is your connection to Lily-May Murray?"

Silence filled the room. She began to sob uncontrollably while peering out of the window, not speaking at all. I was growing impatient at this point. Perhaps she needed a break, and to resume this in an hour. I sure could have used a smoke break myself at that point, some fresh air would have refreshed my mind.

I never was much of a smoker, but stressful times had caused me to take up smoking and drinking—but not to the point where I would say it was essential, or that I was an addict.

"Justine, let's take a rest, catch our breaths, and resume this in, say, an hour?"

I said this as gently as I could, as she continued to stare and sob out the window. As much as I wanted answers, I also did not want to pressure the only person who seemed to have the answers. It was a difficult situation to balance, and I knew the Captain wouldn't approve of the route I was taking, but my gut was telling me to take it easy with her.

Sometimes we had to break a few rules and go out on a limb to find our answers. Justine acknowledged my suggestion with a nod of her head. It seemed her past had caused her much pain. Our police division was out of her district to be able to assist with the spousal abuse, but I made a mental note to talk to some of the detectives in that division to help her.

I rose from the table and made my way to the door.

"There's a coffee shop across the street if you wish to have lunch," I mentioned before walking out the door.

Justine continued to stare out the window, speaking in only a whisper.

"If you don't mind, I will just wait here."

I didn't have any reason why she couldn't, so I nodded to her and told her I would let the front desk know she was there.

I left the room, leaving Justine behind, and made my way to my cubical on the fourth floor. I informed the front desk that the witness was still in the interview room as I passed by, towards the elevators. I needed a break myself. It had already been a long and emotional morning. As I took a seat in my chair, I stared out the window with my mind drifting to Lily. Where was she? Was she still alive?

ELEVEN

Lily
Past, July 1998

It had been nearly three months in this hellhole, and every day was something new. He let me stroll upstairs on select occasions other than for my meals. The sleeping quarters hadn't changed, and I was still being forced to sleep in the basement, but had now been given an old mattress to sleep on instead of the cold, damp, concrete floor. Only once did he allow me to sleep upstairs— that was only because his manhood was in need of attention. Being handcuffed to the night table had been awkward, and I was thankful it had not occurred again since. After his sexual thirst had been satisfied that evening, he wanted me to sleep next to him, but he didn't trust me, of course—he handcuffed me to the night table. I would have taken sleeping in the basement over having to have myself chained to a night table all night long after what he did to me. I needed to know why he didn't trust Justine and the reasons behind his control issues.

Darren took his time coming down to get me for breakfast that particular morning. It was the weekend, which meant he wasn't working. I still hadn't found out what he did for a living as of yet. When he arrived home after working, his focus was solely on me and nothing else. I didn't bother to poke and prod him with questions, as I thought it would tip him off more about the mistaken identity.

Just as those thoughts left my mind, I heard the familiar sound of heavy foot steps descending the staircase.

I sat up against the wall as I waited for him to enter the room. He had stopped chaining me to the pole in the basement a few weeks after he had kidnapped me, my bold attempt to run caused him to be paranoid. I had the feeling he had started to trust that I wouldn't try to escape the moment he opened the door. Although it was the most obvious thing to do, I had learned it wouldn't lead me anywhere with all the locked doors he provided between me and the outside world. His presence filled the doorframe. It appeared he was holding something in his hand. As he moved into the open space and directly towards me, I could see it was a vase of roses. Why the heck was he bringing me roses?

"Happy Anniversary, here are roses for my Rose. I love you."

Rose?

This man really was neurotic, or maybe he called Justine 'Rose' as a nickname—she did seem to like flowers a lot with the way the rooms upstairs had been decorated. That name sounded so familiar to me, but I couldn't recall where I knew it from at that moment. Processing information was difficult when Darren was present, as my attention needed to be fully on him, watching his every move to try and be one step ahead of his thoughts and actions.

"Thank you," was all I managed to say. How could I celebrate someone else's anniversary? There was an awkward silence as he handed me the vase of what appeared to be a dozen red roses. Setting them down beside me, I peered back up at him.

He smiled—a smile that seemed not to be angered or sly, but genuine. Maybe Darren did have a heart after all, but he had a funny way of showing his kindness.

"Dance with me?" he asked, his voice soft as he spoke, which was rare to hear coming from him. He didn't wait for my answer, but instead reached his hand down towards me.

"Dance...I...umm...don't...I mean...we don't have any music."

Without hesitating, Darren began humming an unfamiliar tune. His eyes met mine, and for the first time, Darren had genuine passion in them—not the desired filled ones that only occurred when he needed something from me, that only I could deliver.

I stood, accepting his outstretched hand. He pulled me close into him. Reluctantly, I laid my left hand on his shoulder. Darren lifted my other hand to hold in his as he led us into a swaying motion, back and forth. I had to concentrate not to step on his toes. I had never danced, other than on my own wedding day. I always believed I had two left feet. I closed my eyes, remembering my real wedding day, with my actual husband—our first dance as husband and wife. I thought it would be less awkward if I focused on something that had actually occurred in my life. It was paining me to think about such a happy day that I had once lived. Now, I was missing my family dearly. Every day I wondered how many more days would go by before I could see them again.

Continuing to dance, he stopped humming to speak to me.

"I will never forget the day I married you, and us dancing to this song."

I shuddered at his words, but did my best to contain my emotions and actions. There was only so much I could take. I had to remind myself I was Justine Johnson now, there was no Lily-May Murray anymore. Times like these reminded me what my life had become, and that I needed to push all other thoughts of my previous life to the back of my mind.

Swaying back and forth on the concrete floor I felt him lean in closer to my ear. I jolted back to reality, just in time to feel him place a soft, but awkward, kiss on my neck.

Pulling away and out of his hold, I realized it had been nearly two months since the last time he had been romantic with me in the bedroom.

"What's wrong, Rose?" he murmured.

"Why are you now calling me Rose? What's wrong with you!" I shouted louder than I had planned to.

"Because that's your name?" he replied, a confused look upon his face.

"I think I know my own name, it's Justine Johnson!" I shot back.

"Justine hasn't been your only name, and you know that. Why are you playing dumb?" he replied, his tone becoming gruffer.

What did he mean? Justine had another name?

I had no response for him and for fear of creating anger within him, which I could already see in his knitted brows, I left the conversation there. With my concern focused on what Darren meant by this other name, I hadn't realized he had moved behind me. He placed his hands on my shoulders and ran them down my arms, his warm breath inches from my neck. He pulled my hair to one side and pressed soft kisses against my skin, descending from my earlobe down my neck.

I shivered. I wanted to scream, run, anything not to have him on me like this. I had learned in these short few months that all of that got me nowhere. I was Justine—or was it Rose today?— whether I liked it or not. This is who I was, and this man was now my husband. His hands roamed my body, starting down my arms, then back up my torso, crisscrossing his arms around me to force me backwards, closer to him. I continued to shiver against him. The discomfort that sat in the pit of my stomach began to rise and caused my breathing to become heavy. My nerves were kicking into high gear. I didn't want him to get angry with me again, so I pretended my heavy breathing was due to enjoying the moment—well, shall I say, he was enjoying.

Shaking my head of the thoughts, I pulled away. I needed it to stop. I didn't care if it caused Darren to be angry, I wasn't going to let him take advantage of me in that   way   again. Literally shaking, I tried to calm myself as I peered over my shoulder to Darren who stood behind me, perplexed.

"What is wrong with you?" he barked, his voice angry and confused, and not allowing me to answer before he continued on.

"You will do as you're told. If I want to hold you, caress you, then you're going to allow it." His tone was firm as he spoke.

"I'm a human being, too. I should be able to control my own body," I shouted back at him.

Even I was becoming angered at the situation. He thought he was in control of everything. He would soon learn he wasn't in control when it came to my body, and that I would protect it.

"Think again, Rose. Think again," he cooed in an antagonizing tone.

"Stop calling me Rose! That's not my name!"

I didn't understand why this name irritated me to the core, it was just another name after all. "It is your name, like it or not. You may not want to remember those days in the orphanage but that's the name your birth parents gave you."

Darren wasn't making any sense. How had he known I grew up in an orphanage? It was all confusing. Everything was meshing together. It seemed as if the lives of Justine and I had been intertwined together at one point in time, but I didn't have the brain power to process it or come up with an explanation in that moment.

Dropping to the floor, weakness took over. The lack of food and water, due to having only two meals a day, began weighing in on me.

"Get up off the floor. I'm not done with you," Darren grunted.

My vision was blurred as I saw his body move towards me. I lifted a hand for him to stay back. I didn't know what was happening. I had never felt like this before. The sickness from my stomach began to rise. I could hear his voice distantly.

"If you're going to be sick, be sick here."

Before I knew it, the pee bucket was shoved under my face, just in time to catch the contents exploding from me. Why was I so sick all of a sudden?

My hair was being held back by Darren's hands, who was now crouched down beside me. At least he knew what to do when someone was sick. Managing to pull myself up to sit properly on the ground, I peered up into his eyes. They were soft again, just like they had been when he first came into the room today. The flowers still sat on the floor where I had left them, next to the mattress. I noticed they weren't in any water though, which meant they were not going to last long.

"Are you going to be alright?" his voice broke the silence, when he noticed my eyes diverting.

"I'll be fine. It's nothing," I lied.

I had learned that's how things rolled with Darren. Everything the last nearly three months had been a bed of lies.

"Come upstairs so we can get you cleaned up," he instructed me.

I almost had to give Darren a sideways glance. Was this man seriously actually caring about someone else for a change, instead of himself?

"That would be nice, thank you," I replied, weakly.

I stumbled as I made my way to my feet. Darren looped his arm around and under mine to assist me as we made our way out the door and up the stairs. I was still feeling weak for some reason. I thought it was possible I had the flu, but I had already received the flu shot nearly eight months ago prior to the kidnapping.

Once on the landing, I turned to Darren to speak.

"I think I have it from here, thanks; but could I get a cup of water, please?"

With a nod of this head, he let go of me as he made his way into the kitchen. I hung to the wall as I made my way down the hallway to the washroom. I turned the tap on to cool, and pulled a face cloth from the pile in the drawer. I wet it and after wringing out the excess water, held it over my entire face. The coolness pressed on my face was relieving, if even for just a moment.

Darren appeared in the doorway with a cup of water, that genuine smile plastered on his face once again.

"Here you go," He said pleasantly, as he handed me the cup he had brought.

I managed to take a sip. I knew if I had the flu or a stomach bug I would need to take things slow and rest.

"Why don't you lay down in the master bedroom? The bed is more comfortable, and if you continue being sick the bathroom is close by."

I was surprised by Darren's offer, and he must have noticed the confusion on my face, because he continued, "You have to promise me this isn't some sort of escape plan, faking being sick. If I find out it is, there will be hell to pay."

You had to love how Darren took the soft moments, and crumbled them instantly. As I took another sip from the cup, I nodded my head. A comfortable bed would be nice, even if it was only for a short while. Right now, it beat the dampness of the basement. For all I knew, it could have been the basement making me sick.

Darren moved from the doorway and began down the hallway towards the bedroom. I followed behind, ensuring not to move too quickly to create anymore waves in my stomach. As we entered the room, I noticed rose petals in a path over the floor, leading to the bed. The smell of the roses overwhelmed my sense, causing more sickness to rise up.

"Darren…I'm going to—"

Before another word, I shot back to the washroom just in time to purge more contents from my stomach. What was wrong with me? I was hardly ever sick, being a nurse had made me accustom to being around germs, and in turn, a better immune system. When I was finally able to pry myself from the ceramic bowl and clean myself up again at the sink, I made my way back down to the bedroom.

Darren had picked up all the petals by the time I made it back, and I found him sitting on the edge of the bed waiting for me.

"Feeling better?" he asked softly, as he searched my face for answers.

"I think so. I'm sure it's just a stomach bug. It should pass," I assured him.

"Let's get you into bed. I don't need a sick woman on my hands."

It sounded as though I was a burden to him, and my next statement came out in a snarl.

"I can take care of myself, you can take me back to the   basement."
It was clear he did not approve of this option.

"No. You will sleep here until it passes. The bathroom is much closer this way, I don't need to be cleaning up your vomit."

Darren had gestured towards a closed door, I assumed this meant there was a master bathroom. I took a seat on the edge of the bed. The waves seemed to have been easing over the last few minutes.

"Sorry to have ruined your plans today," I said meekly, attempting to make small talk with him.

I wasn't really sorry, but I was learning to play his game. I was thankful whatever this sickness was, had come, because it appeared Darren had other plans for us—ones that I doubt I would have enjoyed.

"There will always be other nights. I'll let you rest now."

Darren walked to the door, closing it behind him. I was surpised he didn't lock it, since everything of his was under lock and key.

Without thinking much more of it, I pulled my legs up onto the bed and laid back.

Was I really sick? Or could I be...No. There was no way I could be pregnant and this was morning sickness. I never experienced it with Callie.

TWELVE

Callie
Present, April 2004

Over the years, I felt as though I had seen mom in passing; but every time I looked in the direction of who I thought was there, they were gone. I felt as though it was my imagination playing tricks on me.

"Callie—earth to Callie."

Stan's voice was pulling me out of my thoughts while we sat in the school cafeteria during lunch.

"Sorry, Stan, I—"

I apologized, suddenly falling silent. I've tried not to unload on him about mom, as he had usually taken the brunt of my irritation over the years. I know he always said I could tell him anything, but I felt as though it was all burdening him now.

"What's on your mind?"

"Nothing," I replied, spreading a weak smile across my face and taking bites of my sandwich to create a distraction.

"Do you want to go out tonight? I was thinking maybe the coffee house on 14th Avenue, the one with the board games?" Stan asked.

I had been avoiding his requests every time he asked me out. He never came out and said it was a date, but he didn't have to tell me—I knew. I didn't feel ready for a commitment. I peered down at my food to avoid eye contact with him.

"What are you afraid of Callie?" his tone dropping, realizing what he had just asked me.

How was I to answer that question? I myself didn't even know what I was afraid of. I did like being in his presence, he was a really nice guy, and we seemed to connect well. Maybe it was the fact that he was my best friend—I didn't want us to try a romantic relationship and it not work out. I guess I was afraid I would lose him as a friend forever.

"I don't want to lose you as a friend Stan..." I murmured quietly, while I continued to pick apart my half eaten sandwich and avoided eye contact with him.

"Why do you think you would lose me?" he asked, with a genuine look of confusion on his face.

I was quick to answer him back—perhaps *too* quick.

"Don't most relationships that stem from long-time friendships lead to break ups? Which would then result in losing our friendship."

"That's what you're afraid of? Losing our friendship?"

I guess that's what I was actually afraid of the most. It wasn't the entire reason, but definitely a good chunk of it.

"Partly—"

"Partly? What else is bothering you?" he interjected.

I sighed and started laying it all down in front of him.

"My mom. She's supposed to be the one I go to for advice, to help me handle all of this,"

I said matter-of-factly, while gesturing between the two of us as if it was a normal thing. Stan fell silent and looked down at the table. I wanted him to realize and understand my reasoning.

"Losing her at a young age was hard. It's been hard to grasp the whole dating world, knowing how to handle it all, and to just simply express how I feel about a person I might be interested in."

"Why don't you go with how you feel, and not worry about losing anything? I'm not going anywhere, Callie. We've been through too much," he promised softly.

"That's the problem Stan, if things don't work out, is it really going to be that easy to go back to this? The bond we have as friends?"

He didn't have an answer for that at all. We sat in awkward silence for a few minutes after that. I felt terrible for all the times I had shrugged him off. All the times I had made excuses that I was busy. I hadn't taken into consideration how he had been feeling. I should have been flattered he had taken an interest in me.

"What time are you thinking about hitting up the coffee shop? I don't think dad will have a problem with me being out, as it's a Friday night." I asked, giving him a small smile. His face lit up at the sound of my question.

"How about we head over right after school? Less likely it will be crowded."

"Sure, we can do that," I agreed.

The bell rang, indicating lunch was over. Stan and I had separate classes that afternoon and started heading our separate ways. He called back over his shoulder to me.

"I'll meet you on the steps outside the school after the final bell."

"See you then," I assured him, with a nod and a smile.

For the rest of the afternoon my focus was not on my lessons at all. Instead of listening to my teachers, my mind kept drifting to later that afternoon. Tonight would be my first official date, ever! Even if it was only coffee and board games, I still had butterflies in my stomach.

As the last bell rang, I rushed to my locker to pack away my books, throwing my book bag on my shoulder to head out to the steps to wait for Stan.

I made my way through the hall and out onto the front steps, taking a seat to wait. Just as I sat down, someone at the end of the schoolyard caught my eye— she was wearing an oversized coat, large sunglasses, and had wavy brunette hair.

At first I thought it was my mom. Shaking my head, I blinked fiercely, expecting that it was my mind playing tricks on me again. When I peered back into the same direction I had seen her, she still stood on the other side of the chain link fence. Again, I shook my head fiercely. I had to have been dreaming— but there she was, standing in the same place, staring straight back at me.

It took me only a split second to get up from where I was seated, rushing down the stairs towards her, as she took off running down the street.

"Hey, wait up!" I called after her.

Why would she be watching me? Who was she?

My heart began to race because this was not making any sense to me. If this *was* mom, why would she be running away from me?

She was already halfway down the street hailing a cab by the time I made it to the sidewalk. Neither of us were stopping. I saw her take a glance back at me. I tried calling out to her again between gasps for air, as I ran as fast as I could after her.

"Wait! I need to talk to you," I called out breathlessly.

The woman looked over her shoulder as I closed the gap between us. A cab pulled up to the curb when I was within only ten feet of her.

"I just want to talk to you, please. Are you—"

She cut me off, and I stopped dead in my tracks, practically dropping my book bag from the abrupt stop

"I am not who you think I am." Her words were firm and direct.

She turned and stepped into the cab closing the door quickly behind her. I wanted to stop the cab from leaving, pull open the door and demand an answer. All I could do was stand there, watching the cab take off, carrying within it whoever this woman was.

Whoever she was, she looked identical to my mother, the only difference had been in her voice—it was much deeper than mom's. I shook my head as her words began repeating themselves over and over in my head.

I am not who you think I am.

All I could think was, who was she? How did she seem to know who I was?

I couldn't move from where I was standing. Slowly, shock began to overtake my body. I had been so close to her, yet so far.

Why hadn't I grabbed her? Why hadn't I stopped her?

Even though she looked like mom, she didn't walk or talk anything like her. Then again, it had been years since I had seen mom, things could have changed—*she* could have changed.

As these thoughts swirled around in my head, I heard Stan's faint voice behind me. I didn't move, I couldn't move. I was frozen in place. The next moment Stan was standing in front of me with his hands on my shoulders, attempting to grab my attention. Tears began to stream down my face. I was so close to her, why couldn't I stop her from leaving?

I could hear Stan talking but I couldn't comprehend his words at all, the world felt as though it was falling away.

"Callie, can you hear me?"

I could hear him, but I had no voice to speak. All I could do was stare at him as my eyes blurred from the tears.

"Who was she? Did you know her?" he asked with concern.

Again, my voice was lost. I didn't know who she was, but she looked like mom.

Was it mom? Why would she run, if she had been here the whole time, watching me?

Too emotional, I grabbed my phone from my bag and dialed dad's cell. He would know what to do, and right now I needed him.

THIRTEEN

Murray
Present, April 2004

Nearly two months had passed since Justine Johnson had been at the station. When I had returned to the interview room an hour after we agreed to take a break, she was gone.

Nobody had seen her leave and I was furious. She was our only connection and she vanished without a trace. We had been calling the number she left us to be able to get in touch with her, but the woman who answered insisted we had the wrong number. It baffled me. Why would she voluntarily come into the station claiming to have information, provide us with a random number, then leave? Was she trying to hide something from us?

I had searched the city looking for her. Nothing had turned up. It was as if she had disappeared, and I briefly

112

questioned if she had simply been a figment of my imagination.

I honestly believed she held *all the* answers to the entire case, and now she was gone without ever looking back. I felt hopeless, and that it was time to let Callie know what had been happening lately. She deserved answers about why I had been working extra hour's non stop for the past six weeks, and why I had been vague when she asked me about work. I had wanted to be sure of the information before giving Callie any hope. I knew deep down she still carried hope. I think we all did, until proven otherwise.

As always, I had been keeping my eyes and ears open to the homicides coming in, but thankfully nobody matched Lily's description—which meant there was still a glimpse of hope she was still alive, or it could mean she wasn't even in the province anymore. My only course of action now was to try the last known address for Mrs. Johnson, which was up in North Vancouver. It was like a needle in a haystack to locate anything in Justine Johnson's name. There was nothing in her name to state she lived at the address she provided to us. She had no bills, credit cards, or car registered in her name. All we could locate was a Darren Johnson, her supposed husband.

With the case resurfacing and the Captain allowing me to be a part of it, I was given the go ahead to launch my own investigation and had been allotted two bodies to help me. I thought Gresham would like to be one of the two to assist me in my efforts—after all, she had always told me to let her know if I needed anything; and although I still hadn't asked either of them, I had hoped my current partner Pryce would be the other body on the investigation team.

Picking up my cell, I gave Gresham a call.

"Hey, Murray!" she answered. Her voice was always sweet.

"Hi Gresham, are you busy?"

"Oh no, go ahead, what do you need?"

"I was wondering if you could assist me on an investigation up in North Vancouver? I've been given the go ahead to have two bodies besides me on this team."

"North Van? What's there?"

"A possible lead to Lily."

The phone line went silent for a moment.

"Does Captain know about this?" she asked in a whisper.

"Captain knows what's going on, and has put me on the case. Remember that woman who came into the station nearly two months ago, claiming she knew information about Lily? Well, during the second day we interviewed her she got up and left sometime in the lunch break we gave her. The number she left us isn't for her, supposedly. I wanted to check her last known address in order to tie up all the loose ends we currently know about her."

"Of course I can help, when do you want to go?"

"What about before our shift Monday morning, say nine o'clock? Now that you're on the case, you'll be working the same shifts as I do. It really shouldn't take too long to get there."

A long pause occurred before Gresham spoke again, and agreed to assist me.

"Okay, nine o'clock. Where should I meet you, at the station?"

"Why don't you swing by my place, we'll take my car."

"Okay, see you in the morning."

114

With that, she hung up quickly. I didn't mind at all, as most detectives were in a rush. I turned back to the computer pulling up the file we made on Justine Johnson. I wrote the address she had provided us with in my notebook. 6815 Nashome Drive, North Vancouver, British Columbia.

I tucked it into my briefcase for safekeeping. It was a little after three in the afternoon, and Callie would be leaving school shortly. I had some time owing to me, so I thought that I should knock off early and spend an evening with her.

As I gathered my belongings, I headed to the elevator. The display showed it was on the twenty-first floor. I didn't feel like waiting, in case the Captain saw me ducking out early. I didn't have anything to hide, I just didn't feel like conversing with him much these days.

Making my way down the several flights of stairs instead, I reached the bottom to my cell phone ringing. I checked the display, reading 'Callie' from the screen. As I answered, Callie cut me off with a hysterical cry and mumbling. I couldn't make out anything she was saying.

"Callie, take a breath. I can't understand you," I instructed her, my voice more panicked than I had intended it to sound.

I could hear her taking deep breaths as she breathed hard into the receiver.

"Try again, what's wrong?" I asked, this time speaking in a smooth voice to help calm her. A few seconds passed before Callie spoke again. Her voice cracked as she spoke.

"I saw mom. I've seen her so many times while walking to and from school."

She sniffled uncontrollably once the words were out. I was trying to process what she was telling me, but I was lost.

How could she have seen Lily? If Lily were here, why hadn't she come home?

At that moment, it clicked—was it Justine? I wondered how Justine would have known about Callie. Had she been watching our family? Things weren't making sense—I had lost myself in my own thoughts; forgetting Callie was on the phone. She was now screaming into the phone for my attention.

"I'm sorry honey. Would you like me to pick you up from school? Or meet at home?"

With still a shaky voice, she answered, "I'll walk home, Stan is here. I'll meet you there."

As we hung up, my mind wandered back to Justine.

Why would she have been watching Callie? The thought made me uneasy. Had she been a part of the kidnapper's plan, and just told a story to make me think she was a victim herself? My thoughts blurred together, all that mattered right then was that I got home to see Callie and find out more about these sightings she had been having. I didn't understand why I was only hearing about them now. If it had been happening frequently, why hadn't she talked to me about it? Nevertheless, I would have my answers soon, once I made it home.

As I threw my items onto the back seat of my car, I hopped in the driver's seat and turned the engine over. As I peered in my review mirror, I noticed a woman standing on the corner. Was it Justine? As I blinked to take a second look, she was gone. I had no time to challenge my imagination at this point. Forgetting about her, I backed out and methodically headed towards home. I wanted to collect my thoughts before hearing what Callie was about to inform me of. I knew I too would need to explain some things that I had been keeping from Callie the past couple of months.

As I pulled into the driveway, the front door swung open before the engine was even cut. Callie stood on the porch with Stan at her heels. She was shaking—I could see tears running down her face and my heart broke. Regardless of how old Callie was, I never wanted to see her hurt or upset.

I didn't bother to collect my briefcase from the back seat, and instead focused on Callie. As I stepped up on the porch, her arms reached out and wrapped themselves around my neck in a hold I knew was not going to be breaking anytime soon. We stood in silence, without exchanging any words, but understanding each other's pain. Stan had gone back inside to gather his belongings. As he came back out, I nodded and mouthed 'thank you' to him for being there for Callie. He had always been protective of Callie, and been by her side when she had needed someone.

Stan gave a silent nod of understanding and went on his way. Callie broke the hold first—her eyes were swollen and red. I led her inside, into the living room, and sat her on the sofa. In the same place that I found her on that horrific night six years ago. We had not rearranged our furniture since the day Lily went missing. We wanted the house to be exactly the way it was the day she was taken from us. That way Lily would feel welcome the day she returned home. As we sat on the sofa, silence filled the air. I wanted to know everything from Callie about these encounters, but I also wanted to let her tell me in her own time, without the pressure of my questions. She spoke in a soft whisper when she finally opened up to me.

"This has been happening on and off for the last couple of years. I thought it was just my imagination at first..." she trailed off and peered out the bay window in front of her.

"At first, I saw something out the corner of my eye—a woman who looked like mom, but when I would look back again, the woman was gone. I thought nothing of it, dad. I thought it was me just imagining mom because I miss her."

Her words started to slur together as she began to sob again.

"Today was different, though. I came out of school and the woman was standing at the edge of the school yard. I stared right at her. I even shook my head and blinked my eyes several times, but she was still standing there. When she saw me looking at her and I started running towards her she began to run down the street and hailed a cab. I was nearly within arm's reach of her, dad. I don't understand why she would run!"

At this point, Callie was crying uncontrollably.

"Why would mom run away? Doesn't she love us anymore?"

Those words stung to hear from my daughter. The pain behind her words was evident. I could sense her frustration and the anxiety she had been facing all these years. As we sat in silence for a few minutes, I felt the urge to express my encounters with Justine, but I wasn't sure if Callie was ready to hear what I had to say. However, I knew the longer I held off, the more it would hurt her in the end.

"Callie," I began to say in between her sobs, "I need to explain something to you."

I waited for her to answer, but I could tell she wasn't going to let up anytime soon. I didn't think this was the right time to tell her. I wrapped my arms around her and pulled her close to me. Rocking her like I had done many times before. Her breathing began to slow and her sobs began to ease.

"I know this is very difficult for you Callie, but I want you to know that you are not alone. I miss her too, every day."

My voice started to shake, my emotions were getting the better of me but this was not the time to express them.

"Are you listening Callie?" I asked her in a whisper.

She nodded against my chest but didn't speak. As long as I knew she was listening I could continue.

"Mom would want us to keep fighting for her, and not give up. I haven't given up yet. I fight every day when I go into work. Not just for us, but for mom too. I believe in my heart she is still alive, I still have hope, deep down."

Callie pulled away from the grip she had on me and wiped her face with her sleeve. She stared at me with questionable eyes.

"You still believe she *is* alive, Dad?" Her voice carried confusion.

Had she already lost hope that Lily was alive?

This stunned me a bit, to believe that my daughter could think her mother was dead. I was jumping to conclusions and without point blank asking her, I would be assuming.

"I do, we have to until it's proven otherwise."

Fresh tears began to fill Callie's eyes but I could see the start of a smile forming. Feeling this was a better time than any to let Callie know of my own encounters—with Justine Johnson.

"I don't want you to feel mad or upset I didn't tell you sooner but know I wanted to ensure I had all the facts first before coming to you."

119

I most likely made Callie feel uneasy because all of a sudden she fully stopped crying and was very attentive to what I had to say. I picked her hands up in mine before carrying on with what I wanted to tell her.

"I know the woman you are speaking of."

Her eyes widened, and her mouth dropped open.

"She came to the station two months ago. She claims to know about mom's disappearance."

Before I could even finish the thought, Callie jumped up from the couch and began pacing the living room.

"Callie, please lis—."

"How could you keep this from me, Dad!" she yelled.

She was angry. She had every right to be but I needed her to calm down and hear me out. There was a reason I wanted to wait and I needed her to know that.

"Why didn't you come and tell me this sooner?"

I could sense the tension and anger in her voice. I had been afraid of this. I stood and took hold of Callie by the shoulders to capture her attention, to ensure she was listening to the words I was about to say.

"Because I thought it was my imagination."

She looked puzzled, just as she thought her encounters had been her imagination, I thought mine were, too——that this whole thing was a dream, a very confusing dream.

"I didn't think it was real. I thought I was losing it. I never imagined after all these years someone would come forward with information about mom."

Callie dropped to the floor. I wasn't sure what she was thinking, but it looked as though she was going into shock. Her lips were moving but no sound was coming out of her mouth. I knelt down, lifting her chin toward my eyes.

"It is real though, Callie. The woman you have seen must be the one I have seen at the station. Her name is Justine Johnson. I don't know who she is, or what her connection to mom is, but she is our one and only current lead to finding mom."

Justine was the only answer to all of this. I needed to find her again, and quickly. I couldn't lose her because then I would truly lose Lily forever.

FOURTEEN

Lily
Past, July 1998

It had been two weeks now since the sickness incident, and I noticed my period was spotting, but I took that as my stress levels beginning to weigh down on me. After all, I had been kidnapped. Kidnapped in front of my own child none the less, and was being held hostage. I still had hope that I would get out of this, somehow. I was strong, and nothing was going to keep me here forever. If there was a way out, I would find it eventually.

Darren and I were sitting at the kitchen table having our morning breakfast. This had started becoming a tradition over the past month, once he began trusting me to leave the basement—to always eat breakfast and dinner together upstairs. I never ate lunch because he was mostly at work during those hours, but I didn't mind. I wasn't much of a lunch person to begin with.

Darren seemed a little off, but was still pleasant towards me. I could tell something was bothering him. We continued to eat in silence until he piped up with a strange outburst.

"Are you pregnant?"

The words hit me with force.

Me, pregnant? Was I showing?

Immediately I looked down at my stomach. I didn't have a bump, but then again I never had much of a bump with Callie, either. I was taken aback that he thought this was something that was occurring.

"I don't think so? Why?" I replied hastily.

"You seem different, almost... glowing," he said with a sneer.

I hadn't noticed if I had been glowing. I didn't usually see myself in the mirror unless I was using the washroom, and with how Darren had his finger on me I couldn't take too long in there.

I thought back to when Darren had told me he was giving me the pill every day. After that night I started taking it. I didn't know much about it as it wasn't something Keith and I had used, and I wasn't even sure if there would be any ill effects if I were actually pregnant and still on the pill.

These thoughts worried me, and the concerned look on Darren's face was not easing me.

"Well, I picked up one of those tests from the drug store. I want you to check after breakfast."

All I could do was nod. This whole thing had me on edge.

What if I was pregnant? What would he do—what would I do?

It was bad enough having been raped by Darren, but to be pregnant with his child as well. I couldn't even finish my breakfast because I was feeling so sick from the thoughts. Darren stood from the table and took our dishes to the sink. He returned to the table with the box, handing it to me as he sat back down across from me.

"Well, what are you waiting for?" he asked roughly, after sitting in silence for a minute.

All I could do was stare at the pregnancy test. I felt lost. I wasn't even sure if I wanted to know if I was carrying this monster's child.

Finally, I stood and walked down the hallway off the kitchen to the washroom, closing the door quietly behind me. My back pressed again the door, I stared down at the pregnancy test once again, attempting to believe this was just a nightmare. I couldn't imagine raising a child in these conditions, and especially to have to raise a child with another man who wasn't my husband. What would Keith think of me?

The urge to pee was present. It could have been more of a nervous pee, but regardless, at least I could get it over with quickly. At this point I just wanted to not drag out the process any longer. Wanting to confirm the time lapse needed that I had to wait after peeing on the stick, I checked the instructions on the side of the box—two minutes. I had nothing to track the time, so I decided I would count to a hundred and twenty to obtain as accurate of a count as I could for the reading. I made my way over to the toilet, because peeing in the middle of the floor was not an option, with my nerves settling in as I sat down,

After peeing awkwardly on the stick, I pulled myself off the toilet to place the tester on the counter. All I could do was sit and wait. It felt as though it took an eternity. I tried my best to stay calm, and hope for the best outcome, although, I had to prepare for the worst as well. The time ticked by slowly as I began to count. I was interrupted not long after by a knock at the door.

"Anything yet?" his muffled voice shot through the door.

"Not yet," I called back.

I knew it wouldn't take much longer, but truthfully I was trying to wait it out before I had to discover my fate.

Picking up from where I left off, I continued to count. Finally, I reached the approximate two minute mark and knew it was time to look at the tester that I had set on the counter. Closing my eyes and counting to three, I peered down. Two lines showed in the window. I felt myself collapse to the ground and tears began to stream down my face. At some point I screamed out, because the next thing I knew, Darren was standing over top of me.

"Well, are you pregnant, again?" he barked.

My mind wasn't functioning, I was incoherent, and I didn't understand his question. What did he mean *again*?

"The stick says that I am..." was all I could say.

Tears still streamed down my face.

"Have you not been taking the pill every morning? You know you have to prevent this."

I had started taking it the following day after we had last made love, which was after learning what it was he had been giving me. Had I hurt the baby by taking it? Emotions were flying through me, and I couldn't focus on any one thing.

"I asked you a question, now answer," his voice was stern and cold.

"I... I... I thought you were poisoning me, so no——well, at first no——but after you, umm... after we were together the first time I have been taking it since, for the past two months."

"How dare you do this to me! How dare you go against my wishes!" he screamed, anger plastered across his face. Even his hands were twisting into fists. What had him so angry?

"If I'm pregnant why do you even care? I'm the one who you raped, and I'm the one who has to carry this child and live with this now, not you."

"Rape, who said it was rape? You're my wife, and I made love to you. Plus, you won't be pregnant for very long if I have anything to do with it," he chuckled, his tone filled with mockery.

"What do you mean?" I shouted, my voice hysterical.

He either wasn't making any sense, or I simply couldn't comprehend what he was saying. Everything was blurring together.

"You should know from the last time you got pregnant—you aren't keeping it," he replied, flatly.

What the hell was he talking about? This was my body, my choice. I pulled myself to my feet. There was no way in hell I was letting him anywhere near me, or this unborn child. I needed to escape, and fast. First, I had to get past him, as he was blocking the entrance to the washroom.

"First thing in the morning, I'm taking you in."

"Taking me in where?" I shot back. He couldn't make me do anything I didn't want to do. This was my body and my child.

"Don't use that tone with me, you know exactly what I mean——the clinic." I saw the anger in his face, obviously caused by my assertiveness.

"You don't expect me to get an abortion, do you?" I cried.

126

"Of course I do. You didn't get to keep the baby the first time, so of course you don't get to keep it this time. There is no place for a child under this roof. It. Must. Go." His last three words were punctuated, as if he were giving me an order.

His words hit me like a ton of bricks. I was against abortion. How could I comply with his demands?

"Well…what if I don't want to? You can't force me," I said plainly.

"You are getting the abortion, end of story. Let me tell you now, you better listen to me when we're out there, no escaping or screaming…"

I had begun to tune Darren out as my mind wandered to the unborn child. I felt myself begin to breathe heavier. I couldn't go through with his demand. He would have to kill me first before I would agree.

"No," was all I could manage to say.

"No? What do you mean no? You don't have a choice. You are not keeping this baby."

He was irritated, I could see his fists clenching at his sides. Was he really going to hit a pregnant woman?

I stood there, motionless; I had nothing further to say to him. I tried to stare through him, but his eyes drew me in. I wanted to understand him, understand his ways of thinking, what made him tick. I remembered hearing you could understand a person by looking into their eyes, but all I saw in Darren's eyes was darkness. He was shut off to the world. Something terrible had to have happened to him for him to be this way.

"I would like to go back to the basement," I requested, my voice void of emotion. I looked away as I stood in front of him.

He moved to the side and let me pass, and I quickly walked down the hallway, into the kitchen and back down to the basement. Darren followed behind me, and once I was inside the empty room, he spoke briefly.

"This will all be over tomorrow and we can get back to our regular lives." With that, he slammed and locked the door.

Get back to our regular lives.

I had to laugh——nothing about this was a regular life. Husbands didn't lock their wives up in a basement.

I had no emotions left; I stared blankly at the wall for what seemed like hours. All of a sudden, I remembered the book and box in the wall, although I was not entirely sure why they had come to mind. I still had not managed to find any keys, but was sure there had to be a way to get into them. Every time I had thought about them and attempted to pull them out of their hiding place, I would hear Darren coming down the stairs and needed to shove them back in the wall. I also didn't always have light.

The switch for the light was on the outside of the locked room, and Darren had control over whether it was left on or off. I noticed that when he was angry or upset with me he left it off. I figured this was his way of punishing me, and generally all I could do during those times was sleep or lay with my eyes open staring into pure blackness.

When the light was on, I managed to locate some novels in the boxes to read, but with the little energy I had most days I found myself falling asleep and napping more times than not. The naps helped to keep my energy up to face him when I needed to.

Finding the loose brick I carefully took it out from its space in the wall and pulled its secret contents out. I felt as though they would lead me to some clues about Justine's time here with Darren.

Setting the objects down in the middle of the room, I began pulling the boxes off the shelving unit. Maybe a key was located in one of the boxes. It seemed as though everything of Justine's was here in this room——her childhood and her adult life from the way things were labeled in scribbled writing on the outside of each box.

As I pulled things out, again, I found mostly clothes, but now also some old trinkets. Just as I was ready to give up and return everything to their boxes, I came across a pouch nestled between old sweaters that contained all small locket keys. Taking them back to the book and box, I started trying them one by one. At first, none of them worked. I was down to the last two keys. I tried the second to last key.

Click!

The journal popped open. I tried the same key in the lock on the wooden box, but it didn't work. I had but one key left.

Please, please let this be the right key, I silently said to myself.

With bated breath, I pierced the hole in the lock and turned the key. At last! The lock was open. The last key had opened the box.

I wasn't sure what to expect when I opened the lid. As I opened it, a cloth was wrapped around an object. As I slowly unwrapped it, I felt my heart race.

Discovering yellow baby boots, a rattle, and a small teddy bear with a note reading,

"I love you, until we meet again." I smiled.

I flipped open the book. It was hand written, and the first page indicated it had been written on January 15, 1996. As I read through the pages, they were addressed to a Corrine-Michael. The writing was in script, causing me to struggle to make out some of the words.

129

The letters seemed to be talking to someone, telling them she loved them and she was sorry for cutting their life short.

I sat back and questioned what I had just read. All the letters were signed off as "J", which I assumed to be Justine. Justine must have been pregnant, and that's what Darren was talking about when he said I knew about 'before'. The entire journal was full, appearing that she wrote to Corrine-Michael for a year. I wondered why she had chosen to put these items into the wall; that was the part that wasn't making sense to me. Considering all the boxes in the room were Justine's, why did she feel as though she had to hide these items behind the wall?

I couldn't dwell on this matter; I had my own state to consider. What was going to happen to the baby growing inside of me? I always thought I would only have Callie. I wondered what Callie would think about being a big sister. The thought pained me——how could I be happy? I was pregnant from another man. I couldn't imagine my beloved husband Keith finding out about this, would he think I was a whore?

I placed the contents back inside the box, locked both the journal and box, and placed them back inside the hole. I made my way back to the mattress against the wall, and sat down.

My mind was confused about the whole situation, and for the fact I had been taking the pill for almost two months, every day. I was tired after the day's events, and I leaned against the wall, sleep taking over almost immediately. There wasn't much else I could do, except hope for the best.

FIFTEEN

Darren
Past, July 1998

I was fuming mad, how could she disobey me? Had she not learned from the last time? Why would she stop taking the pill and think it was poison? All these questions clouded my mind. I took a swig from my flask as I stood in the kitchen. It was to settle the anger in me, or so I thought.

My blood was boiling, because I didn't need a scene anywhere. If I could do it myself, I would, but I didn't need anything happening to Justine in the process. I needed her to cooperate, to allow everything to work out for the better.

I remembered back to when this happened two years ago——for the next year she moped around. The baby hadn't even been three months developed, and to me that wasn't a person. It hit her hard though, and I didn't need her overreacting again this time.

Taking some deep breaths, I made my way down the stairs to the basement, entering the room to find Justine asleep on the mattress.

"Justine, wake up," I called out, but it didn't seem to stir her.

I gently nudged her shoulder until she woke, startling her in the process.

"It's time to get ready, come take a shower and prepare for us to go out."

Her eyes perked.

"You're letting me out of the house?" she spoke back, in a half sleepy tone.

"You're not going alone if that's what you're thinking. This will only be for an hour, the clinic is around the corner.

"Fine," was her response.

It appeared she still had some anger against me. She knew we couldn't raise a baby. Plus I didn't even like babies, all they did was cry, poop, and sleep.

"You can take a shower, and change your clothes."

"That will be nice for a change," she replied, her tone sarcastic.

"I could let you go as you are, but I thought for your own sanity you would at least want to be clean for the occasion."

I walked back to the door, hoping she would follow, and she did. As we made our way upstairs, I let her lead the way down the hallway.

"I'll get you some clothes and towels. Go ahead and get in."

All she did was nod as she entered the bathroom.

The shower was started by the time I gathered clothes and towels for her. Taking them into the bathroom I informed her, "Everything you need is on the counter."

A faint "okay" came from behind the sliding doors, muffled by the sound of the shower.

She was taking her sweet time, it had been half an hour already. She needed to know she couldn't take all day, so, knocking on the door to the washroom, I gave her a warning.

"What is taking you so long, our appointment is in less than an hour. Hurry up."

"I'll be out in a minute," she called through the door.

Five minutes later, Justine finally emerged from the washroom. She had pulled her hair back into a ponytail, with loose waves throughout it. It was uncommon for her, but in a way it was appealing.

She stood in the middle of the hallway awaiting instructions. I needed to execute this with minimal problems.

"Once that door is opened you promise me you won't run?" I asked her calmly.

"Yes."

"We will drive to the clinic, have our appointment, and come home, alright?"

"If that is how you wish it to be handled."

Her answers were short, you could tell she was not in agreement with my demands, but she knew what I said was final. I handed her sunglasses and a hat, to give her some sort of disguise. I didn't need the neighbours asking questions, or anyone recognizing us while we were out.

"I want you disguised as much as possible, I don't need our nosey neighbours asking questions. We'll go out the back door and into the garage, and you will lie down in the back seat with your head down. Understand?"

"Yes, sir," she replied.

"Good, let's head out."

When we reached the back door, I placed my hand around her upper arm. Regardless of her giving me her verbal agreement she wouldn't run, I didn't fully trust her. I felt her squirm in my grip, but it only caused me to grip her tighter as a reminder. The door opened and I felt her pull forward.

"Remember our agreement," I whispered to her.

She relaxed and let me lead her to the garage and into the back seat of the car. I had my truck, but there was nowhere for her to sit without being seen, so I took the car instead. It was less likely for her to be noticed.

"Lay down, I don't need anyone seeing you as we leave.."

She didn't answer, but placed the sunglasses and hat on, then positioned herself on the seat as I moved around to the driver's side. I prayed I would not regret this moment, having to take her into public with me. Thankfully we didn't have to go far.

We rode in silence the entire way. Traffic was light, which allowed us to reach the clinic within five minutes. As we pulled into the parking lot, I peered in the rearview mirror. Justine was mumbling to herself, I couldn't make out anything she was saying.

"We're here," I spoke, causing her to stir from whatever she was focusing on. She sat up slowly, and peered around at her surroundings.

Her eyes fell on the sign 'Ryerson Women's Clinic' and you could see her shoulders tense. I exited the car first and went around to open her door. Of course we were in public and I had to act natural, so instead of holding her on her upper arm, I simply held her hand——firmly——to keep her in check.

We walked the few short feet to the door, and I opened the door for her to enter.

"Take a seat, I'll register you," I instructed her.

I watched her as she took a seat in the corner. I kept my eye on her the entire time that I was registering her. I didn't trust her enough to let her out of my sight. She ran before, and ran good. I knew she was capable of doing it again.

When I finished with the receptionist, I made my way over to Justine and sat next to her.

"It shouldn't be too long, they don't seem busy. I mentioned to the receptionist that you want me to be in the procedure room with you, so you would feel more comfortable. What are you going to say the reason is you want this?"

She gave me a blank stare before speaking.

"What do you want me to say?" her voice was irritated.

"Make something up, but don't tell the truth, and don't reveal who the father is. I have a reputation in this city and I don't need you ruining that with your little game here."

"Game? You think this is a game?" This time, her voice was unnecessarily loud.

"Keep it down, don't act like that here," I hissed.

I peered around the room and it seemed the others had been unaffected by my wife's outburst.

"Don't act like what? I'm being forced to have an abortion; you didn't even consult with me about it, considering it's my body."

"You know exactly my reasoning for no children. Why are you acting like this? Don't get into that depression mood like you did after the last one. This shouldn't be such a big deal."

She turned away from me and didn't say another word. We sat for another twenty minutes before her name was called.

"Justine Johnson," A young, blonde woman called out, and I turned to Justine to see her get up.

"Now, no crazy business, you hear me. You go in there and do exactly as I said. You understand?" I whispered to her.

"Of course, there's nothing else I can do except comply with your demands," she sneered at me.

With that, we were off in the direction of the blonde nurse.

When we walked out of the room an hour later, she looked visibly upset, which caused anger to rise in me. I didn't need a basket case on my hands after this. This was all supposed to be a quick fix so we could go back to our regular lives.

I escorted us out of the clinic, quickly. I didn't need anyone to recognize us, I also just wanted to get home and back to the way things used to be.

The car ride home was silent; she laid in the back seat, the same way she had on the way to the clinic. Once inside the garage, I cut the engine, but sat for a moment to collect my thoughts.

"Why are you moping? You know it was the right thing to do," I attempted to put a positive spin on the current events.

"It's whatever you wanted, again," she answered shortly.

"At least you managed to convince her."

She turned to look at me through the review mirror.

"You heard me, I told them exactly what you wanted. I had to lie that I cheated on you with another man. It was all to keep you looking like Mr. Wonderful, as per usual."

It wasn't exactly what I would have said, but it was over and done with now. I couldn't change what had happened. All we could do was ensure this would never occur again.

"Let's move on from this. From now on you better be taking the pill so this doesn't happen again."

"How about you tell me why you don't want children?"

Her question came as a sudden shock because she knew my reasoning. I turned in my seat to look at her.

"You know we only need each other, anyone else would cause me to lose control over you. There would be someone else that would need your attention. I don't need that."

She turned away and didn't say another word. Once back inside, it was time for dinner.

"Do you want to help me with dinner tonight?"

The dead look in her eyes told me she was not interested.

"Or you can wait in the living room until it's done."

Without a word, she walked into the living room. I could hear her sit down on the sofa. She could be as mad as she wanted to be over this, but in the end I was protecting her. We didn't need anyone else in our lives; the two of us was sufficient enough.

The living room was awfully quiet after a while. While the venison was cooking, I walked in to find Justine asleep on the couch. Without wanting to disturb her, I placed a blanket over her. It was peaceful to watch her sleep.

Returning to the kitchen, I finished preparing our meal. Once I had the food plated and set on the table, I woke her up, nudging her shoulder.

"Dinner is ready," I said softly.

She pulled herself into a sitting position and stretched.

"What are we having tonight?" She asked through a yawn.

"Venison, carrots, and baked potato."

"Okay, that sounds fine."

What was she expecting? A five-course meal?

Of course it should be fine. It's food, and I was feeding her, so she should have been happy.

We made our way to the kitchen. I pulled out a chair, and as she seated herself I placed a napkin on her lap. Taking my seat across from her I flashed her a small smile. As time passed, she did not speak.

"Why are you so mad over this situation?" I probed.

I knew it was bugging her. It was written all over her face.

"We are not going to discuss this. There is nothing more to be said, you said your piece."

"You don't agree with my decision? What don't you agree with?"

I knew I was playing with fire and causing more anger within her, but I needed to know why she felt this way. I was the man of the house and I ruled what happened here.

She stared at me, motionless and speechless, for what felt like an eternity.

"Well?"

"I don't believe in abortions, every life is important. We had other options."

We didn't have any other options. If she thought putting the child up for adoption would have been easy, it wouldn't have been. She should have known that, growing up in an orphanage. It was completely time consuming, and I couldn't handle her being pregnant for nine months. I couldn't deal with mood swings, and to actually have to go to a hospital for the birth. This morning had been our one and only logical option; it was best for us—for me.

"What is done, is done. We can't go back, all we can do now is move forward. You better be back to normal by tomorrow, no moping around like you're a ghost."

I needed this day to end; I wanted to forget any of this had happened. I knew she would eventually come to her senses and realize I saved us both.

SIXTEEN

Callie
Present, April 2004

I felt relieved to know that what I thought had been my imagination had actually been confirmed as real, but questions still remained in my mind.

Who was she? What did she want from me? Why was she identical to mom?

I was still attempting to comprehend the news dad had shared with me the night before, that Justine Johnson may be our only connection to mom. Why, after all these years would someone show up, after haunting us from a distance, and feel *now* was the most opportune time to share what she knew?

Knowing that someone knew about that night and why mom had been missing, and had chosen to stay quiet all these years, hurt the most. In my mind, that was a selfish act.

Dad had informed me he was not going to stop searching, and even though this Justine Johnson hadn't been back to the station for almost two months didn't mean he was giving up. He located a last known address for her and was planning to visit it. It wasn't close—it was in North Vancouver, which was a good hour drive from Richmond. Whoever she was, she really couldn't expect to play these disappearing acts and leave us with so many unanswered questions. I was praying she would be there when dad showed up.

Dad had got up early Monday morning and was in the shower, because Gresham was coming over at nine o'clock. She had agreed to go with him to investigate, and I was happy she was the one to go with him. Gresham had been around ever since I could remember, and was like a part of our family. I trusted she would thoroughly investigate this woman, as much as dad would. I knew Gresham loved mom, too, and had been upset about her disappearance since the night it happened.

I had mixed emotions about dad trying to track down this woman. Right then, all I could do was think back to when I had been within arms' reach of her, but let her slip away from me by allowing her to get in that cab. Though, would it have solved much if she hadn't run off the way she did? It wasn't as though her providing the information to me was going to do much, she needed to talk to dad and inform him of everything she knew about the case.

I heard a soft knock on the front door, which I expected would be Gresham. It was a late start that morning at school and I didn't need to be there until eleven. To my surprise, when I answered the door, it wasn't Gresham at all, but Stan.

141

I shifted awkwardly as I stood in the doorway; I hadn't been expecting to see him until I had arrived at school later that morning.

"Hi, what are you doing here?" I questioned.

"I thought we could talk, maybe you could let me know what happened yesterday?" he whispered.

He had really odd timing. I looked down to realize I was still in my pyjamas—not exactly what you would wear around a boy you had no idea whether you liked or   not.
"Well, it's kind of early. Can't we discuss this later...at school?"

I must have offended him, because he began to stare down at his own shifting feet. I had never seen him act like this before, he was usually confident.

"I was worried about you, the way you were shaking…it scared me," he avoided eye contact as he spoke, staring at the ground in front of him. It was nice to have someone concerned about me, I gave him credit for that, but what was wrong with a text or phone call?

I noticed out the corner of my eye that Gresham had pulled into the driveway next to dad's car. I gave her a small smile as she made her way towards the door where Stan and I stood.

"Hey kiddo, is your dad ready?"

"I actually have no idea, you can head inside to check. There's fresh coffee in the kitchen if you'd like some."

"If I plan to get through this day, I sure will need a cup! I'll head inside to wait, let you finish up here," she smiled, nodding her head towards Stan. As she passed by me, she mouthed to me that he was cute. I rolled my eyes and chuckled inwardly. As Gresham headed inside, I turned my attention back to Stan who was still not moving from the porch, despite my request to talk about this later.

"I have to get ready for school, I'll catch up with you at lunch? Okay?" I tried to sound as peppy as I could.

I knew I was giving him the cold shoulder, but it was too early to be discussing things I didn't know everything about, especially since he had shown up unannounced.

"Fine, I'll see you later," he spat back, anger evident in his voice.

He didn't look up again at me until he was on the sidewalk. Had I really crushed him? I had never seen this side of him before. I made my way back inside and down to the kitchen where I found Gresham seated at the kitchen table with a hot, steaming cup of coffee in her hand. She spotted me after I entered the room, as I made my way to the fridge to find something for breakfast. I had my head inside the fridge when she began to talk, "Who's the boy? He's adorable, if you ask me."

She had a cheerful tone, but the question startled me and I ended up hitting my head on the inside of the fridge while trying to stand up. I turned to face her, and the smile she wore could have been seen from a mile away.

"A boy from school. Remember Stan from my grade six graduation, who walked next to me down the aisle?" I reminded her.

"Oh, now I remember! Stanley Wilson... he wouldn't take his eyes off of you. Goodness, he's grown up to be a handsome young man."

I rolled my eyes—this wasn't exactly what I had planned on discussing this morning. I had assumed my eye roll caught Gresham off guard.

"Oh c'mon Callie, you can't tell me you're oblivious to the way he looks at you?"

She was stating the obvious—of course I knew *how* he looked at me. I knew *exactly* how he felt about me, too.

"Well, that's the problem, actually. I *am* aware of it. It's me who's the problem."

She looked puzzled, and patted the table for me to sit beside her. I slumped my shoulders as I walked over and took a seat across from her. I was barely seated when she went on,

"Tell me, what's wrong? The Callie I know can defeat any problem."

I was quiet, trying to figure out what I wanted to say. She had always been a good listener in the past, so why did I feel this would be different now?

"The biggest problem is that I don't have anyone to talk to about relationships. It's awkward to talk to dad about this kind of stuff. I don't know how to act, or think, or even be in a relationship," I sighed as I let out the last few words.

"That's what you've got me for! You know you can always talk to me. I've got your back." Her smile was reassuring and I thought about how she had been around for me and dad all these years.

It was nice that she had stepped in after mom's kidnapping to try and help where she could, but it still always had been dad and I, getting through all the hiccups of having a teenage daughter.

"You know your mother would want to see you happy, Callie, to see you enjoy your life."

That was exactly the problem—mom. I wanted her here to experience my first relationship, my first kiss, all of the firsts. My eyes fell, as the next words left my lips.

"I miss mom, I miss that she has missed me growing up, seeing my graduations from elementary school and middle school. To hear about my first crush and help me through the next steps."

I hadn't realized Gresham had moved and was crouched down beside me. She took one of my hands in hers.

"Callie, I know it's painful. You shouldn't stop living, your mom wouldn't want you to."

I had heard my dad walk in and he rushed over once he saw Gresham crouched beside me.

"What's wrong? Is everything okay?" he asked with slight panic in his voice.

He placed his hands on my shoulders, while Gresham stood from her crouched position.

"Everything is fine dad, we were just talking about girl stuff."

He dropped his hands and began making his way over to the coffee pot.

"I didn't mean to disturb you, let me just grab a coffee and I'll head back to the bedroom to finish getting my things ready to leave. I should be ready in five minutes, Gresham," he nodded in her direction.

I saw her acknowledge dad with a nod of her head, as she pulled her seat around to sit next to me. We waited until dad left the room to continue our talk. It wasn't that I trying to hide any of this from him, I just felt all of this woman stuff would be a burden on him. It was bad enough the day I got my first period, having him drive me to the pharmacy to pick out pads. I was completely embarrassed as we stood in the aisle and he went package by package asking if it was the right thing. I remember grabbing something off the shelf and running out of there in hopes no one I knew would see us. To date, it had been the most awkward moment of my life.

"Your dad cares about you, I don't think you're giving him enough credit, Callie. You would be surprised how much he would want to know about what's going on in your life."

"Now, I think Stan hates me, I gave him the cold shoulder this morning when he was at the door. Now I feel guilty, I know he's concerned about me but I needed the space to think, and figure things out, you know."

"I completely understand, follow your heart kiddo, everything else will fall into place."

Dad walked back into the kitchen with his brief case, and appeared ready to head out.

"All set ladies, time to get across town. Callie were leaving Gresham's car here in the driveway while we head out. It would be useless driving two cars when we're headed to the same place."

Gresham stood but not before she gave my hand a squeeze, I gave her a small smile to acknowledge and silently thanked her for the talk. She may have not been mom, but I was thankful to know she was around if I needed her.

"Do you know when you will be home today? I don't want to cook dinner again and you not arrive home until midnight dad?"

"Honestly, I'll grab something if I'm hungry. We're not sure what we are expecting when we reach the home. I'll call you though, to keep you updated."

"You promise? Any leads, I want to know."

He walked over and gave me a kiss on my forehead,

"Yes, you will be the first to know if anything changes in this case, you have my promise."

Gresham and dad headed down the hallway towards the front door, we stood awkwardly for a moment as our eyes fell on the dent in the wall. It was the only physical reminder of that night. Dad tried so hard to fix it, but he was no carpenter. It had turned out worse than what that horrible man had done.

Dad broke the silence, "We're doing everything we can now to find her, these leads should help us."

Gresham and I nodded, and off they went to begin their day of investigation. I watched them leave in dad's car, then turned to head back inside to get ready for school.

As I climbed the stairs to my bedroom, I began talking to myself, or I should say, began talking to mom as if she could hear me.

"Wherever you are, I hope you're okay. We miss you, we want you home. Come home soon mom, I love you."

SEVENTEEN

Lily
Past, August 1998

My time in the basement alone had made me think back on my life. It had been four months now—although it felt like an eternity—since I had been kidnapped by Darren. I had been sure that I would have escaped by now, or the police would have found me. It made me feel abandoned, just like I had felt during my childhood. Thoughts of my childhood were pushed to the back of my mind most of the time. I never spoke about them because I wanted a better life than the one I'd had all those years ago.

I had been adopted, but not until I was nine years old. I found it difficult to make friends at the orphanage, because I lost them within a few months as they were adopted one by one. It was also a struggle for me to even become adopted, because who wanted an older child, anyway? This was a frequent thought that passed through my mind as each year passed while I lived there. Parents wanted a cute, adorable baby, or toddler, to coo over. My day came, though, and I remembered it clearly.

It was a cold winter morning, when an older couple, in their mid-forties, walked in the front doors of the orphanage shaking off the light snow that had collected on their jackets. The woman looked quiet and stood behind the tall, slender man. Miss Walker was sitting at her desk in the front foyer as I swept the floors. I had been taught not to speak unless someone addressed me. I kept my head low and continued with the task at hand.

The man spoke to Miss Walker in a soft voice with a heavy Irish accent.

"We would like to adopt," I heard the man say. Without looking up, Miss Walker handed the man a clipboard, which held the adoption questionnaire that everyone had to fill out if they were looking to adopt. Miss Walker never guaranteed anyone an adoption, because the orphanage had a strict screening process before letting any of us leave with an adoptive family. That was one thing I loved about that place, they wouldn't let any child leave with just anyone who wanted to adopt. They wanted the best for each and every one of us.

"Fill this out, and bring it back to me when you are done, please." Miss Walker instructed him.

Nodding, the man took the clipboard and turned to the woman who still stood behind him. He motioned toward the chairs on the far side of the room from me for them to sit. I continued sweeping, but it was hard not to hear the man speak about each question with his wife. I heard him ask her the questions one at a time.

"What age group?"

There was a moment of silence. The woman shrugged to imply she wasn't sure. Keeping my eyes on my work, I heard the man ask the woman about me in a whisper.

"What about **her** age?" he nodded in my direction.

I could see out the corner of my eye the woman nodding in agreement.

"She has to be about nine or ten years old," I heard him say.

It was clear he was attempting to keep his voice low, but I was hanging onto every word they were saying. The woman nodded again in agreement and they continued on through the questions. By this point, I had finished my chores and began making my way to my room. I knew for a fact there were not many of us older children to choose from. Maybe I had a chance to finally be adopted after all these years. Just off the foyer was a winding staircase that led to the second floor. As I made my way up the steps, I stopped to try and listen to the conversation again. The man spoke in such a soft voice, I had to close my eyes to concentrate on what he had to say. I heard Miss Walker speaking to the man, which meant they were returning the questionnaire to her.

"Are you sure you're looking for an older child, sir?"

My heart sank, why did she have to confirm? The couple had said they wanted an older child. I had to make an educated guess, because I couldn't hear the man clearly, but the next thing I heard from Miss Walker was, "We only have one girl that meets your criteria." In that moment, my heart began to race and I bolted up the stairs, down the slender hallway to my

150

room, which was at the end, and slammed the door. Was this my day? Was I finally going to have a family?

A tear fell from the crease of my eye. I hadn't even noticed I had begun to cry. Thinking about the days in the orphanage were times that caused my heart to break, from all the years I felt abandoned and unloved. I doubt anyone knew what it felt like to be so broken to the point of feeling unloved. The couple did adopt me in the end, and I left the orphanage two days later without ever turning back. The Hannigan family had been generous to me through the years—they had allowed me to keep my surname, because they knew staying connected to what little I had left of my past was important to me. Lydia, my adopted mother, mentioned if I wanted to try and find my sister, or even my birth parents, she would help me. Nothing came of our searching attempts, and eventually we gave up. We traveled around the world, seeing many places that I had only ever dreamed about visiting or had heard and read about in stories.

When I was eighteen, the Hannigans were in a horrific car accident and died instantly. As the only family who had never abandoned me, I vowed to never forget them. They loved me unconditionally and showed me there was love in the world, if we believed it existed.

My heart began to ache as the memories flooded me.

I stared at the dark walls pondering if my life would ever be the same again. The only thing even half interesting in the empty room was a shelving unit with old boxes. I had been through the ones on the lower level shelves, and they had only produced old clothing, trinkets, and the keys for the secret box and journal to Justine's unborn child. I wondered if the boxes higher up would lead to any clues about my environment,

151

Justine's life, or where I was. At that point I figured I had an hour or so before Darren arrived home from work. I didn't need him catching me going through those boxes, because I wouldn't have an explanation as to why I was exploring them, after he had warned me a few times not to go through them.

I had never given them much thought, really. I had found myself eying them before, but no real urge to investigate—until now, given the other useless information I had already discovered. I had been more focused on trying to understand how Darren functioned and what made him tick. Since I had pretty much figured him out, my focus transferred to learning about Justine and who she actually was.

Climbing my way up the shelves to the boxes, I noticed some writing on them, but they were so old that the writing on them had begun to fade away. Lifting a flap on one of them, I saw stacks of papers, but thought that would be too tedious to go through at the moment. I set the flap back down, and moved onto the next one that sat beside the one I had just peered in. I could faintly recognize what was written on the outside and it appeared to read 'Past Life'. I awkwardly pulled it off the shelf and carried it back down as I tried my best not to fall, and placed it on the floor in front of me.

Dust flew in every direction as I lifted the flaps of the box. A moss green baby blanket with pink roses and a teddy bear in a yellow sunflower dress sat at the top of the box. In the back of my mind, I wondered about the connection to flowers this woman had on everything. Moving pieces from side to side, I found more baby items—clothes, toys, and books. I spotted a ripped book at the bottom of the box, with what seemed to be loose and tattered pages. I thought it may have contained information about Justine.

As I pulled it out of the box, I noticed the title on the front had been written in bright pink crayon, '*Future Home of the Flower Sisters*' with two little stick figures holding hands. As I opened the first page, memories flooded back like an ocean coming in at high tide.

I had made this scrapbook with my sister back at the orphanage, but how had it made its way here? The only person who knew about it was... I put my hand to my chest. I couldn't comprehend at this point everything that was piecing together. Streams of tears fell down my face uncontrollably, and I began to shout out into the empty room.

"ROSE!"

My breathing became heavy as I looked down between the blur of tears. I could manage to read the words 'Rose and Lily's kitchen' with images of sunflowers identical to the ones painted upstairs on the kitchen walls. I couldn't bring myself to turn anymore pages. I couldn't believe what was happening. Out of nowhere, after twenty-four years, I was reconnecting with my twin sister; though, I had known her as Rose, not Justine. Perhaps her adopted parents had changed her name. She had been adopted when we were seven years old. She had been more than just my sister, she had been my best friend, and we had done everything together.

The orphanage didn't want us to believe we were sisters, but merely friends in the same orphanage. As much as they tried to instill this in us, when you are siblings—especially twins—it had been impossible to believe. They warned us many times over the years that the chances we would be adopted together were slim to none. In our case, Rose was adopted first, and then myself two years later. I remembered those years without her. She had been all I could think about, wondering whether she was alright and growing up well.

I sat there with the scrapbook in my lap, sobbing. We had made a pact two years before she had been adopted that when we grew up, we would live together and decorate each room with a different flower. With the connection to our names, Rose and Lily, we loved flowers. In the garden behind the orphanage we picked all the wild flowers that grew. The colours were beautiful—every colour under the sun could be found in the garden. We picked them and placed them in a vase in our room, and Miss Walker even let me put a vase on the kitchen table we used for supper with some in. She used to tell us the aroma was heavenly. The mixture of scents calmed us to a peaceful state as we slept in our room.

Even though we were young, we had spoken like we were grown adults. The day Rose was adopted was a broken day. My heart broke to see her go, because I was losing my twin—my sister—but at the same time I was happy for her, because she was going to have a better life than we had at the orphanage. As the years went by while I still lived at the orphanage, I still picked flowers and placed them in the vase in our room, just like we had every week. It was my way of keeping Rose's spirit alive and with me.

I couldn't believe I had landed in Rose's home, after missing her all these years. There hadn't been a day where I hadn't wondered where she was in the world. Pushing the book away, I stood up and paced the room. I didn't quite understand the connection between Rose and I, and why Darren felt I was Justine. Rose had always kept her hair short, almost like a boy's cut, where as I had always kept my hair long, only having trims to keep the split ends at bay. Then again, that was then, and this was now. It dawned on me that I hadn't seen a single photograph upstairs of Darren and Justine together. I wondered if I would have made the connection earlier if I had known.

Too many thoughts were running through my head, and I was becoming dizzy just thinking about it all. I needed to get out of here, I needed to find Rose— Justine—whoever she was, and resolve this once and for all. My plan from here on out was to figure out how to escape. I needed more time upstairs to survey the area; because there was absolutely no way I could escape from the basement.

Suddenly, I heard loud footsteps banging down the stairs with the jingling of keys in the keyhole. Wiping my face of the tears, I took a few quick breaths to calm my senses.

Darren stood leaning against the doorframe.

"Hi doll, whatcha up to?" he asked in a sultry voice.

Hearing Darren calling me 'doll' nauseated me. Like every other time, I knew I had to act neutral, but at the same time I was wondering about his chipper mood. At that moment, I realized all the boxes with the contents of the past were nearly emptied upside down on the damp concrete floor, and were scattered around. I froze, hesitating, and wondered whether I should move towards them or away from them in order to not draw any attention to them.

As Darren walked towards me, my eyes darted between him and the pile of baby items inches from his steps. Noticing the nervousness in my facial expression, he turned to see where my eyes had been darting to. In the blink of an eye, his mood changed, becoming agitated. The littlest thing set Darren off, it was something I was getting used to.

"I have told you time and time again not to let me see you going through those dumb boxes. Why must you disobey me all the time?"

His tone made me want to take a step back. I could see his hands clamping into fists, something which I was all too familiar with. Darren's breathing became heavy. I took a few more steps back as the situation began to escalate.

"I'm sorry...I...I..." I stammered.

My mind blanked. Why was he so angry about the boxes in the first place? They were a piece of history— someone's life, at least part of their life.

Before I could register what was about to happen, Darren's arm lifted with his fist clenched. I tried to duck away from his swing that was aimed at my head, but I was too late. His fist made contact with the side of my face, causing me to drop to the floor instantly.

I trembled with fear and crawled away from him, along the cold, damp concrete floor, my mind was racing with each inch I took across the floor. I thought that this was it, I was going die, right here, right now. Feeling the vibration of each step Darren took, made the hairs on my arms stand on end. The closer he got to me, the further I tried to crawl away before coming to a dead end at the wall. Turning and curling into a ball with my knees to my chest, I prayed. It was the only thing I could do—pray my life would not end here. If he had really wanted to kill me, I thought he would have done it sooner.

I could hear his footsteps stop right in front of me. His breathing was heavy as he stood above me.

"Look at me," he demanded. I did not move, I was too scared of what was about to come.

"I said, LOOK AT ME!" he voice boomed, echoing in the small room.

156

He reached towards me, pulling my hair to make me look up at him, tears running down my face.

"Get these damn boxes cleaned up, and don't let me catch you rummaging through them again. I already told you, your family doesn't love you, that's why you were given up at birth and placed in the orphanage. If I catch you looking through them again, everything will go in the trash."

He breathed heavily down upon me. As he let go of my hair, I let my head slump between my knees. I wasn't sure what he was talking about, but I did not want any of Justine's—Rose's—items thrown away because of my mistake. Darren exited the room, locking the door behind him. I could hear his loud stomps up the staircase, which seemed to echo louder than usual.

I scrambled to place the items back in the boxes, doing my best to remember where everything had come from. As I picked up the scrapbook, tears began to fall once again. How did I have so many tears to shed, I really didn't want to part with the book. It gave me answers about this whole situation, which was clearly a case of mistaken identity. It was also the only connection I had left to my sister. Not knowing where she was now, and not knowing if I would actually see her again, I wanted to hold onto something to remember her by.

As I finished putting all the belongings back into their boxes, I held the scrapbook close to my chest, and then placed it back in the box—this time on top. I continued to stare at it, remembering the words Darren had said earlier about her not having anyone that loved her. Yanking the scrapbook back into my grasp, I looked around the room. I didn't exactly have anywhere to hide anything, but I didn't want to leave the scrapbook in the box. The shelving unit was one of the only objects in the room besides boxes and the pillow, blanket, and mattress I had been given. Thinking on my feet, I remembered the hole in the wall. I scrambled to the loose brick and pulled it down, setting it on the floor gently. Taking the scrapbook and placing it with the journal and box inside, I took a moment to remember the day we put it together. We asked Miss Walker for an extra printing book, the small half sized books they gave you in school. We covered the pages inside with coloured paper and drew each room of our future house on the pages. Shaking my head, it didn't matter how it was made, it was the fact that she had actually held onto it for all these years. The day she left the orphanage, I remembered running to the room and pulling it out from under the bed. I gave it to her as a reminder of me—of us. At that time she told me our pact stood, but how could it? She was leaving and I was being left behind. She tapped my chest in the area over my heart, and told me that it would live there. To some extent it did, a day never had gone by that I hadn't thought about her.

After replacing the brick, I finished packing the remainder of the boxes and placed them on the shelving unit. I was in shock that everything Justine owned were in these boxes, her life summed up five shelves. I had to wonder the reason why she was not permitted to have her belongings upstairs, where they would be more visible. Darren couldn't really believe she or he could forget about her past life.

By now it must have been close to dinner time, and Darren would return to take me back upstairs to sit with him during dinner, at least that's what had become the norm. Privileges to the main floor were becoming more and more frequent as time went on. I assumed he was testing me to see if I would run. Justine had run away before from the way Darren talked, and frankly I didn't blame her. If anything, it proved her bravery, and I was proud of her for it. I knew I must find an escape, and if she had escaped before, there had to be a way. I couldn't see myself surviving too much longer with him and his temper.

Just as these thoughts were prominent in my mind, the familiar heavy footsteps began their way down the stairs. After opening the door, Darren stood leaning in the doorway, and without moving spoke.

"Dinner is served," he said, stepping aside to signal me it was time to go upstairs.

As I reached the top of the stairs, the kitchen light was dimmed, and the table was set for what seemed like an elegant dinner—candle light with roses. At that very moment, I lost my appetite.

How was I supposed to sit and eat in this manner with someone who wasn't my husband, who was actually the husband of my twin sister?

I almost threw up in my mouth at the thought, it sickened me. As he pulled my chair out for me to sit, I gave a small fake smile to entertain him. Before me lay a place setting of the classiest of displays, including fine bone china plates and crystal glasses. It appeared to be the dinnerware I had spotted in the china cabinet at the end of the hallway leading to the washroom—eggshell, with tiny red roses lining the outer edge of the plates. I didn't recall ever eating off such fine china in my life. Why Darren had such things was beyond me, as it didn't seem to fit *his* style.

Darren placed a steak before me, accompanied with mixed steamed vegetables, and rosemary roast potatoes. It smelled delicious, but knowing my surroundings it continued to make me nauseous.

As he sat before me, our eyes connected. In the candlelight, it looked like he had light brown eyes, with a slight twinkle. Shivers spread up and down my spine. I could tell it was going to be an awkward dinner, I had hoped it would be in silence though. I didn't think I could handle much more of him today.

A few moments into the first couple of bites, Darren spoke.

"Doll, you know I love you, right?" he asked, accompanied by an ugly, toothy grin.

Those words made my stomach flop. Nervously, I nodded my head to acknowledge his words, but kept my eyes on my plate.

"Look at me, Justine," he spoke in a tender voice.

I took a moment and gazed up to meet his eyes. This was a different side of Darren I rarely saw. The only other time I noticed this kind of behavior was the apparent anniversary last month.

The shivers up and down my spine were still present as his stare made me feel dirty. No man except for *my* husband should have been looking at me the way Darren was. I was a happily married woman, after all. This thought sickened me even more, causing a wave of nausea to overtake me. Staring back down, I glanced at my ring finger, the date suddenly flashed before me. It was my anniversary—Keith and I would have been married eleven years today.

My mind flew back to the night of the kidnapping, and remembered that my wedding band had fallen off in the struggle. Ironically, Keith and I were supposed to go to the jewelers the next day to have it re-sized, as it had grown too big for my hand with my, then recent, weight loss.

Darren immediately noticed the concern that was present on my face, and questioned my thoughts, something he did when I became silent or appeared to be thinking.

"What's wrong? Is the dinner not good enough?" he went on to say.

I shook my head, but did not say a word. I caught myself rubbing the underside of my ring finger with my thumb as a reminder what I was missing today. Darren noticed. Of course he noticed, nothing ever slipped by him. His eyes were those of a hawk, seeing everything.

He rose from this chair, which caused me to lose my breath for a moment. I froze, as he walked right past me and down the hallway. I heard a door squeak open before seeing him return to the kitchen. Standing at my side, he placed a gold wedding band on the table next to me, and without a word, he silently returned to his seat in front of me. Not realizing that I was holding my breath, I let it out slowly, taking in what had just happened. This was not my husband, nor was this *my* wedding ring.

"Are you not going to put it on?" he cooed in a smooth voice.

I glanced between the ring and Darren, it was difficult to think with him staring at me constantly. I had been able to play along thus far, but this was taking things a little too far for my liking.

Hesitating, I could tell Darren was becoming impatient as each second ticked past. Staring back down at the ring, I picked it up and held it between my fingers.

"We are married Justine, no matter how much you don't want to be. You were stupid to leave it behind when you decided to run. I assume you didn't think I would follow? The papers you thought you stashed away gave away where you were headed. You can't hide from me. I told you many times before, I'm all you

161

have, and will ever have. Your past life gave you up, and your adopted family died, leaving you with nobody, once again."

Tears began to form in my eyes, but I did not want to show him weakness. Had Justine really been looking for me? This thought alone made me feel overwhelmed—she had actually been searching for me, and she wanted to see me again. This would explain why this man was led to my house, and after what I discovered today, that Justine is my lost twin sister, it confirms why I was mistaken for someone else.

EIGHTEEN

Darren
Past, June 2000

I felt as though things were falling into our old routine again, lately. One of the most significant changes I had noticed was Justine had become feisty with me—definitely felt it to be unusual for her. It was something to wonder about, and what had happened to cause her to develop this type of personality all of sudden.

Trust had still been a major issue with her, and wasn't something I thought I would ever let up on to be honest. She had lost most of my faith in her with all her attempted escapes over the years. To this day, I still couldn't understand what that house in Richmond offered her that I couldn't give her.

I locked up the basement and was headed into the garage to take the trash to the road before I headed into the woods for today's hunting session. I needed to catch anything I could today, because my supply was running low. This was the perfect time of year to pull together my winter supply because the wild life was out in full force after hibernating for the winter months.

There was quite the collection of beer bottle cases shoved in the corner of the kitchen that had piled up over the past few months. I never bothered taking them back to the liquor store. I wasn't that desperate for money considering the rate meats were selling at these days, hence the need to replenish.

Justine continued to inquire regularly why I drunk so much, and I had to laugh because *she* was the reason I drank. The liquid kept me sane enough to deal with her moments of disrespect, which happened much too often. By now, I thought she would have learned, but she continued to be Justine—maybe she enjoyed the beatings.

As much as I savored the taste of whisky, it wasn't always necessary at thirty dollars a bottle my money could have bought more beer to satisfy my needs. You could call me stingy, but my money was worth more than splurging on unnecessary material objects. None of my earnings made it into a bank account, I had never believed in them for the fact the government could track me down—I never wanted to be tracked, by anyone. All that was needed was to pay the little bills we had and buy food—it was all that we needed to survive.

I had been lucky enough that my grandparents had left me their house, and it was fully paid for at the time. I didn't owe a cent, and it was an exhilarating feeling to live here paying only the utility bills. Even my truck had been paid off when I bought it off someone through a reseller's newspaper ad—a thousand dollars, no questions asked. Living simply had its benefits.

I had been meaning to get rid of the car considering Justine neither drove nor worked any longer, and I was not in need of it. I had considered it extensively, for the fact it was my boot around car within the city; the truck was used solely for work, to carry the animals from the cabin to the city, and usually smelled rotten.

I lugged the three cases of empty beer bottles out the back door and through the garage, nudging the automatic garage door opener on the way through. I had placed the cases on top of the recycle bin to roll out to the curb.

After I reached the curb and set the bins and boxes on the grass next to the driveway, I turned to see a cab sitting outside the Adams' home. It was unusual, as I knew Mrs. Adams lived alone after her husband had died nearly a decade ago. That's when Justine and I had moved in. Justine had talked a lot with the neighbours back then, and had been close with Mrs. Adams.

As I moved my way back up the driveway towards the garage, I heard a vehicle door slam. I turned towards the direction it had come from to see the cab outside the Adam's pull away. As it passed my driveway I noticed the passenger in the back seat was blonde and wore large round glasses. Whoever it was, had turned in the direction of my house as the cab rolled by, but abruptly turned away once we made eye contact. I wasn't entirely sure what that encounter had meant, but whoever she was, she made me feel uncomfortable.

As I pulled the rest of the trash to the curb, Mrs. Adams was standing on the sidewalk. I turned to see what she had been staring at, only to see the cab had turned the corner onto Cassandra Drive. I was not entirely sure why the events had suddenly caught my interest. It was not as if I knew the person being carried away, but anything that was remotely different that occurred in the neighbourhood caught me off guard. You could say I wasn't a fan of change.

Suddenly, the voice of Mrs. Adams could be over heard through my thoughts. Automatically I changed into my defensive self, where I hated people, and most of all hated talking to them unnecessarily.

"Darren! How are you? It's been so long since I've seen you and your wife," she said in her sickeningly sweet voice.

Great.

Talking with the neighbour wasn't in the cards for today, or any day for that matter.

"Life is busy," I shot back curtly, as I continued to head back up the driveway.

She was the only nosey neighbour on the street and it had annoyed the shit out of me why she thought it was necessary to constantly strike up conversations with me. Regardless of how rudely I acted towards her or my attempts to brush her off, she continued to try and talk to me. The only theory I had come up with was that she was lonely without her husband, and needed someone to talk to. Even if that was true, couldn't she have bugged other people on the street, rather than me?

"I would love to see Justine again, maybe you can tell her to drop by sometime?" she asked.

She had become more annoying with each passing minute; I needed this woman to shut up asking about my wife—my wife was nobody's business but my own. She wasn't going to see her again, and I needed this woman to know that. If I gave her an excuse, maybe she would finally leave me alone and move on with her life and stop butting her nose into my business.

"She died last year from pneumonia," I offered bluntly.

"Oh, I'm so sorry to hear that. I wish I had known, I could have helped you around your house if you needed someone."

"I don't need anyone. I'm late for work. Good day," and with that, I stormed up the rest of the driveway to my truck and jumped in, hitting the garage door remote rapidly to close it, as I jammed the key into the ignition and backed out. I needed to get away from her. The way she stared at me created friction and rage inside me, something not many people did to me. The sense I got from her was that she knew more than she was letting on—but about what exactly, I had absolutely no idea.

I sensed Justine had disclosed information to Mrs. Adams during their encounters they had years ago. It was a huge reason why I made her stop going around to her house. Knowing full well she shouldn't disclose anything about us. What happened behind closed doors was our business, and our business only.

Coming back down from my apparent rampage of thoughts, the last few minutes had already begun to become a blur.

Regardless, I needed to focus on getting to the cabin and feel my gun in my hand. Whenever I was under a lot of pressure or stress, holding and firing a gun relieved that.

As I pulled away, I peered in my review mirror. Mrs. Adams was nowhere to be seen, which was a relief. Maybe the diversion I had given about Justine, would keep her from coming around anymore.

As I drove, my mind wandered back to the woman in the cab.

Who was she, and why was she staring at me?

NINETEEN

Lily
Past, April 2001

It had been three years since I had been abducted from my home, Things had changed since the first day I was brought here. For the first year I was condemned to the basement—Darren's way of punishment for my escape; well, Justine's escape.

Now, I was able to roam the house freely when Darren was home, sleep in the bedroom each night, and prepare breakfast and dinners for the most part. The only time I was taken to the basement was when he went to work—eight hours a day during the week. Darren worked five days a week, with the occasional Friday off. Since he was his own boss, he was able to set his own schedule of work because he had no one to report to.

I had finally discovered during the first year of my kidnapping that he was a hunter; he brought home all sorts of meats. Some of which I never knew you could eat. He would reference constantly that his clients enjoyed the rare selection he provided them with.

Darren had installed a freezer in the basement where he kept the frozen meats to sell at markets and restaurants around the city. As he said, work was picking up and he needed more space to freeze the meat. Wherever he had been storing them previously was not suffice to keep with the demand any longer.

I had to admit it was gross; the smell the basement now held began to cause me to feel nauseated whenever I had to sit down there. The day he brought home a full deer and said he needed to dry it out in the basement, I freaked. I wasn't exactly a vegetarian, but I definitely did not want to see my future meals hanging from the ceiling of the basement.

Venison was something new to me, but it was very tasty and I didn't mind it. Other than the odd chicken or some beef, deer was pretty much all we ate. Once, he brought home a rabbit, and told me it was one of the more rare meats, and was in high demand. He could make a good buck on selling rabbit meat. That was something I never imagined people actually ate—rabbit.

Darren never elaborated beyond the work he did as a hunter, but it was our only source of income that I could see. We didn't live extravagantly by any means, just simple, 'the way he liked it' as he put it. I caught him several times shoving bills into canisters and placing them behind a picture frame in the hallway that led to the washroom and bedroom.

I never once dared to ask him about it, but at this point nothing should have surprised me. His life was completely controlled by him, and no one else—that was evident. I had to wonder on occasion, if he truly had all this money, why wasn't he spending it? Why would he stay here, in the middle of the city, when he could be living elsewhere, more secluded? That was the lifestyle he always talked about, and harped on the fact that he didn't need anyone but me, well, Justine. He never spoke about having friends, and we didn't even have a home phone from what I could tell. He carried a cell phone, though, because occasionally I heard him on the phone with a potential client, but other than that nobody ever called or text.

I had eventually realized that Darren suffered from a mental illness. I couldn't put my finger on what exactly he had. Working as a nurse for many years, I had some experience with psychiatric patients. It was obvious by the way he acted—the way his mood could swing drastically from one minute to the other. He had been taking a pill almost every morning. I had tried my best on several occasions to see what they were, but he would snap them away before I could ever get a proper look at the vile. All I could see, is that it was labeled from a pharmacy. Without prompting, he frequently told me they were his property, none of my business, and that he would take whatever they were when he wanted to—not when I wanted him to take them.

I had no idea what he was talking about considering I didn't know anything about them, but it must have been something Justine had nagged him about for that type of reaction to occur.

Regardless whether he was taking it regularly or not, this medication was not working one hundred percent of the time, if my assumptions that he suffered from a mental illness were correct.

The sense of living normally still haunted me as much as things were becoming more routine. Living in someone else's shoes at any point in life was difficult, let alone living in the shoes of your twin. Not seeing her during our adult lives had made this more difficult, until I had learned her ways through Darren and my surroundings. I figured I had to have been complying and acting well enough for Darren to still believe that I was his wife—especially this many years later.

There was one thing that I still wanted to question, which was the fact of why the windows were donned with heavy-duty blinds—which were never touched. I was told to never open them under any circumstances. Instead, we used lamps and ceiling lights to move around, and Darren had grown accustom to using candlelight at dinner. If it was late at night and Darren wanted to watch a movie, we would sit in the dark with the TV brightness on the lowest setting. To me, it was not even worth watching because the picture would be too dark to make out. Darren had gone to great lengths to protect himself from the outside world, to hide himself away for the most part.

There were only three windows that had sheer curtains in the entire house—the front door, back door and washroom. Out of those three windows there was only one which I could actually see out into the world somewhat—the washroom that faced the neighbour's backyard. Darren never let me anywhere close to either the front or back door. The reason, he stated, was that he didn't want anybody seeing me. I never understood why, but it was another thing I had to go along with. Was he ashamed of Justine, had she committed some crime that he was trying to cover up? I doubted it very much, and it was most likely something Darren was making up in his mind, it was evident that not all of his actions could be accounted for.

I had come down the hallway to the washroom to wash the floors while Darren was in the living room. While he was home, I would have rather completed chores than sit around with him. The less I was around him, the less he was angry, and the less I would get beat up over the smallest things. It always made him happy to see me working around the house—it almost always put him in a better mood.

Anytime I was in the washroom I tried to take a peek out the window. I had to stand on my tippy toes to be able to see out properly. Most times, I had no longer than two minutes to complete my business. It usually entailed Darren standing guard monitoring me. Darren had removed the door to the washroom after I continued to throw what he called hissy fits over the years. I tended to try and lock myself in there to get away from him, when he was being his angry self. If I needed the washroom for my business, it was now aired for him to hear—privacy was something I had lost—I should have known that and learned it early on but I still had a glimpse of hope it wasn't. This was a man who if given the world to control, he would, in a heartbeat.

I had set the mop down against the wall, placing the bucket inside the bathtub under the running faucet to make Darren believe I was filling it. I had wanted to steal a glance out the window briefly. It had been awhile since I was able to check what was occurring outside.

When I had reached up on my tiptoes, I spotted a shed in the neighbour's backyard. It wasn't something I previously had noticed, but with the quick glances I had taken previously, I could have missed it. Something about that shed was off; the tiny, clouded window appeared to have been painted on. I squinted to see if it was my imagination, but I swore I had seen a figure inside with binoculars pointed towards the house.

Not wanting Darren to hear me, I moved quietly away from the window to grab the stool from under the cupboard. Once I had it in place and had taken a step up, I peered across to the shed once again. Whatever was there, in the tiny shed window was now gone. I blinked and shook my head. It had to have been my imagination. Suddenly the door swung open and a woman with brunette hair tied back in a bun rushed out and into the back door of the house. There was life on the other side of these walls, I saw another human being! I gave a single bang on the window to grab her attention but it was too late. She was gone.

"What the hell do you think you're doing?" Darren exclaimed, which nearly knocked me off the stool with a startle.

He grabbed me from behind and roughly pulled me off the stool, swinging me around to face him, with his hands firmly planted on my upper arms.

"What have I told you about the windows in this house, stay clear of them!"

"I...I...I thought I saw someone."

"I don't care what you think you saw, the outside world does not concern you anymore. Only what happens inside these four walls. Do you hear me?"

"Yes."

"Now clean this bathroom like you said you would, and don't let me catch you by that window ever again."

He shoved me towards the bathtub where I had placed the bucket to fill; which had now over flowed. Darren stood by the window and peered out, his eyes narrowed while he scanned around whatever was on the outside.

He didn't leave the washroom while I cleaned, instead, he stood by the window and continued to stare out. Out the corner of my eye I could see that he had been stealing glances at me. I found it uncomfortable when he would watch me, I had no idea what was going through his mind.

The fact he couldn't realize I wasn't his wife was something that haunted me, even all these years later he still continued to believe I was someone else. Wouldn't he eventually know I wasn't who he claimed I was?

"I'm done in here," I announced to him.

He appeared he was lost in this own world with the stare he had off into la-la-land. He grunted and peered over to where I was standing in the doorway of the washroom.

"Are you sure you haven't missed a spot? Do I need to get out the white glove for inspection?"

That was something he always threatened me with when it came to chores around the house, but never did I actually see a white glove. I'd often wanted to question it but thought better of it.

"I am sure it is to your liking, you were standing here the entire time, remember?"

"You don't need to remind me of what I am doing, if you hadn't tried to draw attention to yourself I wouldn't have had to watch over you like a child."

"I thought I saw someone, they appeared to be watching the house."

The moment the words were out of my mouth Darren was back at the window, aggravated, peering around abruptly.

"What do you mean, they were watching? Why?"

"I don't know, that was what I was trying to find out."

"What did they look like?"

"I didn't exactly get a good look before you pulled me away, appeared to be a woman, with brunette hair."

"That nosey neighbour, doesn't she have anything better to do than watch me and what I do."

He said this more in a mumble, and it wasn't clear if it was directed at me or not. I stood silently while he continued to mumble away, peering out the window until he turned and walked towards me.

"You stay away from that window, do I make myself clear?"

"Crystal clear," I growled back.

"Don't give me that tone; you will regret that you have a voice to speak if you keep that up."

If Darren thought his words would spook me, he thought wrong. He threated more than actually following through with the actions. I had begun thinking that he thought I was that same woman as several years ago, the one who cried at every insult he shot at me. I had grown accustomed to his remarks and rolled with the punches he gave. It had truthfully been the only way to survive. That was if I wanted to survive at all.

TWENTY

Murray
Present, April 2004

We had pulled up to the house. I peered back down at the address I had scribbled in my notebook confirming the address matched that of the house that stood across the street from us. The house appeared to be well kept, with no over grown weeds or grass. A red truck, covered in rust and dirt, sat in the driveway. From where we were seated in my car across the street, we were barely able to make out the license plate. I pulled out a pair of binoculars from the glove compartment and peered through them. I rambled off the plate number so Gresham could write it down. I needed everything I could on this guy, to help fit together all the missing pieces of this absurd case.

Since we had pulled up, I had been completely astounded at the surroundings of the house—it appeared to be in a well-developed community complex in North Vancouver, lined with manicured gardens and expensive cars in each driveway. My mind was lost, completely forgetting Gresham was even present until she asked, "What are we waiting for?"

Taking my eyes off the house for only a second to turn to face her, I shrugged and replied, "Nerves, I suppose."

I was thankful I had her with me as backup, because I didn't know what we were getting ourselves into. We didn't have a warrant, only for the fact we were conducting a preliminary investigation on the Johnson's, collecting what we could, to know for sure if what Justine had told us was factual. For all I knew, I could have been strung along in some mind game of two completely neurotic people. If I wanted a warrant to search this home, I needed to provide the judge with solid evidence as to why and what for. I wasn't sure if this address would be accurate, or if we would find Justine or Darren there, considering the phone number she had given us was a wrong number. For now, this was part of the investigation—trying to piece together the entire mess that had been dragged out for six years.

Without any further hesitation, I pulled myself out of the car, with Gresham on my heels. As we walked up the driveway, we noticed all the curtains were drawn on every single window that faced the street. As we neared the front door, I noticed it had a large strange double lock on it, which I had never seen before, along with a security kick plate. I couldn't find a doorbell, which resulted in me giving the door a good pounding.

I listened for any movement inside, but with the noise of traffic traveling along the street with several of the neighbours' dogs barking, it muffled out any sounds that I might have been able to hear. Nobody was coming to the door. I tried peering through the small side window that had a sheer curtain. I could see down a hallway that had rooms veering off either side. I thought I saw a shadow to the right of the hallway, but blinking my eyes to clear my vision I still didn't see anything. I couldn't make any assumptions, and took a step back to peer around—again, nothing could be seen.

I gave the door another pounding, and within seconds someone opened it, with the security door chain still attached. Although the door was only open a few inches, I could tell that a tall, dark haired, broad shouldered male stood behind it. He spoke in a low husky voice,

"Can I help you?"

I cleared my voice before speaking.

"Yes, hello! We're looking for Justine Johnson, is she home?"

He appeared agitated, as if we had disturbed him.

"There's no one here by that name. Who's asking?"

"I am detective Murray with the Vancouver Police Department, she came to the sta—"

He cut me off before I could even finish my sentence.

"I don't know who that is, and there's nobody living here by that name."

Without a description, or anything to go by, I couldn't make any assumptions, and needed to investigate the identity of this man at the door.

"Are you Darren Johnson?"

"No, the Johnsons moved. Have a good day." He slammed the door and locked the dead bolt abruptly.

I walked away from the house confused. I had been hoping this would have been her correct address. Why wasn't Justine here? In my search, a business address

179

showed up for her where she had been listed as a receptionist at a medical center. When I had called, they informed me she hadn't worked there in close to eight years, but provided this address as the last residence on file for her. She had no other listings in the system for current employment.

We passed the overflowing garbage bin that had been left at the curb. I thought it was a little odd how one person could create that much garbage. I spotted a can on top and instantly my mind shouted *evidence*. Without hesitation, I whipped out a tissue from my pocket and pulled the can out of the bin. Gresham gave me a sideways glance as we walked back to the car and I opened the trunk to snatch a paper bag from the 'supply kit' I always carried. If this man didn't want to tell me who he was, I would find out myself.

"What exactly do you think that's going to prove?" Gresham asked with a hint of sarcasm in her voice.

"I'm not sure, but something inside me told me we needed it."

I closed the trunk and made my way around to the driver's door. Before I sat down, I took a brief look over my shoulder to eye the house one last time. I noticed the curtain next to the door was drawn and the man's eyes stared me down. I was certain he couldn't have seen me take the can out from his trash, because his driveway was lined with trees and shrubs, which blocked the view of the curb where his garbage bins were placed. He seemed apprehensive and fidgety, but without court papers I was unable to demand he let me in.

"I think we're missing something here Murray. Did you notice how he didn't make eye contact and was quick to shoo us away?"

I know what she was hinting at, but we had come here on a preliminary investigation with no search warrant. I, too, felt something was off about the situation, but without proof I had to walk away. The next step was to find out what we could about Darren Johnson.

As we pulled away from the curb, my eyes drifted to the house on the left of what we thought had been the Johnson home. There was a figure standing in a window on the upper floor, who appeared to have long, wavy hair. As I slowed the car and glanced back, they were gone—had it been just a figment of my imagination again?

My mind continued to ponder the actions of the man who had answered the door. Shaking the thoughts away, I focused on driving back towards Vancouver. Other than to discuss stopping at a diner to grab lunch it was an eerily quiet drive back.

Although we weren't due back at the station until early afternoon, with the lack of new leads on my wife's case, our timetable was in a bit of disarray.

Gresham stared out the window on the drive from the diner to the station, without speaking a word. We pulled into the parking lot of the station. I bowed my head and closed my eyes as I cut the engine.

"It's time to give up, isn't it Gresham?" I sighed.

My voice was shaky, trying to hold in the emotions that were eating away at me.

"No. It's never over Murray."

She even had a quiver to her own voice. I looked up to see her eyes welling up with tears. As I reached my hand over to console her she flinched. Her eyes landed on something behind us in the rearview mirror.

"Murray...Murray...LOOK!" she screamed, while pointing to something behind me. As I turned to see what Gresham was screaming about, I saw her standing next to the entrance of the side door. In barely an audible voice I breathed,

"Justine?"

She was the one and only person who seemed to know anything about this whole mess. I fumbled as I hurried to get out of the car, nearly dropping my keys and phone as I shoved them into my pocket. As I approached her, I made mental notes not to rush to avoid scaring her.

She removed her sunglasses once I was within a few feet of her—it was scary to feel like Lily was the one staring straight back at me. In the blink of an eye, I had to reach my hands out, as Justine almost fell to the ground, shaking uncontrollably, tears running down her face.

"I'm sorry...I'm sorry..." she repeated over and over.

I wasn't exactly sure what she was sorry for, but all that mattered right then was that I got her inside, away from the public eye. Gresham held the door open as I helped her to her feet. It was becoming difficult to support her weight, so I quickly made the decision to scoop her up into my arms and let her lean on me.

I didn't need anyone seeing us like this. I chose to take the back hallway towards the same interview room I had previously interviewed her in. As I rounded the corner of the hallway that split into two directions—one to the main lobby and the other to the interview room—I heard someone call out,

"Do you need a paramedic?"

I ignored them and continued carrying Justine towards the interview room. I heard Gresham's voice informing whoever had asked that everything was okay, but that was all I could hear.

Since the day Justine had stepped foot in the station, everyone had wanted to know what she knew. Regardless of how many times I asked everyone to stop airing my business, they still did.

I had always been a private person and didn't talk much to my co-workers, except Gresham and Pryce. All anyone else knew, was this woman seemed to have answers to Lily's disappearance. Those who worked the case in the beginning stages of the kidnapping wanted me to hand over the new leads, but I refused too. Captain Sullivan rearranged the teams and allowed Gresham, Pryce, and myself to work on the leads that were slowly trickling in through Justine's information. I was not about to let what little glimmer of hope I had left in the case fade. It had already happened once, and I was not about to let it to happen again, that was, Justine disappearing on us again.

Finally, we made it to the interview room, where I assisted her into a chair. She let her arms fall into her lap, and nearly slumped over the table in front of her. I wasn't exactly sure what was going through her head or why she had come back, but I wanted to ensure she wasn't going to run away again. I would sit here all night long to hear just two words from her if that's what it took.

I motioned to Gresham for a cup of water and box of tissues for Justine—I wanted her to be as comfortable as possible. Once I felt Justine was comfortable, I asked Gresham to leave, silently signaling for her to go into the viewing room to watch. I wanted Justine to have as little distraction as possible. I wasn't sure if during previous times we had interviewed Justine, she had felt intimidated having anyone in the room.

Gresham exited the room, quietly assuring me she would be around if I needed her—in the small viewing room next door where she could listen via a speaker. I closed the door gently behind her. I paused briefly before I turned and made my way back to sit in front of Justine. She looked as though she hadn't slept for days, or eaten in just as many.

For an instant, I saw her eyes drift to meet mine, the sadness and heartache evident even through the strands of hair that covered most of her eyes. Her mouth began to move, but there were no words to be heard. To comfort her, I placed my hands on the table that sat between us, to show I was relaxed. The silence had begun to eat away at me, but before another thought entered my mind, she found her voice.

"I can explain," she said.

TWENTY-ONE

Lily
Present, April 2004

The bruises upon my body told the story of the last six years in this God forsaken place. With each escape I had attempted, I never managed to get further than the driveway, if that far. I was ready to give up, ready to throw in the towel and finally accept the fact this was now my life—I was Justine Johnson, 'wife' to Darren Johnson, my kidnapper. It had come to the point where I had done everything he told me to do, with no questions asked, just to save the little strength I had left. Each blow he delivered to me caused one less ounce of strength within me to survive.

Eventually, I found a spare set of keys that had been left on the counter under some newspapers, which I swiped one morning after breakfast. I stuffed them in my bra, thinking they wouldn't make a sound amongst the padding. Of course I had no idea which key opened which door, however I did notice a number pattern, although I was unable to break the code to determine any matches very quickly.

I suspected he thought he knew me well after this long, and things would be safe, that I wouldn't try anything stupid—like escaping. I proved him wrong. Regardless how long I had been held captive, every day I was planning an escape. The keys were my escape route, so I hid them carefully in the basement, in the hole in the wall with the journal, wooden box and the little book Rose and I had made when we were five years old. When I had time alone while Darren was at work, I would inspect the keys. Upon closer examination, I was able to see the keys had been labeled at one point in time. In faded lettering I could see one key labelled 'back door'. He must have changed his mind, to using a numbered system instead. I had pulled it off the key ring and kept it in my bra until I found the perfect occasion to put it to use. I prayed it was still the key to the back door.

Coming back to reality, I shook my head from the thoughts—they were nothing but memories now, because he had beat me until I gave up the location where I had his spare set of keys, which resulted in him finding the scrapbook, journal, and box. He took them all away, and I never saw them again. All I remembered was that I had smelled smoke one day from the fireplace. I never questioned him, but instead let those memories of my sister fade away.

That day I felt I had let her down, that I had given up her hidden treasures, ones that she had held on to for a special reason that I knew nothing about. If I ever escaped and found her, I wouldn't know what to tell her about what had happened to her treasured belongings. I would feel ashamed telling her I led Darren right to them and let him burn them. I should have fought harder to save them. I should have lied and never given up the keys' whereabouts. I had been selfish and had only thought about myself and *my* need to survive.

Why? Why had it been so important to survive all these years? What had I been surviving for?

I had been unsuccessful in finding an escape route and nobody had even come looking for me; at least not to my knowledge.

Hadn't Darren left fingerprints at my house? They could have connected them to him, couldn't they? Had I really believed that nobody but my own daughter had witnessed the whole ordeal? I had been sure Callie would give my husband every detail she could remember, but I had to remember she had only been a child then, and a scared nine year old child for that matter.

I was washing the breakfast dishes, as Darren sat reading the newspaper the same way he did each morning. Due to my attempted escapes, Darren had placed locks on the inside *and* outside of the front and back doors. I remembered watching him take apart locks and building his own from scratch. He was determined to keep me from escaping to the 'outside world' as he called it. I thought back to all the strange occurrences around the house—the windows had been glued shut since the day I had arrived, at least the bathroom had. It had been the only one that I had managed to easily gain access to. If that one had been sealed shut, I could guarantee all of them had been sealed. Why? Had been my question all along.

Why had Darren been such a control freak? What was it about being in control that he found thrilling, or even exhilarating?

I had a lot of unanswered questions, ones I never thought I would obtain answers to. I thought I had perfected the image of Justine well, considering this man still had no idea about my real identity six years later. What helped the most was discovering the person's shoes whom I had been forced to live in, they were at least shoes I had some connection too. It had made this whole process a tiny bit more bearable, but not by much.

Nobody should have had to live the way I had for the last six years. It wasn't normal to keep someone in almost solitary confinement, without causing them irreversible mental trauma. I knew that to be true, because I had fought my mental capacity deteriorating every day that passed. Most days I had to look deep within myself and pull up the very little strength I had left, just to get through the day.

My mind wandered back to the task at hand, cleaning the dishes. Darren had moved to stand behind me, pushing my hair off my neck as he breathed my name along my neckline,

"Justine," he whispered breathlessly into my ear.

Goosebumps instantly popped up along my arms, his breath on my neck causing me to nearly jump out of my skin; but as always, I accepted his advances and prepared myself to adapt to whatever horrific actions were to come. As he reached around to place his hands on my forearms, we heard sirens roll by the house. It had been a normal occurrence and never seemed to faze Darren at all. Each time I heard them, I felt as though I should have screamed and run, but everything around me was locked down; just the way Darren liked it—it kept me exactly where he wanted me to be. From what I was able to gather, Darren lived on a busy thoroughfare in a city. Traffic could be heard at all hours of the day and night, along with other typical city sounds.

That had been another question I had wondered about—where the hell had he been keeping me? The day I discovered his name, I hadn't had time to read past whom the mail was addressed to. From that day forward, I never saw another piece of mail again. He had told me it was none of my business what mail he received, as he was the sole provider and took care of the little bills we had. The question of my whereabouts lingered in my thoughts daily.

Had we stayed in Vancouver, or had he moved me out of the province, or worse, out of the country?

It wasn't a far-fetched thought, considering the border into Washington was just south of Vancouver. Darren's grip on my forearms tightened as a subtle reminder I wasn't going anywhere, as the sounds of the sirens faded into the distance. Darren let go of his grip, which allowed me to finish washing the dishes in the sink. I noticed him peering out the back window across to the next-door neighbour's backyard. When he caught my eyes watching him, he let the curtain drop out of his hands and turned away.

He seemed to always be paranoid, and watched out the back window whenever we were in the kitchen. I never could understand what, or who, he thought would come after us. I assumed he thought the police watched us, from the many paranoid mumblings I heard from him day in and day out. I had hoped the police would eventually come, that someone would have witnessed the whole event of my kidnapping and would walk into a police station to finally set me free from this man.

Suddenly, an abrupt pounding was heard on the front door, which interrupted the silence in the kitchen. Instantly, my mind was frazzled—who on earth would have been knocking? We never had visitors—ever. Momentarily, I froze in place, merely for the fact that what was occurring was extremely out of place.

Darren was equally as shocked as I was, with his demeanor change instantly, as if trouble had started. In a split second, I shook myself out of the apparent haze I was in to realize what this meant—I could be rescued. I could be *free*. I bolted towards the front door, but didn't even make it to the doorway of the kitchen before Darren's hands were around my waist, lifting me off the ground—his reflexes were responsive at a moment's notice.

I didn't plan on giving up the fight, and did everything I could to free myself from his tightening grasp. I kicked and screamed, in hopes of whoever was at the door would hear me,

"Help! Please help me!"

Darren silenced my cries instantly by shoving his hand over my mouth, similar to how he had the night of my kidnapping. In that brief second, I felt the chance of freedom that had presented itself vanish, just as quickly as it had come.

I continued to struggle to fight him off as he pulled me towards the basement stairs pounding down them all the way to the damp, dark room. Once we were inside the room, he dropped me to the ground. I shot myself back up onto my feet and charged at him with my fists drawn. It was no good because he was always one step ahead of me and placed his hands up to catch my fists. He spoke briefly before he slammed and locked the door behind him.

"You will regret that stunt when I return, you hear me? You know you don't go screaming around here. You will pay for that outburst!"

I hated the basement, for a number of reasons, but my number one reason right then was that you couldn't hear anything from down there—no voices, knocking, outside sounds, nothing. It was as if the whole room was sound proofed; nothing could ever be heard except the thuds of Darren's feet on the stairs as he traveled up and down them.

What felt like hours, when in reality must have been bordering on thirty minutes, passed by before I heard Darren's loud footsteps pounding down the stairs in a rushed manner.

The door swung open and I could sense something was not right, because he marched right inside and met me eye to eye with clenched hands.

"Who the hell have you been talking to?" he demanded.

What did he mean, who had I been talking to? He knew very well I couldn't have talked to anyone the way he had me held up in this house.

 In a small voice I answered him,

"No one."

I began to inch backwards towards the wall, but with every step back *I* took, Darren took two steps forward. He stayed silent, his breathing heavy, and raised clenched fists. I felt I couldn't handle him if he decided to take a swing at me. I thought it could be the last night of my life, because I simply did not have the energy to fight back anymore. Instead, he turned around and marched out of the room once again— slamming the door without another word spoken.

I hadn't realized how much my body had been shaking. I could have sworn he would have beaten me right then, but clearly he had more important things to consider.

I slid down the cold, damp wall, and began to ponder who could have been at the door, and what Darren had been all riled up over. It had to have been someone looking for Justine obviously, for him to question if I had been talking to anyone—but there was no way Darren could be that senseless. Who the heck would he think I could have talked to, and when? Even when I had attempted to run, I hadn't made it far enough to talk to anyone.

I often wondered if a neighbour had seen anything suspicious and called the police. It seemed as though what I had learned over the years was that Darren kept to himself, he never talked about friends or even family members for that matter. He was definitely a loner. With his attitude and temper, who would have been able to stand him, anyway? Justine obviously couldn't, that was clear.

TWENTY-TWO

Murray

Her words began to run together as she spoke. I took a breath before I broke my own silence,

"Take your time, Justine. I am here to listen."

I tried to keep my voice soft and calm in order to keep her comfortable. She bowed her head, as her eyes dropped from my gaze before she spoke again.

"My husband, he is sick. He doesn't understand his actions sometimes. Not always does he take his medication. I'm sorry."

She paused only for a minute, which allowed me a split second to ask a question.

"What kind of sickness does he have?" I inquired, with a slightly puzzled voice.

I felt uneasy knowing he could be mentally ill, because his actions would not stand trial—he would be deemed 'not criminally responsible by reason of mental disorder' by the courts.

"He's mentally ill. Schizophrenic."

It was evident Justine did not want to maintain eye contact with me as she spoke.

"What happens when he doesn't take his medication?" I asked tentatively.

I was worried how she would answer, because it was clear that she was scared of him. You could tell by her words and in her demeanour.

"He gets violent due to his bouts of hallucinations. He never wants to take his medication, though. I literally had to force him to have the pills by grinding them up and hiding them in his food or drinks. He was much better if I kept up regularly with it."

She sucked in a deep breath as she finished her sentence. Thoughts began running through my mind. I rose from the table and began to pace about, but quickly realized I had to stay neutral and stopped. I believed Justine could feel the tension that began to swell within me.

"I'm sorry to have caused all of this. If it wasn't—" I cut her off quickly.

She needed to realize that blaming herself would not get us anywhere. Blame and self deprecation was the problem with domestic violence cases, the victims always felt they were at fault. She needed to know that.

"His actions were not your fault, Justine. You did everything in your power to ensure he took his medication," I stated, yet keeping my voice soft; but, Justine's attitude changed, it instantly held anger.

"If I hadn't run away to find my sister, that bastard wouldn't have followed me and we wouldn't be in this mess."

The room fell silent. What did she mean, sister? She had never mentioned a sister to me before now. Words continued to fall from her mouth,

"As much as you are trying to tell me it's not my fault, detective, it *is* my fault."

She slammed her fist onto the metal table in front of her. I couldn't seem to process what she was telling me, partly because she talked in fragments, but also because it was as if she was dancing around something— perhaps the truth.

"If I hadn't run—" I cut her off immediately.

"You ran away for a reason, a damn good reason, because someone was hurting you."

She paused and I could see her eyes well up as she fought back tears, but she couldn't keep them from spilling over. I had sensed she hadn't let out how she really felt about what had happened to her in some time, possibly never.

As much as I worried for the woman before me, my mind continued to think of Lily, considering this was the whole reason this woman had come into the station in the first place—she had information about Lily's case.

I had become lost in my own thoughts, when I was interrupted by Justine calling out.

"Detective Murray?" she asked.

I immediately returned my attention to her, and made my way to sit down again in front of her.

"You were at my house today, weren't you?"

The words she spoke were almost a whisper.

How did she know we had been at her house? Had she been watching where I had been going? Was she the person the man kept looking back at? If she had been in the house, how did she escape?

None of this was making any sense. It had been proven that she could appear without warning, considering she had been haunting Callie and I for many years, or so it seemed. It took me a moment to figure out how to respond, and then what question I wanted answered. With my delay in determining what I wanted to ask, Justine interrupted.

"You did go. Was Lily there? I know she was there."

She rambled her statement quickly, and I couldn't comprehend everything she was asking.

"Yes, I was at your house, though, I was looking for you. A man answered, but he indicated there was no one by the name of Johnson who lived there."

I barely had my response out before Justine continued, slamming me with her questions,

"Lily *is* there! Did you see her?"

How would she know if Lily had been there? Had she been watching the house? Had she been the figure in the window of the house next door? Everything was running together at this point in my mind.

I shot up from the table, and excused myself from the room temporarily. I needed another officer or detective in the room to hear her statement.

I didn't have my recorder because I had only arrived at the station when all this began, and I hadn't had a chance to make it to my desk. I pondered quickly who I would ask, possibly the Captain if he was around?

No, no, no. Not Captain.

He would pull me from the case if he knew we had a new lead such as this, and I couldn't afford to lose this lead.

Suddenly, Gresham walked out of the viewing room as I entered the hallway walking towards me, at a quickened pace.

"Is she okay, Murray?" she asked with concern in her voice.

"Yes, she's okay, I think," I replied slowly.

"Why are you out here if she's still in there stating information?" Gresham raised an eyebrow in the direction of the interview room.

"I need another detective to witness her statement. The woman is pouring things out left, right, and center. I can't comprehend it all, and I don't have my recorder with me," I admitted.

"I'll do it. I'm not tied down with anything. I've been listening to everything from the viewing room," she stated with a small smile. I was glad she had offered. She was the only person I felt comfortable hearing Justine's statement at this point.

"Okay. Can you bring a recorder, pad and pen? I'll head back in."

"I've got you covered. Seeing the direction it was going, I was headed up to my office to retrieve them anyway. I'll be back in five minutes!" With that, Gresham walked away from me, towards the elevators, leaving me to ponder for a second and take a breather before I headed back into the interview room.

Once inside, I found Justine staring out the window. She seemed to always be watching out the window. I reclaimed my seat back at the metal table. As I did, I must have startled her, because she jumped away from the window ledge as I screeched the chair on the floor, nearly clenching her chest.

"I'm sorry. I didn't want to disturb your thoughts," I apologized.

Flashing me a small smile, she returned to the seat across from me, leaving her thoughts at the window. She hadn't even made it back to her chair before words began falling from her mouth again,

"Since I left him, I've been paranoid he will find me. That's why I have stayed hidden and wear this disguise," she motioned towards her sunglasses and large hat that were sitting on the table.

I nodded, not sure exactly how to respond. I figured at this point, all she needed was a listening ear, and that was something I could give her.

"He must have realized by now who he has isn't who he thinks she is. Then again, he's probably off his medication and had been hallucinating too."

What did she mean—he has someone who he may think is someone else?

"Can you elaborate on that?" I was curious to hear this story.

"It's best we start at the beginning. I think I owe you that much," she sighed.

That was true—the more history I had, the better I could continue to piece together what information she claimed to have had about my wife's case. She didn't hesitate, and started right into informing me of what she needed to tell me.

"Once Darren and I were married, I began to notice his condition. In high school, I didn't make the connection, but as I looked back I could see it had been a part of his disorder. He would become jealous of other boys who simply talked to me, and was extremely over protective as to whom I hung out with. He wanted control. At the time, I thought it was because he was a jock and wanted to show me off to his jock friends. After high school, we attended different colleges, seeing each other only on weekends. He never wanted me to leave his sight when he was around. He drank, but not excessively, just socially with his guy friends— you know, it's normal for college students to drink when they are among their peers. As we neared the end of our four years of college, his drinking increased. During his bouts of consumption, he would reference events and people as though we were back in high school, such as bringing up boys who I no longer had contact with. It confused me, though people say stupid things under the influence, and I had passed it off as him being drunk and that he didn't really mean anything by his comments."

A single tear fell down her left cheek, but she ignored it and took a deep breath before continuing.

"We married six years after we moved in together which was the year we finished college. About a year after that was when the abuse started. At first it was verbal, and then after another year he became physically abusive. At this stage, we had only just discovered his issue as being a disorder. That's when I was finally able to drag him to see a doctor. He never liked the medication they prescribed him, as he always felt uneasy and less 'in control' as he put it. It also made him sleepy—it was knocking him out for at least twelve hours at a time in the beginning. When he wanted to give up on it, I learned how to administer it to him without him knowing. Giving up would result in the aggressive behavior returning, and I wasn't about to let that happen, again. It gave me a small sense of security when I took those great lengths to protect myself. One year into our marriage, I found out I was pregnant. We had never talked about a family, but at that stage I didn't want anybody else having to deal with his behavior that was becoming increasingly aggressive each day. A child did not need to be brought into the world, into that situation. Though abortion was out of the question, I decided if anything, I would carry the child full term and offer it up for adoption. The morning I was going to see the doctor, Darren questioned where I was going. He wouldn't take anything I said at face value and kept calling me a liar. I finally broke down and told him. He was livid. He ranted about how I was supposed to be on the pill, so why was I coming up pregnant, and that I must have stopped taking it and was trying to ruin his life. I don't think he realized that the pill doesn't offer a one hundred percent guarantee of preventing pregnancies. He told me he was taking me straight to the women's clinic for an abortion—he didn't want children. When I tried to tell him that I wanted to give the baby up for adoption, he ignored me."

Silence filled the room. *This woman has been through hell*, I thought. I couldn't imagine what she must have felt going through everything she had just told me; and worse, to be forced to go against her wishes. My imagination wondered what life would have been like if a child had been introduced into the picture, but I shook those thoughts away, knowing that would have been a terrible situation.

Justine stared at the floor. You could feel the weight she carried and sense she still wasn't at peace. She wouldn't feel safe until her husband was caught. My eyes diverted to someone sitting in the corner by the window, it was Gresham. I had completely forgot I had asked her to come into the interview, but never heard her enter. I was too invested in what Justine was saying to pay any attention to what was going on around me.

She looked completely shocked as she sat there, listening to what Justine had to say. She had been by my side the entire time Lily had been missing, and had gone beyond her duties as a friend, a constable, and now, as a detective. I truly appreciated her more than I probably ever told her. I brought my attention back to Justine. I wanted to understand the connection of this sister she mentioned of earlier. I needed to know the answer. It had been burning on the tip of my tongue,

"You mentioned earlier you had a sister. Who is she, and what relevance does she play in this ordeal? "

I know I sounded blunt, but it was something I needed to know. The way Justine had said she had a sister earlier made it sound as if that would change everything. She was quick to answer, as if this whole time she wanted to come out and say it,

"She is Flower, from the orphanage. Flower is your Lily!"

I stared blankly at Justine, as my eyes darted between her and Gresham. Even Gresham couldn't fathom what was said, I could tell by the puzzled, shocked look across her face. Lily never spoke about having a sibling, ever. This would make complete sense as to why this woman looked identical, but how could I actually know this was the truth, and not some fairytale?

TWENTY-THREE

Lily

Hours had passed, and I had been nodding off to sleep sitting in the dark. I was awoken promptly at the sound of familiar footsteps on the stairs, with the door swinging open and the room flooding with light seconds later. Darren stood in the doorway, not taking another step inside the room. His words were stern when he spoke.

"Let's go."

I rose slowly from my place against the wall, and took my time as I walked towards the door. Darren was not taking my reaction to his request lightly. He finally reached out when he had enough of my dilly dallying, and grabbed my upper arm before I was even at the door. He shoved me in the direction of the stairs, and began to push me up them. I was sick of his attitude, so I ensured I climbed the stairs extra slow. As I reached the top of the staircase, I spotted two suitcases on the kitchen floor. I was confused, but stayed silent, not wanting to irritate Darren any further. Whatever was happening, and whoever had been at the door yesterday, had really upset Darren, and was causing him to flee quickly.

He still held a grip on me as he placed his hand on the handle of the back door,

"You keep that trap of yours shut, you hear me? Do as I say for a change."

He turned the handle and the door popped opened. Instantly, my mind told me to run, but I knew running was useless because he would find me. Darren lifted one suitcase in his left hand, placing it under his arm to retrieve the second suitcase. With his right hand he pulled at my arm to lead me outside and through the back door of the garage. Although it was dark outside, during my brief time outdoors I could see light on the horizon, which meant daybreak wasn't too far away. He set the suitcases down on the floor of the garage as he opened the hinged covering of his truck's bed. Meeting my confused gaze, he nodded in the direction of the truck bed.

What was he expecting me to do?

A few seconds passed in silence before he finally spoke again,

"Get in the truck, now," he demanded. He said it slowly as, if I was stupid and didn't understand.

I moved slowly as I crawled into the darkness of the bed, which smelled horrible from rotting meat. I wanted to gag from the stench. Before closing the cover, he issued me a warning,

"Don't make a single noise, or it will be the last noise you ever make."

The cover slammed closed, and I was left feeling confused. Everything was happening too quickly for me to fully comprehend, or come to any conclusion about what had happened yesterday. It seemed like ages before the engine turned over and I felt him back out.

The whole time, I managed to stay quiet, as much as I wanted to scream and bang in case someone could hear it on the outside. I feared for my life, once again. I didn't know where we were headed.

It felt like it had been hours before the truck came to a rolling stop. I must have been dozing off due to the darkness and lull of the truck's movement. As soon as the truck bed cover was off, bright sunshine blasted the darkness in which I had been kept in. Darren was obviously still in a foul mood, and with no care whatsoever, began pulling me by my arm to drag me out of the truck bed. I didn't know what had his panties in a twist, but he was beginning to piss me off.

Although it was early morning, somewhere around eight o'clock I was guessing by the sun in the sky, I was exhausted from the way we had traveled here and being shoved in the truck as I was. Even attempting to breathe had been difficult, causing me to breathe slowly to save what oxygen I had available.

I was hoping that the person who knocked on the door yesterday scared Darren into running because he thought I was being sought after. Even if it were a far fetched dream, at this point I wanted to indulge in such a fantasy. Given Darren's paranoia after the visitor yesterday, it dawned on me that I could be very close to being found and he was now on the run. I was completely and mentally exhausted. I was done pretending, done with this fake marriage, and the games this creep had wanted to play all these years.

Darren clenched his fingers around my upper arm tighter as he led me to the tiny house we had arrived at, which appeared to be nothing more than a cabin. By the size and appearance of it, I would have referred to it as more of a shack. I was already too weak and would not stand a chance of defending myself today, if it came down to it. Complying with his physical demands, I shuffled along the trodden down dirt path towards the door.

I began wondering if anyone knew about this hideaway as we approached the worn, wooden front door, but from the way it was tucked away in the trees, my hope faded. All the trees, bushes, and grass were well over grown, and camouflaged the cabin. If someone had been walking by and not paying attention, I doubt they would even know there was a cabin there.

Darren wasted no time shoving me inside, leading me into an open area, and throwing me into the seat of a chair right in the center of the room. I could feel the dust and dirt that covered the inside of the place crawling onto my skin. I looked up and saw Darren's facial expression—he was pissed, his heavy breathing synchronized with his pacing. I sat quietly for a few minutes, before Darren spoke.

"Who the hell are you?"

He swung around briskly to look at me. I thought long and hard before answering.

Did he want the fake me, or real me?

I chose to go with the fake me, Justine, because that's what he had believed for the past six years. With one word, I answered his question,

"Justine."

His eyes grew larger, then narrowed instantly.

"Bullshit. You are not Justine."

His voice was irritated as he spoke. The room fell silent once again as he began to pace the room.

What did he expect me to say? How did he know I wasn't Justine after all this time? Was it all going to be over, because he had figured out I wasn't Justine?

"Are you telling me that for all these years, you have just been pretending to be my wife?" He asked in a shocked tone.

His eyes were wild, and I wondered where these sudden accusations were coming from.

Had the person at the door yesterday somehow told Darren I wasn't Justine? How would they have known?

It didn't take me long to answer his question.

"Yes," I replied flatly.

I wanted to leave my answer short, because I didn't believe he would have given me the time of day to even explain. To my surprise, he did question this,

"Why?"

I thought for a moment, but knew my answer would be the truth and to the point.

"To save my life."

I felt tears beginning to form in my eyes, and I wiped them away with the back of my hand as they spilled over, one by one.

Darren finally stopped pacing and walked over to stand in front of me, lifting my face towards him.

"Your game is over."

He said the words as he stared into my eyes, sending shivers through my body. Abruptly, he dropped his hand from my chin, and left the room. My heart sank, and I was more scared now than I had been on day one of this journey; when this nightmare all began. My thoughts instantly flashed to my family—Keith and Callie.

Did they even remember who I was? Or had they moved on with their lives?

I tried to remove the thoughts from my mind, as they upset me too much. Darren's words were on repeat in my head, *'Your game is over'*. What did he even mean by that? I had managed to stay alive for this long, which I had hoped would have allowed me to escape successfully. Now, it seemed my chances of escaping were over. I had absolutely no idea where we were, or which direction anything was even in. My life was truly coming to an end, all these years later

I sat in that chair for hours, practically all day, alone and crying. I had cried all the tears that were left in my eyes, and heart, leaving nothing left to cry about.

If everything was truly over, why was he taking so long to return? Had he left me here to fend for myself? To die?

I was too scared to move. I was numb from his words. Finally, I heard movement from the other room, my breath hitched as the heavy footsteps sounded closer to the entrance of the room I continued to sit in. It was dark, and the only light emanated from the room where Darren's footsteps could be heard. As he neared the room, his features were increasingly frightening, illuminated by the lantern's flame he was holding. He stopped and stood in the doorway. I felt his eyes burning through me even in the midst of the darkness. For once, his breathing seemed under control. His reaction to most situations had been anger, and usually what I expected whenever he spoke to me. He began to walk towards me, stopping about a foot away, and with a deep, throaty calm, he spoke,

"Where is Justine?"

How the hell was I supposed to know?

I wasn't sure exactly what he wanted to hear, because frankly I didn't know where she was. Darren gave me no time to respond, because suddenly he stomped his foot, which caused me to jump out of the chair. I thought quickly, and gave the best answer I knew—the truth.

"I don't know..." my voice trailed off at his angered expression.

Without skipping a beat, he asked his question again, as if repeating himself would give him a different answer.

"Where is Justine? She went to your house, *Lily*, and I want to know why."

This statement scared me.

How did he know my name?

He was a ticking time bomb waiting to go off, and I despised his unpredictability. I really had no idea what he was going on about, either, because I hadn't known Justine was trying to find me in the first place. What baffled me the most was if Darren and Justine had still lived in Vancouver, how had our paths never crossed?

My thoughts were interrupted as Darren grew impatient, tapping his foot while he waited for my answer.

"I don't know why she was searching for me. I thought when we separated at the age of sev—"He cut me off before I could go any further.

"I want her back," he barked.

He paced the floor in front of me. He was being irrational. Why would he assume I knew where she was? I wasn't sure how he expected to find her, because frankly six years was enough time for someone to run away—far away for that matter. I had really hoped she was long gone, out of this country and stayed wherever she was forever. Her life depended on it, and I couldn't imagine what she had been going through with Darren for so many years before this whole mistaken identity occurred.

I had closed my eyes to keep the tears from falling. Like so many other times, I did not need to show weakness. To know this was my sister's life for so long, broke me. Nobody deserved it, nor deserved the wrath of Darren. He was sick, mentally sick for that matter, and needed desperate help. Nobody should have to be living with him. His anger gets the best of him. His hallucinations scared me the most because I knew it was not exactly him, but the disorder that he suffered from that made him the way he was.

Time felt as though it was standing completely still, not knowing what was going through his mind or the mood he was in. I had learned to be quiet in most cases, merely for the fact it had saved my life numerous times before.

Without another word, Darren walked out of the room again. I assumed he was done—it was his way of coping in most situations. He always walked away from situations to keep his temper in check—I didn't mind that, because it kept my life intact a little longer. When he reached the door, he turned and instructed me to follow him with only a single fingered motion.

I felt my breath escape me because I had no idea what I was walking towards. I slowly rose and walked towards him, as he turned to move through the small cabin. We passed what seemed to be a make-shift kitchen, with a mattress directly across from it on the floor—two pillows and a ratty old blanket laid on it.

Darren pointed towards the mattress with a jerk of his head.

What was with the silent treatment? Was he really expecting me to sleep there? Though, I really had no other options.

I moved in front of him and sat down on the edge of the mattress. I watched him make his way to the cabin door and lock it with his intricate, customized system.

He really had invested a lot into these high security locks of his. I wondered why, though. I figured it must have just been his paranoia, but perhaps something else had happened in his past to make him extra cautious. When he finished with his security checks, he walked over to the opposite side of the mattress, kicked off his boots, sat down, and swung his legs up onto the mattress.

As he laid his head down, he spoke the final words of the night,

"Don't think of anything stupid. Just sleep. I don't have time for your games anymore."

There wasn't much left to do but sleep now. I turned away from him to stare at the wall, the only thought in my mind at that moment was that my chances of being found now were slim to none. Nobody even knew we were out here.

TWENTY-FOUR

Murray

It was late-evening now and Justine had completely lost it, there was no way I was going to be able to coax any further information out of her. I needed to find the Captain and inquire if there was any way we could put her up in the motel across the street with an undercover squad car watching her, for the night. I couldn't lose her again—she was the golden key to this entire investigation.

I had asked Gresham to stay with Justine in the interview room while I went to locate the Captain. I found him in his office mulling over some paperwork. I was surprised to see it was Lily's case file. I could see her photograph paper clipped to the top of the file folder.

As I motioned to knock on his door, he glanced up to see me standing in his doorway. He gave a small smile and waved his hand for me to come inside and sit in one of the chairs that faced his desk.

The Captain spoke first, before I fully was seated, "I was wondering when you would enlighten me with today's events, Murray."

I knew what he was after. I should have informed him of the interview that was taking place, but I didn't exactly have time to find him with how quickly everything had transpired. At the time, I felt her statement was needed right then and there, and that she was the most willing she had been thus far to provide a statement. If I had delayed it, I was afraid she would have closed up again.

"That's what I'm here for now, this is the first chance since making it back to the station that I've had to let you know of the outcome of our inquiry at the house Gresham and I went to earlier."

He gave me a look of *'get on with it'* and I didn't hesitate to elaborate and inform him of what had occurred earlier that day.

"We were told by the gentlemen that opened the door that there was nobody there by the name of Justine Johnson. He was short with us, and when I inquired if he was Darren Johnson he snapped and told us the Johnsons had moved, and slammed the door in our faces. As we left, I pulled out a soda can from the trash, hoping we could run it for prints, because I had a hunch that something wasn't right. He was too quick to shoo us away at the time."

Captain rested back in his chair with his arms crossed over his chest. You could tell he was contemplating a question in his mind.

"What happened once you arrived back? What is this I heard about you carrying Mrs. Johnson?"

I cleared my throat before answering, he had obviously already heard about my return that afternoon through the grapevine. Nothing could happen in this building without everyone knowing about it instantly, there was no keeping anything quiet.

"She nearly collapsed in the parking lot, I helped her inside. I didn't want a scene to erupt if I could help it."

He was quick, not allowing any time to pass between my answers and his questions.

"What new information could she provide us with? I figured you've been questioning her this entire time?"

He leaned forward onto his elbows and peered over at his clock to indicate the time. I knew that it was late, he didn't have to remind me.

"Mrs. Johnson—Justine—is Lily's sister, and Darren Johnson, who apparently has Lily, has a mental illness—schizophrenia, she claims."

Captain's attention lifted from the case file in front of him to me. I hadn't noticed his gaze drop back down to the file.

"You're telling me that woman is your wife's sister? How did you not know of this before? As far I knew, Lily never had any siblings?" his tone was exasperated, but also quizzical at the same time.

"Because Lily was adopted, she never spoke about her childhood. I didn't know she had a twin sister, but right now that doesn't matter."

Captain didn't miss a beat, "It does matter, *that* changes a lot of things, Murray. How can you think that it doesn't?"

I didn't understand how he felt that information gave us anything new, and he must have seen the confusion on my face, because he glared at me questionably. I shook it off, because I had no time to sit here and argue with him.

213

"There is no way we will be getting any more information out of Justine tonight, can we set her up across the street at the motel with an officer for the night? I'd like to reconvene the interview first thing tomorrow morning."

It took Captain a few minutes before answering, "Do you believe she has more information to provide us?"

Of course she did! There was no way she had told me everything. Personally, I thought she was holding back. Holding back on what exactly, I didn't know, but I was sure to find out.

"Yes, I believe she does. That's why I want to ensure we have her close by. You know as well as I do we can't afford to lose her again," I stated matter-of-factly.

"I will see what I can arrange, we don't have many available officers, but I'll do my best."

My eyes fell to the file folder that sat on his desk, and I was still curious about why he had Lily's case file open. Captain noticed my gaze upon his desk.

"I thought I would go over what information we had, and see if we had been missing something this entire time. Though, we only had so much information to go on, with the little evidence we gained from that night."

He was correct—we hadn't had much evidence, because whoever had taken Lily was meticulous about protecting themselves. No finger prints were spotted, no hairs, not even a footprint. The only item found was a cellphone battery in the street outside the house. When we ran the fingerprints we found on it through the system, nothing had come back, and it ended up being a dead-end lead."

"Hopefully Justine can provide us with more information tomorrow which will help us with this case. I know we're dragging things out and making special accommodations, but something tells me if we push her, we won't get the answers we need."

Captain seemed to dismiss my statement and launched in with questions about the soda can I had brought back. Perhaps he realized I was right, even though I wasn't sitting here arguing over who was right or wrong.

"Have you dropped off this can you pulled from the trash at the lab, yet? I know it can take a few days to process, but I could put a rush on it if you feel its findings will give us more information."

"Actually, it's still sitting in a paper bag in my trunk. I can drop it off before I leave for the night," I felt sheepish, and knew I had broken protocol in terms of maintaining the integrity of physical evidence. I was glad the Captain didn't ream me out about it. Instead, he seemed to ignore this aspect and continued,

"Do that as soon as you can. The sooner we get it processed, the sooner we may have another lead." He nodded while giving me a knowing look.

I was not entirely hopeful anything would come of it, but the Captain seemed to have more hope, which was encouraging.

"I will. I'll head down now after I let Gresham and Justine know that we will be putting her up for the night."

With that, I stood and excused myself from his office, remembering about the license plate of the truck in the driveway as I walked away.

"I don't know if this information will be useful, but there was a truck in the driveway of the address we visited. Maybe it could lead to something? I haven't had time to run it through the system yet." Captain motioned with his hand for me to give him the paper that housed the license plate information.

I tossed the piece of paper I had shoved in my pocket onto the Captain's desk before I turned and made my way back down to the interview room. I pulled Gresham into the hallway to inform her of the next steps. She assured me it would all be taken care of.

Once I was at my car, I rummaged through the trunk and pulled out the paper bag that contained the can. I quickly made my way back inside the station to the forensic department to drop it off. The Captain must have already spoken with them, because they were aware I would be by and were informed it was a top priority. They hoped it would be back within a few days at most, and at that moment it hit me that this may give us a real, solid lead—or not. I tried to hold onto what little hope I had left, if not for me, then for Callie, and for Lily—wherever she was.

After speaking again briefly with Gresham I was pleased Captain was helping and moving things along by already arranging for a room across the street for Justine. I assisted Justine over to her room, and ensured she was settled before I made the trek home. I warned the on-duty officer that he was to keep a strict eye on her—she was not to leave her room under any circumstance, and she was not permitted to have any visitors, either.

Justine had become a key witness, and as lenient as I was being with her, now knowing she was family, I still had to take every precaution I could to protect her and the case. Considering it was gone midnight already, she would literally be sleeping and coming straight back to the station within the next eight hours.

I was completely exhausted myself and needed desperately to sleep. I made my way back to my car, not bothering going back to the office. Whatever was needed from me, or whatever needed to be completed, could wait until tomorrow.

As I drove home mundanely, my mind drifted to thoughts of Lily. What had she done to deserve this? She didn't deserve to be taken by a monster, and endure whatever she had endured for all these years. I was speculating she was still alive, but we were always told to until proven otherwise. It had been six years, and I knew realistically the chances were slim to none, but a flicker of hope still shone within me keeping my faith alive.

I made it home within thirty minutes—I hadn't been in a rush and took a slow, calming drive. The entire house was dark besides the porch light that Callie had left on for me. I expected Callie to be asleep, well, more like I was hoping she was asleep. I could tell all of this was taking a toll on her, and without being home much, I had no idea what exactly was going through her mind since we had discussed Justine. I couldn't imagine how she would feel finding out Justine was her aunt.

Peeling myself from the driver's seat, I made my way to the front door. Slowly and quietly, I unlocked and closed the door behind me. I placed my keys on the small side table and my shoes at the front door before I moved down the hallway towards the kitchen. Knowing Callie, she would have prepared supper for both of us and left my dinner in the oven, but I was completely exhausted and couldn't bear the thought of eating at this point.

I pulled the plate from the oven, and wrapped some cling wrap around the plate before I placed it in the fridge. As I made my way up the stairs to my bedroom, I stopped along the way to look at the pictures Lily had insisted we hang on the wall next to the stairs. There were images of Callie as a baby, all the way until she was nine years old; family photos, and even photos of Lily and I when we first met. I thought how disappointed Lily would be that I hadn't continued to hang Callie's school pictures each year, and made a mental note to dig them out and hang them next weekend.

I didn't realized a tear had escaped me, until it was running down my cheek. I was missing Lily terribly, more than I ever had let on before. I felt we were close to finding her with all these new leads, but so far we were back at square one when it came to locating her—or at least finding out what had happened to her all those years before. I couldn't dwell on that right now, I needed sleep so that I could question Justine once more tomorrow, praying she had more information that was useful.

TWENTY-FIVE

Lily

The cabin smelled of old, rotten meat, and was filled with cobwebs. How could anyone live here? It was disgusting, at least to me. It was a small enough space that it only took me the morning to clean. Was this where Darren came whenever he left me during the day? It didn't surprise me if it was, considering that he was a hunter, which was where all the odd meat came from that he had forced me to cook for him over the last several years.

At first, he required that he cooked for me, but as I took an interest in helping with things around the house—merely for the fact it helped me scope out the place—he let me help prepare dinner most evenings.

It was early morning and I swept the floors as Darren sat at the table with a coffee in his hand. His stare bore right through me, as if he could clearly see to the other side of the room. A small smile played on his lips as he sipped at his coffee. I tried my best to ignore him, praying he would get the hint that I wasn't playing along anymore.

It surprised me that even when Darren had discovered my true identity last night, he hadn't hurt me—I had sworn, once he figured out that I was not who I said I was, I for sure would have been rendered useless to him.

How Justine handled this man, I honestly didn't know. I often thought about her, and if the theory about being twins was true? If it were, we would have a deep connection even if we were miles away. Thinking back, I was sure it was true, as I had felt strange at times, but couldn't explain why. The sensation had faded over the years, and they were nowhere near as strong as during the first couple of years after she had been adopted, but something in me still glowed enough to give me hope. When I had found out during the first year I was kidnapped that I was being mistaken for my sister, I did everything I could to fight to stay alive. All I hoped for now was that she was okay, and living a better life away from Darren.

Suddenly, Darren barked out a question,

"Tell me why you lied to me for so many years?"

It caught me off guard, causing me to drop the broomstick I held in my hand.

Hadn't I just answered this question last night?

I stared into his angered eyes—something that almost never seemed to ease. I gave myself a moment to collect my thoughts. My mouth opened, but no words would escape. It had never dawned on me that one day my true identity would surface. I thought I had left that person behind six years ago, after this man chose to take me from my family.

I had grown accustomed to investing my waking hours attempting to discover everything I could about Justine Johnson. All I had known was that she lived simply, and that her childhood memories were stored in a few old boxes in the basement—I could almost say even her adult life lived in that basement as well. She had existed, but only barely. From what I could tell, she had done exactly as she was told by Darren, at least until the day she decided she'd had enough and found a way out. With a husband like Darren, I could definitely see her not being able to voice her own opinions, considering that was how I had felt all these years.

Finally, I found the voice within me to speak. It felt as though time stood still as the words left my mouth— I decided I wouldn't hesitate any longer, if he wanted the truth, the truth was what he would get.

"I wanted to live. I had hoped all these years later I would get to see my daughter and husband again."

My voice shook as I spoke. I had stopped suddenly, because I didn't want fear to be heard in my voice. Darren was suddenly standing in front of me with those angered filled eyes that I had come to know all too well.

"I doubt they are looking for you. It's been far too long. Your husband, or shall I say *ex*-husband, would have moved on by now."

Tears began to well in my eyes, but I wasn't going to let this bastard see weakness in me. I blinked them back and stood a little taller.

"Who came to the door yesterday?" I asked with confidence.

The question had been burning inside me since the moment I heard the knock on the door. I needed to know if they had come to find me. Darren's expression changed and I took a step back.

"Why do you care who it was? Did you send them yourself then?"

"Of course not! How could I? You've kept me locked up like a prisoner. It's no wonder Justine wanted to get away from you."

The words had already left my mouth when I realized what I had said. I should have known it would push Darren over the edge.

"Stupid bitch! I should kill you now! How dare you speak to me like that! You don't know my wife, she deserved to be locked up—to teach her respect!" The words roared out of him, and his eyes were wild.

I had never seen Darren this angry before. He wasn't making sense. Why did he feel as though Justine had no respect for him? Seeing his anger flourishing, I knew I had bigger things to worry about in that instance, one being my life. I knew I was about to be in serious danger unless I made an escape right then and there.

I eyed the door with all its locks. It didn't look as complicated as the ones back at Darren's house, but my thought was short lived when I realized I didn't have the keys—he had them. He must have sensed my idea, but he was quick to shoot it down,

"Don't you dare think about that now, there's no way you're going to escape from me. You are mine now," he informed me, his tone angered.

I had every right to think about it. I would do anything to save myself. I quickly scrutinized the room considering what I had at my disposal—which wasn't much. I had never been a violent person, and I had never used any force on Darren except for my own body weight before, but times had changed. If I didn't do something to stop him, he would do something worse to me.

I darted around the small room, my eyes never leaving the door for long—it looked to be the only true escape I had. I also needed to know Darren's every move and be one step ahead of him. That was how I was going to survive. Between Darren and the doorlock, I was becoming dizzy attempting to keep myself moving and not stand in one place.

"I can see wheels turning. Whatever you're drumming up in that pretty little head of yours, you can forget." He laughed at his own statement, though I paid no attention to his sarcastic comment, as my intention was to continue to move about and find something to defend myself with.

When I reached the kitchen, I immediately considered grabbing a knife, but I discovered he kept that drawer under lock and key.

Control freak.

"What are you thinking about woman?" his voice was impatient.

When wasn't he impatient?

"Well, I was just thinking about my options, and you know what? It would be considered self-defense if I killed you." I shot back at him, as my mouth seemed to have no filter now. I knew it may get me into trouble, but now that my identity was out in the open, I felt that being honest and staying in survival mode at all costs were my only options.

"Not if I kill you first!" He roared.

With that, Darren ran towards me at full force. At the last second, I ducked and darted across the room, which caused him to fall into the counter with a loud thud. I scanned the room to locate something I could hold him back with. I knew he could squash me in the blink of an eye if he wanted to, but if I was to fight, I wanted it to be a good fight.

As I looked around for a weapon of some sort, a strange thought entered my mind—if Darren was a hunter, why wasn't this cabin equipped with standard hunting equipment? I didn't have long to ponder this, as Darren turned around and inched forward towards me with his hands clenched into tight fists. The only thing I had next to me was a pillow—as if that was going to protect me—but it was enough of a distraction for Darren to stumble, laughing.

"You think that will protect you? Get a grip woman! I don't know which is a worse weapon choice—a hairdryer or a pillow," he keeled over, laughing, remembering back to my first week in captivity. Somehow he thought this entire thing was a joke, and was enjoying mocking my survival strategies, but if the roles were reversed wouldn't he try anything he could to survive an attack?

With the split second my mind had drifted, it caused me to take my eyes off Darren. In that short amount of time, his fist had connected with the side of my head. I was thrown to the side and smashed into the wall. I felt dizzy as I attempted to balance myself. If he thought that blow would cause me to give up, he was wrong. Once I had myself balanced on my feet again, I saw Darren taking steps back and forth. He was ready to beat me to a pulp, I could see it in his eyes. Regardless that I was seeing double vision, I was able to follow his movement.

He had moved back in front of my face with his hand reaching for my neck. Remembering what Keith had taught me about self-defense, in that split second I took the leap—I drew my knee up in one swooping motion, connecting hard into his crotch. Immediately, he stumbled backwards, falling to his knees, while holding himself. I gave myself a quick smile, and some

224

mental credit for that move. I had known that would not keep Darren down long enough to get away, thus I needed to find a way to keep him down for good.

Darren was still doubled over, holding himself with his head nearly between his knees. He was mumbling something, but I couldn't make it out. For all the abuse I had taken over the years, he deserved to have a taste of his own medicine—and that was exactly what he was going to get. With a swift kick, my foot connected with his head, which caused him to lose his balance completely and fall to his right side. It wouldn't be enough to keep him down for long. I knew well enough that Darren was too tough to be bogged down by me.

I bolted from the living room and grabbed the keys I had spotted on the night stand—he clearly thought I wouldn't try to escape, otherwise he wouldn't have left them out in the open. Normally they would be in his pocket, but I was happy that his sudden naiveté had occurred.

My hope didn't last long. There were too many keys on his key ring, causing me to feel anxious that all the work I had done to get Darren down was going to be useless. I had to keep glancing over to Darren who was slowly beginning to pick himself up off the floor. When I peered back down, I noticed tiny labels on each key, similar to the spare set I had swiped off the counter years ago. I could barely make them out as the labels were worn, but I saw one labeled 'cab' and prayed it was the correct one. I inserted it into the keyhole and turned the doorknob, with the door gave way from its latch.

Instantly, I was hit with a million emotions. I hesitated for a moment before swinging open the door. Had I just escaped after all these years? I stole one more glance over my shoulder to see Darren had finally made it to his feet, but was still wobbly as he began to regain his balance. Time stood still, but I broke the stillness caused by the mental chains that were holding me back and turned—without looking back, I bolted out of that tiny cabin.

It had rained the night before, causing it to be muddy. The more I ran, the slower I felt. My feet were sinking deeper into the mud, which was slowing me down as I pressed forward, but Darren's voice broke through my adrenaline rush,

"You won't get away! Get back here!" I heard him bark from the front door of the cabin.

I was too afraid to look back to know truly how close behind he was, but I needed to know. I needed to know if my efforts of escaping were pointless.

I looked over my shoulder, and my fears were confirmed. He was suddenly hot on my tail. As I turned back to focus on what was in front of me, I tripped, landing face first into the mud. I was only down for a mere second when I felt a hand grab me by the hair and pull me backwards.

"You thought you could get away from me? You're wrong woman, and now—your life is over!"

I couldn't hold back my emotions any longer, and I sobbed as he spoke those words. He dragged me back to the cabin by my hair as my legs dragged along the ground. I took extra care to dig my feet into the ground to leave a track that I had been there. If anybody came out here, maybe they would see my attempts of a struggle, as much as I knew it was a far-fetched idea. Truthfully, the woods were abandoned from what I could tell, and we were completely secluded. During the short time we had been out here, I hadn't heard anything other than the wind rustling the trees or the chirping of a bird.

My head continued to bounce around as my body was dragged over the fallen branches and roots. I tried my best to look around me as I moved backwards, to find something I could use to defend myself, but nothing was within arm's-reach. The only hope I had if I wanted to survive, was to get Darren down—down for good—I couldn't let him end me this way.

I brought myself back to reality to realize we had passed the cabin and Darren was now headed to a set of wooden doors planted in the ground.

No, I won't let him.

I needed to distract him enough to loosen his grip, but it felt as though his grip had been tightening with each passing minute. I stopped focusing on the pain I was enduring, and reached my hand out as we passed along the back side of the cabin to see if I could feel anything that I could use to free myself.

My hand finally stumbled upon something long that had a square bottom to it. It definitely had weight to it, I grabbed it with all the strength I had as we passed by. I held it tightly in my grip and dragged it along the ground with me. In the position I was in—being dragged on my back—I had no idea if I would even have any leverage. At some point, I needed to knock him over the head, but I was far from being able to reach his head in my current position.

Darren grunted and mumbled the whole time, but I couldn't make out any actual words being low to the ground and having mud stuck in my ears. I assumed he wasn't really paying attention to me anymore, and was simply fed up with me.

We stopped abruptly and for a split second Darren let go of me, with my head dropping forcefully to the ground. Life stood still briefly, but I wasn't going to waste this opportunity. Darren was roughly pulling at the object I had been dragging along with me.

"Give me that fuckin' shovel," he spoke with heavy breath.

I knew I was not giving up, I had kept a grip on the handle of what I now knew was a shovel. I managed to lift the shovel high enough and swing it to hit him in the knee-caps. As I watched Darren fall to the ground, I quickly scrambled to my feet.

He continued to mumble, but his words weren't making any sense. I saw him lay there on the ground below me, our eyes connected, all I saw was rage in this eyes, but still, he managed to shout at me,

"If you think you will get away with this you are wrong! Dead wrong!"

His words made me take a step back. I still held a firm grip on the shovel, while he began pulling himself up off the ground, but stumbled. Darren held his knee where I had wacked it hard. He screamed out like a little boy in agony, as I continued to step back in fear he would actually make it to his feet. I started to draw a blank on what I should do next. Finally, making it to his feet, he had his back towards me, bent over to rub his knee. I didn't think, just reacted.

I pulled the shovel up with both hands on the handle into a baseball hitter's stance. My breath heavy, I counted to three.

One…two…three…

As I swung the shovel, he turned. It hit him square in the side of the head. He fell to the ground immediately, not moving an inch.

I dropped the shovel instantly and pulled my hands up to my mouth in disbelief of what I had just done. Darren was not moving—he was out cold. This was supposed to be a good thing, but part of me was completely freaked out that I had possibly just killed a man. I paced back and forth around his body, which still didn't move. Had I really just taken out the man who had been my captor, after all these years?

TWENTY-SIX

Murray

The alarm blared next to my head. I turned over and slammed my hand down on the snooze button to mute the annoying voice of the reporter relaying the breaking news from overnight. I knew I would learn about the city's crime when I arrived at work in the next few hours, so I didn't need to wake up to it.

It had been one heck of a week, and I had finally broke the news to Callie a couple of days before about Justine. She had taken the news pretty hard, but at least understood the latest developments.

Callie was growing up, and quickly, therefore keeping secrets from her was next to impossible. After all, it was just her and I to hold each other together. I wasn't ready to enlighten her about what we had discovered—or rather, not discovered—at the Johnson house we had visited the day before, or the fact Justine had come back to the station last night.

The alarm blared once again and I turned over to slam the snooze button once more, but stopped my hand in mid-air as something the reporter said caught my attention.

"It is believed that the case of eighteen year old Kennedy Daniels, brutally killed in the lake side murder six years ago, has been connected to the disappearance of Lily-May Murray, wife of Keith Murray of the VPD, that occurred during the same year. Detective…."

The woman's voice pierced my muzzy state of just waking up and I shook my head, I couldn't have heard her correctly. I jumped from the bed not bothering with my slippers, as I dug my phone out of my pants pocket I had thrown over the chair the night before.

9 Missed calls
3 Voicemails
1 Text Message

I stared at the screen, scrolling through the missed calls. Some were from the station, and two were from Gresham. I had no time to listen to the voicemails, and instead dialed the switch-board at the station. With only two rings, a familiar voice spoke through the receiver.

Vancouver Police Department Headquarters, Detective Pryce speaking, how may I help you?"

"Pryce, its Murray. What are you doing on the switch board? I need to speak to the Captain urgently." My voice was cracking like an old broken record, and my questions ran together.

"Murray….the Captain's having a news conference…" he trailed off.

That still did not answer my questions about why a detective was on the switch-board, and he didn't continue with his train of thought. I literally had to scream my next words into the receiver of my cell phone.

"Can you tell me what is going on? Why am I hearing about a connection to my wife's case on the radio?" My voice had become impatient. I hadn't realized what I was saying as the world seemed to fall away from me.

"We've been trying to reach you for the past two hours..." he trailed off again.

I could see they had tried to reach me, but my phone had still been set to silent from yesterday while I had been interviewing Justine. I wanted to collapse on the floor, but knew I needed to get to the station to find out the truth. Without hesitation I hung up, without a goodbye or even letting Pryce continue.

I turned around, hearing the creaking floorboards, to see Callie standing in my doorway with a confused and sleepy look on her face.

"What's wrong, dad?" she asked between yawns.

I knew I had promised Callie she would know every detail that transpired from leads on this case; however, I still needed to be careful what I told her, and how I told her. I know I had promised her no secrets, but she was still my daughter, and I wanted to protect her.

I cleared my thick throat before I spoke,

"It seems there may be a connection between another case and mom's case."

The look on Callie's face told me she wasn't coherent enough to understand what I was saying. I tried giving her a few minutes to understand what I had said, but knowing there wasn't time to waste, I finally blurted out,

"Be ready in fifteen minutes. We're going to the station."

I had no time to sit around and wait. I needed answers and to be fully briefed on the new developments. Callie made her way back to her room while I had a quick shower, with both of us meeting in the kitchen a short time later.

We had no time for breakfast, but the automatic coffee percolator's timer had already gone off, providing fresh hot coffee. I poured black coffee into a travel mug, nearly slopping it down my shirt with the way I roughly jostled it around before lidding it.

Callie and I hastily shoved our feet into our shoes. As I placed my hand on the front door she turned to face me.

"Dad, do you think we finally have the answers we've been looking for?"

I didn't want to be overconfident in that heart pounding moment, because I didn't have all the information to make that conclusion.

"I believe we are getting closer, Callie, but let's make it to the station and find out the real story before we jump to any conclusions."

With that, I pulled on the front door handle and swung the door open to be abruptly met by the scene outside—News vans and reporters littered our front yard. My eyes darted between them and Callie, who was staring blankly into the openness of the front door. I could see her eyes tearing up.

"This reminds me of that night dad… Make it stop…" Her voice was shaky and tears began to escape from her eyes.

I could see her chest heaving as she tried to catch her breath, but tears continued streaming down her face. News traveled fast in this town, it was hard not to

233

in a city that never slept. I turned to Callie and placed my hand on her shoulder.

"Let's go back inside," I said as calmly as I could.

I didn't want to scare her anymore than she already was. She nodded without another word, with sunken shoulders she turned to go back inside. As I followed her, I could hear reporters shouting from the sidewalk towards us.

"Do you have anything to say?"

"Do you know who it is?"

"What's your thoughts after all these years?"

I ignored them all, as my focus had shifted to Callie and ensuring her well-being was taken care of. As we entered the living room, my phone buzzed in my back pocket and I pulled it out to see Gresham's name flashing on the screen, I answered it before it could go to voicemail.

"Hey, Gresham," I sighed.

"Murray! I've been trying to reach you. Don't leave your house—" Her voice had worry plastered all over it. I shook my head at her words, and interrupted her.

"It's a little late now Gresham, you need to get officers here, stat."

Anger was beginning to set in at this point, and I didn't mean to shout at her.

"I'm ten minutes out. I'm on my way."

The line went dead as the call dropped. I peered out of the shear curtains, watching the mob of newcasters grow. Only hearing the brief report on the radio and not knowing the whole story, I didn't want to jump to any conclusions regarding the case. I had contemplated whether to turn on the TV, but opted not to for Callie's sake.

She was rocking on the sofa. I had no idea what was going through her mind. Without certainty myself, I couldn't give her more information until Gresham or the Captain updated me.

I sat down next to Callie and placed my arm around her as I drew her into my chest. Tears continued to stream down her face. With her near me, in my embrace, I felt her breathing begin to slow. A hiccup escaped her as she began to settle into my hold.

My mind wandered to how exactly they could say these two cases were connected? The same person who killed that innocent child had also kidnapped my wife? It sounded like something out of the movies. Had there been a serial killer on the loose? I didn't want to draw any conclusions, but it sounded grim...

My mind was brought back to the present by the sound of the doorbell chiming throughout the foyer and front hallway. Callie gripped me when I attempted to get up from where we sat on the couch to answer the door.

"I'll be right back, Callie, it will be okay."

I gave her a reassuring kiss on her forehead. When I finally was able to reach the door, I gingerly peered through the glass window to see Gresham and Captain waiting outside. Being in a bit of a daze, I hesitated, when the doorbell sounded again to remind me of their presence. I quickly pulled the door open and ushered them inside, catching them in my eagerness to slam the door behind them to keep the reporters' questions at bay. I stole a peek through the window to see officers placing police tape around our trees to keep the reporters on the sidewalk, away from the house.

I pulled myself away from the door and stepped back into the living room, reclaiming my seat next to Callie, while Gresham and Captain took up standing in the door way. The room fell silent, but I didn't want silence, I wanted answers, and fast. I motioned for them to sit on the love seat, then proceeded to ask, "Will someone finally tell me what is going on here?"

I kept my tone as neutral as possible, but the anxiety was evident in my voice. Gresham and Captain stole a glance at one another and then in the direction of Callie, who still sat shaking next to me. I pulled her closer to me before I spoke again.

"What you have to say, you can say in front of Callie. There will be no secrets moving forward."

I spoke with a firm tone to my voice, and then Captain spoke.

"Murray… Callie… the pop can that you provided," he motioned towards me, "from the Johnson house, Murray, came back with a match. The system matched it to the print found on the cell phone casing by the lake that was recovered that morning Kennedy Daniels was discovered. We also matched it to the cell phone battery we found on the street outside your home the night Lily was kidnapped."

Immediately, I had questions flying through my mind, he had just connected two cold cases to each other in front of me. The only question that I managed to coherently put together in my mind and voice out loud was simple.

"What does this mean?"

I was completely confused, and wasn't sure what our next steps would be. Before I allowed anyone to answer my previous question, I was throwing out questions left, right, and center.

"Will we be granted a search warrant for the Johnson house? Can we get the ball rolling on handing in the evidence to a judge?"

I had a million questions running through my head, but knew I had to choose them carefully—as much as I wanted Callie involved and promised her no secrets, I still had to keep her safe.

Captain finally spoke, "Early this morning, I took the liberty of presenting the evidence to a judge to look over. I submitted the request for a search warrant as urgent, and we should hear something in a few hours—the odds are in our favour that it will be granted after the new evidence that has connected the two cases."

I nodded to show I understood the information, and Captain continued with his explanation.

"The truck in the driveway belongs to Darren Johnson. We believe the man you encountered was him. With that information, I don't believe it will be hard to get a judge to grant a search warrant for the house."

This was all great news, but I still had a question looming. I took a glance at Callie, who was still nestled at my side.

"What is the likelihood Lily is in that house, Captain?"

You could hear a pin drop with the silence that had filled the room. Captain's eyes darted between Callie and I, and I knew I had asked a sensitive question. He cleared his throat, and spoke very slowly.

"Well, we don't want to make any assumption right now, Murray, but let's keep our hopes up."

I felt relief at the thought we may finally find Lily. Though fear was still present as to whether or not we would find her dead or alive. If this man was capable of murdering an innocent child, who knows what he could have done to Lily?

I looked Callie in the eyes—all that filled them were fear and sadness.

"I know this is hard right now and a lot to take in, but know we are doing everything we can," I assured her.

She gave us a small nod as she continued to rock on the sofa. Gresham walked over and sat next to her as she embraced her in a hug. Gresham had always tried to be there for Callie, knowing it wasn't easy for anyone to lose a mother, let alone a nine year old child.

I stood and motioned for Captain to follow me in the direction of the kitchen. I needed to find out more information, but away from Callie. I knew Callie would be okay with Gresham.

The moment we entered the kitchen, questions began flying out of my mouth before we had even settled in at the table which I motioned for Captain to take a seat at.

"How did we get a print from the lake side murder? I thought it was only a partial print?" I asked huffily.

"That partial was enough to make a connection on the print from the pop can," was all of Captain's reply.

I continued with questions and suggestions without missing a beat, and without letting the Captain get a word in edge wise.

"We should set up a team to go in as soon as we receive the papers, we don't have any time to waste."

Without hesitation, I pulled out my cellphone from my back pocket to dial into the station. Captain placed his hand on my hand just as my fingers found the numbers.

"It's already been done, Murray. You just need to take care of your daughter right now. Let us handle this."

Was the Captain implying I would not be part of the operation, after all this? If he thought that, he was absolutely kidding himself. He put me back on this case. He couldn't pull me off it now!

"If you're trying to tell me that I will not be on this case or participate in the search warrant, you are wrong. I will not let this sick son of a bitch get away."

I realized I had nearly shouted the words, and toned myself down. I felt the rage begin to build inside me.

"You're too close—"

"I am going in. End of discussion," I interrupted him.

Without a second for him to answer me back, Captain's cell phone rang.

"Hello?" he answered.

Of course I couldn't hear the person on the other end of line, but Captain's actions made it seem like good news from all the nodding and 'mhhmmm's I heard from him before he told whoever was on the other line, "Thank you, someone will be right over."

I felt my anxiety build as the anticipation grew. Captain hung up, and looked to me before I completely lost it.

"That was the Judge's office, the search warrant was granted. I'll send Detective Pryce across town to pick it up and he can meet us at the house with it."

Those were the words I had been waiting far too long to hear. While the Captain dialed the station, he gave me a long look of despair. He knew I was going to ignore his orders regardless how much he talked it up.

Walking back into the living room, I didn't give Captain another glance. It appeared Callie had calmed down and was sitting talking with Gresham when I walked in.

"Callie, I must go, but I'll be back. Gresham will stay with you. If you need me, call me."

"But Dad, I need you… here."

"I know, but mom needs me too. You'll be okay, you're a strong young woman."

Kissing her on the forehead, I walked away. I knew that if I stayed it would be harder on both of us. As I made my way to the front door, I grabbed my keys from the hook. Everything else I needed was at the station. Captain walked down the hallway to meet me at the front door.

"Nothing I will say will stop you, but hear me out— you need to be careful. We don't know what we will find there, or if we will even find Lily. I don't want you getting your hopes up."

I knew not to get my hopes up, but every lead meant we had a little more information on the bastard, and to me that was better than no leads at all.

"Thank you for your concern Captain, but I'm ready to find him and Lily."

With that, I opened the front door. A sea of reports began shouting questions at me as I made my way down to the Captain's car in the driveway. I could hear cameras clicking a mile a minute. I ignored them, and was focused solely on getting to the station to receive some much needed answers.

As Captain drove, my thoughts drifted… How had it been six years and we were only now obtaining a proper lead? I never imagined it would come to this, after this long most people gave up hope. Part of me had, but part of me still felt connected to Lily, and *that* part of me never gave up hope. I knew Callie hadn't given up hope either. She told me countless times how she felt a connection and that Lily was alive. Maybe it was mother-daughter intuition, or maybe it was just Callie's way of coping. Regardless, we now had a chance to find out for sure.

Once we finally made it to the station, reporters lined the stairs to the front doors. It was enough to have them at my house, but at the station as well? It was becoming too crazy to handle. Officers attempted to hold them back as we pulled up, but one slipped by and ran directly towards me as I exited the car, shoving a microphone into my face.

"What are your thoughts all these years later, do you think your wife is alive?"

Anger boiled through me as I swatted at the microphone. I didn't realize the strength behind my efforts and ended up knocking it out of his hand. In a way, it served him right to be pulling crap like that.

"What the hell man—"was all I heard as I made my way up the steps and into the lobby.

Eyes began darting into my direction from nearby officers and colleagues. It seemed everyone had lost their voice the moment I walked in. It was as if everyone assumed if they said anything I would break like a pane of glass. I turned around to find Captain making his way through the front doors. Without hesitation, I followed him.

"So what's the plan?" I demanded.

"I'm going with you. Suit up."

With that, he disappeared through the stairwell that led upstairs to our offices. I wasted no time and rushed into the locker room, yanking open my locker. It wasn't every day I suited up. Pulling my bullet-proof vest over my head, and holstering my gun to my belt, I felt pumped and ready to go. For good measure, I stuffed my spare weapon in my sock around my ankle. I was hoping we wouldn't be met with violence, but we were walking in blind after all. We had no idea if he had weapons of his own, so I needed to be prepared.

Other officers began filing into the room. At first, they didn't notice me standing there as they began talking about the case.

"Can you believe this many years later there's a lead?" a young male said.

"Are we even going to find her alive? It seems... unlikely, if you know what I mean," another male responded.

"We won't know unless we get a move on now, will we?" I slammed my locker closed. I didn't want to bother giving them the time of day, though, I did make sure they knew who the boss on this case was now, and that I was not planning on taking a step back like I had before.

"I don't have all day to wait, hurry up if you plan to be on this mission. We leave in five minutes," I barked before storming out of the room.

Captain was in the lobby when I returned.

"The boys should be out, I sent them in to suit up," he informed me.

"I know. If they did less gabbing, we would be out there by now" I grunted, giving a nod in the direction of the front doors.

I was baffled when anyone thought these kinds of situations were a joke and was not taking their job seriously. It was irritating me beyond words but I had to stay level headed.

"Murray, I understand you want to nail him, but we need to ensure we're following protocol. I'm already breaking it by allowing *you* to participate."

You had to admit, Captain was pretty laid back. I knew he meant well, but nobody was going to stand in my way, especially when it came to my family.

The officers who were assigned to the search finally made their way to the lobby where Captain and I had been waiting for them. Captain gave them their instructions before we made our way out to our cars.

Reporters still lined the stairway as we fought our way through them, with microphones shoved at me from all directions. I made it clear I had no time to stop and give a statement or answer their questions. For what it was worth, my wife needed me more. There would be plenty of time to discuss the case when we had more solid leads. Whoever had leaked this information to the media would be paying for it later. I still wondered how exactly the news had spread to the media so quickly. Was there another connection we were missing?

TWENTY-SEVEN

Lily

I couldn't stop running. I knew it was the adrenaline that had taken over, because I was physically and mentally exhausted, yet I continued to run. I had absolutely no idea if I had knocked Darren out cold, or if he would be coming after me any minute. The further I ran from the cabin I felt as though I was finally free, but I wasn't going to be free until I found help.

Not knowing which direction I had been running in, I became more anxious, as night was falling quickly. I buried that anxiety deep down and continued running. I finally slowed my pace after another fifteen minutes of running, realizing Darren wasn't behind me. I could stop glancing back over my shoulder. Part of me felt he would jump out of the trees and tackle me at any second, because I felt it was impossible for me to have killed him. Then again, I *had* knocked him over the head with a shovel.

Dusk turn into night, meaning I had lost my daylight. There was no way I would be able to continue without being able to see where I was going. I literally only had the clothes on my back at this point, with no source of light to lead me onward.

My pace slowed even further into a slow walk, as I struggled to keep my legs moving, only to find myself collapsing after a few more steps. My entire body felt weak, and I could barely move my limbs. I struggled into a sitting position, after crawling along the ground in the dark to a tree, and leaning my back up against it.

I was exhausted to the point where I couldn't keep my eyes open any longer. I took one last glance around the darkness expecting to be able to see if anyone was around.

Was I actually safe?

I couldn't think anymore, and I was shutting down from the events and exhaustion of the day.

Morning rose early, but that was what happened in the middle of the woods when the bright sun flooded through the trees. My body still felt tired as it had the night before, although, I felt as though I was more alert mentally. All I could think about was that I had survived the night, and it was the first step to being free—at least that's what I thought. I wouldn't be truly free until I could find help, someone to get me out of here and back to civilization.

I attempted to stand and gather my bearings as I peered around at my surroundings. I was in the middle of the woods. All that I could see for miles were trees, without any inclination of which way was north. All I knew was that I had to keep going straight on this path that I had walked the day before, I couldn't afford to turn around and head back in the direction of the cabin. I needed to get further away—anything was better than the cabin, and Darren.

The path I had walked on seemed to have been a traveled route as it was not covered with any debris and was fairly even to walk on. I kept up my hope that someone would come along eventually if I kept traveling the path, although, I hadn't seen any fresh track marks yet.

My mind drifted to Keith and Callie as I began walking again. I feared I had lost them forever, believing they must have moved on with their lives by now. Callie would be celebrating her sixteenth birthday this summer. I almost cried at the fact that I had missed half of her teenaged years. As for Keith, had he moved on? Had he met someone else? I wouldn't blame him if he had found someone else, but part of me still had to wonder how he had dealt with the last six years.

As much as I had played this role of being Justine in order to survive, it had been an exhausting experience. Darren was unpredictable most of the time, and I had to focus on his actions and tone to foresee his next move. As for Justine, where was she, and why had she been trying to find me? I was glad she wanted to find me, but it just seemed strange after all these years. From the day I lost her when I was seven years old, it wasn't something I thought would ever happen,

I could see now that her years with Darren couldn't have been sunshine and rainbows. Experiencing the way Darren treated me, I could only imagine how Justine had been treated—I wondered if all the times I had felt anxious or upset for absolutely no reason, was feeling my own twin's emotions from being mistreated. All I wanted to do was find her, hug her, and tell her I never wanted her to leave my life again.

I felt that every tree I passed, every bush I brushed up against, was the same as the last. My surroundings had become a complete blur. I figured I would eventually have to meet someone, or get to a road to flag someone down.

Growing tired with each step, I felt weak. I hadn't eaten in over a day, and my body was taking the brunt of the lack of nourishment. I didn't know how long I would last out in the woods, but I knew I needed at least water to survive. Thus far in my travels, I had not heard any running water I needed to change my direction if I wanted to continue trying to survive. I knew I wasn't going to give up, considering I had made it this far.

The worn footpath came to a fork. I stopped and surveyed both paths—left and right. Both routes appeared to be heavily overgrown wooded areas. Without over thinking or hesitating, I veered to the left, praying it was the right decision—for my sake, I needed it to lead me to someone.

I had been traveling for what seemed close to another thirty minutes when in the distance I could faintly hear the sound of running water. I used that sound as my guide. As I moved through the heavy wooded area, branches were scratching me, but at that point my skin was numb—I was numb. Nothing fazed me anymore, I was too used to it all— these tiny scratches were nothing compared to the unexplained beatings and the pain that I had sustained for years.

A lone tear ran down my cheek. You would think by now, I wouldn't have had any tears left to shed. Crying in front of Darren had been impossible, and usually ended with him in my face, or worse—his fists in my face.

My mind couldn't stop thinking about had happened back at the cabin, more for the fact I still had no idea if he was dead or alive. If he was alive, he would have come after me by now. At the time, all I was worried about was getting him to the ground—to disable him for an escape route. I wasn't capable of murder, or at least I didn't think I was. Then again, being kidnapped on the assumption of being someone else, and living— or attempting to live—in another person's shoes to stay alive long enough to one day see your family again, took guts and will power. Over the past six years I had learned that I was a stronger person than I thought I was—both mentally and physically.

The running water I had faintly heard was becoming louder with each step I took. I could nearly see the water glistening through the trees ahead of me as I continued to approach a clearing that lead down to a shallow stream. Once it was in sight, I practically ran to it, falling to my knees and scooping up a handful of water. Bringing it to my lips, I felt its coolness refreshing me. I continued to scoop much needed handfuls of water, slurping them back as I felt the wonderful liquid run down my throat. I didn't have anything that I could fill to take water with me, so I needed to drink what I could, now. My eyes darted around the landscape hoping to find something to fill, but of course there was nothing.

I gazed at the scene around me—it looked as though the river ran in both directions, as far as I could see. The width looked to be at least a hundred meters wide. It was shallow near the edge, as I could see the rocky bottom of the river clearly. I debated whether it was safe and logical for me to cross it. I imagined the water would come to my knees, if even close to that.

I tried to use the river to figure out what direction I was facing. As I thought back to the ride here, I couldn't recall crossing over a river when we pulled into the wooded area. All I remember was that we drove for what seemed like a few hours before reaching the cabin with me falling in and out of sleep near the end of our journey.

Without any further hesitation, I dipped my toe into the water, testing the temperature—it was cold, but nothing I couldn't handle. Taking a deep breath, and nearly not exhaling, I ran through the river towards the opposite bank. The further I made it into the water, the deeper the water rose on me.

Well, that was very misleading from the water's edge, I thought.

I was waist deep before the water began receding away from my body as I reached the other side. Shaking myself off, I knew a little water wouldn't hurt me. It was a warm day, which meant I would be dry in no time. I glanced around, wondering which direction I should head in. A growing feeling inside me indicated to continue straight. At this point, I had just as much luck finding someone or a highway as the next lost person.

When would I be completely free? When would I be able to find someone?

Those were my thoughts as I began to climb my way up the steep hill I had come to. I was not about give up—there was still hope.

TWENTY-EIGHT

Murray

As Captain and I made our way through the city with the siren blaring, my heart raced. Was this finally the moment I had been waiting for? I had to realize that Lily could be in bad shape when I found her, or maybe she wouldn't even be there at all.

I had to keep my mind clear, but it was difficult in this type of situation. I was kicking myself because I knew walking away from that house had drawn me in even closer. The man who answered fidgeted and avoided eye contact with me the entire time, but without a search warrant I had no business stepping inside as much as I knew I needed to. I could have been in Lily's presence the whole time I was there, and I never knew it.

I couldn't dwell on the past. All that mattered was that I was headed back to where she was or at least where I hoped she was. I wondered what her mental state would be like when we found her, I didn't want to imagine what this man could have done to her. I knew how kidnappers worked, and I didn't want to think about what torture and trauma my wife had endured.

With the sirens running, it didn't take us very long to reach North Vancouver. Captain insisted on driving. I was informed as we were leaving that officers had been dispatched to the house to stay with Callie so that Detective Gresham could join us.

Callie had told me over the phone when I checked in with her before leaving the station, that she would be okay with other officers staying with her. You had to admit, Callie had become a strong young woman. I knew she had her weak points—as we all have our weak points—but she was incredibly strong for her age and I admired her strength throughout this whole ordeal.

Gresham pulled in behind us, following us the rest of the way. If we found Lily, depending on her condition, I thought she may have needed to see a familiar female face.

Rounding the street of the Johnson house, I felt a lump form in my throat and my breathing become heavier. I noticed Pryce had already arrived and was sitting in his car as we all surrounded the house with our cruisers. We had no time to waste. I jumped out of the car, pulling my gun from its holster, drawing it up towards the house that stood before me. Pryce came running up beside me with the search warrant in his hand, snatching it from his grip I held onto it firmly.

We had no idea what type of man Darren was other than he was supposedly schizophrenic and had beat his wife. Justine had never elaborated whether Darren kept any weapons inside the house, thus we had to prepare for the worst. Gresham, Pryce, and I were placed on the front door, while three others made their way around to the back of the house. There were no vehicles in the driveway, but that didn't mean someone wasn't parked in the garage. I waited for no one and began banging heavily on the door.

"This is the Vancouver Police Department, we have a warrant to search the premises. Open up."

No sound could be heard from inside, and I called out one more time. I was ready to kick in the door any minute, but knew I had to wait and follow protocol. When we heard nobody after our second verbal statement, it was time. With the battering ram in hand, Pryce breached the door with one fell swoop, splintering the wooden door from its hinges and Darren's three key, high security, deadbolt locks—I knew this was why Captain had put Pryce on the front door—solely for that ability. It took skill, and it had been something he and I practiced heavily, because the quicker you were able to gain access to the inside of any building, the more ground you covered quicker and swarmed in on whatever was happening inside.

I began shouting throughout each room we cleared.

"Lily! Are you here?"

The home was a bungalow, which meant everything was on one level with the exception of the basement. Nobody was inside, at least not on the ground floor. I noticed the entire house looked spotless—almost as if nobody lived there and it was staged for an open house.

The last place for us to check was the basement. I remembered seeing a door in the kitchen and wondered if that was where it led to. As I approached the door, I placed my hand on the handle and turned it, holding my breath in the process. What appeared behind the door was a long, straight staircase that led down to a small landing.

I made the trek down the steep staircase to a single door off to the right that was ajar. I didn't know what to expect, what I would find, or if I would even find anything at all. This was my last hope and the final room that needed to be searched.

The door squeaked open loudly as I shoved it abruptly, revealing a pitch black room. I felt around on the wall inside for a light switch, but found nothing. I took a single step back to feel on the outside wall while I called out,

"Lily, can you hear me?"

I received no response, and located a single switch outside the room. I was beginning to wonder if anyone was here at all, or if they had been tipped off that the cops were coming.

As the light shone full strength, I peered around the large, empty room. There was an old mattress and bucket across the room from where I stood at the door. A shelving unit stood against the left wall with old boxes filling the five shelves.

I didn't know what was happening.

Where was Lily? She was supposed to be here.

I heard footsteps descending the staircase behind me.

"Murray, the house is empty." Gresham's voice rattled me.

I had no words. He must have been tipped off when we had come yesterday, and moved out. To know I had been in the presence of my wife and I couldn't do anything about it, left a pain in my chest. I knew we needed this place processed for any evidence.

"We need to find them, Gresham, this Darren guy and my wife. Get forensics in here now, I want this house processed top to bottom."

"Yes, I can get them in here now that we've completed the search," she replied with a heavy voice.

Gresham turned and made her way back upstairs, which left me completely alone. Before another thought entered my mind, I lost myself. I dropped to my knees in complete agony and cried out, mostly in anger. He had stolen my wife from my daughter and I, told me he didn't know a Justine Johnson, and that the Johnsons had moved. He knew he had been playing me, but I couldn't see past what he told me, because we had no other solid lead.

"Murray, are you alright?" I was pulled out of my despair by the Captain's voice, where he stood over me while I continued to kneel on the floor. I couldn't speak, and kept my face pointed towards the ground.

"We won't stop until we find him, I can promise you that." His voice was firm, yet reassuring.

I knew the Captain was on my side, and was working with me instead of against me. It was nice to have my team back me up for a change instead of trying to push me aside. I found my voice and gave a single statement as I peered up towards him,

"We don't sleep until that bastard is found, you hear me?"

I pulled myself off the floor and brushed my pants off, composing myself before I spoke directly to the Captain.

"What's next? I feel as though we're at a dead end..." I trailed off as I glanced around the empty room.

"If they're not here—" Captain cut me off.

"I have already arranged for Mrs. Johnson to be brought in for more questioning and be ready in an interview room as soon as we make it back to the precinct. She must have more information, perhaps another place Darren goes to. I don't believe she has given us the whole story, she must be holding back something, and it's time to find out the whole truth."

I had been very compassionate towards Justine up until now, but maybe I was being played. Regardless of the fact she had mentioned she was Lily's sister, I was going to have to be much more stern with her once we arrived back at the station. Everything she fed us could have been her way of making us believe she had been a victim. With the way she had come into the picture, and always been on the run…it just didn't add up—but I had been blinded by the fact that she seemed to hold the only information about Lily, and was my only connection to her disappearance.

"I'm sorry Captain, for putting all my trust in her. Not following protocol—"

"You were doing what was best for your wife, it's understandable," he assured me quickly.

"I broke protocol, I shouldn't have—"

"We can't go back on what has already been done, all we can do is move forward and nail him."

I didn't have any other words for him, and none needed to be spoken. I was beginning to feel at ease knowing that we were on the same side for a change.

We made our way back upstairs to see the forensic team arriving on the scene and setting up their equipment in the living room.

"I want every inch of this house dusted for prints, every hair collected. Nothing goes untested. Everything is evidence," Captain barked out.

There wasn't much more that I could do, and left my trust in the hands of the forensic officers. I knew I would receive a detailed report when they had finished their investigation.

As I stepped out of the house, I was met by another line of reporters who were being held back by officers. Before I could process how they had managed to find us, voices began to shout from every direction, and all I could do was take a deep breath to keep myself centered. I was not prepared to give a statement, but I needed them to take a step back and give us space to work through the new developments. Without thinking, I walked straight up to the first reporter I could reach. Soon, the rest of them had huddled around me, shoving their microphones in my direction. I cleared my throat and spoke with authority.

"I will not take any questions, I will only give a statement. Please respect the decisions made, and respect the family that this situation effects."

I really didn't have much to go on, but I thought it would at least keep the reporters out of our hair until we had more information.

"Earlier today, a discovery was made between a murder investigation from 1998, and the sudden disappearance of Lily-May Murray during the same year. It is believed, from the evidence recently discovered, that the same male who committed the murder of the young eighteen year old, Kennedy Daniels found beside the Wandle River, is the same man who kidnapped Lily-May Murray. We have been working closely with a witness over the last few months, which has led us to this home. Our discovery today came up empty handed, though we are confident we will track down the person of interest. All we know at this time is that his name is Darren Johnson. If you know the whereabouts of Darren Johnson or Lily-May Murray, please come forward to the Vancouver Police Department. All information provided assisting in the location of Lily-May Murray and Darren Johnson will be kept in the strictest of confidence and hopefully answer questions bringing closure of the horrific murder for Daniels family."

This was all that I felt I could say and didn't have anything more to add at the time. My time was needed back at the station to process and figure out what our next steps were. This was only the beginning of a long journey still ahead of us.

I stayed true to my word and didn't answer any of the questions the reporters began to shout at me. Regardless of telling them you won't answer any questions, they will still always try to wriggle themselves into having you answer. As I walked to Captain's car, Gresham exited the house in a rush.

"Murray, wait up!" she called out.

I gave her time to catch up to me before entering the car to head back to the station.

"They found long brunette hair on the pillows in the bedroom. We need something of Lily's to match. Do you have anything on you we can—"

"I'll find something at home. I have her DNA on something." I cut her off, whispering, before the reporters eavesdropping on our conversation could piece together that Lily was my wife.

I realized she had mentioned the hair had been found in the bedroom, which didn't make sense when there was a mattress found in the basement. Where had Lily been kept? Or was there more than one woman involved? I knew the hair would be Lily's, as there was no way Justine's would be on the pillows this long after the fact—unless Justine was involved in the

257

disappearance in some way. My worst feeling overtook me, and I needed to know more. I hesitated before asking Gresham my next question.

"Was anything else found in the bedroom, Gresham?"

"I don't know, they're testing the sheets as we speak," she whispered, so as the reporters wouldn't overhear us.

I was trying not to read into statements too much, but it was very hard not to jump to any conclusions.

"Keep me informed if anything more develops. I'm headed back to the precinct; Justine is coming in for more questioning."

"Murray, do your job, find the answers you need. Lily's life depends on it."

Gresham had faith, even after all these years later, which made me find the little faith I still had and hold onto it. It was just a matter of time until I located Lily, but I was sure now that the media had leaked details about the case that her time was running out. If they were on the run, anything could happen. I needed to get roadblocks in place, but not knowing when they had left, we were probably too late for that to be any help. I needed to put in a call to border patrol to flag his vehicle in case he thought he could flee the country.

The entire drive back I felt every emotion possible— since the Captain wasn't a very talkative man, I had some time to process the events of the day thus far and think about what questions I needed to ask Justine when we arrived back. We needed the truth, and all of it—no more of these bits and pieces she had tried to give us the last few times we had interviewed her.

As we pulled into the parking lot and parked in the Captain's stall, I thanked him and exited the car, but gave myself some extra time before I walked into the station. I noticed that there were no reporters outside this time, which gave me some relief that they had taken what I had said earlier seriously.

I knew once I walked into the station everything would go quiet. It was just the way things went around here. When things hit any member of our police force personally, everyone was on edge.

I took the side entrance, feeling as though it was the safest bet. As I walked through the hallways and past my colleagues, they gave me a simple head nod to gesture they understood, but gave me the space I desperately needed.

I had no idea if Justine was here already, Captain usually had her brought in before I even mentioned it to him, but this time he had been out with me. I also wouldn't have Gresham as a witness to the interview. With the way I was feeling, I knew this interview would be different. She would answer my questions, regardless of how upset she was, because I was done playing games. Lily was still alive, I could feel it, and I wanted to ensure she stayed alive by finding her in time.

My cell rang as I reached my desk, gathering the items I would need to conduct the interview.

"Hello, Murray here."

"Murray, it's Officer Falcon. Mrs. Johnson is in the main lobby."

I lost my breath but recovered it quickly, remembering I didn't want her spotted or hounded by anyone.

"Have someone take her down to interview room three, please. I don't want anyone to see or speak to her, you hear me?"

"Yes, I understand, sir. I'll have someone take her down right away."

I hung up abruptly as I didn't have much time to prepare. I retrieved the necessary items that I would need from my desk and headed down to meet her. As I made my way back down, I stopped at the duty desk to give a quick call home to Callie to ensure she was alright. I hated that I'd had to leave her home alone with officers she wasn't familiar with.

Once I finished the call, I travelled down the hallway of interview rooms and reached for the door handle of the one that I had asked Falcon to take Justine to. Before opening the door, I paused as I took a deep breath to calm my increasingly tense nerves. I needed to keep calm if I wanted any answers. I couldn't let my anger overtake me, not now when time was of the essence.

I found Mrs. Johnson sitting by the window—I really didn't understand her connection to the window.

"Mrs. Johnson," I greeted her shortly, with a quick nod of my head.

It took her a moment to turn and acknowledge my presence. Without speaking a word, she gave me a nod. I contemplated whether to have her move to the table, but my compassion won me over again. I realized I couldn't be that soft person I had been with her in the past, and chose against it and went with protocol. It would work better in my favor, I thought.

"Let's take a seat at the table,"

I kept it professional. I could tell she sensed something was different in my demeanour today.

Her voice was weak when she spoke, but I could understand her.

"Is everything alright? You seem different today."

I was different because I had just raided a house in which my wife was supposedly at, but no longer was. How else could she expect me to act?

"Everything is fine, let's take our seats."

Without a word, she made her way to the metal table, as I set the recorder and pad down. I wanted to get down to business.

"Mrs. Johnson, do you understand this interview will be recorded and can be used as evidence in the case of Lily-May Murray's disappearance?"

"You can call me Justine, detective. You know we're family now." Her voice was sweet, but I was not in the mood for bonding right now.

I repeated my question, "Mrs. Johnson, I will ask you again—do you understand this interview will be recorded and can be used as evidence in the case of Lily-May Murray's disappearance?"

"Yes," she replied meekly, and I assumed she sensed I meant business.

It was a better time than any to jump right into questions. All I hoped was that she actually had answers to my questions, or else this would be a complete waste of time, once again.

TWENTY-NINE

Callie

Dad told me not to worry about the investigation, but it was all I could think about.

Was he close to finding mom?

I had no idea what had been found at the house, but when nobody had called, I feared the worst. I wanted to call dad, knowing full well he would call me when he had any new information. The reporters had dispersed, but two officers still sat outside, more or less to give me a sense of peace and security while I was home alone. My phone rang on the night stand as I sat on the edge of my bed. I didn't bother checking the caller ID before answering, which I probably should have done.

"Hello?"

I started saying into the receiver before I had even raised the phone to my face.

"Hey Cal, it's Stan. I heard the news—"I cut him off before he could go any further.

"I know the news is broadcasting, if that's why you called, I don't have anything further to say. I don't know anything more than what you know." My tone was sharp.

I was irritated. If that was why he had called, I didn't need it. I was trying to keep myself occupied, which was already hard enough being home alone while dad was out there doing all he could to find mom.

"Okay, I just called to see if you were okay and if you needed anything."

I breathed out a heavy sigh. I felt terrible about jumping to conclusions about why Stan had called in the first place. All he wanted to do was check on me, and instead, I lost it at him, thinking he had wanted the inside scoop to sell to the six o'clock news.

"I'm sorry Stan. You can imagine how stressful all of this is. Dad isn't here, and besides the two officers outside, I'm all alone."

"Do you want me to come over?"

My mind drifted to where dad might be, considering he was headed to a place that was supposedly the kidnapper's house. This caused tension in my chest. Somehow I had forgotten that Stan was still on the phone until I began hearing his voice again.

"Callie, are you still there?"

"I'm still here, sorry. My mind was drifting."

"Do you need me to come over? You shouldn't be alone during a time like this."

I hesitated before answering him.

Stan was right though, I was here alone while dad was attempting to catch the man who had kidnapped mom. It had never dawned on me that this was actually real, that the investigation had been reopened and was

263

now an active investigation. After six years, I had never expected a cold case with no evidence to resurface in this manner.

"You can come over if you want. I don't know how great of company I'll be, though."

"Don't worry about it, I want to," he quickly replied.

I could tell he had a grin on his face by his chipper voice.

"Okay, I'll see you soon then."

"I should make it to your place in less than half an hour."

"Not a problem, I'll let the officers know you're coming, that way they won't be alarmed. Bye."

I hung up my phone and continued to sit on the edge of the bed, staring out into thin air—that was, until my phone began to buzz in my hand again. I didn't recognize the number calling, but I picked it up anyway.

"Hello?" I asked.

"Callie, its Dad…"

"Hey dad, where are you calling from? It didn't come up your number?"

"I'm using the front desk phone at the station. I wanted to check in on you and see if you're alright."

"I'm fine, but what happened with the search warrant?" I asked quickly.

The line went quiet, but I could still hear my dad breathing heavily through the receiver. After a few seconds, he answered in an all too cheery voice.

"We're still trying sweetheart, making progress."

"How much progress? What was found at the house? Was M—"

Dad cut me off before I could continue with my question.

"We won't stop searching."

It felt like a flame had ignited inside me. I had never been one to be easily angered over things, but with this case flip flopping between hot and cold, I couldn't handle all the pressure it was throwing my way. I could tell dad was beating around the bush and not giving me straight answers, but I couldn't pressure him into giving me them, either. I would eventually find out when he felt the time was right.

"When will you be home, then? Stan is on his way over to keep me company."

"I don't know, Justine—ahem—Mrs. Johnson has just been brought in for further questioning."

Whoever this Justine person was, I didn't like her very much. It seemed we had only ever got half assed answers and never any full details from her—at least that's what I sensed whenever dad spoke about her. I also felt he was keeping things about her from me, but I simply couldn't pinpoint what exactly.

"I hope she provides you with some more solid information this time."

My statement came out more harshly than I expected, but dad didn't seem fazed by it.

"We're doing everything we can as we work with her. Give us some time. I have to go now, but I'll see you tonight."

He was done talking. As much as I knew this was my dad, I was done talking, too. The entire situation was irritating me. There were always lingering questions, but never enough information to answer any of them.

"I guess I'll see you when you get home then."

With that, we hung up, but I still hadn't moved from my bed. I was motionless and moving from this spot was the last thing on my mind. All I could think about was mom, and whether she was still alive. Was she somewhere in the city or had they fled? It was all too much to think about, and I felt my whole body tense.

A tear spilled out from my eye and down my cheek. I swiped at it with the back of my hand. I felt stupid for crying at a time like this—I was angry and wanted answers about my mom. I was drawn out of my anger by the sound of the doorbell ringing through the house. I realized I had forgotten to tell the officers that I was expecting company. I made my way down the stairs and peered through the peep hole. It was Stan, but he was blocked by one of the officers.

I opened the door just enough to tell the officer Stan was a visitor, and for Stan to slip inside; I was not ready for the world to see me, and even with no reporters around, you could never take a chance because someone could always be lurking about.

"Hi," he said, with a small smile playing on his lower lip.

"Hey…" I mumbled in reply, while looking down at the floor.

The few seconds that we stood awkwardly in the hallway, killed me.

"Is everything okay, Callie?" he spoke softly, in a tone that was soothing.

However, his soothing tone made me feel defensive and I snapped at him.

"Of course—I'm not a little girl anymore. I'm nearly sixteen after all, in just under four months. The last six years have been a huge weight on my shoulders, but I've tried my best to press on."

As strong as I tried to act, I broke down after hearing my own words. As I finished snapping at Stan, I began to heave and tears seemed to overflow from my eyes. Over the six years of my life my mother had missed, I had to grow up and become a strong young woman.

Not only for my own sake, but dad's too. I needed him to know that I was alright and that I could take care of myself.

I hadn't seen Stan move, but all of a sudden he was at my side and had placed a hand on my upper back.

"You know I'm always here for you. I know this has been such an emotional time for you, but know that no matter what, we all love you and want the best for you. That includes your mother."

"But how do we know she is even still alive?" I wailed.

"It's been way too long, and they found nothing at that house earlier today. As much as I've tried my best to keep my hopes alive, it's fading Stan."

"Don't underestimate your mom, and your dad. Your dad is doing everything he possibly can to find her. Only time will tell. I know it's been many years, but have faith and believe Callie. Find that strength I know you have. Don't give up."

It was strange hearing from him about faith and beliefs, considering we had never had any talks about religion. I didn't know where he stood on that front. Regardless, faith had kept me together for the most part—it was the one thing that I felt I still had control over.

"Why don't we watch a movie in the living room? You need to take your mind off today's events and breath," Stan suggested.

I really didn't know what I wanted to do, but I knew I wanted to get my mind off the investigation. Maybe Stan's suggestion was for the best, as I did need to do something to ease my mind.

"That sounds good, I can do that," I nodded and gave him a weak smile.

My voice was weak and Stan tugged at my hand as we stood in the hallway. Before I knew what was happening, he had pulled me into a hug.

Being close to him sent a sensation through me like no other I had ever felt before. Don't get me wrong, Stan had hugged me before, but *this* was different. It felt as though there was more passion involved with *this* hug.

I was still on the fence about actually agreeing to date Stan. All I had agreed to was that we would take things slow if we did start dating. As the days and weeks had gone by, I had begun to feel a deeper connection to him. He was generally a good guy, I had lucked out with him. He had put up with a lot from me over our years of friendship, never seeming to be burdened by it.

Instead, he just waited—what guy nowadays would actually wait for a girl. Pretty much all the popular girls at school had some male hanging off their arm every week. I couldn't understand how they could change boyfriends monthly as they did. Whenever I heard about dating, or relationships I pictured a couple getting to know one another, their interests, their fears, and whatever they wanted to learn about. I never pictured it as just a phase; you couldn't play with people's emotions that way.

I guess I had zoned out, because the next thing I knew, Stan gave me an extra squeeze. I peered up at him and noticed a sparkle in his eye. Being friends, I had never looked at Stan in any other way but as a friend, but, at that moment in time I felt I was getting a glimpse into his soul.

"Callie, you are incredibly beautiful."

His words flowed off his tongue suavely and danced through my mind. I didn't want those words to disappear from my ears, and I replayed them over and over in my mind. I couldn't take my eyes off him. I leaned into him, allowing myself to lead in that split second as I reached up to place a kiss on his lips. Maybe it wasn't traditional for a girl to make the first move, but it felt right and it didn't seem to bother Stan in the least.

I took a step back unexpectedly, breaking our embrace.

"I... I..." I stuttered.

Stan cupped the side of my face and spoke softly with a smile on his face.

"It's okay. I've been waiting for that moment for a long time."

I felt my cheeks flush with colour as we stood in the hallway. My eyes darted everywhere except at Stan, as I processed what I had just done. I had kissed a boy, and not just any boy, but my best friend. Of course, doubt began to wash over me, but I pushed it to the back of my mind.

I broke the silence that had crept upon us,

"I guess this makes things official then."

I realized I couldn't kiss the boy and expect to go back to being friends. It was obvious to me, and to him, that we had a special connection. I don't think mom would want me to hide myself away for the rest of my life, without experiencing everything life had to offer—which included romantic relationships.

We had stood in the hallway long enough. I thought a change of pace would be good right about then.

"Why don't we head into the living room and pick a movie?" I finally said to Stan.

The investigation would still be on my mind, no doubt, but there was not much more I could personally do at this point. In the meantime, I had to keep on living. Time hadn't stood still, so why should I?

THIRTY

Murray

"Mrs. Johnson, when was the last time you saw your husband?"

Silence filled the room as I sat patiently for an answer from her, though what surprised me was her quick answer to my question.

"In what capacity, detective?"

I wasn't completely sure what her question was referring to, but I repeated my question in case she hadn't understood what I was asking.

"When did you see your husband last?"

I had no other way to pose the question to be honest, it was simple. I just wanted to know the last time she had seen this man she claimed was her husband; and claimed to have kidnapped Lily. She took some time before she spoke, but when she did, it shocked me.

"A few days ago.

Was this woman actually telling me she had seen him just a few days ago?

Of course I instantly had a comeback question ready.

"What do you mean, Mrs. Johnson? How did you see him a few days ago? You told me you had run away. Have you returned to him?"

By her body language, I could tell a sense of hostility had come over her, a side I had yet to see from her, until now.

"No, not at all! I could never return to him!"

I was confused by her answer, but didn't want to alarm her. Instead, I continued on to the next question to dig deeper into what she was trying to tell me.

"Did you speak to Mr. Johnson when you saw him a few days ago?"

"No." Her voice was flat.

"Where were you in order to have been able to see him, but not talk to him?"

I needed to be poignant with my questions, I was done with mind games and I didn't want to beat around the bush any longer. The answers needed to be straight and to the point.

"I was standing behind a tree."

"Alright… and what was Mr. Johnson doing when you saw him?"

"I'm not sure, I saw him moving about in the kitchen."

Did this woman have binoculars for eyes? Where the heck had she been standing in order to witness what was occurring inside the Johnson house, and see specifically into the kitchen of all places?

"Where were you again Mrs. Johnson, when you were watching him?"

"Behind a tree in my neighbour's backyard. You can see through the kitchen window when you stand in her yard."

I had to take a minute to understand what she was telling me.

Did her neighbour know what had happened? Why did she not come to the police herself and report all of this?

"Does your neighbour know that Mr. Johnson kidnapped someone?"

"Yes, she does, she has been helping me. This is how I know Lily is still alive." I was amazed at how calm and matter-of-fact her voice was.

That was a pretty big claim unless she had seen Lily herself. My next question rolled off my tongue without hesitation, but quickly came to pain me when I realized what I had asked.

"Have you seen Lily?"

"Yes, I have seen her at different times throughout the years," she answered, just as plainly as she had before.

Before I could think of anything else, my following questions rolled out altogether in one lump.

"When did you see Lily last? Is she okay? Has she seen you?

I must have overwhelmed her because she began shaking her head vigorously.

"I didn't see her this last time I was there—only Darren. I had been watching her to know that she was safe…"

She trailed off, stopping mid-sentence. My heart began to beat quickly, I needed to know if she was okay.

"Is Lily okay?"

"I don't know, but I have seen her with bruises sometimes in the past."

That answer shot through me like a bullet—bruises, on my Lily. I could only image the pain she had gone through. I understood well how kidnapping cases worked. The victim almost always suffered some type of abuse from their kidnapper. To know she was still alive gave me hope, something I had begun to lose a few years ago when the investigation went cold.

Now, I sat here with the only witness who said she had seen Lily alive with her own two eyes within the past six years. I had to keep asking questions to find out the full truth.

"What else can you tell me?" I asked, with bated breath.

I didn't really know what to ask next, but whatever she wanted to tell me I was prepared to listen to.

"When I returned to keep an eye on Lily the week after Darren kidnapped her, my neighbour was outside. I thought I hid myself well under my big glasses and oversized coat, but apparently I could be seen from a mile away. Being the nosey neighbour she was, I had a million questions being directed at me. Not to draw any more attention, I pulled her into her home and explained the situation."

That explanation cleared up why I had noticed a woman standing in the window next door when I was driving away from the Johnson house. I had never thought to question the neighbours, but I was not really on the case to do so until recently. Justine continued with her explanation.

"After I explained to her what had happened, she promised me she wouldn't tell anyone where I was, and that I could use her house for surveillance and as a home, too, if I wanted. She wanted to keep me safe."

She paused, and I jumped at the chance to intervene and ask a question. To me, knowing someone else actually knew what was going on sent chills down my spine. Although we couldn't change the past there had obviously been a reason why both Justine and the neighbour thought it was the best decision for the situation.

"Is this where you have been living all these years? With your neighbour?"

It was a valid question because she never elaborated where she had actually been staying for the past six years.

"No, not permanently. I don't stay too long in one place. I'm fearful I'll be seen. I go back once a week to keep tabs, to know that my sister is okay. I was there the day you came knocking, I wanted to come and tell you that Lily was there. She was in the kitchen washing dishes when you knocked. He pushed her downstairs before coming to answer the door."

My mind began to swirl knowing my intuition had been correct. Lily *had* been there, within my reach. I shook my head at the thought. I had walked away, when I could have had her back in my arms again right then. What came next from Justine caught me off guard.

"I'm sorry. I know I have messed up. I was trying to save us both... but I failed."

My heart became heavy. This woman needed to know she had not failed, and that she had her sister's, and her own, best interests at heart. She was a victim herself and she was doing what she thought would save her life.

"You haven't failed, you lead us to the house where he was keeping her. It was very brave for you to even return and watch your husband with another woman."

The room fell silent. Justine stared at her hands—fidgeting. I felt as though I may have struck a nerve with her. I could see she was closing off to the world due to her actions. I needed to keep her here, in the present, to discover more. She looked up and stared me in the eyes with her next statement.

"She is my sister, I don't want to see her hurt."

Her words were mumbled, but I could make out what she was saying. She had a point—as much as Lily was my wife, and Callie's mother, she was Justine's sister, too. If Lily came out of this alive, it wouldn't be just us she reconnected with, Justine and her would be reconnecting as well.

"Does Mr. Johnson have any other property or residence?"

It was an important, burning question I'd had, since the start of the interview. If he had taken Lily, they had to have gone somewhere he knew and felt safe. We had cops staying outside the house in case he returned, but I didn't think he was coming back anytime soon.

"His work cabin, but I don't know where it's located. Darren is a hunter, he hunts deer for the most part. He used to go on trips to it and bring home a lot of meat—enough to last us an entire winter."

Her head fell, and I assumed her thoughts matched mine in the sense this might be a place he would have taken Lily. I didn't even know of any hunting places around here, we were in Vancouver after all.

"How long would he be away for on these hunting trips?"

She shook her head, but didn't answer.

"Was it a few hours, a few days?" I prompted.

"A day, maybe two at most. He worked there Monday to Friday and would be home within eight to ten hours."

Knowing that time frame, I assumed it couldn't be too far from Vancouver. I stood as I pulled out my cell phone from my back pocket. I needed someone investigating this, Gresham was still at the house to my knowledge, but Pryce had come back to the station.

"Pryce, hey, can you look for any hunting grounds in and around Vancover?"

"I can search, but why do you need to know that?"

I pinched the bridge of my nose. I hated when someone questioned an order. Regardless, this *was* my partner. Every second was precious right now.

"Possibly a cabin that Lily has been taken to."

For a second, I thought the line had gone dead, but I could hear him breathing into the receiver.

"You realize we live in Vancouver, right? We don't exactly hunt here?"

"I know it sounds strange but, Mr. Johnson is a deer hunter and used to go on day trips to a cabin. There has to be something around here—maybe even just on the outskirts of the city."

"Okay, I'll look into it, but I can't promise it will lead to anything."

"I know, but we have to take every lead seriously at this point."

With that, I ended the call, slipped my phone back into my pocket and turned back to Justine.

"Would you like some water, Justine?" My tone had lost its edge, and I asked her this softly.

She nodded '*yes*' and went to open her mouth to say something, then closed it. I gave her a minute, and sure enough, she spoke.

"He doesn't believe me, does he?"

I was taken back by her question. How could she sense that from a one sided conversation?

"Everyone is trying to process all the events of this case, that's all."

I wasn't expecting her next response.

"I'm sorry I caused your wife to go missing. I truly am."

"It's not your fault in the least. With the knowledge you have, we will find her."

I gave her a reassuring smile as I sat back down in the chair across from her to continue our interview. I wanted to know every last detail in hopes that we could close this case quickly.

There was not much more information Justine could provide us with that we didn't already know. We were both exhausted, and the investigation was still going on to locate any nearby wooded areas that had cabins and allowed hunting.

I found myself driving down McNabb with Justine in the passenger seat. I didn't know what I was thinking taking a witness home with me, but in a sense she *was* family now—she was Lily's twin sister, after all. I didn't know why it took me so long to realize this. The day I found out she was related, I should have taken her in, but I had been so worked up about finding Lily, and thought of Justine as simply a witness in the investigation.

The entire trip home was quiet, with Justine constantly looking out the window, and me lost in my thoughts. I didn't know how Callie would react when we arrived home. I hadn't called her to warn her at all, and I knew Callie felt bitter towards Justine after the incident at school. I thought I could calm Callie down enough to realize that she was now family, whether we liked it or not.

I peered over to see the nervousness in Justine building. I couldn't imagine what she had been through while on the run for six years. I had no idea what she did for money, or food. I broke the silence that had filled the car.

"Are you alright?"

"I'm fine," she answered in her flat, emotionless tone.

Her eyes never left the world outside the car window. I knew she genuinely feared being caught by Darren, because she insisted on wearing her sunglasses as we drove home, regardless that it was overcast and nearly dusk.

Did she not realize I wouldn't let anything happen to her?

"I don't want you to feel awk—" She turned and cut me off before I could finish.

"I'm afraid of what Callie is going to think of me."

Her tone was even and didn't waver. The last time Justine and Callie had an encounter, Callie was running after her thinking she was her mother.

"I'm sure she will understand, it may take her awhile, but she will come around. Trust me."

I gave her a reassuring smile to ease her mind. She turned to look back out the window, but continued to speak.

"She has every right to be mad at me. I took her mother away, but that's why I've been watching over Callie—from afar. I wanted to ensure that Callie was protected. She is such a brave young woman, I can't imagine what she has gone through."

Justine was right—even I couldn't fathom how Callie had made it through these past six years. To lose her mother, and be a witness to the kidnapping… It was astounding that she managed to still function normally. I was not able to comment on this before Justine asked me another question.

"Is that boy I see her with all the time her boyfriend?"

I burst out laughing. I knew exactly who she was referring to. Stan was Callie's best friend. He protected her when I wasn't around, although lately I had noticed them becoming a little closer than normal, but I hadn't questioned anything. I knew dating was a topic Callie found hard to talk to me about, and for sure was a mother-daughter conversation. I gave her space when it came to that, and I would support her in any way I could.

"I actually can't say, but they are very close friends. They met just after Lily disappeared and they haven't been apart since. I know Stan has deeper feelings, but Callie has been struggling without having her mother around to talk about boys and relationships. I can only do so much when it comes to that department."

I could hear Justine exhale, as if she was holding her breath.

"They would make a cute couple if they were. I hope Callie will forgive me."

My heart broke. I could truly hear the sincerity in Justine's voice. As much as we wanted to blame her for not coming to us earlier, we had to realize how difficult it had been for her to show up at the station and give us the information she had. Without her, we wouldn't have been where we were today in locating Lily.

"I want you to know that I thank you for coming forward, I can imagine it hasn't been easy to tell your story."

She turned in my direction and spoke firmly,

"I am not doing this for me, I am lost already. I did this for Lily, because she deserves to come home to her loving family. For me, I have nothing. I don't want to go back to Darren."

I had no words for her. I didn't know how she had survived on her own this long, but sticking this out all alone was brave, and I was sure Lily would agree with me if she knew. Even if she didn't want to admit it, escaping your abuser was one thing, but staying alive to tell the story was a completely different one. I wanted to help her once we found them—I wanted justice not only for Lily, but justice for Justine as well. Darren would be going away for a very long time when I got my hands on him, that was for sure.

We pulled into the driveway, and I cut the engine. I could feel Justine tense as she stared at the house. I hadn't even noticed that the reporters were nowhere in sight, but police tape was still up around the perimeter of our property. The officers who were stationed here were still standing on the porch, which put me at ease to know my daughter was alright.

I turned to Justine to see her nearly pass out from the shock she was displaying, just from staring at the front door, but you could tell she had something to say. I gave her the time she needed to speak if she wanted too.

"I never imagined I would come back. That night... I replay it over and over every day."

I was slightly confused and wanted to tread lightly in questioning what she had meant by that statement.

"What night?" I asked in an almost to chipper a voice, in my attempt to lighten the mood.

"The night Lily disappeared."

I was taken back by her statement—why was she only telling me this now?

"You were here when that happened?" I asked in an exasperated voice.

She nodded, but didn't speak. Tears filled the brims of her eyes.

"When I ran away from Darren, the next two days I tried to be brave enough to knock on your door. I only made it up to the front door once, but nobody was home. I felt as though she would have forgotten about me and moved on with her life. I was standing over there, behind those trees," she gestured towards the two giant oak trees our neighbour had on their front lawn, then continued with her recount, "and Darren had staked out the house the entire day. Once he got out of the car, everything was a blur and happened too quickly. He had Lily in his grasp as he pulled her outside, and Callie—poor Callie—she was trying to pull her mother back inside, but Darren was focused on Lily. I don't even think he noticed the child, but then again, he hated children to begin with."

The words both shocked and pained me, all at the same time. This woman had witnessed everything. She truly was the missing piece to the puzzle we had been searching for all these years.

"We can't change the past. All we can do is move forward and change the future. Right now, you're going to stay with us until we find them—and we *are* going to find them. We're close, I know we are. I can feel it."

"I hope you're right," she sighed.

I opened my driver's door, with Justine following suit. As we both made our way towards the front door, we met at the hood of the car. I could see her take a deep breath in. I put my arm around her shoulder to walk her up to the front door. As we approached the porch, I pulled my keys from my pocket, unlocked the door, and called out,

"Callie, I'm home."

THIRTY-ONE

Callie

I had to admit, this had been one of the best nights of my life. I felt free, and it was amazing to spend the evening with Stan. I finally felt like I wasn't giving him the cold shoulder anymore, that I was letting myself open up.

"Thanks for coming over tonight Stan, I really enjoyed myself."

"It was nice to finally have a date with you, even if it was in your living room." He nudged his elbow into my side playfully.

I knew I had brushed him off for years, but he had to realize my life had turned upside down—that I was turned upside down.

Stan turned on the couch and gave me a small peck on the lips before pulling away and standing up, just as

I heard the front door begin to open. I jumped up, knowing it had to have been dad coming home.

As dad made his way in, I noticed he had a woman with him—the same woman I had run after who got into the cab. This couldn't be happening right now!

Why was she standing in my house?

"Dad, what's going on?" I asked in a low voice.

Dad could tell I was angry and confused.

"Callie, I need you to focus right now. This is Mrs. Johnson."

I couldn't understand why dad had brought her here. This woman had been haunting me for years, and now she was standing in my house. I continued to shake my head, but dad stepped towards me and sat me back on the couch.

The woman couldn't even look at me, she just looked down at her fidgeting hands.

Why couldn't she look at me?

This angered me inside and I shouted at her.

"Look at me!"

My words scared her, which caused her to jump.

"Callie, calm down now." Dad's voice resonated vaguely in the back of my mind, but my focus was on her and why she was here, in my house. She had been the one who had caused my mother to be taken away. She was the reason mom had been gone for so long.

"How could you come back here, after everything you've put us through? How?"

Panic took over me and my breathing became shorter as I tried to catch my breath. The woman continued to avoid me, but why?

Was she scared of me?

"Why can't you look at me?" I spoke in barely a whisper. I was giving this woman hell, but somehow I was able to realize she was just as scared as I was right then.

"I am… sorry… I deserve to be hated," she heaved out.

Her words stung, she thought I hated her. In a sense, part of me did, though the longer I stood there looking at her, I realized she was scared, and even hurt. It was evident from her body language.

I took a deep breath and exhaled before I spoke again. I hadn't realized dad had moved to stand next to her, and was comforting her with his hand on her shoulder.

"I didn't mean to yell, but you've scared me for years. You've been watching me. I thought you were my mother's ghost."

The room fell silent. Nobody said a word. Her eyes rose to meet mine and her mouth opened to speak, but no sound came out. She tried again, and in barely a whisper, she spoke.

"I'm sorry to have scared you, that was not my intention at all. I was trying to watch out for you, to make sure you were okay. I never imagined that I would get caught. All those times that you turned and saw me—I had to run. I didn't need you finding out who I truly was. The person that made your mother disappear."

I needed to know answers to the questions I had. I had told myself I would ask her if I ever saw her again.

"Why did you run from me when I finally caught up to you? Why did you leave me standing there on the sidewalk as you rode away?" I was surprised by the hurt I could hear in my own tone. Continuing to meet my eyes, she answered in a more confident voice.

"I didn't know what to say to you, or if you even knew who I was. I hadn't realized that I would look identical to your mother, and that you would recognize me," she paused for a few seconds before posing her own question,

"Do you know who I am?"

I didn't really understand the question she asked, but the way dad reacted, it seemed he knew what she was talking about.

"Justine, can you excuse us, please? I think I need to explain further to Callie what this is all about. The kitchen is down the hallway, make yourself comfortable."

I watched Justine as she made her way down the hallway and out of sight. Stan followed her and I heard them talking. I immediately questioned dad, as to why he sent her out of the room.

"What is it dad, why did you have to send her out of the room?"

"Because I think it should come from me what needs to be said next."

Those words worried me, what did he mean?

"You see, mom never spoke about her childhood very much. All we know is that she grew up in an orphanage, right?"

I nodded to acknowledge this was what mom had told us when I was little.

"Well, you see Justine was also in the orphanage."

"Is Justine mom's long lost friend then? But…that wouldn't explain why they look so similar?"

After I finished my thought, I realized what he was trying to say without dad even having to tell me.

"Is Justine mom's… sister? Are they twins?"

"Yes sweetheart, they are sisters. They were separated when they were seven years old."

Now I felt horrible for treating Justine the way I had.

Did I have to call her Aunt Justine now? It wasn't like I really knew her?

"What does this mean now? Is she staying with us?"

Dad nodded.

"She's going to stay here until we get this case sorted out. She helped us with some new leads about the possibility of a cabin today."

"You mean to say, mom is still alive?"

You could see dad take a step back mentally in what he was about to say.

"Yes, we believe she is still alive."

"How though, what evidence do you have to prove that?"

After mom had gone missing, dad and I used to play detective and try to solve cases. I felt like this was one of those games.

My dad normally never fumbled, but you could tell he was trying to choose his words carefully. I knew why—to him I was still his little girl, even though I was practically a young woman that was taking care of him.

"She was seen just a few days ago, the day I went to the Johnson house."

My world stopped. What did he mean she had been seen just a few days ago? This was not making any sense.

He must have seen the simultaneous confused and horrified looks on my face, because he continued on quickly.

"Justine has been keeping a watch over the house, she saw her."

My mood changed back to anger immediately. Justine had known where my mother was, that she was actually alive, and hadn't told anyone until now?

"Why didn't she come forward sooner?" I blurted out.

Thinking that it was impossible to cry any more tears at this point, I was surprised to feel more spill out from my eyes. Dad was speechless, he had no words to answer my question. All of a sudden, Justine appeared in the door way of the living room and spoke.

"Because I was scared. I thought if I came forward that Darren would hurt your mother. I thought I was protecting her, protecting everyone, by staying quiet. I know you're upset and angry with me; I deserve that, but I'm here now and working with the detectives to find her and bring her home."

Dad and I looked between each other and back to her. I think I finally understood her motives.

"I'm sorry for taking my anger out on you Justine, you can imagine how much pain dad and I have gone through all these years."

"I know, I completely understand. I hope one day you can find it in your hearts to forgive me. I am cooperating and answering every question that I can. I'm not going anywhere, as I want to find her just as much as you both do."

I could sense she was truly sorry, and was willing to work with dad and the rest of the detectives to find mom. At this point, none of us knew what else to say; we were exhausted, and everything that had needed to be said, had been said. I think we all just needed time to process all the changes.

I wanted to make amends with Justine to let her known I truly accepted her apology. I rose from the couch and walked over to where she was standing in the doorway. I peered into her eyes, and I could see the hurt that was hidden behind her gaze. As much as dad and I had been hurting, Justine was too, it was evident.

"We are in this together, we're a team now, and teams stick together. We will bring mom back—Lily back."

She nodded and I could see her eyes well up, and in that moment I pulled her into a hug. Dad joined us as we stood in the doorway of the living room. We needed each other equally, this was what was going to get us through.

Though, I couldn't stop asking myself if we were too late, and if all our efforts would prove fruitless in the end. I actually didn't know if I could honestly believe whether we would find mom alive or dead at this point.

THIRTY-TWO

Murray

I had barely slept at all the night before, I was completely restless. All the events from the last couple of days had begun to wear me out. With the new developments surrounding the case, we had everyone working around the clock. I had never seen the police department work together as a team as they were on this case, but I knew it was because it was one of their own family members. While I knew that shouldn't have been an excuse, as every case was important, it was the truth.

Regardless, I needed to get up and go to work. I didn't really know what to do with Justine, though. Obviously I hadn't thought this through well, or what I would do with her during the day when I made the split decision to bring her home last night. I was obligated now to ensure her safety. I know Lily would want me to ensure she was safe if she knew.

As much as Callie seemed to have forgiven Justine, I wasn't certain she would be up to staying with her all day while I was at work. I sensed I wasn't going to be faced with Justine running away again this time, so I contemplated leaving her at the house alone. I believed she had finally understood how important her side of the story was in this matter, and that she was the piece to this puzzle that we had been longing for all these years.

I realized lying in bed wouldn't do much good. I finally stretched and pulled myself to the edge of the bed. I sat for a few seconds , when a knock sounded on the bedroom door.

"Come in," I replied groggily.

I turned to see who had knocked, to see Justine's frail body standing in the doorway.

"Sir, I made you breakfast. Would you like it in here, or at the table?"

I was confused why Justine felt as though she had to make me breakfast, she was not obligated to do anything during her stay here… and why had she called me sir?

"That is very nice of you, but you didn't have to go to the trouble, and please, call me Keith."

"I can't do that, not yet. You don't know how much it means to me that you took me in like this, I actually finally feel safe for the first time in a long time."

I sunk a little; her feeling safe was one of my top priorities. Even with that, I needed to be careful with my words and actions. She had been through enough already.

"I'll be out in just a few minutes. I'll meet you in the kitchen."

Standing to pick up my cell phone to check for messages I peered back over my shoulder. I saw Justine staring around the room. I could see emotions rise inside her as she took in her surroundings.

"She painted it exactly how we drew it when we were children…."

A tear escaped her, but she quickly wiped it away from her cheek. I wasn't entirely sure what she had meant by that statement.

"What do you mean? Lily loved to paint and told me the day we moved in she had to paint the bedroom like this," I told her, gesturing around the room.

"We made a scrapbook back at the orphanage and promised that when we were older and had our own home, we would paint each room with different flowers…" she trailed off.

The only room that had painted flowers on the wall was our bedroom. It had roses and lilies, but I never understood why. All she told me was that she had to decorate it with those specific flowers.

"This is how the bedroom looked back at Darren's house, I didn't want to forget Lily. I have never forgotten her."

You could sense the passion, and the heartache, that Justine was feeling. I didn't know how to respond. Lily had never spoken about having a sister, let alone a twin for that matter. Then again, Lily had never elaborated about her past, especially her childhood. I had never pressed her for information, but I sensed something wasn't right or that something happened all those years ago that made her not want to talk about it.

"I'm sure Lily will be thrilled to see you."

This comment seemed to shake Justine out of her daze and continued to peer around the room

"Are you sure? If she never told you she had a twin, then she must have forgotten about me."

My heart was breaking for this woman. I stood and made my way around the bed to stand in front of Justine. I placed my hands on either side of her shoulders, and looked her straight in the eyes.

"You are welcome here, you're family. We will all get through this. She's out there, and we will bring her home. Lily will be happy to be reunited with you—that I am sure of."

Suddenly, Justine put her arms around me and squeezed me in a way that pulled at my heart strings. I was relieved she trusted me. I couldn't imagine how hard it must be to trust another man after what Darren had done to her. Now, I needed to protect her and ensure her safety. Justine pulled away first from the embrace, and wiped away the tears that had streaked down her face.

"Thank you."

It was all she could manage to say between tiny sobs.

"Breakfast smells delicious, why don't we head down to the kitchen and enjoy what you prepared."

We made our way down the hallway and stairs to the kitchen. Callie was already awake and sitting at the table when we walked in. I gave her a smile and a kiss on her forehead.

"Morning sweetheart, did you sleep well?"

I made my way to the coffee maker and poured a cup, while I awaited Callie's answer.

"I was restless, but I'm okay."

Walking over to the table, I sat with Callie as Justine pulled pancakes, eggs, and bacon out of the oven where she had been keeping them warm.

Callie smiled as Justine placed a plate full of delicious breakfast foods in front of her. You could tell she was amazed, because her eyes widen. I wasn't much of a cook, and I knew Callie did her best with preparing the meals when she could, but this was something Lily would have done on a regular basis—she loved to cook. I realized how similar Lily and Justine actually were while watching Justine move about the kitchen. I always knew twins had a special connection and wondered if the theory, that twins had an inner bond was true, and whether Justine could actually feel what Lily was experiencing? I shook my head at that crazy thought, knowing it must have been a myth. With that thought leaving me, I dug into the plate in front of me, but peered back up to where Justine was hovered over the kitchen sink.

"Are you going to join us, Justine? There is plenty here for you, too."

She looked hesitant, but spoke.

"I need to wash these pans and dishes, sir."

"We can worry about that later, please, come join us."

She still stood almost stone-like, staring at me. Had she really never sat down for a meal? Had she been made to clean every minute of the day? I realized that I really didn't know anything Justine had gone through. The little things we took for granted seemed huge for her.

I gave her a reassuring smile and waved her to join us. She moved slowly, pulling out a chair and taking a seat between Callie and I. I loaded a plate up for her, just as she had ours, and watched her eyes widen. It made me realize Justine probably hadn't eaten in some time, or if she had, it must have been very little. I stopped piling it up and smiled at her for reassurance that I meant what I said about her being accepted into this house, and that I would keep her safe—that included feeding her properly.

We all sat in silence, enjoying our breakfast together, when my cell phone began to ring faintly in my robe pocket. I excused myself from the table and made my way up the stairs to my bedroom. On the last ring, I answered without checking the call display.

"Hello?"

"Murray, it's Captain."

I plopped down on the bed as I realized it was never a good sign when the Captain called you directly.

"What's going on?"

"We seem to have narrowed down the area for the cabin to three possible wooded areas. We've been working all night to figure this out."

Any news was always a relief, and I slumped forward to listen more closely to what he had to say.

"Just outside North Vancouver there's a wooded area, north of West Vancouver there is another, and the third is further north, about 2 hours from here that could also be a possibility."

"Do we know which is the more likely place to begin with?"

It was great that we had narrowed it down, but we could be completely wrong all at the same time—there were a lot of wooded areas here in British Columbia, and that was assuming the cabin was even in the province. I wasn't ready to put all my hope in the fact that we would actually locate her at any of these locations, but it was a start, a very good start.

"That's what I was hoping you could tell me, or maybe Mrs. Johnson could tell us."

Oh crap.

I hadn't told Captain that I had brought Justine home, and I had pretty much backed myself into a corner now.

"Well…maybe start with the two outside North and West Vancouver, since they're the closest. Do we have enough bodies to hit both at the same time?

"No, we don't have that kind of man power, Murray. Looking at the map, both places are pretty large areas. It's going to take us days to get through just one, I believe. We're going to have to set up shifts in order to cover all three areas."

"Let's start with the closest one that seems the most logical."

"I'll have someone go over to the motel and pick Mrs. Johnson up, that way she'll be here when you get here."

The line went silent as I attempted to figure out how to break the news to Captain. Regardless that Justine was related, she was a witness and protocol stated you could not take a witness home with you.

"Well, is that alright?"

"I have her here. I'll bring her in and we can talk to her about the locations."

Captain's heavy sigh was heard over the phone. When he spoke, his voice was laced with anger.

"You know you can't be taking home witnesses. This goes against protocol! I don't care if she is family, you could be suspended for this!"

"I know, but she's my sister-in-law—family."

"I understand. This doesn't look good Murray, it doesn't look good one bit!"

"She is family now, I need to protect her."

I don't think Captain knew what to say, because the next words out of his mouth were still laden with anger.

"The both of you had better get in here right away, and I am not done with this conversion. You hear me?"

"We will be there within the hour."

The Captain hung up first, without a goodbye, but I didn't take it personally. I tossed my phone onto the bed and pulled some clothes off the chair. It didn't seem as though I had much time for a shower, considering the demands of the Captain.

I made my way back down the hallway towards the stairs and then into the kitchen where I found Callie and Justine laughing—it was a pleasant sound and both seemed to be happy. I wish that I hadn't had to break it up, but Captain would have my head if I didn't present Justine to him soon.

"Ladies, I'm sorry to have to break this up, but Justine and I are due at the station within the hour."

Callie's smile dropped suddenly.

"Is everything okay, do they have new information?"

She always knew when something was going on, I couldn't hide anything from her.

"They've found three possible wooded areas where this cabin might be. Justine and I need to go in and try to figure out which one is the most likely place we think Darren may have taken mom."

"Why can't they just search them all?"

"We don't have enough units to do that sweetheart, we have to choose one and work from there. It's not easy."

I could see the disappointment in her face, but there was nothing more I could do. Justine fell silent. I knew I had told her I didn't think she would be needed anymore, and I felt as though I was going back on my word.

"I'm sorry Justine to have to pull you back in, it's Captain's orders, though."

"I know sir, it's the only way we're going to find her. I'm willing to do anything it takes to bring this family back together."

We all looked between one another as those words left Justine's mouth, it was the first time we realized that we were a family even if it had only been discovered within the last few days. We all wanted the same thing at this point—the return of Lily.

"We're doing everything we can, all we can do is keep going. Nobody is giving up until we find her— and him, too, for that matter."

This seemed to ease the tension growing in the room. Justine stood and gathered all the plates and piled them in the sink. She didn't have much when she came here, so I offered for her to wear some clothes of Lily's. At first she didn't want them, but she couldn't keep going around in the same clothes that I had seen her in over the last few months.

Once I pulled my briefcase together, Justine and I climbed into my car and made our way to the station. The car ride was silent, just as it had been when I had brought her home the night before. I needed to warn her about Captain—I didn't need her to get spooked by his temper.

"I broke protocol when I brought you home last night. My Captain is feeling the pressure now."

I glanced out of the corner of my eye to gauge her reaction to what I had shared with her. It didn't seem to faze her. She stayed silent.

"He may ask you some hard questions. Just answer them the best you can. I'll be there to support you through it all."

I could see her biting her lip as I glanced between the road and her. I hadn't wanted to scare her, but I needed to warn her. I had been very soft on her, but Captain wouldn't be. He wanted answers, and he would make sure he got them right away. That had always been his moto. The fragility Justine had shown from the beginning is why I had tried to conduct all the interviews myself. Truthfully, if I had let the Captain conduct and lead the interviews, I don't believe we would be where we were today in this investigation.

"I understand. I'll give up all that I know—if it will save Lily."

That was the entire point now, to save Lily. We knew she had been alive several days ago, but anything could have happened between then and now. All we could do was be hopeful that she had either escaped, or was still being kept alive.

THIRTY-THREE

Lily

It had been another day of walking these woods, and I felt as though I was not getting any closer to civilization. If anything, I felt I was moving away from any sign of human life. I had come upon a few clearings, but nothing had lead to anywhere in particular. I tried walking in all three directions, attempting to remember which way I had already been. Using the direction of the sun as my compass to navigate through these woods had been the only hope I had.

I spotted nobody and heard no vehicles, but had come across much wildlife. In the back of my mind, I did fear bears lived in these woods, but we were too close to the city for bears, or so I hoped. I actually had no clue how close to the city we were. I sensed we hadn't driven too far, but I couldn't get a sense of my surroundings when I was stuffed in the bed of Darren's truck under a cover. I had been focused on breathing because of the lack of oxygen and smell of animal residue it had.

My legs were growing tired, and I needed to rest. Finding a log, I plunked down and rubbed my legs and feet. They were cramping and going numb from all the walking I had done. I had been forcing myself to keep going even when I grew tired. Right now, I was running on pure adrenaline, as it was my only way to keep my hope alive and keep pressing onward.

As I sat there, looking out into the dead woods, my mind began to wander back to a couple of days ago.

Had I actually killed Darren?

I knew I used to have the strength to do something like that, but after fighting him for years I never expected I could actually knock him out. I was sure he would come after me eventually; he knew how to hunt and find his prey easily enough.

I had been with him for six years—six *long* years for that matter, where I endured everything under the sun. I would never have imagined lasting as long as I had. I was sure that he wouldn't keep me around once he realized I wasn't who I said I was. With Darren's hallucinations, it never seemed as though he caught on, that was until that knock on the door a few days ago.

What stuck out the most during my dreadful stay with Darren, was when he had taken me to the abortion clinic within the first few months of my kidnapping. I knew he wasn't my husband, but that day continued to haunt me even six years later. To know I had ended a poor child's life that day and it hurt me. Part of me ached to take that moment back, but part of me was relieved because raising a child under those circumstances would not have been good. I had to continue to remind myself that it was the best decision under the circumstances; even if I'd had no say in the decision—a true blessing in disguise.

As I sat there slumped forward, I felt as though all the energy in me had drained. I needed to eat. Water was only going to do so much before my body would completely shut down on me.

Suddenly, hearing a noise, I jumped up from the log I was seated on. I had already crossed paths with enough wild animals, but every sound still echoed through me. As I peered around, I saw nothing. Suddenly more rustling of leaves and branches could be heard.

I began spinning around in circles, setting myself into a daze. My breathing became heavier and I was becoming dizzy. I was most likely panicking for no reason, it had probably been the wind or a squirrel. I slowed down, and really looked around me to discover absolutely nothing was there. I brought my breathing back to a steady pace and assured myself it had just been my mind playing tricks on me.

I turned back to take a seat on the log to continue resting for a little while longer, when I came face to face with what had been making the noise—it was not my mind at all. It was real, and he was standing right there, only a few feet away from where I stood.

"Did you miss me?" he snarled with a sarcastic smile upon his face.

I moved away, taking several steps back while my mind was attempting to process how Darren had managed to find me here. It was next to impossible! It had been two days since I had run from the cabin, thinking that I had killed him. I kept taking steps back until I tripped backwards on a tree root. My focus was not to let Darren out of my sight, landing on my ass as I fell backwards, I immediately crab walked as I crawled backwards along the ground until I hit my head against a tree. I pulled my legs towards my chest as I continued to stare him down.

Fear over took me as he stared at me with anger in his eyes. I couldn't say a word. I was completely focused on his movements. I didn't know what to say but, in my mind I had been certain Darren would not be getting up off the ground when I had been done with him back at the cabin. I truly thought the deed had been done and my focus had been on finding myself help and getting back to my family.

"Well, aren't you going to answer me?" he taunted.

Darren stepped closer. I could see him limping slightly. He obviously had some damage to his knees, but not enough to keep him down. I was truly surprised he had been able to track me down. It dawned on me that he had his truck, and perhaps that was how he had found me so quickly, but I hadn't heard any engines around before I heard the rustle of leaves and branches.

"You know you can't out run me, you're lucky you even made it this far. Did you really think you were going to get away successfully?"

I remained silent. My mind was thinking a mile a minute and had become confused. I felt as though I was trapped, officially trapped, and this was going to be the end of me—end of my life. After what I had done to him, he had every right to kill me, right here, right now.

"I… I…"

I couldn't even form any words. I was shaking. My whole body had begun to tense because I had absolutely no idea what was to come next. I knew Darren was extremely volatile and unpredictable.

"Cat got your tongue now? You were all words the last time we spoke, what's changed?"

He laughed a hearty, evil laugh as he spoke his words. I tried to find words to speak, but nothing was coming to me very easily.

"I… I…thought you were dead."

I don't even think he heard me, because my voice was as small as a mouse.

"Well I'm here, aren't I? So you couldn't have killed me like you thought you did. If you thought a blow to the knees and a blow to the side of my head was going to stop me from coming after you, you were dead wrong. It had me down for a bit, but I bounced back, didn't I?"

I thought I had done quite a number on him, and was sure the force had knocked him out cold—dead cold.

"I can see that, clearly."

"You haven't lost your attitude I see, but I'm sure you will lose it when I get ahold of you."

He moved forward, but I already had my back against the tree and nowhere else to go unless I tried to get up and run. As he moved closer and was only mere inches away from me, I darted to the side, stumbled, rose to my feet, and bolted. I didn't know where I was headed, but I knew I needed to get out of there and run like the wind.

I had a pretty good idea about what his intentions were, but I wasn't ready to find out for sure; and regardless of how weak I was, I found the strength to keep running, and run fast. In my case, my life mattered more than being tired and weak. It was difficult being in the woods because of all the debris beneath my feet. I was concentrating on my footing while I attempted my escape.

I tried my best to peer over my shoulder to see where Darren was, but I shouldn't have. He had jumped back in his truck, which he had hid behind some trees, and was mowing down the brush as he came after me in his truck. Branches were flying in every direction as he moved his way through the narrow opening of the woods.

Thinking on my feet, I decided to weave my path. I was taught if someone was running after you with a gun, it would be harder for them to hit you if you were zig zagging. Obviously he didn't have a gun on me, but he did have a big truck coming after me. In my eyes, it was the same thing.

I could hear him yelling at me but I couldn't make out his words, I don't think I really would have wanted to hear them even if I could.

Not stopping, I continued to weave. It was causing me to become dizzy, but I fought it. I was not about to stop, not even for a split second. I gave up looking back because I could hear his truck ripping through the brush and the sound of his engine gaining on me.

Am I going to be able to out run his truck?

Were the types of thoughts invading my mind, despite how hard I tried to shake them away. My chest was becoming heavy, and my legs felt weak and wobbly. I could feel myself slowing down—running in zig zags takes up a lot of energy.

I heard a short popping sound that I thought came from the truck running over branches. I turned back to investigate, wishing instantly that I hadn't—the sound had been produced by what was being held in his hand. He had it pointing directly at me—a gun. I was close enough to see Darren had his finger on the trigger, which meant he could, and would, pull it at any time now. I turned back to face the direction I was running in and continued my zig zagging pattern through the woods as I prayed. By some grace, I needed faith on my side at that very moment. Having a gun pointed directly at me made me feel queasy.

The sound of multiple shots rang out all around me—he was firing at me. With my mind becoming confused as to what I should do next, I wasn't paying attention to my footing and stumbled over a root, causing me to land on my hands and knees, hard.

I turned back quickly to see Darren's truck rolling to a stop about twenty feet away. I tried to get up, but kept stumbling. Finally, making my way to a standing position, I was shaking like a leaf, mainly for the fact Darren had gained so much ground on me, and so quickly. He had already hopped out the truck and was coming at me with his gun still positioned in his hand, with his finger on the trigger. His arm was outstretched pointing directly at me as he moved closer. He didn't flinch, but rather held a steady grip on his weapon as he moved his feet over the broken twigs and branches.

I was finally able to make it to my feet with my back to him, but another loud 'pop' rang through me. I felt weak, dizzy, and a warm liquid beginning to drip down my leg. As I looked down towards the warm sensation that was enlightening my body, my vision blurred as I saw a dark red trail leading to the ground below me.

He shot me. The bastard actually shot me.

I couldn't move at all, I was affixed to the ground beneath me—frozen in time. I felt hands around me, as I was now being pulled backwards. I looked up towards the sky, but it was darkening as my eyes began to close on me. I could hear the door to his truck open, and felt as though I was being pushed up onto the seat, though I found myself slumped over once he had me inside. I was too weak to hold up my own body weight any longer. My body felt numb, with only a feeling of pressure in my leg escaping.

I heard the truck engine start up, and Darren beginning to drive away, jolting me around in my seat as he drove over the uneven surface of the woods.

"Maybe that will keep you in one place now. I didn't think I would have to use that type of force on you, but you left me no choice."

Darren's voice echoed through my throbbing head as I tried to focus on what he was saying, but my mind was completely lost.

"Did it teach you a lesson? I don't know how you thought you could outrun me. Nobody outruns me, not my wife, or you."

I managed to say a few words, but I had no idea if they were actually audible or not.

"I had to try, I was trying to save my life... and for your information, you wife *did* outrun you. She isn't here, remember?"

I figured it didn't matter what I said to him anymore, because at this rate I was sure I would be dead soon enough. I wanted my last words to be memorable.

Darren wasn't giving up, though, he always had to have the last word.

"Saving your life? Do you know where you have been for the past six years? I am your life, or at least I was your life."

I couldn't comprehend him, falling onto the door as the weakness completely overtook my body. I wanted to move, but it was as if I was turning to stone. Every limb felt heavy, even blinking had become a struggle.

Was this it? Would he finally end me like he said he would all those years before?

My eyes finally closed and I drifted out of the world around me, maybe I could have the peace I had been desperately longing for.

THIRTY-FOUR

Callie

Dad and Justine had left and headed to the station, leaving me at home alone, again. I hadn't expected the news I had received last night, nor expected dad to bring Justine back to our home. A warning may have been helpful, but then again, would I have mentally lost it at him over the phone?

From the sounds of things, we were getting closer to a possible location. I didn't know much of what had transpired at the house dad had gone to with the search warrant, but if it had been anything substantial, I'm sure he would have told me.

Finding out mom had been alive all these years had been a huge relief. As disappointing as it was to know the kidnapper had left the property before they arrived with the search warrant, I was sure they would find the man. I understood where Justine was coming from with her attempt to keep everyone safe; but part of me was torn about being angry at her, knowing that mom had still been here, close by, and alive.

I walked down the hallway to my father's room, the master bedroom. I didn't like going in there too often, because it reminded me of mom. She had painted beautiful flowers on the walls. I remembered back to when I had asked her why she had painted them, with her telling me it was in memory of someone, but never elaborated past that. I took a seat on the bed and looked around. Dad had maintained it just the way mom had left it all. We hadn't change much about the house overall, because we wanted it to be the same for mom when she returned, in hopes it would be comforting for her.

Pictures of mom lined the tall dresser across from the bed. I stood and walked over to inspect them more closely. Some were of mom when her and dad and had first met, another was of their wedding day, and there was even a picture of me when I had been born and was lying on mom's chest. Even though he didn't have any of the three of us as a family displayed, I knew we had pictures taken, but I had never seen them framed or hanging around the house as these others were.

A tear fell from my eye onto the dresser. It had been hard to move on, to keep living, when an important family member was no longer with me. Dad and I tried our best to be strong for each other, attempting not to show weakness to one another in fear we would weaken the other's faith.

As I moved along the dresser, I spotted a small box, the size and likeness of a jewellery box. I didn't recall ever seeing it before. It was secured with a lock, but no key accompanied it on the dresser. Feeling around the box for any other opening, I felt something taped on the underside.

Blindly pulling the key free from the tape on the bottom of the box and setting it down on the dresser, I saw it was a small silver key. It looked to be the size that would fit in the lock. I took the box and key, and sat on the bed.

I slowly inserted the key into the lock, making a single turn to the right. I felt the lock give way, and I removed it from the latch. I didn't know what to expect when I opened it, but as I pushed the lid back it revealed what appeared to be envelopes. There had to have been at least thirty or forty of them crammed inside the box. They were all small, letter sized, and none of them had mailing addresses or stamps on. They were all addressed to a Rose-Marie Sinclair.

I hesitated as to what I should have done next. These were obviously not meant for my eyes, but who was Rose-Marie? My curiosity got the better of me, and I pulled one out, setting the box with the rest of the letters still enclosed within its tiny walls down next to me.

Slowly, I turned it over and pulled out a single sheet of notepaper, recognizing my mother's neat handwriting across the page, I was hesitant to go any further, however I had made it this far and I needed to know why the box had been locked. I felt that reading whatever this was would give me that answer. With a heartbeat that was growing faster by the minute, I took a long breath in and peered down at the words written.

August 19, 1988
Dear Rose-Marie,

311

It has been twelve years since I was adopted. A nice family by the name of Hannigan took me in when I was nine. They died three years ago in a car accident, a private service was held. I miss them dearly.

I was their only child, and they provided me with the best years of my life. They only wanted the best for me, even though they struggled themselves. I was sent to a private school until I was sixteen, but then I dropped out, finding a job to help with the bills and put food on the table. They had given me a lot, and I owed them for their sacrifices. Being selfless individuals, they taught me that having each other was enough, and to never give up on my dreams.

I never moved away from Vancouver, I am still living here. I moved to Richmond to obtain a nursing degree. I have been a nurse for the past two years and I enjoy what I do, but am still learning. Every time I walk into a patient's room and see flowers, I think of you. Whenever I see any flower, the memories of us at the orphanage come flooding back.

I have tried searching for you, but I don't know if you have changed your name. I couldn't find any documents under Rose-Marie Sinclair, except your birth certificate. The only name that has been close is a Justine Sinclair Johnson. I do hope you are doing well, and enjoying the life you have now.

All my love,
Lily-May

Tears fell as I picked up and read letter after letter. Mom was writing letters to Justine, proving she remembered and cared about her. My heart broke even more. My mother had been hurting, hurting deeply that she had lost her sister from her life. It was obvious by the numerous letters that had been written that she had missed Justine very much.

I placed the letters back inside the box, in the order in which I had taken them out, one by one. Locking the lock and placing the key back on the underside of the box, I placed the box back on the dresser. To us, it had just looked like part of the dresser, but to mom, it had been a very special item—a part of her private, lost world.

Since dad had told me about Justine, I couldn't stop wondering why mom had never spoke of her past. Growing up, she told me she would tell me one day, when I was older and could understand. Now that I was older, I wanted to know what it had been like for her growing up. I couldn't imagine what life had been like growing up in an orphanage. I imagined it felt as though you were unwanted. All I could gather was that she had been nine years old before a family took notice of her.

An abrupt knock on the front door brought me out of my day dreaming. It startled me. I wasn't expecting dad and Justine home for some time. Before I could react, it sounded again, this time louder and more urgent.

I made my way down the stairs to a muffled voice coming from the other side of the front door. I froze, remembering that night mom had disappeared—the man's voice had been muffled through the door.

"Callie! Callie, open up, it's Detective Gresham."

Feeling relieved, I unlocked and opened the door. She looked out of breath standing there, panting. It was unusual for her to come in this manner. I couldn't imagine what the urgency was.

Moving to the side, I let her in closing the door behind her. I directed her to the living room.

"What's the matter? I've never seen you like this?

"We believe we located the woods the cabin is in, we're only ninety percent sure but that's closer than we have ever been before"

Had we entered the final step in locating mom? The question drifted through my mind.

"What does that mean? Are they going in to find her?"

"Right now they've mapped out the area, it's not small by any means. The only way in and out is on a single main road. It's rural, but believed to have man-made trails once inside the area. We're covering all our bases. Unfortunately, we don't have the man power to cover the entire place in one go, but we're going to do our best with what we have and keep going forward. It could be a few days before we locate anything, or anyone."

In a way this was good news, but also bad news.

What if this wasn't the correct woods and they had wasted all their efforts in that one place?

I had to push these thoughts to the back of my mind, stay positive, and have faith this would all work out.

"What can we do in the meantime? You're going to be out there looking for her, right?" I asked her excitedly.

"Not exactly…" Gresham looked down at the floor, almost as if she were ashamed.

"I was asked to watch you and Justine, to ensure you're both kept safe. We want you both here in this house while the search is being carried out. If the man who kidnapped your mom gets any tips that the police are close, we don't want him coming after you...or Justine."

314

"What about Justine? Does he know she's staying here?"

"We don't think so, but we can't be one hundred percent sure. This is why we need to keep you both safe. I need you to tell Stan while we move forward on this lead, he can't come around here. While I'm stationed inside here, we're also going to have an unmarked car parked outside for extra measure."

How dangerous was this man if they were going to all this trouble to protect us?

It was another serious question I had, and I knew Gresham would be truthful with me. We had a bond, and I trusted her.

"How dangerous is he, the man you're searching for, the one who's with mom?"

It took her a moment before she answered. I felt she was choosing her words carefully. Everyone seemed to choose their words carefully lately when they spoke to me about this case. I felt as though they thought I was made of glass and would shatter if they told me the truth, but I had a strong soul and was prepared to hear anything—good or bad.

"He could be very dangerous. We don't know much about him, though from the information Justine has provided us with, it seems he can become violent very easily."

I think she realized what she said and wanted to take it back, but she had already said it. The man that had my mother was dangerous and it confirmed my fears that mom had not been in a safe place for all those years. I couldn't imagine what condition she was in right now, or how she had even survived through all of this.

"I'm sorry, I shouldn't have said that." The colour had drained from Gresham's face, and she looked as though she had seen a ghost.

I answered her with a smile on my face, with the most confident tone I could muster.

"I needed to know. I more or less realized mom could be in rough shape. Who would kidnap someone for this long and not harm them?"

She gave me a shrugging gesture of '*I know*' but couldn't actually speak the words. I had come to realize that mom had to have endured some sort of harm, but to what extent I didn't want to think about.

I pulled out my phone to text Stan, but felt this was worth a call instead. I felt terrible having to tell him he couldn't see me already, what with just recently starting this whole dating and officially calling ourselves a couple. His phone continued to ring until the last ring before his voicemail was to sound.

"Hey Callie! What's up? How are you?"

"I'm okay…" I answered tentatively.

I needed to cut to the chase and not drag it out, otherwise it would be more painful.

"Hey, so, Stan… you won't be able to come by my place for a few days, and I won't be at school either. Would you mind taking notes and collecting my homework for me?"

The line went quiet. I didn't normally miss class unless I had the flu or was terribly sick, which was pretty much never.

"Are you feeling okay? Are you sick?" Clearly Stan knew me better than I had thought.

"No, but there have been some new developments in my mom's case. They think it's best I stay at home until this is all over."

"What's going on? It doesn't sound safe."

I didn't really know what to say, or how to say it, because I knew he wasn't family but he had been there for me through everything over the past six years. I looked to Gresham for answers, but she shrugged her shoulders with uncertainty.

"They think they located the woods my mom is in, but they don't know the condition she is in or if the kidnapper will come back. It's more just a precaution. I won't be alone, I'll be with Justine and Gresham."

"Justine? Who's Justine?"

I realized I hadn't filled him in since this whole ordeal had occurred last night. After Stan had followed Justine to the kitchen, making sure she was okay, he had slipped out the back door as to not interrupt dad and I talking in the living room. I wish he hadn't done that.

"Well, she is sort of like family, I guess. She's my mom's sister, her twin actually."

Stan didn't say anything.

I felt the awkward silence growing, so I jumped in.

"Remember that woman I ran after that day a few weeks ago?"

"Yes."

"That's Justine."

"The one who's been watching you for years, and causing you to be concerned when you walk to and from school?" His voice sounded almost accusatory.

"Yes, her. I know it's a complicated story but I'll be okay. I'll keep in touch with you."

I peered over to Gresham who carried a confused look on her face. I realized dad may have not told her about my sightings of Justine.

"Okay, well... I'll catch you later," I chirped into the phone, and hung up abruptly; tossing it onto the couch.

317

Gresham immediately began questioning my conversation.

"What do you mean Justine's been watching you for years?"

"On and off I would see someone out of the corner of my eye who appeared to look like mom, but when I would turn to look, they were gone…"

I trailed off and looked down at my hands, which were becoming increasingly fidgety with each passing minute.

"I thought I was seeing mom's ghost, as if she were actually dead. I found out a few days ago it had been Justine. I got close to her one day just as she got into a cab, but other than that she had been watching me from a distance."

"If she had been watching you for years, why did she not come forward sooner?"

I felt this was not my place to say.

"Maybe dad can explain it, I don't think it's my place to say and I probably don't know all the details. I know this is all very confusing. This kidnapper has a lot of explaining to do when dad gets his hands on him, that's for sure. Do you think you will find them alive?"

She paused before speaking.

"We hope to, but of course I won't sit here promising you that we will. We're all hoping it all works out for the better."

Without warning, the front door swung open and dad walked through it with Justine in tow. She looked exhausted, and her eyes were red and puffy, as if she had been crying. She didn't look at me, but instead, walked down the hallway and into the bathroom. I gave dad a look of raised eyebrows to see if he would give me any information. Instead of offering me any clues, he stood with his head down.

Gresham got up and walked over and began speaking to dad in a low whisper, which irritated me. Anything that could be said to dad, could be said to me. This case affected me just as much as it affected him, and I wanted to be in the loop.

"What's going on dad?" I asked sternly, interrupting their conversation.

I wasn't going to continue to sit by and not be in the know of anything that pertained to mom any longer.

"Nothing, dear."

"It doesn't sound like nothing dad, I know when you're trying to hide something. Please. Tell me what's going on."

They both looked at each other and moved further into the room.

"Justine is going to be taking a rest. I don't want you to disturb her, or ask her questions. She's been through enough. Do you understand me?"

I still didn't know what was going on but dad's tone said it all. I had to respect him when he asked me to obey.

"Yes dad, I'll help her if she needs me."

"That would be great; I know you will keep an eye on her. All she needs is some rest."

"Where are you going now?" I asked, hoping he would actually provide me with an answer.

"I'm headed with the rest of the team to the woods we believe the cabin is in."

"Where mom and her kidnapper are? Where's that?" I prodded, attempting to lure a location out of him.

"We can't speculate, but we hope to find something," he replied, clearly catching onto the purpose for my line of questioning. I decided to give up and let him provide me with the details when he felt comfortable.

"When will you be back?"

"I don't know, could be a few days. It depends if this is the right place and we find what we're looking for. I won't stop until the whole place has been searched. I'll call Gresham with updates as I know them, I promise. I know you will be okay here, keep your strength up. Everything will work out."

What could I really say to that? Tell him not to go? I was afraid of what this kidnapper would do if he was out there on the loose.

"Can you promise me one thing, dad?"

He looked at me with confusion, as I had never asked him to promise me anything before but this was important.

"I can try, honey. What is it?"

"Can you promise that you will stay safe, because we don't know what this man is capable of?"

He looked at Gresham and then back at me. I guess he didn't think Gresham would have told me their opinions of the man, but I was thankful she had kept me in the loop that this man was not exactly a bed of roses and he was extremely dangerous.

"I will do everything I can. Don't worry about me."

Justine appeared in the doorway next to dad, and spoke in a soft voice.

"I'm going to take a rest in the spare room."

Immediately I wanted to help her, you could tell she looked weak.

"Is there anything I can get you? Water? Something to eat?"

She shook her head silently and turned to walk up the stairs. Whatever had happened at the station had hit Justine hard.

I looked back at dad. I wanted to ask him what had happened so I knew how to best help her. She didn't look herself. I mean, we had just been laughing this morning.

"What happened at the station dad? Justine doesn't seem right at all?"

He fidgeted before speaking, and a few seconds went by with an uncomfortable silence looming over the room.

"Captain lead the interview, he was asking her some tough questions, even making assumptions that were not true. It was a hard interview, one of the hardest she's been through. I know she will pull through, but please, leave her alone until she's ready."

There was not much more I could say, but respect dad and let it go. I was sure Justine would come around eventually

"I'm going to head up and pack an overnight bag, I really can't say how long I'll be out there, but I have to be prepared for anything."

I watched as he went upstairs, and then turned to Gresham. I wasn't sure why my emotions were running high all of sudden. A tear escaped me and Gresham pulled me into a hug, rubbing my back in circles.

THIRTY-FIVE

Murray

Driving on the highway towards the outer part of Vancouver took much longer than I had expected. The rest of the team left before me. With me having to take Justine back to the house and pack an overnight bag, they wanted to get started as quickly as possible. I wasn't planning on leaving the woods until I found them; we were too close to let any mistakes slip. However, I was simply going on the assumption that this was the correct forested area we were headed to and that we weren't about to waste any time searching the wrong area.

The interview with Captain and Justine had not gone as I had expected it would have. Even though Captain seemed to have calmed down by the time we had arrived, he drilled Justine for answers to the point of Justine breaking down. I had seen her cry on a number of occasions, but this time had been different. She was shaking uncontrollably, and nearly hyperventilating at points. Captain insinuated and pretty much accused her of partaking in Lily's kidnapping and disappearance. When that happened I had to step in—I had sat there quietly up to that point, allowing Captain to ask his questions, but I was not going to allow him to make these assumptions and accusations any longer.

Without Captain present during the previous interviews, he had not learned about her childhood and the past abuse she had endured at the hands of her husband, Darren. I wanted to console her, wrap her up in my arms to let her know she was not alone, but I couldn't—even thought she was now family, she was a key witness, the *only* witness, in this investigation.

When we had finished and were back in the car, I assured her that everything would be alright, and that the Captain had just been doing his job. She was quiet and didn't talk the entire way home. I was worried that Captain had gotten into her head, and closed her off even more than she already had been.

I knew Callie would look out for her while I was away; their relationship was already growing and it was evident, with how Callie was concerned for Justine when we arrived home. I was sure they had things in common and could work off each other's strengths to get through this waking nightmare. It affected them both in different ways, but at least it was a family situation and we had each other to lean on for support.

Dusk had begun to set in the distance—I knew at that point we wouldn't be making much progress. The anxiety of the events had begun to take its toll on me. I hadn't really stopped to think that every new piece of information we had received could be bringing me closer to seeing my wife again. What kind of condition she would be in, and her mental state were points of high concern for me, as well as her physical well-being. She may not even remember me—could that even be possible?

Spotting the exit sign to Brownie Lake Conservation Area, I pulled off the highway, noticing officers were immediately stopping vehicles to check each one as they were exiting the highway. We had roadblocks in place in the hopes that whoever had Lily may come to and from the city, or travel around town for any number of reasons. If they had been tipped off, we wanted to have those measures in place—we didn't want them attempting to run again.

Rolling down the window, I presented my badge and stated where I was from.

"Detective Keith Murray with the Vancouver Police Department."

"Thank you sir, we've been expecting you. Go right on through."

Nodding my head, I rolled my window back up and was off down the road towards the entrance of the woods.

From what we knew, there was only one official entrance and exit into and out of the area. The staff at the information booth had already been alerted of our arrival and briefed on the situation. We needed their co-operation if we were to find Darren Johnson and Lily, assuming this was the correct place we needed to be. Yes, we were taking a chance by choosing this area to search first without simultaneously searching the others, but this had seemed the most logical place of the three for us to start with to locate the cabin, Lily, or Darren Johnson.

Captain was at the main gate when I arrived, ensuring the staff knew which officers and members of the Police Department were authorized to be there. Off to the side, I could see another Detective had a map of the woods laid out on a truck bed, placing markers to indicate which teams were starting where.

Our plan was to start from the entrance and work our way in. As we did, we would need to spread out wider to cover more ground. Pulling my car off the road behind another cruiser, I exited it while placing my holster on my hip and pulling my bullet proof vest from the back seat. The detective who was mapping the area called me over, and briefly spoke to inform me of the actions that were going to take place.

"Murray, I think we're ready to proceed."

I looked over to Captain, who was headed our way—my nerves were setting in. Captain noticed this as he approached, placing a hand on my shoulder.

"We're all here for you and Lily. If at any point you need a break, you radio in. You know how much I don't want you on this case, but I doubt anything I say will change your mind."

It was comforting to know that Captain had my back, but he was right, nothing was going to stop me from being here. I was going to be the one to find her and take her home—where she belonged.

"We're losing light, but I'm ready to move forward. Let's begin."

The VPD had brought ATVs for some of the members to use, realizing we could get into some dangerous rough patches and needed the ability to travel around the expansive area easily. Besides seeing it on our map, we were informed by the grounds officials a river ran through the woods. We also had a few police horses available to assist us if the need came.

I hopped onto an ATV, which I had been given permission to use. I chose to not partner up with anyone, but had a GPS equipped radio for assistance if needed. We were to radio in if we spotted anything suspicious or concerning.

The last time it had rained here had been several days ago. The earth would have had time to dry out, but it was still possible to see foot prints or tracks left while the ground had been wet. If any vehicles were being used on non-marked roads, we hoped there would be an increased chance we would notice tire tracks or footprints.

We were told the residential cabins were three quarters of the way through the woods, north of where we stood, but the information booth didn't have records of who owned them. That would have most likely helped us in our search efforts, but we would take what help we could get at this point. They informed us the cabins were spread apart across a few acres, and that some were set back from the roadway and not easily seen by passers-by.

All that mattered now was that I got in there and started searching. Every minute was precious at this stage.

It had grown dark, and visibility had become impossible. Only the headlights of the ATV and handheld flashlights could be seen. We were in the first hour of searching, and nothing had come over the radio yet from any other officer or detective. Since this caused me to feel slightly paranoid, I thought to check in to ensure my radio was working.

"Murray to Captain," I whispered into my radio.

"Captain, go ahead." My anxiety settled down a notch hearing the Captain's voice.

I met up with a few other units; now that it was dark I wanted to be close by to other people, for safety. Even though we were all fully equipped, I knew we should work together and not against each other, as much as my mind kept telling me to move ahead on my own.

I pulled out the map to indicate to the others where we were, and point out where we were headed. The map only helped us so much though—it didn't inform us of any obstacles we might encounter, such as fallen trees or debris that covered any paths we were travelling on.

"Looks like we haven't even made it half way through yet," I reported to the surrounding unites. Just as I finished my sentence, a call came over the radio.

"All units, we have tire tracks on the upper west side, approximately twenty-five kilometers north-west of the entrance. They look fresh, perhaps made within the last day or so."

Anyone could have made those tracks; so it didn't cause me to jump for joy. Checking on the map where we were compared to where the call came in from, I saw that we were east of the location by at least ten or fifteen kilometers.

It didn't appear a direct path travelled in that direction, which meant the vehicle had to have been off the main road. Of course, that raised some suspicion in my mind, but I had to stay positive and keep an open mind. These woods were heavily travelled, and a common place for hiking and hunting. Anything was possible, but the call caused concern in me; that it was a connection to why we were here.

It took us nearly half an hour to drive across to the location. I hopped off my ATV and walked over to another officer, who I figured, was the one who had called in spotting the tire tracks.

"Murray, it appears the tracks go east, but here's the strange part—they also originally came in from the east."

He pointed behind us to show me. I pointed my flashlight in the direction the officer had gestured. Looking around, it appeared as through the brush had been mowed down by some sort of large vehicle, but the question remained—why would someone be attempting to get through this heavily wooded area in the first place with a vehicle? It was a tight spot to begin with.

"The tracks don't appear to be deep, and we couldn't find any foot prints."

I waved him off, and started my own survey of the area for any other evidence, when another officer called out through the dark.

"There's blood over here!"

My heart sank. Blood was not a good sign. Fear began to set in that it was possible Lily was not alive, however I had to consider the fact that it could have been animal blood. We wouldn't know until we got a forensics team out here, but they wouldn't arrive until daylight broke.

Taking steps over to where the officer had called out from, I saw the small trail. It wasn't a lot of blood, but it was smeared across the ground, then a few drops here and there, and then the trail disappeared. It was an odd pattern. Whatever it was, it looked like it had been dragged, then picked up. It could have been an animal that had been hunted and put in the back of a truck, an animal that had been wounded by another—or a human.

Without any further hesitation, I called the findings into the Captain.

"Murray to Captain." I waited. His lack of response made me nervous, but finally, I heard his voice through the speaker in my hand.

"Captain. Go ahead, Murray"

"We have found what looks like fairly fresh blood about twenty-five kilometers north-west of the entrance. It is smeared along the ground, then has a few drops, before the trail ends. When is the earliest forensics can be out here?"

"Not until 0600, when day breaks; but Murray, we need to call it a night. Nobody can see anything. Come back to the entrance with the rest of the team, we'll start fresh in the morning."

I couldn't argue with the captain, it was pitch black and realistically, nobody could see anything. We could have been missing crucial evidence.

Doubling up on the ATVs, we all made the trek back to the front entrance, which took us close to forty-five minutes. I had not planned to go back to a hotel with the other officers. I was fine with sleeping in the car until day broke and getting back out there to search as soon as possible.

As I made my way to my car, I spotted the Captain standing against it, waiting for me. Once I reached it, he pushed off and spoke firmly,

"Murray, I want you to go back to the hotel to get some decent rest. You will need it for the full day we plan to put in tomorrow."

No. There was no way in hell that was going to happen.

"No, that won't be happening Captain. I'll sleep here in my car until daybreak, which is only five hours away. I want to be close by to get things rolling again early."

Something told me that the Captain wouldn't push me into anything, because I would come back fighting. Instead, he gave me a look of displeasure and continued on informing me of the plan for sunrise.

"I called in to forensics, they will show up at 0530 to get a briefing and be taken to the location…"

He trailed off, but continued.

"What is the likely hood you think this is human blood, Murray?"

The question caught me off guard. I really couldn't say. Considering we were in a wooded area that was known for hiking and hunting, tire tracks from large vehicles were common out here from what the front end staff had told us. However, I couldn't imagine that finding these type of tire tracks through a heavy brushed area with everything mowed down as if something or someone were being chased, was common. It was the way the scene had been displayed that had especially caught my attention—I didn't want Captain to know this, though. Not just yet.

"I don't want to speculate, I really don't know."

You could see in his eyes he knew I was lying. At this point, after witnessing the bloody scene, I could feel this was the right place and we would actually find her here.

I wanted to call home and check on the girls. I had hoped they would be able to be each other's strength as we moved forward on the case.

As I slipped into the car, I pulled my phone from my breast pocket. I immediately noticed I had missed texts from Callie.

CALLIE: Dad, Justine is still in her room resting. I'm worried about her.

CALLIE: She won't come out to eat the dinner that I made us.

CALLIE: Justine has now locked herself in the bathroom. What should I do?

The texts ended there, and the last one shook me. Immediately, I dialed home. In less than two rings, Callie answered, blurting out a response without even a hello.

"Dad, I know you're busy and I shouldn't have sent you those types of texts. Everything is okay now."

I was relieved everything was okay, and part of me relaxed hearing Callie's voice. I knew I was not ready to tell her about what had happened tonight, she didn't need to freak out unnecessarily.

"I'm glad everyone is doing okay, I know all of this is very stressful on everyone. We just have to be patient with one another, and support one another."

"Justine and I have been bonding…"

Her voice lowered as she continued.

"She carries a lot of guilt dad, she believes this is all her fault."

I already sensed this about Justine, but being a male I thought perhaps she may have felt uncomfortable talking to me. I was glad Gresham and Callie were there to support her. She had a long road ahead of her in terms of rebuilding her life and relationships. It was not going to be easy, but I was willing to support her until she got back on her feet.

"I know honey, please don't bother her too much, though. She is sensitive, and we don't know the true extent of her past. I need to go now, but I will call tomorrow. Love you."

We hung up, and I was ready to call it a day and grab a nap. It wasn't going to be long before we headed back out.

THIRTY-SIX

Darren

Her pulse was weak, but at least it was still there. She felt like a dead weight as I dragged her from the truck to the cabin. It appeared she had lost consciousness, but I didn't expect it to last long as it was purely due to the amount of blood she had lost; and I had already wrapped it with enough pressure to stop most of the bleeding.

If she hadn't tried to run, or attempted to kill me, I wouldn't have had to shoot her. It was her own damn fault I had to use that type of force to stop her. She had brought it on herself—that was for sure.

I needed to re-bandage up the wound once I had her settled on the bed. My intentions were not to shoot to kill her, but merely to stop her from running, for both our sakes. I knew she would bounce back; it was just a matter of time because, where I had hit her in the leg, just below her knee, there weren't any major organs or arteries— at least to my knowledge.

I did have to question why she thought she could out run me, or better yet how she thought she had actually killed me. If she thought giving me a whack to the knees and the side of the head would be enough to knock me out dead cold, she was wrong. I had been in worse bar fights in my early adulthood and still walked away unharmed. Yes, it had knocked me out for a few hours, but I had come to—obviously.

I was finally able to make it to the bed, and lie her down. I had grabbed some clean towels from the tiny bathroom and wrapped them around her leg tightly. I could tell the wound was already clotting, but I needed to keep it clean so she didn't form an infection.

I pulled up a chair and sat back in it next to the bed. All I could do was stare at her. I couldn't believe that for all these years I imagined she was my wife, Justine. Justine never told me she had a sister, and a twin sister for that matter. She was pretty quiet about her childhood, but kept all those boxes in the basement from her younger years telling me they were keepsakes.

Both sisters carried the same traits—Long, brunette hair, piercing green eyes, and the fact that they were fighters. Lily was more vocal, mind you. For all these years I noticed small things that didn't add up to being Justine's normal personality, but I thought it was just me losing my mind, as usual.

I knew my mind was not right, considering I misinterpreted the couple at the plaza to be Justine and the man she cheated on me with years ago, which ended up being a huge mistake.

Why did this woman want to live so badly? Why had she spent all these years playing the role of my wife? Did she really think that would help her save her life?

She had pretty high hopes if she thought she would be able to get out of that house alive and in one piece. I'm surprised I hadn't tried to kill her sooner. I wanted too, because she was becoming one feisty woman at times and I found it difficult to control her. Even though it had crossed my mind, something about all of this caused me not to commit the act sooner.

Lily's body lay there, motionless on the bed. Her skin was pale, and I had found myself checking her pulse every few minutes. It was still weak, but seemed to be slightly stronger than when I had checked it back in the truck.

There was nothing I could do until she regained consciousness, I was confident this was just temporary...at least I was hoping it would be. I wouldn't even know where to begin if she didn't make it. We were in the middle of the woods, after all.

Being out in the middle of nowhere, it would still take me a few hours to get back to the city to get supplies. I needed to locate things around the cabin instead, because leaving was not an option. Something about that cop who had showed up at my door a few days ago, told me things were going to begin to turn on me. If cops were coming around, it meant they were investigating something.

This happened to be twice I had mistaken someone as my wife, but at least the first one had never been pinned on me. I remembered the first couple of weeks when it had been all over the news—they said then they had no suspects or DNA to prove it was anyone specific, and no suspects they were looking at. That case went cold within a few months. What was done was done and I couldn't change what had happened back then. If I was ever caught, I would most likely gain immunity, because I would play the insanity card.

It was the truth—I had been told by numerous doctors that I was mentally ill, but I never let it define me. I hated the medication they put me on, because I felt I wasn't myself at all. They caused drowsiness, which just made me sleep all the damn time.

How were people expected to live like that? I needed control over my life, over the people in my life. If I slept my days away, nothing would have got done.

Finally, I stood, knowing she merely needed time to heal and staring at her would not wake her any faster. I began to put the cabin back together. I had left it the way it was from when we had fought just a couple of days earlier. When I had come to, I guessed it had been hours since the blow to my head. My focus instantly turned to finding her, and hoping she hadn't made it to the main path to hail someone down.

Picking up various items that were littered across the cabin floor, I noticed an old lamp which she had used to hit me over my head. She had good tactics mind you, but I was stronger and had more determination than what she could handle. I was twice the size of her, and I was pure muscle. It would take a hell of a lot to knock me completely on my ass, and she could not do that at all—well, not usually.

I swept up the glass from the bulb into a dustpan and dumped everything into the trash. As I moved about the cabin, my mind began to wonder. It tended to do that a lot lately, but I couldn't stop it unless I took the pills—something I would not give in to. My mind went back to the night I approached the house where Justine had gone. I wanted to relive it to see if at any time I had noticed anything that would tip me off enough to realize that it wasn't Justine I was taking after all.

I staked out the house for several hours once I made it back to where I had last seen Justine. I knew that I couldn't do anything in broad daylight, and had to wait until night fell. A male had exited that morning, dressed in suit clothes—button-up fitted shirt, black slacks, and carried a brief case. The thought came to mind that this was the man Justine was after, but he seemed as though he was nothing special. If anything, maybe he had more money than I considering his attire?

At the time, he was on a cell phone, but I was too far back to figure out anything he was saying. They kept their blinds drawn, which made it more difficult to see any other movement within the house. A girl, who looked to have been about nine or ten, ran to her school bus that had pulled up along the curb outside the house. There was a figure at the door waving to her, but I was blinded by the sun and couldn't make out who it was. Whoever it was, they never stepped foot outside or left the house for the rest of the day.

Eventually, the girl who had left that morning returned home after school. I hadn't seen the male return at all. No movement had been seen inside, either, but that was because the blinds were still drawn.

I must have eventually fallen asleep sitting there, because I woke to pitch black darkness outside. When I peered back at the house, there were lights illuminating the front lower section of the home, but nothing on the second floor could be seen. It didn't mean someone wasn't at the back of the house in a room, though.

This was my time to go, and I began to prepare myself for the mission I had come for. I pulled out my gloves, cloth, and a bottle of chloroform from the bag that I had on the floor on the passenger side. I was prepared to bring Justine home any way I could. Figuring she would put up a fight at this point, I needed some type of force to keep her in check, and silence her enough to get her home.

Slipping on the gloves and dropping some of the chloroform onto the cloth, I shoved it into my coat pocket. It was only supposed to be enough to knock her out—not actually kill her. I wanted her back home alive, not dead, but it depended on what state she was in once I had her in my grip.

I waited a few more minutes before exiting the car and walking up to the house. I had scoped out the surroundings and the street was quiet, which would work in my favor. I didn't need to cause a scene or have any witnesses as I proceeded. To them, this would look like a kidnapping of some sort, when really I was just here to retrieve my wife who had escaped me.

When I approached the door, I wasted no time, banging on it abruptly several times. I wanted to be heard and get the process over with, because I had no time for playing games—I was done with them. It seemed as if it took forever before someone answered.

A female answered the door, but she wouldn't open the door all the way. I caught a glimpse of her hair and side profile, and immediately recognized it was Justine—at least, it seemed like it was Justine at the time.

"Did you think you could run and not be found?" I asked her gruffly.

I wedged myself into the small crack of the door she held open, then pushed my way inside. She fought back by trying to

"I don't know you, please leave. Get out of my house."

She was distracted by something as she kept looking back down the hallway. I wasn't worried about who else was there. Did she think the lover she had run away to would save her?

All of this was taking too long, and she was beginning to cause a scene—I didn't need a scene. I grabbed her by her arm and began pulling her outside. She continued to look down the hallway. I didn't understand what she was focused on, but at that point it didn't matter to me. All I cared about was getting her back to the car and driving her home, where she wouldn't see the light of day for a very long time.

Suddenly, the young girl I had seen leaving and coming home earlier that day was running down the hallway towards us, screaming; but my focus was on Justine and getting her out of there before anything more could happen.

Yanking on her harder, I managed to get her outside, but the girl latched onto her arm. I was strong enough to keep pulling and didn't stop until Justine was freed from the little girl's grasp.

Justine screamed.—she knew I hated when she screamed—and began kicking and throwing her free arm at me. I couldn't take this any longer. I reached into my pocket and pulled out the cloth, placing it over her mouth in one motion. At first, she resisted; but the longer I held it to her mouth, the weaker she became.

Once she stopped fighting, I picked her up and carried her to the car, placing her down on the backseat. My eyes darted around the neighborhood to see if anyone witnessed the scene. Luckily, nobody was out and I hadn't seen anyone standing at their windows, either. For now, I was safe.

The girl had dropped to her knees outside the house. She wasn't my problem, but I didn't understand why she was crying her eyes out. What was her connection to Justine? That was the only question that came to mind, but left me just as quickly. I put the car in drive and drove off, not looking back at the house again.

I shook my head of the memory, but now I know that young girl must have been Lily's daughter. Did I have remorse? Not really. This woman had chosen to lie to me for all these years. Maybe if she had been truthful from the start, things would have been different. I may have considered letting her go then, but now—no way. She could land me prison, and it was a well-known fact that men behind bars were not treated well when those inside with them learned what they had done to a woman.

I thought back to those intimate moments and it bothered me—I had been making love to another woman other than my wife. I dropped the broom instantly and began pacing the room back and forth. My blood was boiling, as I thought about how I'd had a sexual relationship with someone other than my wife. I peered back to the bed where Lily laid resting without any movement.

All I could think about was how she had let me make love to her, and then my mind remembered all the times we had been together. Her reaction to my touch now made perfect sense, why it seemed she was afraid of me, of my touch.

I walked back to the bedside, taking a seat while I stared at this woman that now lay before me. She looked peaceful. I reached over to check her pulse one more time—it was still weak. I didn't think it had changed much since I had brought her back to the cabin and onto the bed.

This woman has endured the last six years trying to survive as someone else, and now we were on the run together. If I was to run away, she was coming with me. She was too valuable to the cops now, and she would easily give me up.

As those thoughts left me as she began to stir, mumbling as she came to. I knew that she would wake up eventually, it was only a matter of time, but she had to realize things were going to be different from now on—very different.

THIRTY-SEVEN

Callie

It was Sunday morning, and Dad usually made pancakes. I thought to carry on the tradition that morning and get up to make Gresham and Justine some breakfast. Gresham had stayed the night on the living room couch, with a cruiser parked outside for extra protection. I wasn't worried, because I had to be strong for Justine and I, for us to get through the next few days together—or longer.

We'd had some time to connect last night; it was awkward at first because I had never had an aunt before. Dad was a single child, and to my knowledge, mom had been a single child herself—that was, until now of course. The awkwardness was mutual, I could sense Justine was confused over all of this as well, having a niece.

In a way, I felt she knew me because of how she had watched me for the past six years. I wondered what she had learned from me during those years, but that was a conversation for another day.

As I flipped a pancake over in the pan on the stovetop, I heard someone enter the kitchen behind me. I turned to meet the gaze of Justine standing there.

"Good morning!" I greeted her, "I'm making pancakes. I hope that's okay with you, it's something dad and I do pretty much every Sunday."

"That sounds good, thank you," she replied weakly, with a tight-lipped smile.

She made her way to the coffee maker; I had already made sure the timer was on to brew a pot to be ready for them. She slowly poured herself a cup, but didn't add any milk or sugar—black coffee. I remember mom would drink black coffee on occasion but she was not really into coffee, more of a tea person. The memory had dazed me. The next thing I knew Justine was screaming at me for my attention from across the room.

"Callie, it's burning!"

Peering down suddenly, I saw a burnt pancake smoldering in the pan before me. *Oops.*

"Well, thankfully there's more batter!" I laughed.

A set of giggles escaped me, which turned into Justine laughing along with me, as I danced around the kitchen towards the garbage can with the burnt pancake on the end of the spatula. I made my way back to the stovetop and ladled another scoopful of batter into the pan to cook.

Justine had taken a seat at the kitchen table as Gresham groggily made her way in, yawning as she took her own seat across from Justine.

"I thought I smelled burnt pancakes." She let out a small laugh.

343

At least we could all find something to laugh about and enjoy considering the current circumstances. I was thankful to have them both here with me. I couldn't imagine being alone while dad was away, not knowing how long he would be gone for.

I stacked the last pancake on the warming plate and carried the platter over to the table, placing it in the center.

"Dig in!" I exclaimed.

Pulling up my chair between the two of them, I piled two pancakes onto my plate. I looked at each of them to see them both devouring their breakfast. I knew that we would need to find something to do to pass the time, as we surely couldn't sit around all day wondering what was happening with the search. I spoke up to cut through the dead air that began to linger around us.

"What shall we do today?" I asked in a peppy voice.

Justine shrugged with indifference as I looked to Gresham, who was shaking her head.

"I have to stop at the station for a few hours, but the cruiser is going to be outside the whole time while I'm gone."

It wasn't as though I had never been home alone, but Gresham gave me a look as if I was supposed to know what she was thinking. It dawned on me that it would be the first time Justine and I were completely alone.

Turning back to Gresham, I assured her we would be fine. If we need anything we had someone stationed outside but I didn't believe it would come to that.

"We'll be fine. I'm sure we can find something to do around here, right Justine?"

I looked over to see her quietly staring at us, but giving me a small nod to indicate she had heard me.

Gresham finished her plate before excusing herself and making her way down the hallway towards the front door. I followed her to lock the door behind her.

"If you need me, remember, I'm only a phone call away. I won't be too long and will head back as soon as I can."

"We're going to be fine, trust me," I assured her.

I flashed her a toothy grin to let her know I genuinely meant what I had said. She gave me a hug before she headed out the door. I watched her through the side window as she pulled away from the house.

When I made it back to the kitchen, I found Justine still seated at the kitchen table. She appeared as though something was bothering her. I know dad said not to press her with questions, but I felt as though she needed someone to talk to. I couldn't imagine losing a sibling in the manner she had and then feel responsible for having her go missing.

I began to clear the dirty dishes from the table, placing them in the sink. I decided I would wash them later. I stood back against the counter for a brief second before I spoke to Justine, who still had not moved from the table.

"Do you want to watch a movie?" I asked.

All Justine could do was shake her head and continue to peer down at the table in front of her.

"Would you like some tea? You've barely touched your coffee. I can make us some?"

She looked up from the table briefly and spoke softly, "Maybe some tea, tea was always soothing."

I smiled. At least she still knew how to talk.

"We have a variety here. Mom loved tea and pretty much collected all the seasonal teas from the specialty shop down the street."

I didn't realize I had brought up mom without taking Justine's emotions into consideration. I turned to see a tear fall from Justine's eye and realized I needed to be careful with what I said around her from now on. I knew this was a sensitive matter—for all of us.

"I'm sorry, I didn't mean to upset you," I tried to comfort her.

She shook her head before speaking between her small sobs.

"Don't be sorry, this is not your fault. If it's anyone's fault, it's mine."

My heart broke for her. This was no one's fault but that man's who took mom. No one else should have been blaming themselves for the events that had happened.

I walked over to the table and sat down in front of Justine, taking her hands in mine.

"Please don't blame yourself for what that man did."

"That man was my husband, so it is my fault your mother is missing," she whispered.

My heart continued to ache for her and I didn't need her to be upset. I quickly thought on my feet, to put her at ease. What I had to say was the truth, not just a way to calm her.

"I don't blame you for what happened."

As the words left my mouth I noticed a flicker of hope in her eye as she stared back at me with nearly a gaping mouth.

"Really? I truly thought you hated me."

Hate was a strong word. I didn't hate her. I may have not been happy with the way she had withheld the important information she had known for so long, but I didn't hate her. After all, she was my aunt, and part of me felt close to her—even if we had only met a few days ago, officially, that was.

"I don't hate you. I could never hate you!" I exclaimed.

That was the truth. I wouldn't have said it if it wasn't something I truly believed.

"But...I took your mother away. You lost her because I decided to run away, to find my sister. I thought she could help me get away from Darren, to save me from my own life."

This poor woman was harbouring a lot of guilt. I needed her to know she was helping us now, and that's all that mattered.

"You have given us new hope by knowing that you've seen her recently. That's all we can think about right now."

Justine looked away from me before she spoke again. This time she *couldn't* look at me.

"She has not had it easy Callie, by any means. It's been a tough and long road for her."

I'm not sure why she would have thought I wasn't already aware that mom may have gone through a very tough time. I needed to reassure her that it was because of her, the investigation was now open and active again.

"Dad will find her, he will bring her home. It's because of you and your bravery to come forward that reopened the case."

Justine turned to face me. The next words out of Justine's mouth were simple.

"You have a lot of faith in your father, Callie."

It was the truth. I *did* have faith in my father, because he had never stopped fighting for mom—that was evident. Now, with this new information he was more determined to finding not only mom, but the man that had taken her and bring him to justice—justice that certainly needed to be obtained.

"I do, he has never given up hope. He has stayed strong all these years and told me he would bring her home one day."

Justine pulled away from where I held her hands and stood. Her body language had changed drastically. Anger was intertwined in her voice.

"If it wasn't for my attempted escape, this wouldn't have happened."

Up until now, I had not known much about Justine's history, nor this detail that she had been trying to escape her apparent abusive, manipulating husband. A part of me remembered what dad had told me about asking questions, but Justine had laid it out in front of me. To me, that was an open invitation to inquire. My words were calm when I spoke, because I didn't need to fight anger with more anger.

"Why did you escape, what happened?"

Justine's shoulders tensed as she turned back towards me.

"You need not hear what happened to me, no child should hear of those awful things."

Her words shocked me. Yes, to some I would be viewed as a child, but I had grown up much quicker than others my own age under the circumstances. It was just the way things had been after mom was gone. Without waiting for an answer, Justine began blurting out statements.

"I had a not so very nice husband who hurt me. I couldn't handle it anymore and I tried to runaway, and more than once. I began searching for Lily, my sister, because I had hoped if I found her she would help me get away from him. When I managed to finally get away and felt I was not being followed, I thought I was in the clear—but obviously I wasn't."

I didn't have words to reply to what she had poured out. If this man had hurt Justine as badly and horribly as she had stated, what would he have done to mom? I had a question, but didn't know if it would be too personal to ask. Since Justine was being so brutally honest, I thought I would take a chance and ask. I knew if they were identical twins that meant they looked the same, but would the man have known the difference?

"Do you think he knows mom is not you?" I posed.

She fidgeted with her hands and you could tell she was contemplating her answer.

"I can't say for sure. From what I could see, it seemed he believed it was still me, but who knows at this point."

I was suddenly reminded of the letters I had found in the box on mom's dresser. I knew it was not my place to bring it up, but I felt as though it might bring some closure, or at least some assurance, to Justine that mom had thought about her as well.

I stood from the table and left the kitchen without another word. I walked down the hallway, up the stairs to the master bedroom and over to the dresser. I stared at the box for a moment, I was being pulled in opposite directions, but my sense of duty to let Justine know mom thought of her took over. I snatched up the box and made my way back down to the kitchen.

I found Justine seated back at the table and as I sat down, she eyed the box I held.

"What's that?" she whispered.

"Letters…letters mom had been writing to you for years."

I had pulled the key off from underneath the box and began to unlock the wooden box, turning it to face Justine once it was open. You could tell she was completely baffled at what I had just presented her with.

"What do you mean she had been writing me letters?" she asked incredulously.

"It looks that way. I only just discovered them myself the other day. To be honest, mom never mentioned anything about having a sister. She never spoke much about the orphanage, and dad and I knew not to bring it up. It upset her. It seemed as though it was a sensitive matter. We never liked to press her for information for fear of upsetting her. We knew she would tell us when the time was right. It seems she still remembered you. Why else would she write all of these?" I gestured to the filled box.

Silence fell between us as Justine stared down at the box of letters before her. I couldn't imagine what was going through her mind considering I had just told her that her long lost sister had been writing letters to her and remembered her. You could see her hands shaking as she pulled the first one off the top of the pile. Turning the envelope over, she pulled out a single sheet of notepaper—the same one I had, just the day before. With shaking hands, she started reading the letter. Her eyes started leaking. Tears began to roll down her cheeks.

Justine's head began to shake, and between sobs she attempted to talk.

"She remembered me, she actually remembered me. Are you saying all these letters are written to...*me*?"

Looking back up at me with tear filled eyes, she searched for confirmation.

"Yes, every single letter is for you. She may have not mentioned anything to dad and I about you, but she remembered you, and that's what is important...but, why did she refer to you as Rose?"

350

"Rose is my birth name, Rose-Marie. My adoptive parents changed my name when they adopted me. I didn't have much of a choice in the matter."

My mind started to make a connection to mom and dad's bedroom, and perhaps why the trim on the walls were painted with only roses and lilies.

"Is that why mom has roses in her bedroom?"

She nodded to confirm while mustering a weak smile.

"We made a scrapbook when we were kids about our future home. It's back home, and I never got rid of it. It was a book that we put together on what our dream home would look like some day. I can't believe after all these years I would be here, experiencing all of this. To know she had been thinking of me this whole time gives me more hope that she is fighting to escape him."

Mom had always been a fighter; she wouldn't let someone take advantage of her. Even if every bone in her body was broken, she would still fight back. I knew she would—I believed she would.

I stood there in silence as I watched Justine. You could tell she was trying to piece everything together in her head. I spoke softly to reassure her that everything was okay, and that we would all be okay once this was over.

"I'm sorry this has happened. As much as this effects dad and I, it affects you just as much. You haven't seen her in a much longer time than either of us have. I'm glad you came forward, to help bring her back, for all of us."

Before I knew it, Justine rose from the table and stood over top of me. She leaned down before I could even move, suddenly wrapping her arms around me.

"Lily created a beautiful family, and I'm glad to witness the true love of a family—one that will stand by each other through thick and thin."

She squeezed me tightly and I returned the hug, but I was at a loss for words. I found myself tearing up from the pure emotions of our conversation. Justine whispered in my ear as she continued to hug me.

"You are one strong young woman, Callie. Your mother would be proud of the woman you have become."

I melted into her arms. I had hoped mom would be proud of me. Everything I did, I did to make her proud. I managed to speak, with my voice shaking from the emotions that were coursing through me.

"She will be home soon, dad will bring her home. We have to stay strong."

Justine pulled away, but kept her hands on my shoulders for a moment longer.

"Your father is determined; he won't stop until she is brought home—until justice is served."

I had to agree, dad was determined and that's what made this all easier—his determination to not give up. Suddenly, my phone began to ring from the counter top where I had left it earlier this morning. I rushed over and answered it breathlessly.

"Hello?"

"Callie, its dad."

I felt at ease to hear his voice, but at the same time was he calling because they found something, or had news? I moved into the living room to speak with dad, away from Justine.

"What's happened, have you found anything?" I asked eagerly.

"Not yet, I wanted to check in and see how everyone was doing this morning."

The line cracked and his voice wavered—I knew he was holding back information about something.

I repeated my question, a little for firmly, "Did you find anything yet?"

"We're investigating as we speak, but nothing to share at this time," he replied, just as firmly.

Part of me wanted to hound dad for answers, but dad knew when the right times were to speak. I let it slide, even though I knew there was more that he was simply not telling me. He must have noticed my pause, because he changed the subject.

"Is Gresham there, let me speak to her please."

"She isn't here. She was called into the station for a few hours." I was short with him, as I had really hoped for some answers, and was annoyed at his stubbornness to withhold information from me.

"Then who *is* there with you and Justine?"

You could hear the concern in dad's voice as he spoke. I knew he was irritated because he had specifically told us she would be with us the entire time.

"There's a cruiser outside, we're fine, really."

"Gresham was to stay with you. I don't want either of you on your own. We don't know—"

I interrupted him, he needed to realize we were okay.

"Dad, we're fine. We're just talking, getting to know each other."

"You better not be bothering her with a ton of questions, you know what I said before I left."

"I know dad, she just offered the information," I told him in an exasperated tone.

I realized what I had said and instantly wished I could have taken it back, but it was too late.

"What has she been saying? I need to know if it has anything to do with the investigation."

I assured him it wasn't, but somehow he seemed not to believe what I was saying. I realized he was under a lot of stress, but I was kind of glad he was annoyed at receiving a taste of his own medicine. I decided to let it go, given the situation, and tried my best to keep calm and give him the facts.

"She thinks this is all her fault, she's blaming herself for mom's disappearance."

I could hear dad blow out a long breath through the receiver.

"This isn't her fault," he finally stated.

"I know dad, I tried to tell her. I keep telling her we're going to get through this together and that no one is mad at her."

"I'm glad she has you there, I know this may be awkward for you, but imagine how she feels. She has nobody but us right now. We need to be strong for her."

"Dad, just bring mom home, okay?"

There was a pause, as I knew dad was processing my last statement.

"Yes, I know, I will bring her home."

With that, we said our goodbyes. As I hung up, I turned to see Justine in the doorway of the living room with her arms crossed.

"You didn't need to tell him what I said Callie, I thought I could trust you to keep this between us." She looked angry, which was a new emotion for me to see from her.

"I...he...I'm sorry."

I had no idea she had been standing there. I questioned in my head how much of the conversation she had heard. I should have been more sensitive, but it just came out, and I never kept things from dad—we had a standing deal to always have an open line of communication. We had to, considering the circumstances.

"What is done is done, eventually he would have found out anyway. It seems like it's hard to keep anything from him," she finally spoke.

Justine was right, but it was for good reason. Dad had a good head on his shoulders and he knew what to do in most situations. I knew things would turn out for the better, at least that's how I was thinking these days. It was really hard to think of anything negative, even though there was a chance this wouldn't end the way we all thought it would. All we could do was have faith and hope.

THIRTY-EIGHT

Lily

I felt groggy. My limbs felt even heavier. I couldn't open my eyes, but I could hear myself moan. Was I actually alive? Had I actually survived? He had shot me in the leg, and I was sure I was not going to survive and live.

I began moving my hand, then my arm. My eyes felt as though they were glued shut. I felt something wrapped tightly around my leg, but I couldn't figure out what it was.

A hand rested on my shoulder and someone began to mumble. They could have been talking to me, but my ears felt like they had a constant ringing in them or they were clogged—but I couldn't decide which one. I had no idea whose voice I could hear, and couldn't make out if they were even talking to me.

I slowly managed to open my eyes. The room was dark, with only a flicker of light floating from the nightstand. Was I back at the cabin?

I tried to focus on something to determine where I was but, as I tried to sit up, weakness won over, and I found myself lying flat on my back once again. The voice that was mumbling was becoming more coherent—it was a male voice.

"You're going to be okay, but don't try to move," he instructed.

I assumed it was Darren standing over me, but couldn't make out the tones in his voice to clarify if it was definitely him or not with the way my head and ears felt.

Moving was not my intention, I felt like a tractor-trailer had run me over by the way my entire body was aching. I tried to wet my lips, but my mouth was as arid as a desert.

"Do you want some water?" He spoke softly.

Before I could answer or give an indication that I did or didn't want it, a straw was placed at my mouth. I couldn't push it away, and instead took a couple of sips before I turned my head away.

My eyes had finally adjusted to the world around me, confirming I was back at the cabin. Which only meant one thing—Darren was still alive and he still had control over me.

I turned in the direction of the flickering light beside me, and there stood Darren, towering above me and caressing my head. If I could have shivered at his touch I would have, even after learning who I was, why did he feel the need to still touch me?

Turning back, I stared at the ceiling.

Why was I still alive? Why was I back here? If he shot me, why wasn't I dead?

Questions continued to circle through my head, but I didn't have any answers to them. Instead, I shouted at him out of frustration.

"Stop touching me!"

He pulled his hand away to give me the space I desperately wanted.

"You will need to rest; your strength will take some time to return."

All I could ask myself was, why wasn't I at a hospital? After all, I had been shot. He should have known he needed to get me medical attention.

"I need to get to a hospital, I need this bullet out of me." I attempted to stay calm in an effort not to tip Darren off, knowing his questionable moods.

"No you don't, we can't get to one right now. Plus, the city is a few hours away. You'll be fine here. It was a through and through, nothing to worry about."

Nothing to worry about? Did he really just say that to me? He had shot me! He took a gun, pointed it at me, and shot me.

He was acting as though this was an everyday occurrence. I knew he hunted and all, but I was not an animal. Plus, from the feeling in my leg, it felt as though something was still lodged inside it.

"I still need medical attention, I have a hole in my leg, thank you very much," I practically snarled at him.

"I have some fishing line, I'm sure I can find a needle around here and do it myself if you're that concerned. It was already clotting before I wrapped it up. You're fine."

The thought started making me hyperventilate; I didn't need him doing that. It would not be sterile by any means and an infection could set in very quickly.

"No, no you won't. You won't be touching me again—ever again. Now, get out."

Realizing that was a useless statement to make considering this was his cabin and I was still his prisoner, I thought maybe he would at least leave me alone enough to gather my strength, and my thoughts.

"I will let you rest, that's what you need right now. You seem to still be out of it."

I could see him walk into the kitchen area and disappear around the corner. I felt as though I could finally relax—but knowing I was still alive and now unable to escape, made me feel helpless once again. Would they even find me out here? What was Darren expecting us to do? We had no food, water, or other basic necessities that I was aware of.

I had drifted off back to sleep at some point after Darren left the room, because the next thing I knew the sun was shining through the tiny window to the left, flooding the bed with light. Darren was fast asleep next to me. As I tried to move, I realized my right hand was handcuffed to the night table.

You had to be kidding me.

Did this delusional psychopath believe I was capable of escaping? Had he completely lost his marbles?

I hadn't even tried to get up which, I felt was going to be a disaster if it did happen, because I still felt weak.

Darren stirred as I tried to move side-to-side on the bed. I was trying not to disturb him so that I had a longer time to think, but my body had begun to cramp.

"'Morning, how are you feeling?" his voice echoed through the empty air.

His eyes were barely open, how did he know I was awake? Was he psychic?

"Fine. Why did you handcuff me?" I shot back. I was short with him because I didn't understand why he thought I was capable of getting up.

"For your safety," he said slowly, as if I was incapable of comprehending his words.

My safety, what the heck did he mean by that?

"Well can you unlock it, I need to use the washroom…you're going to have to help me up to do that, considering I'm unable to move properly."

He didn't say a word. Pulling himself up, he reached out to his jeans pocket that were draped over a chair, then looked through the ring, key by key, determining if it was the correct one.

"Can we hurry this along, otherwise you'll have wet sheets in a minute," I said flatly. That comment made him find the correct key instantly.

"Don't think about doing anything stupid when I unlock it. Stay calm and nobody will get hurt." His voice was stern and full of exasperation.

I had to shake my head at his stupidity.

He had shot me, had he forgotten that?

Once he unlocked my hand from the night table, I attempted to slowly get up, but slipped. Darren placed his hand under my arm and around my back, pulling me upright as carefully as he could. Once I was able to make it to my feet, I gingerly placed some weight on my injured leg. Pain seared through it. Passing me a large, thick piece of wood, Darren instructed me to use it to lean on so as to not put any weight on my leg. Still holding on to him, I hopped to the only washroom in the cabin.

As we reached the washroom door, I turned to stare at him—there was no way he was coming in there with me.

"I can take it from here, I need some privacy."

Without a word, he stepped back, allowing me to finish the rest of the way myself. I had to hold onto the wall with my free hand for support, otherwise I would have surely fallen over.

Once inside, my first action was to check my wounds. Being a nurse, my first thought was to prevent an infection if I could. I had no idea what Darren had done while I was unconscious, and the thought scared me so much I shivered thinking about the possibilities.

I slowly removed the towel he had wrapped around my leg, which was half soaked in dried blood. That sign alone explained my weakness, as I had to have lost a lot of blood to have been unconscious.

I revealed a hole a quarter inch in diameter on the left side of my leg, just below the back of my knee. It was difficult to see the back of the wound due to not being able to lift and move the lower part of my leg properly, but I could see it had clotted, and that no new blood was seeping from the wound. Though, like any gunshot wound, it needed stitches. If I waited, it could become infected. I was not about to take Darren up on his offer of using fishing line, due to being unsanitary.

Rummaging through the small cabinets, I couldn't find another clean towel to use. I was not about to use the blood-soaked one again. I opened the door slowly and called out, "Do we have another towel?"

It took a second for Darren to answer. I could hear him rummaging around the cabin.

"Yes, under the sink."

Of course, I hadn't looked under the sink because it was too painful for me to squat or try to bend my leg. I found a stack of towels, but they were significantly smaller than the one he had originally wrapped around my leg. At this point, I would make it work. Before I could attempt to wash and apply the new dressing, the door to the washroom swung open with a slight bang.

"I would really like to sew you up, we don't need you getting an infection."

I stared blankly at him—I had already told him he was not touching me.

"You are not a doctor, or a nurse. I don't trust you. It won't be clean." I tried to keep my voice calm, I didn't need to piss him off.

"I found some rubbing alcohol in the emergency kit. I can sterilize the needle."

I was at a loss for words, he was actually trying— but why?

What would he get out of it?

"Why do you want to help me? Why didn't you leave me out there for dead?" It was the truth, he could have just left me. Why had he chosen to bring me back here?

"I couldn't do that. Plus, I knew you wouldn't die from where I shot you. Remember, I'm a hunter," he said with a small laugh.

"You knew where to shoot, just to stop me?" I was puzzled, but right now everything was too much for me to process and I was just trying to stand up right long enough to get through this conversation with him.

"Yup, and it worked didn't it?"

He was a cocky one, always had to be right and in control. It irritated me. I didn't feel like he was going to take no for an answer. Maybe I should tell him I was a nurse, and I would only agree if he listened to me.

"I will only agree if you listen to me, can you agree to that?" I stared him in the eye to convey that I meant business. My life depended on him listening to me—if I had lived through all of his abuse the past six years and being shot, I wanted to live longer.

"What is it first? I need to know what I am agreeing too."

Of course he needed to know, he had to be in control of every situation.

"I'm a nurse at the hospital in Richmond; we will do it my way if we do this at all."

He just stared blankly at me. Finally, he responded.

"Well…okay…I can't fight you on that. You're the professional."

I wanted to burst out laughing at the way he spoke. My convincing had gone easier than I thought it would, but I was still petrified of the method he wanted to use.

Regardless of his semi sterile equipment, I really didn't know how to do this, even though I had stitched patients all the time. To explain it to someone else was completely different. Maybe I *could* actually do it myself, but without any anesthetic, this was going to be a bitch.

THIRTY-NINE

Murray

It was morning, and we had been back in the woods for the past few hours, but nothing new had turned up. We had a police helicopter come in to assist us from the air in hopes they would be able to spot any movement within the woods. We knew we had to get back to where the cabins were situated, but the only way in was by foot. The ATV's could only go so far into the dense brush and skinny man-made pathways. Even if they located Darren and Lily from the sky, we would still have to make our way to them. If they saw any movement from up there, it would at least give us a starting point, letting us know which direction we should head in.

Saying that I was tired was an understatement, but regardless, I pushed forward. I was lucky to get one of the ATV's again that morning, it made me feel as though I was moving forward more quickly. Again, there was no information being heard over the radios.

The forensic team was at work taking samples to determine the blood we had discovered the night before. I knew it would be some time before we got word from them, and as time ticked by I was becoming more impatient. I picked up my radio to call into the command center, hoping they had some news to share. Before I could take my radio off of its holster on my shoulder, the urgent, crackling voice of the Captain could be heard through it.

"All units, we have found the cabins and a truck parked behind a tree close to one of them. We are unsure of the colour of the truck at this time, but further identification is in the process of being made."

I had an unnerving feeling wash over me. A part of me knew the colour of that truck would be red. Without thinking, I questioned the Captain, realizing afterwards he already stated they didn't know the colour.

"It wouldn't happen to be a red pickup, would it?"

"I'll let you know as soon as we can confirm. In the meantime, focus on moving forward. We're getting closer to those cabins."

With the Captain telling me in not so many words not to worry about it, it irritated me more than I thought it would. It had been a very long time since we'd had any leads, and we might have been close to ending all of this—and I wasn't supposed to worry?

Suddenly, someone was shouting my name, which brought me back to reality.

"Murray, pull over."

The sound of Pryce's voice became loud and clear. I had forgotten my own partner was beside me due to my mind drifting off for a few seconds.

Shaking myself from the state of mind I was in, I cut the engine to the ATV immediately. I slumped myself over the steering wheel, breathing heavily. I had closed my eyes to pull myself together, when I felt my partner's hand on my back.

"Are you alright? Are you sure you don't want to go back to the command center and wait?"

I barked back at him—there was no way I was heading back. Not a chance.

"No, what I need to do is keep going, she is here. I know she is here."

He stepped back abruptly and I realized the tone I had used towards him was rough, but I needed everyone to stop telling me either not to worry, or to take a step back. I was done taking steps back, I was done waiting around. I was here now, and I would finish what I came to do.

My head was spinning with emotions and I didn't even know which one I was truly feeling right then. I spoke in a much calmer tone when I spoke to Pryce next.

"I need to take a breather for a second. I'm not turning back now. We're too close."

"I understand if you need to break, just let me know."

"Let's keep going, I'll let you know if I need another break."

With that, I started the engine of the ATV again and began moving forward when the radio on my shoulder went off once again.

"Captain to Murray"

"Murray, go ahead, Captain"

"We have confirmation on the pickup truck that was spotted from the helicopter. It is indeed a red pickup truck, but we can't get a visual on the license plate to make a positive identification that it belongs to Darren Johnson."

Immediately my heart sank, that comment alone confirmed to me that they were here. At least, Darren was here, who knew if Lily was with him.

"Keep a visual. That is Darren Johnson's truck for sure," I spat into the radio.

"We are. Stay focused, Murray. We have eyes everywhere."

The news caused me to speed through the woods as my mind willed my body to hurry to get closer to the location. With my focus lost in my thoughts, I didn't realize I had hit a tree stump, causing me to crash into a tree ahead of me.

"Murray, you okay?" I could hear Pryce's voice behind me.

I looked up and shook my head. I couldn't believe I had managed to let my emotions get the better of me and cause me to lose my focus on my surroundings.

"I'm fine, nothing major," I shouted back at him.

Turning the engine over, I discovered it wouldn't start. Panic rose in me, as I desperately needed it to start; it was a minor crash into a tree, how much damage could have been caused?

I pulled myself off the ATV and inspected the front end. It looked as though the front had been swollowed by the tree I had crashed into.

"Great, just what we need now, a busted vehicle," I shouted out at no one in particular. Suddenly, I heard Pryce over the radio. This was not going to be good at all. Captain was going to lose it, I had wrecked police equipment."

"Pryce to Captain."

"Captain, go ahead, Pryce"

"Captain, we had a minor accident with one of the ATV's. The location is 45 degrees north latitude, and 121 degrees west longitude. We're going to leave it here, and were going to be down to one ATV. No injuries to report."

"Make sure you keep an eye on Murray. You better be driving, Pryce."

Did Captain really think I didn't have ears? It was as if he was treating me like a little kid. I was a grown man, and I knew what I could and could not handle.

Right now, I could handle a lot, at least that's what I thought.

"Murray, don't sweat it. We're only looking out for you," Pryce said through my thoughts.

"Yeah, sure. Let's get going then. I'm driving."

Before I had made it over to his ATV, he was already slinging his leg over the driver's seat.

"That's not a good idea, hop on the back," he instructed me.

Did he really think I wasn't capable of driving now? I had driven over a root, which caused the minor crash. It wasn't as if I was drunk or anything.

I was in no mood to argue, after pulling a few belongings from the ATV we were abandoning, I complied by hopping on the back of his ATV.

As Pryce road ahead, my eyes darted from side to side, in a sense I felt as though everything was moving too quickly and I was not being able to take in my surroundings. Pryce must have sensed what I was thinking. That's when he spoke up.

"Why don't you look one way, and I'll look the other. It will allow us to scan the area more quickly and thoroughly."

Immediately I choose to look over to the right, when static crackled into the air once more. With each radio call that now came in, I was on edge. Information was now moving too quickly, but I couldn't move quickly enough to where I should be.

"All units please indicate your locations. I need to know where all my units stand."

"56 north latitude and 125 west longitude," Pryce shouted into the radio.

"Why, what's going on?" I demanded.

The Captain wouldn't be asking this information unless he had a reason. Once all the units informed him of their locations, he presented us with more information.

"Movement has been spotted at the cabin we have had surveillance on. Someone was spotted covering the windows."

My heart sank at his words. Why would someone be covering the windows unless they knew someone was after them? The Captain continued to speak over the radio, "That puts you about ten kilometers south of the cabin in question, Murray and Pryce. I want a central meeting place set up five kilometers away. Nobody is to go in alone, do you hear me?"

Captain knew I wouldn't listen, but in this case not knowing if Lily was still there we wanted to ensure her safety.

"Yes, I think that's best. We'll meet and disperse as needed. We need to regroup before we take any action," I agreed.

"We should all be making it to that point within 15 minutes, just as dusk is falling. This might give us better coverage as we move in, and not be seen easily. We have asked the helicopter to keep an eye from a distance, but not directly over top in case whoever is operating the cabin becomes suspicious."

Captain was talking as if we didn't know who was there. I knew who was there—it was obvious.

"We know it's Darren Johnson, Captain. We don't have to act as though we don't know," I shouted through the radio.

Not realizing what I was saying, I really wanted to take it back. I knew Captain was simply adhering to protocol, where as I was going on instinct.

"Until proven, Murray, it's still classified as 'unknown person'."

I didn't bother signing off. What I needed to do was collect myself. We were closing in on another day and we had yet to make it to the cabin. We were running out of time, but Captain was right, the darkness would disguise us enough that whoever was in the cabin wouldn't be tipped off too quickly. However, they might have already been suspicious if someone was covering the windows. It was quite possible the helicopter had tipped them off.

My mind drifted off in remembering things about Lily, was I going to recognize her if I found her? Would she remember me, or Callie? I had absolutely no idea what state I would find her in, and all I could hope for was that we were not too late already.

FORTY

Lily

At least I didn't have a gaping hole in my leg anymore. It had been painful, though. Stitching yourself up was one thing, but doing it without any anesthetic was another. The whiskey Darren held to my lips, demanding I drink for a partial pain remedy as they did in the old days, didn't help much; but at least I was patched. It was a temporary fix, though, and eventually I would need to be seen by a doctor. I was hoping Darren had realized this too. You couldn't expect to shoot someone, sew them back up with fishing line, and believe they would be okay.

I was worried about an infection, especially being out here in the woods with nothing around us to properly clean my wound. Using a dab of the left over whiskey was the only idea I could come up with.

Although it wouldn't prevent an infection one-hundred percent, at least it would ward any off temporarily.

Now that I was able to get up, I was tired of lying in bed, even if it had only been for half a day. I couldn't move quickly mind you, but I managed to fix us some food that Darren had in the freezer and do a little cleaning up.

Darren never left the cabin; his eyes were glued to me, which made me feel uncomfortable.

"I can't believe you pretended to be your sister for all these years," he laughed out suddenly.

Turning from the stovetop, I had no response for him.

Why was he still fixated on this? Didn't he understand, I had pretended to be Justine all these years to protect myself.

He continued with another question without giving me a chance to even respond to his first question.

"Why would you do that? You don't even know her."

The accusation struck a nerve in me; I didn't need to know her to still love her, though I wish I had known her, because I could have possibly helped her sooner knowing the torture she had been enduring all those years.

"You don't need to know someone to still love them," I stated bluntly. Darren looked displeased.

"Love? You think you love her? Now who's the delusional one?" He began laughing hysterically, nearly keeling over in the chair he was sitting in. "The only person who could love and care for Justine was me, and I plan to get her back, too."

I tried to hold in the laughter that wanted to spill out of my mouth at that comment. Justine was long gone, that was evident.

372

"She's probably long gone. If I were her, I would have run for the hills and never looked back."

Darren should have known by now that I would speak my mind. That probably didn't sit well with him, because he always wanted control over everything, regardless of what the situation was.

"It's only a matter of time before I find her. She couldn't have gone far as she doesn't have any family or know anyone but me."

I doubted she needed to know anyone to get away from him, if she was anything like me— determined— she would have found a way. I hadn't had much of a chance to escape through the years, as Darren proved he was much smarter with his locks and keys.

Turning back to the stove, I hadn't noticed tears forming in my eyes. I attempted to keep them back with a few quick blinks. I had done all of this, the last six years, all for my sister, and to keep myself alive to be reunited with my daughter and husband.

Darren sat in a chair by the only exit, which was the front door. I assumed he believed if I had run once, I would run again; which was the truth, but in my current condition it would have been a lot harder. There was no way I could run without the wound surely opening up on me—it was only a temporary fix.

I truly thought I would have come across someone during my few days of freedom, but it seemed I had only been submerging myself deeper and deeper into the woods. What I didn't understand was, how had Darren found me? I had crossed a river. Was there a bridge somewhere further along that I had missed?

Suddenly Darren shot up from his chair and began yelling.

"Turn the stove off, now!" he snarled at me

At first I wasn't sure what the issue was until I heard a faint sound coming from outside. I couldn't make out what it was, but whatever it was, it had Darren riled up.

"I said turn the stove off, now!" He stared me down until I finally switched it off.

I closed my eyes and tried to distinguish what the faint sound I was hearing could be.

A helicopter.

Darren wasn't stupid—he knew exactly what was going on. He pulled his rifle from the corner of the room where it stood against the wall.

"Get in the closet now, and don't say a word. You hear me?" He was angry and it caused me to freeze. This was my chance to get out of here, and he wanted me to hide in the closet. He gave me no choice or time before he was at my side with his hand wrapped around my upper arm. Flash backs of being in the kitchen when the doorbell rang came flooding back to me—I was not going to miss this opportunity to be rescued.

Reaching the tiny closet, Darren opened the old creaky door and shoved me inside. As he closed the door he muttered at me, "If I hear a peep from you, you are done. You hear me?"

Without any other words, he shut and locked the door. The closet was not big at all and I struggled to find a comfortable sitting position. What I really wanted to do was try and listen to whatever was happening on the outside of the door.

Pressing my ear to the door, I closed my eyes to concentrate. I could hear him pacing heavily across the wooden floorboards with his heavy work boots. I couldn't hear the outside noise anymore. It had to have been still there for Darren to continue to pace around the cabin so frantically.

Falling back onto the tiny floor space, all I could do was wait. It could mean something, or it could mean nothing at all and it was simply someone flying overhead that had nothing to do with us.

I don't know how long I was in there before I heard the door swing open. The room was dark, with only the lantern in Darren's hand, the same one from the first night he had brought me to the cabin.

"Get up, and come out here." He still had anger in his voice.

Slowly, I pulled myself up. As I did, I felt the incision rip a touch as I moved to my feet and I let out a tiny yelp. I had to remember the hack job Darren had attempted was only a temporary fix; it was not going to be the final result. However, I could feel dampness on my pants, and feared I had begun bleeding again from the sudden movement. Darren noticed the blood first and ensured I was aware of it.

"You're bleeding. Fix it."

I wasn't sure what had him all riled up, but I knew if I didn't want anything to happen to me I needed to comply with him.

I found a seat on the bed once I hobbled over without any help from Darren. I lifted my pant leg to see a trail of blood dripping down to my ankle. Three of the stiches had loosened, which was where I was now bleeding slowly from.

"We aren't safe here," he shouted out, while pulling out a towel from under the washroom sink. "We need to get out of here, and right now is the perfect time, because it's dark." His voice was frantic and panicked, and I wondered if he was suffering from an episode delusion.

On the run again, I thought. Did he believe he could out run them all the time? If it was a search team they would have this entire place covered, and we would not get out of here undetected, that was for sure.

"Where are we going to go? We can't go back home, we can't stay here? So where do you plan to run to now?"

He contemplated my question while he handed me the towel he had pulled out.

"We're close to the border. I'm thinking we can get through to the US and then be free of them."

"Them?"

"Yes, them, the people you have after us."

I had to think about this, as I hadn't done anything to bring this on. If anything, they were probably trying to find me, to get me away from him. I also didn't like the fact he wanted to flee the country. If that plan worked, I would never see my family again—ever.

"No. I need to get to a hospital. This wound is going to get infected."

"Pour some alcohol on it, you'll be fine. There's still some rubbing alcohol in the bottle on the night stand as well as some whiskey, pick your poison. You're not going to a hospital, so use that nurse's knowledge you have and fix yourself up."

That was exactly the point—I was a nurse, not a doctor. I was lucky I had paid enough attention to even mange to fix myself up, but it was only temporary. Why couldn't he understand that?

I knew arguing with him was pointless. Whatever he chose to do, I had to go along with or risk being killed. I was under his control, again.

Darren began pacing around the cabin as I sat quietly on the bed. I didn't bother trying to change his mind. He was in a mood that I didn't want to mess with. Since coming back to the cabin, he hadn't become violent. He had kept his temper for the most part.

Maybe that knock to the head readjusted something in him, although I was not holding my breath.

All I could do was hope for the best, because what else could I do at this point? I sat quietly on the bed, because I was clueless what he wanted me to do. I held pressure on my leg to help clot the now bleeding wound.

I hadn't noticed that the only window in the cabin was now covered by a garbage bag. Whatever Darren had in mind, he really didn't want anyone seeing us. It scared me to death that he was going to this much trouble to hide himself.

"Why is the window covered?" I nodded in the direction of the window next to me.

"Because it has to be, that's why," he shot back.

He continued to move about the cabin as if something would pop out and give him all the answers as to what to do next. Darren normally knew exactly what to do, but right now you could tell he was worried. Even if he didn't want to show it, I could sense it. I would even go as far to say he was actually scared of what was to come.

FORTY-ONE

Darren

Trying to mentally figure out my next steps was frustrating. Why was there a helicopter out there? We were in a secluded wooded area, and I didn't think we had left any tracks. Nobody knew about the cabin other than me. Not even Justine knew where this place actually was. All she knew was that I traveled a few hours for work and that I was a hunter. The location had never been discussed.

Lily was now the only other person to ever know the cabin's location, besides my grandparents, who had left me everything they owned in their will when they died while I was still in highschool.

Now, I had to figure out how to get us out of here undetected. I knew these woods like the back of my hand, you could say I could travel them with my eyes closed, because that was how familiar I was with the grounds. The only problem I had was where these people were, and how they had found us.

If they found us, I would be done—I'd most likely die in the process, because I would put up a fight before I would surrender to anyone. The logical thing was to get to the border, if we crossed it, we would be home free. Obviously I was now stuck with this woman, but it was a sacrifice I would make. Justine was gone, long gone from the looks of things. Where she would have gone to, I had no clue, because she didn't know anyone else. Now thinking back, all those papers that I found stashed away in her basement boxes had been her trying to find her sister, not her running off with another man. Maybe if I knew about her desires, I could have done something. She was so quiet about her past and the orphanage that it seemed she didn't want to remember any of it, that's why I never brought it up with her, because she would always get upset over it.

Peering over to Lily sitting on the bed, I thought again about how they were identical, and that's how I was tricked for so long. Even though there were subtle differences, I could never pinpoint them at first. For her to want to pretend all those years and live like that, meant she was determined to survive.

"We're going to leave tonight. If we want to escape, we need to do it while it's dark. Lucky for you, I know some back ways out of this place. Before you know it, we'll be living a new life in a new country."

She didn't say a word, just stared me down. Regardless, it was her and I now. I was not here to kill her, that was never my motive, but I was not about to get caught and be faced with prison time over this misunderstanding. I didn't need her approval, anyway. She would do as she was told, because at this point I didn't care that she was not my actual wife. If anything, she would be my new wife, because Justine was long gone, supposedly.

The helicopter over head was causing me to become antsy, even though I could tell it was in the distance. In my head, the sounds were magnified beyond belief.

I needed to pack the little that we had here and ensure I had weapons on me to fight with if it came down to that. In the back of my mind, I knew eventually that's what it would come down to. I rummaged through the kitchen to locate some black garbage bags. I unlocked the kitchen draws and pulled out several knives to inspect. I turned to see Lily standing directly behind me, holding the upper part of her leg to stabilize herself.

"Woah, what are you doing with those knives!" she exclaimed.

Slowly, she began to back away from me. To her, it appeared I may have pulled them out to hurt her, but for me most of my conversations occurred in my head, so she didn't know my intentions were only to collect the weapons to use on whoever was outside. Right now, she was alive, and I intended to keep her that way, at least for now.

"I have to be prepared for the outside world, we don't know how many there are and what type of weapons they have. We need to be prepared for anything."

Nodding, she didn't say a word, but instead made her way back to the bed. I began filling the garbage bag with food, towels, and anything else I thought we may need. Pulling the rifle from the night table and leaning it against the door, my mind was whirling and starting to throb. I didn't like when that happened. I needed to find my spare cloth pouch I used for my knives, but I couldn't remember where I had put it last. It was probably in the cellar at the side of the cabin as that's where I cut the meat most of the time.

I peered over to Lily to notice her shaking while she sat on the edge of the bed. She looked as pale as a ghost. I was no doctor, but I could clearly see the woman was unwell. Then again, she could have been playing tricks on me to try and convince me to do things I simply wasn't going to do for her.

"What's wrong with you now?" I stood with my hands on my hips, facing her.

Her voice shook as she spoke, "I think I have an infection, I need to go—"

I cut her off, I knew where she was going with this. She couldn't play the sick game, and there was no way in hell she was going to a hospital.

"If you think you're going to play that card, you're wrong. You know the hospital is not an option for you. How many times have told you that?"

"But I need a doctor!" she wailed at me.

"You're a nurse, can't you fix yourself?"

Surely they were trained the same, or at least she would know what she needed.

"I don't understand. *You* shot me. *You* insisted on sewing me up with fishing line. The germs in this cabin have caused an infection in the wound and it's making me sick inside. If I don't get to a hospital…eventually I will die!" She was annoyed, you could tell.

I breathed heavily. Could I actually believe her, or was she acting? She had played her game of acting as Justine for six years. This could all be a hoax just to get herself out of here.

"The answer is no, and that's final." I had spoken my final words on the situation.

Turning, I walked away, needing space from her. She was not going to ruin my plan of escaping. I was not going to get caught for this. If she died, then so be it—it would not be my problem. If she had listened to me in the first place, she wouldn't be in this predicament, would she? It was her own damn fault I had to shoot her. She's lucky I didn't kill her right there and then in the woods. I could have, I could have ended all of this and ran off on my own.

I didn't really know why I needed to keep her. I knew if she got out that she would be running her mouth off to the authorities about me the first opportunity she had. Then again, she didn't really know that much personal information about me. The police obviously had my home address if that detective had showed up at the door. I still had to wonder how they had located me and my house. Lily never left the house, ever. She never used my cell phone as I kept it locked with a numerical code, nor had she had her own cell phone to make any calls.

Shaking my head, I didn't need to go backwards in time and worry about that now. I couldn't change the past, only what happened from here on out.

Peering over my shoulder at Lily, who still sat on the bed, I noticed she was now slumped over to her left.

"If you're going to puke, at least let me get you a bucket," I offered her.

"What I need is a damn doctor!" she snarled back at me, but I ignored her comment and instead pulled over a bucket to her side of the mattress.

"Here, at least be sick in this if you plan to."

Giving me a scowl, she yanked the bucket from my grasp.

"You're welcome!" I shot back loudly so she knew I couldn't be ignored.

If she wanted to act like that, I would let her be. All I knew was that she would need to settle down by the time we needed to get out of here.

I headed to the door of the cabin and pressed my ear firmly to it. Listening intently, I couldn't hear anything coming from the outside, but that meant nothing. If the helicopter was the police, it would only be a matter of time before they would have units deployed to where we were located in this part of the woods. By then, I hoped we would be long gone.

Until then, I was going to finish packing what little we had here to make the escape easier. I lived simply out here, so it wasn't hard. Out the corner of my eye, I checked on Lily—she still sat slumped over on the mattress and wasn't moving.

"Maybe you should lay down. That might help you," I suggested.

Peering up between strands of her hair, she tried to stand, but instead collapsed backwards down on the mattress with a thud.

"Let me help you, you need to save your strength." I ran over to her, feeling the urge to help her.

She stayed silent, but nodded. Picking her up, her weakened body went limp laying across my arms. As I laid her down gently flat on the mattress, I noticed her body was warmer than usual. Moving my hand to feel her forehead, I immediately regretted it—she had a fever.

"Let me get a cool cloth to help, in case you're running a fever."

I only had a rag, and a dirty rag at that. With the little soap I had left, I tried to clean the cloth off the best I could. I ran the cold tap for a few minutes to ensure the water was ice cold, which would hopefully help her fever.

Wringing the rag out, I approached the side of the mattress, placing it on her head. She didn't move, or wince. Instead, she merely lay there motionless with her eyes closed. Maybe this was worse than I thought; maybe she was telling the truth, that she needed a doctor, but at this stage that was not an option. That would cause me to have to go back into the city and drop her off, which would surely get us caught.

I left the rag on her head and walked away, I had to think.

If she died, what the hell would I do with her body? Just leave it behind for them to find later? Dig a hole in the ground?

Nothing was making sense and my plan was spiraling down the drain, fast. Time was running out, for both of us. I needed to act fast with whichever plan I would try and execute.

FORTY-TWO

Lily

Feeling my weakest during this whole ordeal, I couldn't even move now. I felt nauseous and Darren was not listening to me that I needed a doctor. To him, he thought this was all a joke, a game even. As much as I wished it was, this was the truth. I could feel my body shutting down, feeling dehydrated and fatigued. I sensed a fever, but of course we had nothing at the cabin to check any of my vitals with. The good thing was at least Darren washed out the rag he found, before using it on me. Who knew what anymore bacteria near me would do at this point.

The thought of making it this far, and to die now, after all these years, played heavily on my mind. I was free for a few days, but even that had turned into my worst nightmare, resulting in being shot by my captor, something I never expected to happen. I knew he could be violent, but he had never showed me physical harm with a weapon, unless you called his fists a weapon.

He paced the floor and continued to press his ear against the door. I assumed he was checking the status of our helicopter friends. From the makeshift bed, I couldn't hear anything.

"What do you plan to do now?" I called out in a mumble.

"What do you mean? The plan still stands. As soon as it is completely dark outside, we're out of here." He turned back to listen at the door.

Did he really think he could move me in my condition?

Clearly he had never taken care of someone who had been shot.

"You will have to leave without me, there is no way I can walk, or even sit for that matter. I promise—"

Darren cut me off before I could finish.

"You're coming with me. You can lie down in the back of the truck if you need too. I'm not leaving you here to rat me out."

"I promise. I won't, I'll tell them I didn't know who took me. I won't give up your name, I'll lie," I pleaded.

I was tired of running, tired of being dragged from here to there. I wanted this all to be over, and finally be free, whether that was alive here on this earth, or dead.

"There is nothing more to discuss. I told you the plan, and you will obey. Do you hear me?"

I nodded. That was all that I could do, I had no words left. Anything I wanted to say would be wasted breath.

I closed my eyes to think about everything that had happened. I had no idea about Keith or Callie. Had they given up hope I was alive? Did Keith even work for the police department anymore? I had no idea what they had done for the past six years.

Callie would be turning sixteen this year and I wondered if she had already begun dating. I missed her so much, I had lost so many years with her. She was probably such an independent young woman by now, that she wouldn't need me like other little girls need their mothers. Besides, Keith and Callie, I also had a long lost connection with Rose, now known as Justine. I knew I was thankful she had run away and stayed away from this monster of a 'husband', but I couldn't help but wonder where she was now. Knowing she was out there, looking for me, I hoped I still had a chance to meet her and build a relationship again, if somehow I escaped Darren.

I barely heard Darren's voice while my mind drifted in and out of memories. He was standing over top of me, screaming my name, but I could hardly hear him.

"Woman, aren't you listening? It's time, get up."

How exactly did he expect me to jump up instantly whenever he barked orders at me?

I was weak and fragile and barely coherent at this point.

"Give me a few seconds, you can't just expect—"

"I can expect anything I want, now get up." He grabbed my upper arm, trying his best to yank me up from the laying position he had put me in. I pulled back, causing more stitches to be pulled out with blood oozing down my leg.

Just what I needed, more blood.

You would think by now I would have had no more blood to shed. I pulled myself the rest of the way to a sitting position. My head whirled with dizziness. I couldn't adjust my eyes, and instead closed them to gain my balance. The room was still spinning, even with my eyes closed. Darren obviously didn't realize the state I was in, that my body was going into shock, and that I wouldn't be able to travel the way he wanted me to. I was done, completely done. I decided that if he wanted to kill me now, then I would let him, but I was not going with him or moving from this bed.

"Dar—" I tried to reason with him, but instead he cut me off with a wave of his hand.

"No more excuses woman, it's time to go, now! Nothing you say will change my mind. I don't plan to get caught or plan to have you found. Do you hear me?"

It was hopeless, as though I was talking to a brick wall—stubborn as could be.

What did he want from me? I wasn't his real wife, so why did I matter to him now? Was it because he knew he could be sentenced to serious prison time for what he had done to me? Did he fear he would be ridiculed by cellmates? Was he scared for his own well-being while behind bars?

Whatever it was had him scared. Somewhere in that muddled brain of his, he thought he could out run the law. Eventually, the law would catch up to him, it was only a matter of time.

I placed my hand on the wall to steady myself as I pulled myself to a standing position.

"Are you going to help me or just stand there watching me struggle?" I snarled at him.

"You can stop with your sassy remarks right now," he barked back at me, as he stormed towards me.

I was going to be however I wanted to be, because I truly was done with him.

Darren wrapped his arm around my back and let me use his body like a crutch. Even if we made it outside to the truck, how did he expect me to get in it, and ride comfortably? I assumed he would have thought of this before we got outside.

"What do you have for me to lie on?"

He gave me a sideways look, as if I should know he didn't have anything.

"I'll get the covers off the bed, that's all we have.

It won't be a long ride I hope."

I couldn't believe I was actually planning to leave the country with him, and lose absolutely everything in the process– and all for what, exactly? What was the point in surviving with this man, knowing I would never see my family again if we left the country?

Darren pulled me towards the door, but I wanted to stall a little longer. If it was a helicopter we had overheard, and it was actually here to help, the police could be on their way and could stop Darren from his crazy decision of hopping the border.

"I need to pee first," I said, speaking as confidently as I could.

I knew there were no windows in the cabin washroom. Darren had no fear in me trying to do anything stupid, such as escape on him. I had no energy to attempt an escape at this point. Knowing full well it was no short drive to the border, I wanted to ensure I didn't soil my clothing on the trip.

"Fine, but don't take long," he agreed.

Nodding, he helped me to the door of the washroom, and by holding onto the counter top, I managed to shuffle my way towards the toilet. Once seated, I could feel pain from my thigh down to my left foot—I couldn't sit without extremely discomfort and pain. I took a few minutes, purposely not being quick to gather my thoughts.

I had made it this far in keeping myself alive all these years. I couldn't imagine why I felt this was the best thing for me. If anything, I had endured pain—physically, emotionally, and mentally—by a man who had believed I was someone else. I had been kidnapped based on a mistaken identity. I chose to live like this, pretending to be someone else, because I thought that was the best way to live at the time and it would enable me at some point to escape back to my family—but here I was, over six years later, still with the man who had kidnapped me.

What I had learned was that he was evil, supposedly the husband to a lost sister of mine, and he was off his rocker with a mental illness. Plus, he was a controlling human being when it came to women.

I often wondered if it would have been better if he had just killed me when he discovered I was not Justine.

While all of these thoughts were rolling around in my head, a loud knock pounded on the door.

"Hurry up, we don't have all night, you know," his muffled voice vibrated through the wood door.

When was Darren never in a rush, or demanding? I had grown accustomed to his behavior. Finishing my business and washing my hands, I slid my way across the floor and opened the door. Darren was standing directly outside the door, tapping his foot when I finally managed to make my way outside. I was still very weak and nearly collapsed into his arms.

"Are you drunk? Why can't you support yourself?" he boomed.

Was he serious right now? I would have loved for him to have been shot, sewn up with fishing line, and expected to make a full recovery without any medical assistance. I thought he must have been joking. I chose to stay silent, saving my strength, because I knew what I wanted to say would most likely end with someone receiving a beating–that someone being me. Keeping the comment to myself, I shuffled along the wall as far as I could towards the front door of the cabin, finally stopping where there was no more support for me to hold onto. I waited for Darren to finish shoving a few last minute items into the garbage bags he had prepared to take with us.

Standing there, I felt a wave of fatigue wash over me and the need to collapse.

"Darren, I need to sit down. How much longer will you be?" I winced through the pain.

"I'm going to take everything out to the truck and check the area first. I need to make sure there isn't anyone spying on us."

"And what if there is someone out there? What will you do then?" I snapped at him.

"They won't be alive for much longer," he snarled.

As he spoke, he pulled the rifle away from the wall near the door where it had been leaning against.

Would he just kill anyone who got in his way? Great, there's a serial killer on the loose now.

"Well, I need to sit down. Can you at least help me to a chair before you go?"

He huffed as he made his way over to me.

Did he think I was faking all of this for a purpose?

Darren finally helped me to a chair, and I sat as he prepared himself to exit the cabin. With a blanket tucked under his left arm, he grabbed the garbage bag, leaving his right had free for his rifle.

All I could do was sit there and hope for the best. It wasn't long before Darren was back inside, still carrying the rifle.

"We're ready, the coast is clear," he reported through gritted teeth.

391

To say that I was not afraid would have been a lie. I was afraid and anxious. Part of me hoped he would get caught, while part of me didn't, because of not knowing what kind of fight Darren would put up. I didn't want anyone else getting hurt at the hands of this monster. He had already hurt enough people in this world. He would not give up easily, that was for sure. Even my attempts hadn't fazed him.

I would never say that I regretted what I did, but I wished I had ensured he was completely out after I had hit him with the shovel, before running. Although, I could attest to the fact that when anyone was put in that type of situation, they wouldn't think things through methodically or carefully.

I pulled myself up from the chair and reached my arm out to Darren to stable myself. My symptoms had not changed, and I didn't know how much longer I would be conscious for. As Darren walked me to the cabin door, I looked back. I wasn't leaving much, but something about this place felt safer than riding in the back of a pickup truck without knowing what would be happening next.

Making our way outside, Darren was on full look out, searching the pitch-black night air as he led me to the truck. The gate of the truck was down and the blanket that had been taken off the bed was laid out.

I tried to sit on the edge, but it was too tall, and I couldn't reach it.

"Here, let me lift you up," he whispered, while continuing to dart his eyes about.

In one single motion, he lifted me with both of his hands and placed me on the flap of the gate.

"Slide back, and lay down. I'll cover you with the blanket. Remember, you need to be quiet. Don't scream. I will get us out of here."

"Dar—" I whispered to get his attention.

"No excuses, it's time we blow this place and go somewhere that no one knows us. It will all be okay."

As much as I wanted to, I couldn't argue with him, I didn't have the strength to. Instead, I laid down on my side. It seemed to help with the nausea that was still present. He covered me and then pulled up the black hard top cover that was leaning against the side of the truck.

"What's that for?" It was my attempt at stalling him in case anyone was watching us.

"Going to cover the whole bed. That way nobody can stop us because they see you."

"What if I need you?" I pleaded.

"You'll be fine, I have to make it look as though I'm weather proofing the bed."

He threw the cover over the bed of the truck as gently as he could, but it made a loud noise as he adjusted and locked it in place. It was completely dark. I closed my eyes and pulled my legs closer to my chest. I felt the engine of the truck turn over and the rumbling underneath me as he began pulling away. This was it— we were on the run again, but this time running to another country.

Fear over took me, and I was shaking.

How could he just pick up and leave all the time? Did my family not matter to him?

The thoughts invaded my mind and tears began to drip down my cheeks. This was it. I had no choice but to follow his orders. I was leaving my family for good this time.

FORTY-THREE

Murray

Pryce and I pulled up to the makeshift meeting ground last—it seemed everyone else had arrived much earlier and was moving about preparing for the take down.

I jumped off the back of the ATV and made my way to the Captain, who was in charge of organizing the crew. Once I reached him, I immediately began to flood him with questions.

"Do we have any more news, did they leave?"

He gave me a blank look, which was unreadable.

"Murray, you need to calm down. Take a few deep breaths. We've had eyes on the cabin and up until now, they haven't been able to detect anything. With it being night, it's harder for them to see. The helicopter isn't equipped with infrared. However, we did hear back about the blood that was found yesterday..."

My heart sank, all this time I had really hoped that it was animal blood and not human, but I knew anything could be possible at this stage, now knowing it was almost for certain Darren's truck outside that cabin.

"Well, what's the news on it?" I asked, irritation evident in my voice.

Captain stared at me with time ticking by before answering me. It was as if he was trying to form his words in his head before delivering them to me. It was unlike him to be at a loss for words, he had never had trouble speaking his mind in the past. I knew he was trying to be sensitive to the matter, but I could handle it, I just needed to know the facts and be kept in the loop.

"It is human blood, but whose blood they can't tell. It doesn't match any DNA currently in the system."

Knowing it was human didn't sit well with me. It was too fresh to be classified as old stains, as they had still looked wet when we had arrived the night before. I couldn't afford to take the time thinking much about it, considering they couldn't even tell who it belonged to.

"What are the next steps? How are we proceeding to take him into custody?" I hounded the Captain.

"Murray, I know you seem very sure that this is Darren Johnson, but you need to remember that it could be anyone with the same type of vehicle as him."

Again, Captain with his reasonable mind was playing a huge part, ensuring due diligence was taken. We weren't supposed to make assumptions, but my gut told me the cabin and truck belonged to Darren, and that Lily was with him.

It was as though we were closing in on the end, we were in arm's reach, but we had to wait for the perfect time to stop him. It wasn't going to be easy if they were on the run. There was only so much we could do to try and stop him with the equipment we had on hand.

Another senior detective stepped forward with a map in his hand. He showed us where he had marked the area of the cabin in comparison to where we were. We weren't that far away, and it was predicted we could make it there in less than 10 minutes. No matter how short the travelling time was, time was of the essence—every second was crucial.

"I think we have enough units to completely surround the area. We need to ensure he can't get out of here. Nobody is to go after him alone, we must separate ourselves into sets of two." The detective flashed his eyes over in my direction.

I noticed while the detective was talking that Captain was suiting up—it was rare to see him in this manner. I wanted to know why he was going in with us.

"Why are you suiting up?" I asked him nonchalantly.

"You don't expect me to just sit out here, do you? We have a dangerous man on the loose, we need all hands on deck if we want to execute this flawlessly."

As much as I thought Captain hated me, and this whole case, he was a compassionate man, even if he didn't come across that way all the time. I had learned that Captain marched to his own beat, and never to question his motives.

Once the briefing ended, we paired up. I instantly moved towards Pryce, but Captain insisted I go with him instead.

"Pryce, if you don't mind, I'd like to pair up with Murray."

He gave me a reassuring smile. It assured me we were working together and not against each other. He might have been the Captain, but he was one hell of a friend, too. He had been through the last six years of battling this case with me. He had experienced my ups and downs through all of it.

A radio call came over the wire from what appeared to be the helicopter. Immediately, everyone covered their radios. If anyone was nearby, we didn't want them to hear the communication.

"We have movement. I repeat, we have movement." The voice was stern.

Captain instantly jumped on the ATV and barked questions through his radio to the helicopter personnelle for more information.

"What do you see, exactly? How many people?"

"One male, he is carrying a garbage bag, blanket, and a rifle it appears."

After hearing those words it confirmed my gut feeling that he was armed and dangerous. He was clearly trying to flee and if I had done what he had done, I would be running too.

Of course, my thoughts went to Lily, wondering if she was okay, hurt, or even alive at this point. That's when another call came through the radio.

"We now have movement with a female. She appears to be using the male as support."

Lily was hurt, I knew it. There was no way she would not be hurt, it was her blood we had found, and by the looks of things, we had hardly any time to get to her. Depending on her condition, things could have turned south quickly.

I turned to Captain, he must have read my mind, considering he was hearing what the operators of the helicopter were saying along with the rest of us.

"Stay calm, we can't over react or someone will get hurt. We need to cut them off, we won't let them get too far."

He placed his hand on my shoulder for reassurance. If I had anything to do with it, they were not going to get far at all. Where they might be headed was unknown, so I knew we needed to act quickly if we were to save Lily.

We had our instructions, and we all got into position. Captain and I shared an ATV, turning off the front headlights to not be seen. We didn't need to tip Darren off, since we were going in from three sides. If he was tipped off by one of the units, another unit would be able to block him from escaping.

We were ready to use spike strips if it came down to it, but I was hoping we would end this in some sort of peaceful manner.

As we drove along, my mind wandered. This was the moment I had been holding onto for all these years. The moment I would recover my wife, regardless of her condition. I was sure her injuries, mental or physical, would be severe. She was a fighter in all sense of the word.

Captain pulled me back to reality, nudging me with his elbow to get my attention.

"Murray, look ahead," he whispered.

As I looked up, I saw the outline of a truck. It was parked, but you could hear clicks coming from its direction. It was pitch black, and my eyes needed time to adjust to the lack of lighting to make out anything.

I could see someone checking the truck bed cover, then step around to seat themselves into the driver's seat of the truck. I wanted to move in, but the timing was all wrong. We sat there for what seemed like forever. That's when we heard the engine turn over, which meant he was on the move.

We proceeded slowly, inching forward. I trusted Captain with my and my wife's lives, as I took his lead and hoped we were not too late.

Suddenly, Captain floored it, catching me off guard. I held on as we sped through the trees. With my hand on my holster, I noticed Captain already had his weapon drawn in his hand. He was steering with one hand, while pointing his weapon at the truck with his other. Words began flying from all areas. Momentarily I blanked, and was not comprehending what was happening. That's when I heard his voice—the man in the truck, the one who had held Lily for all these years. I was finally face to face with the bastard, and this was my moment to save her.

"Stay back, or I will shoot her dead, you hear me!" his voice pierced through the crisp night sky.

We stopped abruptly. We knew we had to gauge the situation and not make any sudden movements or decisions.

We cut the engine to the ATV, but Captain had thrown on the headlights, which illuminated the truck, allowing me to see the face of the man inside the truck. Fear was plastered across Darren's face. You could tell he didn't know what to do and was acting out of anger and disbelief. In his eyes, he had a plan. I doubt he thought he would run into us while he attempted his escape—whatever that escape was.

He held up a rifle, pointing it to the bed of his truck. I assumed that was where Lily was, but from what I could make out, he had the bed covered with a truck cap.

I knew I couldn't make any sudden movements or things would go south quickly. Instead, I thought speaking to him would help the situation. Knowing his irrational mental state from the information Justine had provided us with, I wanted him as calm as possible. I never moved from where I was standing behind the ATV, we didn't need to alarm him in any way. Plus, we needed it to take cover if he did start firing at us.

"Darren Johnson, we are the Vancouver Police Department. Put the weapon down and step out of the truck with your hands up."

I figured I should go with the protocol approach before anything else. I knew it wouldn't work, but we had to warn him and inform him who we were.

"We have you surrounded, come out with your hands up," I continued speaking in a calm voice.

You could see him looking around, noting each of the units. It was hard to tell if this was increasing his anxiety. After scanning his surroundings, he turned back to look directly at me.

"Don't come any closer, I swear, I will shoot her again. This time I will shoot her dead." Anger was very present in his voice.

His words rang through me—he had already shot her once? It *had* to have been her blood we found in the woods, but where we found the blood and where this cabin was didn't make any sense—unless she had run, and he went after her. Right now was not the time to figure out what had happened in the past. I needed to refocus on what was happening here and now.

"Put your weapon down, Darren, and step out of the truck with your hands up," I repeated myself.

In that split second, I saw his finger beginning to pull on the trigger of the riffle. I couldn't act fast enough. I heard a loud pop and the sound of glass cracking, which echoed through the woods.

No one moved for several seconds. I didn't know where the bullet had come from. The windshield, with a single bullet hole through it, was cracked in a spider's web style pattern, causing it to be difficult to see if Darren was moving about inside. I turned to see the Captain slowly lowering his weapon.

"I couldn't let him kill Lily," were all the words he could speak.

With my gun still drawn, I made my way slowly, step by step, towards the truck. Captain was not far behind, and the other units began to move in. Once at the driver's side window, I could see where the bullet had hit him—right in the middle of his forehead. He was out cold—he was dead. I reached through the window to confirm, but nobody could have survived that kind of shot. I assumed the shot was meant to disarm him, but with his position, it had ended up killing him instead. At this point, I didn't give a rat's ass that he was dead. We had followed protocol—he went to pull the trigger, and Captain had stopped him.

My focus was aimed straight at the bed of the truck, as I shouted to the others that we needed to get the cap off.

"Get this removed as quickly as you can. We don't have much time," I pointed to the bed of the truck to indicate we needed all hands on deck to remove the cover and reveal Lily.

I slid my hand along the side of the truck to find the latches. My breathing had become heavy as each passing second ticked by. I knew we were working as quickly as we could, but it wasn't fast enough.

"Lily, hang on. We're coming," I shouted.

I didn't expect to hear a response, but if she could hear anything I wanted her to know she was going to be okay.

We removed the cover in record time and I peered down to see my long lost wife, noting her eyes were closed.

Was she dead? Were we too late?

She started shaking uncontrollably along with incoherant murmuring sounds. I was sure she was going into shock. I scanned her body for wounds and immediatley saw the blood soaked towel wrapped around her leg. Pulling the towel aside to evaluate her condition, I discovered a badly sewn wound on the back of her leg, below her knee.

My breath caught as I stared down at her, I whispered in a soft voice.

"Lily, it's Keith. Can you hear me?"

She continued to mumble but it wasn't anything I could understand. I reached under her and lifted her into my arms pulling her close to my chest. I rocked her in my arms. I hadn't realized my emotions getting the better of me, because before I knew it, I felt a tear fall down my cheek. Finally, after six long, agonizing years I had my wife back in my arms. I cried out in anger.

"Don't take her from me now. Let her live. Let her live!" I started sobbing uncontrollably over Lily.

With my vision blurred, I peered down at her. She was frail and malnourished. Her lips were grey, and her skin was ghostly white. She was in really bad shape, and I was afraid trying to get her back to civilization was going to be a challenge, considering we were not equipped to bring back someone who was this infirmed.

Captain was barking instructions to get an air ambulance to the location ASAP. He appeared beside me at the truck bed. You could tell he wanted to speak, but his eyes fell on Lily instead. After a few silent seconds, he finally found his voice.

"I've radioed for an air ambulance. We should have a back board at the command center, we can send someone back to get it while we wait, but they may take some—"

I cut him off—we didn't have any time. We needed to get her medical assistance right away.

"I'll carry her, and hold her. We need to get her out of here quickly. She doesn't have much time, Captain."

He nodded. He knew as well as I that she didn't have much time. I couldn't stop looking down at Lily. In her face, she was the same person, but she looked nothing like how I remembered her. She had already been a tiny woman to begin with, but now she looked as though she had lost an incredible amount of weight. It was possible, it didn't seem as though there was very much out here to survive on if they truly had been out here for several days.

I shimmied my way to the edge of the truck and slid off the tailgate, carrying Lily in my arms. I pulled her close to me, hoping the heat from my own body would keep her warm. Another officer had pulled out an emergency blanket and assisted by wrapping it around her.

I realized it was going to be awkward to get her back to the city in her condition, but we didn't have a choice. If we waited for EMS, she may not make it. At least if we managed to meet the air ambulance half way there, she would have more of a chance of surviving.

I placed two fingers to her neck to check her pulse. It was weak.

"You need to fight Lily, fight for life, fight for Callie, fight for your sister, Justine, fight for me—for us. I'm here, you're going to be okay," I whispered into her ear.

It was all I could say, she needed to live. We had finally found her and she needed to live to say she fought her way back.

Climbing on the back of the ATV, we pulled away from the scene, leaving Darren in his truck—dead.

Now, we needed to fight to keep Lily alive. Every second mattered more than it had before. This really was a matter of life and death.

FORTY-FOUR

Callie

I was being woken suddenly by someone nudging me. At first I thought it was Justine, but it wasn't her voice speaking into my ear.

"Callie, wake up, it's Gresham."

What time is it? was my first thought. My second was, how had she managed to get into the house? She had called to say she was going to be stuck at the station longer than she had expected, and she wouldn't be back tonight.

I turned over to see the time on my alarm clock. It was nearly two o'clock in the morning.

What the heck was she waking me up at this hour for?

Then it dawned on me and I shot up instantly.

"What happened, where's dad? Is he okay?"

Panic rose in me, there was only one reason why I would be woken up at this hour. I searched the nightstand for the lamp to turn it on, and picked up my phone. I had no missed texts or calls from dad.

I turned to Gresham, who was still standing in the center of the room, motionless. Her face told me everything I needed to know.

"Gresham, what's wrong. What's going on? Please tell me."

The room fell silent, you could have heard a pin drop. Justine appeared in the door way, groggy eyed.

"What's going on?"

We both turned to Gresham who was finally opening her mouth to speak.

"They found her, they found your mom. She was alive when they found her. Your dad called not too long ago and wanted me to come over right away to get you. We need to get to the hospital, fast."

Shock set in. Gresham was telling me they had found my mom, she had spoken as if mom had been alive then, but that it was uncertain now.

I looked to Justine, who had suddenly gripped her chest. She was panicking, causing her to hyperventilate. I could see she was struggling to breathe.

"Justine, breath. Take a few deep breathing," I begged her.

I rushed over to her just as her limbs nearly gave out, helping her to my bed to sit. Gresham ran to the kitchen to find a paper bag while I was helping Justine to the bed.

"Here, breathe into this. Only a handful of slow breaths. It's going to be okay."

I turned to Gresham for more answers. I demanded she tell me everything.

"What do you mean she was alive then, what about now?"

My own breathing had become heavy and I had no control over my emotions. Streams of tears spilled out of my eyes and down my face. My eyes darted between her and Justine, noting the emotions in the room were high. We all had been through hell, and here we were finding out mom had been found, but barely alive.

"She's on the way to the hospital. It took them some time to get out of the woods. She was not in good shape when your dad found her…but remember, your mom's a fighter. She made it this far."

I knew my mother was a fighter, she was a damn strong woman and I didn't need anyone to remind me of that. Time was standing still as I stood there. Looking between Justine, who seemed to be slowly recovering from her panic attack, to Gresham, who you could tell wanted to say more, but didn't.

I rushed to my closet, pulled out sweatpants and an oversized sweater. I didn't care that I was throwing my pajamas across the room and shoving on clothes in front of them—we needed to get to the hospital, I needed to see dad—and mom.

Gresham had moved and was standing behind me when I took a moment to breathe. She placed her hands on my shoulders.

"Callie, take a deep breath. Everything is going to be okay."

A tear escaped me as I closed my eyes to breath. I had waited for this moment for a long time, but we still didn't know mom's current condition, and if she was even going to survive. All I knew was that we needed to get to the hospital.

Justine was still sitting on the bed, she hadn't moved. Her eyes were glazed over. I crouched down in front of her. I felt as though I needed to comfort her, but I didn't know how. She was closing herself off to the world as she sat there, staring off into space.

"Justine, can you hear me? We need to go to the hospital, we need to see mom."

She didn't respond, choosing instead to continue to stare off. I lightly shook her shoulders to grab her attention, and all of a sudden she shook her head and our eyes met. I could see the tears welling up in her eyes. I pulled her into a hug where she cried on my shoulder.

Right now, I needed to be strong for the both of us, we both couldn't break down. Someone had to hold us up. I pulled from the hug and held Justine's face in my hands.

"She is going to make it, we know she is a fighter. Right now we need to get to the hospital. We'll know more once we see dad."

She nodded to indicate she understood what I was telling her. I turned to see Gresham standing in the doorway.

"There's a cruiser outside waiting."

Turning back to Justine, I helped her to her feet. We had no time for her to change, but it seemed as though she didn't have a problem with what she had on.

Once downstairs, I felt I should have packed a bag, but why?

What would I have packed?

Gresham was trying to get us out the door. I knew she wanted us to get to the hospital as quickly as possible, to learn of mom's current status.

On the drive, I glanced out the window to see the world traveling by with a blur. It felt as though the last six years had been a blur, just like the scenery passing outside my car window. I had grown up to be a young woman, someone who had lived beyond her years. It was the way I had to adapt to my new surroundings. With dad's job, it had been difficult for him to be home after school, so I had learned how to take care of myself and how to prepare meals.

Looking over at Justine, she too seemed to be in her own little world. I couldn't believe it had only been a few days since she had entered my life. With all the events that had taken place in our short time together, it made it feel as though it had been much longer. So much had happened over the past several days. We both were hurting in our own ways, and for different reasons.

The sirens of the cruiser rang in my ears. I knew riding in a police cruiser would get us there faster, but part of me wanted to slow it all down—just enough that I could fully understand what was happening around me. I didn't know what to expect once we reached the hospital.

Pulling up to the Emergency doors, we exited hastily. It didn't take us long before we located dad in the ER waiting room. Rushing over, I threw my arms around his neck.

We exchanged no words, but held on to each other tightly, more than our normal hugs would have. When I pulled away, I searched his eyes—it was evident he had been through a lot. Between no sleep and running through those woods for a few days, I couldn't imagine how he was feeling.

"Where is she, dad?"

I wasted no time cutting to the chase.

"In surgery, they're having to perform emergency surgery to remove a bullet from her lower leg."

"Bullet? You're telling me mom was shot?" I let out a small scream.

He gave me a small nod, which was enough for my mind to leap in to overdrive. My emotions were flying. I had just found out after six years my mother was still alive, and now she had been shot and could be taken away from me forever?

My eyes darted around the waiting room, noting it was empty except for us. Justine had taken a seat on the far wall, away from us. She had spoken very little since Gresham broke the news in my bedroom. Something was bothering her. Being mom's sister, she, too, needed to be informed and kept up to date with all the information about what was happening. It would save dad having to tell us separately.

I motioned for her to come over, but she wouldn't move, I gave dad a look, and instead we walked over to her. Dad crouched down in front of her, placing a hand on her shoulder.

"Justine, I know this is a lot to take in right now, but I want to thank you."

She looked up suddenly with a puzzled expression on her face.

"Thank me? For what? Getting your wife shot?" she shot back at him.

I was taken back by her comment, why was she angry so suddenly? I could see dad had to take a mental moment before he spoke again. I was sure he was trying to find the right words to speak.

"For coming forward. Without you, we wouldn't have found her alive."

Justine dropped her head, I could see tears flooding her eyes and down her face, onto her pyjamas. I took the seat beside her, putting my arm around her shoulders to comfort her.

"If it wasn't for you Justine, we may never have found mom. You helped save her, you brought her back to us—to all of us."

Dad nodded to agree with what I had said. He moved from his crouched position, taking up the available seat on Justine's left.

"Darren had packed her up in the back of his truck. It appeared he was trying to make an escape. Where to, we don't know. They didn't get any more than a few feet from his hunting cabin before we stopped them. In the back of my mind I really didn't think he would ever give himself up voluntarily. For us to get to Lily, we had to deal with him."

Dad took a breath and gathered his thoughts. As he did so, Justine spoke.

"Where is Darren, was he arrested? Will we finally get justice for everything he put us through?"

Dad didn't answer right away, but when he spoke, he spoke softly.

"For us to get to Lily, we had to kill Darren. He had a rifle pointed into the bed of his truck where he hid Lily, I saw his finger start to pull the trigger."

Justine shot up from her seat in agony.

"You shot him? You killed my husband?"

In that moment, I realized the man that kidnapped mom was never going to see prison time for his actions. Instead, he was dead. In a way, I wished he wasn't, because I wanted him to suffer like he had made mom and Justine suffer. This actually caused anger to rise in me. Dad continued as best he could.

"I didn't. My Captain was the one who shot Darren. If he hadn't, I don't think Lily would still be alive to be honest."

We all exchanged a knowing look, and I concluded we all were thinking the same thing. It was the best decision Captain could have made. If he hadn't made that quick decision, things could have turned out very differently.

We sat there in silence, waiting for news from the medical staff. Mom was in surgery and they had no estimated time of how long it would take. All we could do was wait, and hope for the best.

After waiting over six years, a few more hours seemed like nothing. If mom had made it this far, I knew she wouldn't give up fighting through her surgery.

FORTY-FIVE

Lily

Waking up, I felt like I had been hit by a truck. Everything was a blur, and all I could remember was hearing the voice of a man calling my name and telling me to hang on. After that, I couldn't remember a thing. I opened my eyes to see a white ceiling above me. I was laying on my back. I had an oxygen mask over my face, and the only other sound was a slow, steady beeping.

Turning my head towards what I thought was the door, brought me back to the past, where I had no contact to the outside world. I began to panic, which caused the beeping to suddenly erupt into a quicker, louder noise. Dropping my eyes to the side of the bed, I saw a red button attached to a long wire. I needed someone to tell me what had happened after I lost consciousness. I needed to know if Darren got away, or if they had caught and arrested him.

Before I could reach for the red button, a woman came rushing through the door.

"Mrs. Murray, is everything alright? I'm Karen, your nurse."

So I was in a hospital.

Pulling the oxygen mask off my face, I bombarded her with questions.

"I just woke up, I want answers. Has my kidnapper been caught? Which hospital am I in? Did someone take care of the bullet wound in my leg?"

I felt my eyes begin to well with moisture, taking in everything that had happened in this short amount of time. I needed answers, and someone needed to tell me right away.

"Someone will be right in to see you." With that, she bustled out of the room.

It wasn't long before the door swung open. A short, brunette, middle-aged women wearing glasses and purple scrubs walked in. She wore a big smile on her face as she approached my bedside.

"Mrs. Murray, I'm so happy to see you awake. Your surgery was a success and there are some family members waiting to see you."

As much as I wanted to see my family, my mind was only focused on one, solitary thing —Darren. I needed to know if he had escaped, or if he had been arrested. I needed to know if he was going to go after someone else if I was free.

"What happened to Darren Johnson? I need to know his status."

The woman looked confused, but spoke softly.

"I'm sorry, I don't know who Darren is. Is he a family member? Maybe he's one of the gentlemen outside waiting to come in to see you."

I was not processing what she was saying, and before I knew it I was shouting at her.

"I don't want to see Darren, he kept me locked up for six years! I want him in prison, he assaulted me in more ways than one, and kept me locked in a basement!"

The shock on the woman's face was evident. She took a few steps back to pick up my chart that she had placed on the hospital table as she came in the door. Glancing through, and flipping the page she peered back up at me.

"Did he sexually assault you? Would you like me to run a rape kit?"

Her voice was neutral. All I could do was close my eyes.

"That won't be necessary. I know who the man was who assaulted me—Darren Johnson. All I need to know is if he was arrested."

"I don't have that information, but maybe the detectives can answer that. Can I confirm you do not wish to run a kit, I would recommend it for evidence purposes."

I knew this was standard for anyone who claimed that a rape had occurred, but I had already told her I knew my attacker. There was no point having a kit run now. My only concern was if this man had finally been captured and couldn't kidnap another innocent person.

No other words were exchanged between the woman and I. I hadn't even asked her name, because the moment she walked in, I was after her with questions.

"Do you know who is here to see me?" I spoke in barely a whisper. When she mentioned a few minutes

415

ago people were waiting for me to wake up, I had completely ignored her statement.

Her eyes danced, and she gave me a small smile before speaking.

"Your husband Keith, daughter, and sister Justine. They've been here since you arrived and waited through your surgery. They're eager to see you, though I know the detectives are also waiting to speak with you for a statement."

My husband had been a detective. I knew all too well if he still were, this case would have been a conflict of interest, which meant I had no idea if he would know anything about what I had been through, or would have any information about Darren's status. The mention of Justine's name made me cringe inside. After all the times Darren had called me it, I didn't want to hear it for the rest of my life. I realized this was my sister's name, but how did she even know I was here? That puzzled me more than anything.

How did she know that I was even missing, let alone found?

"I want to see my family first, the detectives can wait. I want to see my husband first, alone please."

I felt as though if they all came in I would become overwhelmed. I needed to see him, to know we were going to be alright. Six years was a long time, and not knowing if he had moved on scared me. I certainly had not, but I wouldn't blame him if he had.

"I will send him in momentarily. Is there anything else you need before I leave?"

I thought for a minute, but nothing came to mind. I shook my head without speaking. Knowing Keith was in the same building as me gave me a sense of panic. I know it was a strange feeling to have, but since I hadn't

416

seen the man I was married to and loved for six years, I felt a multitude of emotions.

Pulling myself up slightly to a more seated position, I prepared myself for what was about to happen. I pushed my hair back, out of my face. I had not had a haircut since I had been kidnapped. I had trimmed my own hair over the years, but it had grown to a great length nearly reaching my hips.

Before my mind could wander anymore, there was a soft knock on the door. My breath caught in my throat. I couldn't speak, let alone answer to invite whomever was there into my room. With the door opening slowly, I closed my eyes to center myself, bracing for what was about to happen.

Would I recognize him? Would he recognize me?

I had no more time to think because as I opened my eyes, there he was, standing at the bottom of the bed. Our eyes locked—his eyes were in a state of confusion, not clear. I felt myself look away, feeling as though he was confused about me.

He walked to the side of my bed, but my eyes would not follow. I stared into my fidgeting hands. No words were forming, but my mind was traveling a mile a minute. I had too many questions roaming around my head that couldn't make any sense of them. Keith could see the struggle I was facing, even if no words were being exchanged. He pulled a chair over and sat down; he didn't touch me, but instead just sat quietly in the chair beside me. It appeared, he was waiting for me to be ready. Part of me relaxed in response to this gesture, but not enough for me to look at him.

Time crept by slowly. It felt as though we had been sitting there for many minutes. My hands stopped fidgeting and I tried to breathe calmly, though every time I felt as though I had the courage to speak, I simply couldn't. He was the one to finally find a voice,

"Lily, it's okay to be afraid."

Afraid? I was scared out of my wits! Scared that he wouldn't take me back, that he had moved on—that everyone had moved on and forgotten about me.

I needed to convey this to him. I needed him to know how I was feeling and what I was thinking.

"I'm scared. I'm scared that everyone has moved on. That if I return, it won't matter."

The words were out, I didn't say hello, or look at him, but instead I blurted out what my heart had been feeling for so long.

I finally looked over to see Keith slump in his chair. I didn't know what that was for, and I didn't ask. I could actually see a tear escape his eye—it used to take a lot for him to show his emotions. He was always the brave one, hardly ever showing hurt, pain, or anguish.

Had the years changed him?

"Lily, we have move forward….but have not moved on. You have been always at the forefront of our minds; I mean, we haven't even changed the house around because we wanted it to look exactly the way it was when you…"

He couldn't finish the sentence, his voice was shaky. He was showing real emotions, emotions I didn't expect to see from him. He was hurting, and it was evident this was taking immense strength to sit here with me.

"I was afraid I was going to be forgotten, that you had moved on. Found some—"

He cut me off with a wave of his hand and his head shaking, not allowing me to continue.

"There has never been anyone else, Lily. You are all I wanted, all I ever want. I waited for you because I believed you would come back someday. It's been one hell of a journey, but no—I never moved on with someone else. You were my everything, you still are my everything."

Tears streamed down my face. This was the affirmation I had been waiting for. All my fears melted away in that special moment and I just wanted him to hold me, to feel his strong arms around me again, to remind me that the past was truly the past and that he had saved me from Darren's control.

Keith stood and leaned over my bed, pulling me into him. My head rested on his stomach as he rubbed my back and spoke softly, "I love you Lily, you are finally home."

It was true, I had beat the odds. I fought, and in the end it had been worth it. At times I felt as though it was all about to end, but I found the strength within me to fight with the little strength that I had left that had depleted a little more each day of the past six years. I ran when I could, and fought back with violence when I needed too.

"I love you Keith, I love you with all my heart, but we need to talk."

He pulled away, confusion written all over his face. He sat back down, pulling the chair to the edge of the bed, then placed his hands over mine. He waited for me to speak, giving me the time I needed to collect my thoughts.

"I need to know what happened to Darren, did he get away or has he been arrested?"

As the words left my mouth, panic soared through me. That question alone would give me closure, I needed to know his fate.

"Darren would not give up without a fight, and that was clear from the get-go. You don't remember anything from last night do you?"

I felt this was a trick question. He seemed to be dancing around *my* question. Though I would answer his, I would ensure I would ask him my question again.

"I remember hearing a male voice coming towards me, calling out to me. Other than that, everything is foggy and blank. What should I know about last night?"

Keith took a moment before answering, I could see him thinking, contemplating the words to use, how to answer. Something was not right, and I feared the worst.

"Tell me, tell me where Darren is. I need to know, please," I pleaded with him.

I pulled my hands away from him and stared him in the eye, awaiting his response.

"He had a weapon, a rifle, in the cab of the truck. When we pulled up in front of him, he immediately raised it and pointed it towards the back of the truck. At the time, we didn't realize that was where you were. We told him multiple times to put it down, but he wouldn't. I could see his finger begin to pull on the trigger and before he could fire, Captain fired his weapon. I didn't know at the time whose bullet had hit the windshield. It was only meant to disarm him, but the truck's window shield shattered from the impact…"

"What happened to him Keith…"

"Captain shot him Lily, he's dead. Bullet to the head."

My heart stopped, was he actually gone? Anger filled me, that bastard was not going to receive any punishment for what he had put me through.

"What about what he did to me? I needed justice served Keith!"

He sensed the pain I was feeling, and assured me that it had been for the best.

"I understand, we always want justice, but sometimes *our* lives are more important and I wasn't going to lose you because of his actions. Captain killed him to save you, to give you your life back. He had no reason to live, but you, you have all the reason to live."

I couldn't argue with him, all of what he had said was true, after all. Now, I felt as though I needed to tell him what Darren had done to me, about the assaults, and about the abortion. He needed to know.

Placing my hand on his, I lifted my eyes to his face. I needed to look him in the eye when I told him what I was about to tell him. I wasn't sure what the best way to tell him, but found myself blurting it out all in a jumbled mess.

"He raped me, multiple times. He hit me, bruising much more than just my ego. I had hit him over the head with a shovel. I thought I had killed him, but I hadn't. I escaped and ran for a couple of days. He tracked me down and found me again. When I tried to run away from him, that's when he shot me. Keith, I was pregnant too, he made me have an abortion."

I dropped my gaze, what I needed him to know was out. It was his choice to take it or leave it. Keith stood and motioned for me to move over in the bed, I was still sore and it took me a minute to actually move myself over.

Once he was on the bed, he pulled me into his side and rested his head on my head. Speaking very softly he placed his arm around me and rubbed my arm.

"I know you've been put through hell these past six years, I never thought that it was all sunshine and

421

rainbows. When someone is kidnapped the captor does everything to control their victim. I hoped that it wouldn't come down to sexual abuse, but in the back of my mind I knew in those circumstances it usually happened. This doesn't change anything, Lily. I love you, and I will love you regardless of what happened when we were apart. None of it was your fault, so I can't hold any of it against you. The control was in Darren, he chose to do all of those atrocious things to you, regardless if he thought you were his actual wife or not. If someone doesn't want to do something, they're not supposed to be forced."

I didn't think that Keith would have this sort of reaction. He seemed calm and collected over all of this, and was taking it better than I ever thought possible. He *was* my husband after all, and at that moment I looked down to still see the band that Darren had asked me to put on all those years ago. I had actually forgotten about it.

Instantly, anger raged through me and I pulled the ring off, throwing it across the room with tear filled eyes.

"It wasn't my ring to wear, and I wasn't his," was all I could manage to say at that point, but Keith was right there, consoling me.

"It's going to be a rough road recovering from this ordeal, but we are all here to help you, every step of the way."

I needed to see my daughter. I needed to know she was okay.

"Where's Callie? I need to see her."

"She's outside in the lobby with Justine."

That name caused me to cringe and shout back at him, "I never want to hear that name again! Her name was Rose, Rose-Marie!"

Keith realized he had hit a sensitive spot with me, and immediately stood. You could see he was contemplating something in his mind.

"I'm sorry, I just can't hear that name anymore. To me, she was Rose. I didn't know her as her new name. It's nothing against you."

"I understand, I'm sorry, too. Let me go out to Callie and bring her in. I know she's been waiting patiently to see you. Remember, she turns sixteen this year, she might not be who you remember her as. She's grown up…a lot."

I was thankful he was warning me, but part of me knew I couldn't forget my daughter. Keith walked out the room and the wait for him to return was dreadful. I wanted it all, right then and there. I missed them, but knew we had to work on building our relationships. It wasn't going to happen overnight, and some adjustments would be needed in order to bring myself up to speed to today's society. I obviously had lost my job as a nurse, but in my present state, working was the last thing on my mind.

A knock interrupted my thoughts before the door swung open, Keith walked back in towards the bed while two others stopped inside the door. Immediately, my eyes were drawn to Callie—she had grown into a beautiful young woman. Tears were in her eyes as she stared back at me. I wanted her in my arms, to hold her and tell her how much I missed her, but she wouldn't move from the doorway. Keith returned to her side and escorted her over to me. It was clear her apprehension grew with each step. Was she afraid of me?

"Callie, it's okay. It's mom."

Keith literally had to introduce us, but as she stood next to the bed I saw the tears starting to stream down her face, and then her mouth opened to speak. Before I knew it she was pouring herself out to me.

"I've missed you. I thought you would never come home. I needed you so many times but you weren't there."

The tears continued to stream down her face, as she collapsed on the side of the bed falling into me. I wrapped her up in my arms for the biggest bear hug I'd had in six years.

"I'm here now, and I have missed you every day I was gone. I love you."

Finding myself choking up, that was all I could muster to say. As Callie lay in my arms, my eyes diverted back to the door where another tall, slender woman stood. She wore an oversized coat and was staring down at her fidgeting fingers. Keith noticed my diversion and nodded for confirmation. The woman standing there was my sister, my long lost sister, Rose-Marie. Our eyes finally met, and my heart melted. All I could do was mouth 'I love you'. She acknowledged with a single head nod and tear filled eyes.

The three most important people in my life were right here, in the same room. I had a long recovery ahead of me, and it didn't promise to be an easy road. I would probably need counseling after the ordeal I had been through. To me, it was worth it if I could have my life back. Callie pushed up off of me and Keith had escorted Rose closer. I had plenty to say to them, but right now I had no voice and this was not the place or moment to speak of it at all.

I stared into each of their eyes—silently pleading. Was it possible to rekindle the love with Keith, be the mother Callie had missed, and reestablish my lost relationship with Rose? I was not sure if any of it were possible, but I was willing to try—if they would be patient with me. I was ready to fight for the life I had been dreaming for, and forget about the one I had lived for the past six years. However, the ultimate question remained—could these relationships be salvaged, even after all these years?

To Be Continued....
Oil Lamp (Conquering Series Book 2)
Coming Summer 2017

ONE

Rose

I had to excuse myself from her hospital room the day Lily was set free from Darren. The pain I felt after only a few short minutes of being in her presence caused me to feel as though I didn't belong and that I was interfering with the family reunion that had taken place before me. Even though she seemed to have acknowledged my presence, it hadn't eased the tension that my chest and heart were feeling in those moments of reconnection. No words were exchanged between us, but then again I hadn't allowed much time for her or anyone to speak to me before I had walked out of her hospital room.

As much as I carried guilt about my involvement in the disappearance of my sister, I also carried the guilt of the Kennedy Daniels murder that Darren had committed. He was angry, and at times a violent man, but I had never imagined he would actually commit a murder. The boyfriend of Kennedy had come out in an exclusive interview with one of the local stations months after his encounter with Darren. That man was lucky to even be alive today, considering the brutal beating Darren had given him. I followed the news to keep tabs on cases—specifically Lily's case, but the news had only broadcasted her kidnapping for about six weeks. After that, it wasn't mentioned again; which only meant it had gone cold at that point.

When Keith told me Darren was dead, I had mixed emotions. Part of me was relieved because he couldn't hurt anyone else, but another part of me realized Lily, Kennedy Daniels, and her boyfriend wouldn't get the justice that they all so very much deserved. He should have survived instead of being killed so that he could feel what his victims had gone through, because he was a criminal now in my eyes, and always would be. I knew that he would have had a terrible prison experience but that was the least of my worries now, because he wasn't going to serve any time. I had wanted to know how Darren had been taken down, but Keith wouldn't elaborate. All he told me was that he was gone, and I and everyone else didn't need to worry about him anymore.

Now in the after math, there were memories that my mind was reliving over and over again. I had started to believe there was a possibility I could have changed the entire outcome. There were a few times I felt as though my efforts were going to blow up in smoke, as it had become harder to travel around without being noticed. Several times I had nearly been caught, or at least tipped Darren off, enough to warrant him the need of double takes. I managed to duck away before he could get a better look in most cases, except for two instances. The day the cab came to pick me up at Mrs. Adams one afternoon, I thought that Darren had left for work, but he must have been delayed. I had learned his schedule and he had never veered from it.

I had disguised myself as a blonde, which Mrs. Adams had come up with. If Darren ever questioned her about it, she would tell him it was her niece. Of course, Darren didn't need to know that wasn't the truth, because Mrs. Adams had no siblings. I never disclosed anything that Mrs. Adams and I spoke about while I was still living with him. With his controlling ways, he always tried to ask, but I kept it neutral. She was God sent, because when I told her about the orphanage and how I wanted to find Lily, she immediately began to help search the city records on her computer. Darren and I never had one because it was not a necessity in his eyes, which is why I begun spending nearly all my free time with Mrs. Adam—but Darren began to take notice and ensured I was kept inside. That was after she gave me the papers that she printed off. I kept them stashed in the boxes in the basement for safe keeping until I felt I could execute my plan to leave him and find Lily.

I had planned many escapes from Darren's controlling grasp, but he was much more experienced than I and had the ability to hunt, it didn't matter if he was hunting animals or hunting me—it was all the same to him. What kept me going and kept me trying was that I was running on adrenaline to find my long lost sister.

When I first went to her house a few days before the kidnapping, nobody was home and I had to turn away. The courage to knock on Lily's door had been hard to find. The second time I came to Lily's house to find her, I was in shock. That day, I hadn't seen him behind me. I truly thought I was home free. It was short lived when I saw my car parked under some trees, and I knew there would be trouble. I couldn't shake the thoughts that I had watched Lily be taken away by this man I called my husband, and all I could do was stand there—motionless—watching the events unfold. I often thought if I had come out from hiding things would have been different, but I couldn't keep thinking in the past, only the present and the future.

Another day that had continued to play on my mind was when Lily had discovered someone in the yard at the neighbour's when she was in the washroom. She was desperate for an escape because she had risked her life by banging on the window for someone to save her—for me to save her. I wanted to turn around and help her but I simply couldn't. I remember crying to Mrs. Adams until night fell and how at that point I wanted to find a way to help her escape Darren's wrath. That's when I started investigating who may have been in charge of Lily's case or at least the department where I could inquire.

The day I walked into the Vancouver Police Department headquarters was the day I took a stand against Darren. I knew it was not going to be easy and everything I had done up until then would most likely be condemned, but I had my reasons for staying quiet.

Meeting Keith, my nerves had settled in, considering I had come face to face with my sister's husband and to know I had a part in the disappearance of his wife gave me cold feet after the first interview with him. That was why I ran and hadn't looked back for nearly two months, because I couldn't face him. When I had to give them my contact information, I gave them Mrs. Adam's phone number and a random address. I requested that if anyone called about me that she say they had the wrong number. In a sense, I also did it to see if I was valuable to them, which obviously I was, because Keith called several times. Once, I was sitting at her kitchen table in her house when a call came through. He was desperate, that much I could tell.

Callie was another guilt of mine, for everything I had put that poor child through. I thought we were on mutual terms and believed we understood each other, but to have caused her to feel scared was never my intention. When I made a commitment to myself to keep an eye on her, I didn't want to fail myself again. No little girl should have had to go through what Callie did, but she was a fighter, and it was something I admired about her. I hadn't come to full terms that this was my niece and I was not going to force her to call me her aunt, because those titles were reserved for true family, not someone who had just stepped into your life.

I shivered at all my memories that I was reliving and couldn't get the image of Darren's eyes out of my mind. The day Keith went knocking on our door Darren was in the kitchen and I had not moved fast enough out of site. Our eyes met—for him, he was staring through my sunglasses, but for me, I could see the confusion settling in his facial features and eyes. I was surprised at that moment he hadn't come storming out of the house, but then again he may have just assumed it was his schizophrenia playing him up. He hadn't known I even had a sister, so he wouldn't have suspected I had a twin and that she was the one standing beside him in the kitchen. He wouldn't have known any of that, because he didn't need me to continue to be depressed over my past as he had been since the tragic death of his grandparents, the people who raised him and the only people who he ever knew as family.

I sat on the bed of the motel room contemplating my next steps. When I had left the hospital days before, it had been my intention to get away and let Lily and her family reconnect—allowing them to start their lives over. I was running, again, but this time for a different purpose. To me I was not a part of the happiness surrounding the fact that Lily was home, because I was the reason their family had been broken apart in the first place. The longer I kept away, the stronger my twin intuition had become. It was as if Lily was trying to connect with me.

When Lily was in surgery and recovery, Keith indicated that I was welcome to stay with them for however long I may have needed to get back up on my feet. He had gone as far as to say I was welcome to move in with them. After seeing Lily in that hospital room with her family, everything changed in my mind. I was happy that she has been returned to them, but I knew the guilt I felt would never leave me for what I had put every single one of them through, and that was something I had to learn to live with for the rest of my life.

The last few nights I hadn't been able to sleep, because every time I closed my eyes Darren's stare pierced through the darkness. Even though the man was dead, he was still haunting me. *How long would his memory continue to haunt me? Would I ever be able to come to terms with myself?*

Discover their continuing stories in *Oil Lamp,* Book 2 in the Conquering Series by J.C. Rochford, releasing Summer 2017.

ABOUT THE AUTHOR

J.C. Rochford was born and raised in Toronto, Canada. Besides being half Canadian, she is also half British with many family members still residing in England. J.C. began her writing journey in her early teens, writing poetry and song lyrics. Currently, you may find J.C. Rochford titles under the young adult and contemporary fiction genres.

'Orphan Flowers' is J.C. Rochford's debut novel, and was written over the course of two years before setting it to release to the world on July 23, 2016.

J.C. Rochford holds additional interests in photography, graphic design, and jewellery design. She also enjoys the outdoors and visiting rural Ontario with her family during the summer, with a special fondness in her heart for Presqu'ile Provincial Park.

FACEBOOK
www.facebook.com/authorjcrochford

TWITTER
@jcrochford

INSTAGRAM
@jcrochford

EMAIL
authorjcrochford@gmail.com

www.ingramcontent.com/pod-product-compliance
Lightning Source LLC
Chambersburg PA
CBHW020500260626
47156CB00006B/1801